BUZZARD'S BOWL

TRAGEDY OF CEDAIN
BOOK TWO

JOHN PALLADINO

For Mom, who's constant encouragement and support continues to propel me to greater successes.

And for Lezlie Smith (also known as The Nerdy Narrative on YouTube), who took a chance on an unknown author and continually spreads praise and awareness for book one. You are amazing, and I'll forever be thankful for our friendship. Even if you hate this book.

CYROK
THE FROSTED SPINES
VOX
COLDRIDGE
TIMBERGLADE
THE S
ALEKI
GYRLOFT
BRYN
ZEMUR
CALRYM
ANEPOLIS
PINECREST
LOCHWALL
LARGOS
VALKRYND MTS
KELM
ILIDROS
VESSIA
ARGOA
VALAKUR
HATHORAN

R SEA
ARGATE
QELT
WARWIN
OOTHE
YORDIV
MACEPORT
ANDORA
BARIO
REMERIA
ASHMOUNT
THE ASHWOOD
SULTIVA
AUCHESTER
RIVANE
N
W
E
S
CEDAIN

THE SHIT PEOPLE DID

DEMRI SLARN

Five years ago, Demri, along with his companion, Caius, slaughters everyone inside a tavern—including a man named Elizer Corbéo. In the present day, Demri, scarred and disabled, finds it difficult to navigate the world, and often requires assistance. He's on a mission: to kill Doram Quandis, a man who, back when Demri was a student at Ashmount, continuously tortured and humiliated him. Demri also wants to expose the Magicai at Ashmount for their many hypocrisies and lies they've told to maintain a stranglehold on resources, power, and manipulate who can learn what. Glaouse, a Magicus tasked with hunting down rogue Magicai, captures Demri, intending on returning him to Ashmount. They stop at the Velvet Mother's to secure passage to Ashmount. Caius takes this moment to intervene, killing both Glaouse and the Velvet Mother to take over the role of the Velvet Mother. The two of them visit their gladiators in Buzzard's Bowl, promising them better living conditions, and possibly a way to win their freedom. Demri then visits Scayde Haklon, a man with the resources necessary to restore Demri's body. In exchange, Demri must convince Caius to relinquish the Velvet Mother's deed to Buzzard's Bowl and turn everything over to Scayde. Demri agrees and is healed, but two important pieces of information are revealed. The first, that Doram Quandis is actually a teacher at Ashmount, and not in hiding as Demri had originally thought. The second is that Caius is actually Tythus Corbéo. When confronted, Caius admits everything. He has killed two members of his former family—the Velvet Mother and Elizer. Caius agrees to relinquish his role as Velvet Mother and continues to aid Demri on his quest to get revenge on Doram Quandis. Through Scayde, they secure passage to Ashmount, but suspect a potential set up. When they meet with their guides, Myri Celioh—the woman Demri loves—reveals herself to be one of them. She's a member of the Elkavich and persuades Demri to come with her. He agrees, much to the dismay of Caius.

EDELBROCK BRENDIS

A minor nobleman with dreams of becoming more, Edelbrock hatches a plan: seduce and murder one of the owners of a deed to Buzzard's Bowl, a gladiator arena where he can earn a boatload of money, then steal the deed for himself. Unfortunately, his wife Jaylena isn't a fan of the plan herself, and turns him in to Scayde Haklon, owner of Buzzard's Bowl. Scayde Haklon imprisons Edelbrock, revealing he and Jaylena are lovers. He murders Edelbrock's son, Gordane, with Jaylena's blessing. Edelbrock endures a lengthy period of starvation and abuse, an attempt to shape him into an obedient gladiator. When it's determined he's learned enough, Edelbrock and his other captors enter the Draft, where the various House Heads make their picks to add new fighters to their House. The Velvet Mother, ignoring Scayde Haklon's demands, drafts Edelbrock. He spends his days training with various weapons, waiting for the next season he'll take part in to begin. When Caius visits the compound as the Velvet Mother, Edelbrock gains a sense of renewed purpose. The Velvet Mother had promised the gladiators a chance to win their freedom, and this becomes Edelbrock's new goal. Unfortunately, when Caius gives the organization up to Scayde, the House is turned over to Scayde Haklon's rule. Edelbrock is selected to take part in a preseason battle to mark the beginning of the next season in Buzzard's Bowl. At the behest of Scayde, Edelbrock's opponent, Anditus Roberon, stabs Edelbrock fatally after the battle ends, but because this is a rule break, a Healer is summoned to heal Edelbrock. Edelbrock then enters Buzzard's Bowl for the first battle of the season and is surprised to find the normally sandy arena is filled with water and two large ships. He boards the one assigned to his side.

VILLIC THE IMBUER

Villic lives a nomadic life, avoiding his other clansmen as much as possible. Shy, introverted, and nervous, Villic prefers the company of his camel, Dunecrest. But the gods have plans for Villic, and he finds himself with a mysterious entity haunting his mind. Villic calls him "Speaker" and accuses Speaker of being a god. Speaker, resolute, denies these accusations. The Camel Clans, generally a group of warring nomads, decide to come together and declare war on Calrym and Remeria—the two countries that have forced the Camel Clans to remain in Vessia, a barren desert with very little farmable land. During their journey, Villic discovers more about his powers and begins to trust Speaker a tiny bit more, though always remains skeptical. Throughout their invasion of Remeria, the Camel Clans raid villages, killing those in their path. During one of these raids, and ambush of Magicai is set up by the Remerians. Imbuers and Magicai battle, but the Imbuers win, although Villic is knocked unconscious. When Villic awakens, the Camel Clans are gone, and he finds himself facing an injured Magicus. Speaker helps Villic understand and speak the foreign language. Ultimately, Villic decides to help the Magicus and goes in search of his allies. When he finds the Camel Clans, he leads them back to the Magicus. They kill the Magicus, then arrive at the capital of Remeria—Andora. They surround the city. Not long after, the Falcon Knights crest a nearby hill.

KELDEN STOOLE

Kelden, the son of a baker, believes he's destined for a much better life than living in the poor town of Warwin. When his father, Hillion's, old friend resurfaces, Kelden receives a chance to journey to the magical university called Ashmount to test his potential. It's determined he has the Trace and is admitted to participate in the Trials. During the Trials, it becomes increasingly clear to Kelden the Magicai are shady and doing things that aren't adding up. When he eventually passes the Trials, his dreams are dashed when it's determined he isn't going to be an Enforcer, but instead, he's to be a Glyphist—one who tattoos the ability for Enforcers to use their power. He trains and learns about the Magicai, and when he isn't taking part in official school business, Kelden decides to start researching on his own. Following in Demri Slarn's footsteps, and uncovering notes Demri left behind, Kelden learns the awful truth about the Magicai and the university. They lied about everything, manipulating the Magicai to do as they wanted and pretending Magicai can only access the one field of magic they were assigned. Unfortunately, there's not much he can do about it because shortly after his discovery, three members of the Elkavich arrive at Ashmount. When Kelden confronts the strangers, they stab him, leaving him for dead, before they walk into the center of the university's grounds and self-immolate, destroying Ashmount and every Magicus there, including Kelden.

SERADAL WINTLOCK

Seradal is a gyrfalconer living in the cold northern country, Cyrok. When the Cyroki military arrives, led by Captain Blago Adavir, Sera and her family—along with the rest of the town—flee for their lives. However, they've been deceived. Adavir and his men are bandits hired by Calrym's crown to initiate a war. Adavir murders Sera's mother and brother, taking any surviving villagers captive, including her father, Jaidik. Sera escapes her imprisonment, arriving at the Cyroki capital, Vox. She's healed, taken in, and named a Falcon Knight. Her father is saved, and she spends her time training. Meanwhile, the Calrite forces have landed on both eastern and western fronts, and they quickly make their way through Cyrok, pillaging and murder all in their path. As the army closes the gap between themselves and the capital, Sera and her father escape the city just in time. On the way to Coldridge, where ships are being prepared to evacuate everyone they can, Sera is mortally wounded. A Healer sacrifices her life to save Sera. At Coldridge, they meet up with Royal, a drunken captain in the Cyroki military, and the Old Vulture, the oldest member—and current the leader—of the Falcon Knights. Boarding ships, they escape Cyrok, leaving their colleagues, friends, and family, to die in the war. The Falcon Knights flee to Remeria, in search of a safe haven, but when they reach the Remerian capital, Andora, they discover the city is besieged by the Camel Clans.

PEOPLE WHO MAY DIE

Alondo Sedoa – King of Remeria.

Alora Couliac – Sister of Jaspard.

Althier – A poetic rebel captain serving in the Redcloaks.

Alyst Garcovi – Nephew of King Mikas Garcovi.

Anditus Roberon – Gladiator in Buzzard's Bowl, fighting for Mikas Garcovi's House.

Arena Hyrel – Duchess of Calrym and adviser for King Mikas Garcovi.

Argdis – Gladiator in Buzzard's Bowl, fighting for Mikas Garcovi's House.

Ashen/Cithrial Hyrel – Former urchin living with Jaspard, tasked with bringing down Calrym's nobility.

Atticus Crenshaw – King Alondo Sedoa's adviser.

Bartlesby Flatchett – Quartermaster of the Redclaws.

Bertrand – King Mikas Garcovi's
  chancellor.
Bethinda – Jaspard's house servant.
Blago Adavir – Cyroki bandit leader,
  initiated war between Cyrok and
  Calrym.
Caius / Tythus Corbéo – Loyal friend and
  ally of Demri Slarn's.
Castede Varono – One of the five House
  Heads of Buzzard's Bowl.
Ced – Member of the Elkavich.
Chance de Gault – Magicus.
Chardaine Hugomes – Barrister working
  for Roachford and Singleton's, a law
  office.
The Chell – Quintuplet gladiators in
  Buzzard's Bowl, fighting for Scayde
  Haklon's House.
Dashiki Magoro – Shaman from the
  Camel Clans.
Delicourt Ramses – One of the elite
  guardsmen tasked with guarding
  Mikas Garcovi and Calrym.
Demri Slarn – Magicus criminal on the
  run hunting Doram Quandis, intent
  on exposing the Magicai.
Doram Quandis – Former teacher at
  Ashmount and Demri Slarn's enemy.
Edelbrock Brendis – Former nobleman
  forced to fight in Buzzard's Bowl.
Everic Deywin – Under the employ of
  Scayde Haklon.
Exildar Alcart – A Calrym baron, married
  to Iadura Khyst, and distantly related
  to Mikas Garcovi.

Faith Ennings – A Glyphist.

Harlem Maccaro – Duke of Calrym and adviser for King Mikas Garcovi. Sent to Cyrok to lead the war campaign. Also, Jaylena's father.

Hemmel – Duke of Calrym and adviser for King Mikas Garcovi.

Hershen – Rebel captain serving in the Redcloaks.

Iadura Khyst – Noblewoman from Lochwall, married to Exildar Alcart.

Jafe Valendar – Officer in the Calrite military.

Jaidik Wintlock – Seradal's father.

Jaspard Couliac – Nobleman who took in Ashen, scheming against King Mikas Garcovi and the other nobility.

Jaylena Haklon – Wife of Scayde, former wife of Edelbrock, one of the five House Heads of Buzzard's Bowl.

Jedkah of the Splintered Manes – Leader of the Splintered Manes, one of the Camel Clans.

Khlaux Corbéo – One of the elite guardsmen tasked with guarding Mikas Garcovi and Calrym.

Kolb Wickam – Officer in the Calrite military.

Lekhan Roelk – One of the five House Heads of Buzzard's Bowl.

Lucky – Gladiator in Buzzard's Bowl, fighting for Scayde Haklon's House.

Madam Zeitwitch – Owner of a brothel which provides many questionable services to its patrons.

Mauve Hardeen/The Bloody Duchess –
A Remerian citizen and leader of the
Redcloaks, a group of rebels who
want better living conditions.

Mikaeus – Guard captain in Anepolis.

Mikas Garcovi – King of Calrym.

Myri Celioh – Member of the Elkavich
and the woman Demri loves.

Nauc Othepi – Gladiator in Buzzard's
Bowl, fighting for Scayde Haklon's
House.

Old Vulture/Vecchio Rizurri – Current
leader and oldest member of the
Falcon Knights.

Patrika Jorst – Falcon Knight.

Renard – Seradal's personal page.

Rickets – Soldier in the Calrite military.

Royal/Decklin Hoarst – Former captain
in the nonexistent Cyroki military but
has remained with the Falcon
Knights.

Savakkis – Gladiator in Buzzard's Bowl,
fighting for Scayde Haklon's House.

Scayde Haklon – Owner of Buzzard's
Bowl, one of the five House Heads,
Duke of Lochwall, married to Jaylena.

Seeker Korran – Gladiator in Buzzard's
Bowl, fighting for Jaylena Haklon's
House.

Seradal "Sera" Wintlock – Falcon Knight
who's just trying to do what's best for
her and those she cares about.

Speaker/Githandus Felimar Mydenwold
– A mysterious and very old being.
Grants Villic his powers as an Imbuer.

Sturgeon Gothal – Duke of Calrym and adviser for King Mikas Garcovi.

Tallas Taybold – Mercenary hired by Jaspard to protect/escort Ashen.

Tanibris – Head servant of Scayde Haklon.

Tauven Shekt – Officer in the Calrite military.

Uva the Shaman – Shaman from the Camel Clans.

Velturo Ondakka – Duke of Calrym and adviser for King Mikas Garcovi.

Villic the Imbuer – A nomadic warrior who cares most about his camel, Dunecrest. Imbuer of the Camel Clans.

Vithor Bane – A disgusting man who helped Seradal, Jaidik, and Renard escape Cyrok during the invasion.

Watchtower of Calrym/Zervan – One of the elite guardsmen tasked with guarding Mikas Garcovi and Calrym.

Whisper – Calrite military messenger.

1st Cycle of
Spring
232nd Reign of Garcovi

I

STURGEON GOTHAL

Lochwall, Calrym

S low and methodical, Duke Sturgeon Gothal lowered his wretched body into the cushioned chair. His shaky, liver-spotted hands reached out and took the mug of chilled water from a side table. He sipped, eyes darting around the balcony, examining his enemies. There were no friends here, even King Mikas Garcovi—a man he'd known for decades—was someone he wouldn't trust.

Shivering, he wiped cold sweat from his forehead. It couldn't be the temperature—there was no breeze and bright sunlight reflected off the water below. Nobody else shivered. Nobody else complained or had warmer clothing. *Must be an illness come to claim me.* Sturgeon pulled his cloak tighter.

"With the decimation of Cyrok, Duke Harlem Maccaro requests your leave to return to the Mainland," the council's chancellor said as he rolled up a letter sent from Harlem himself.

"Must we . . . discuss . . . matters of state . . . now?" Sturgeon wheezed, took a moment to catch his breath. "I'm sure . . . our Lord Haklon . . . would prefer . . . we watch . . .

the games . . ." He gestured below, where two enormous ships loaded with gladiators were about to set off from the docks. The crowd cheered. Sturgeon had never viewed a Buzzard's Bowl event before. He had to admit he wasn't impressed, but things which didn't line his pockets or satisfy his other lusts often didn't make an impact.

"Yes, we must. Besides, *Duke* Haklon can manage, I'm sure," Duchess Arena Hyrel said.

Scayde Haklon and his wife, Jaylena, sat a few seats away. Neither indicated they'd heard the discussion, though Sturgeon knew this to be impossible—he was mere feet away. Regardless, the king and Scayde had agreed to allow the meeting to take place here, in the King's Stand of Buzzard's Bowl.

The council's chancellor cleared his throat. "Should I send a message requesting Duke Harlem return then, Your Highness?"

"Ridiculous. Mere weeks after completing a campaign and your lapdog is already whining to come home with his tail between his legs because his cock and balls are half-frozen. It is pathetic. At least have the decency to put forth enough effort to *expunge* any survivors," Arena said. Sturgeon could assent that the duchess was a pretty woman—smart, too—but there was something about her he disliked.

Sturgeon drew in a deep breath. He felt odd, as if breathing was a more laborious chore than usual *What is happening to me today?* He didn't have breathing issues. He took another sip of his water and looked around. Duke Velturo Ondakka, the slob, was wiping at juice that was dribbling down his chin. Sturgeon's stomach turned. He wasn't one to dislike somebody. Well, he disliked Arena Hyrel. And Velturo *was* disgusting. Also, the council chancellor was annoying. After consideration, Sturgeon realized he didn't like any of them; never had.

"Well, in all fairness, *my lady*, if you were in Cyrok, I can't imagine you'd want to remain, ah-hah." Duke Velturo dabbed at his chin. He missed the drip and caused it to fall onto his white doublet, staining it orange. "*Damn!*"

The end table near the king's side banged with a sudden force—the king's fist. Sturgeon jumped, his heart rattled. The king rubbed a reddened hand. "Velturo, by Mother Avani's last good grace, you damned well need to clean your fucking self up. You are a disgrace!"

"Your Highness, I apologize. I can't help it. I'm clumsy, ah-hah," Velturo said.

Sturgeon cleared his throat. It was time to offer his advice. "My Liege . . . if you were . . . to lift . . . the . . . restrictions . . . regarding the servants . . . we may well be able . . . to offer . . . Duke Velturo . . . a servant . . . who may . . . feed him . . . with a steady . . . hand." This garnered a laugh from everyone except Duke Velturo.

"It would appear a wise decision," Scayde Haklon said, turning to look at Velturo. "Perhaps the good Duke Velturo would prefer lessons on how to behave more like an adult and less like a child?" More laughs. Duke Velturo shrank in his chair. Scayde chuckled, offering a half-wave—more like a flick of his fingertips—in Velturo's direction. "A jest, Lord Ondakka. I apologize." He swiveled in his chair, peering down at the sloshing waves and bobbing ships. Any moment now, he'd order his Magicai to commence the battle.

"My Lords, it's important I send a response to Duke Harlem. His messenger is awaiting a reply. What should I tell him?" The chancellor stood, hands splayed before him. *The least effective diplomat in the history of diplomacy, maybe.*

King Garcovi, of course, did not like taking orders. "Quiet yourself, *Bertrand.*"

The chancellor stepped back, fading into shadows as usual. It was a wonder the man still lived, as often as he angered the king.

Speaking of living . . . Sturgeon winced. He felt the throes of heartburn beginning. He reached for his water again, but a burning sensation in his chest flared up and his arm convulsed. He tipped the mug over, spilling water across his end table. Sturgeon grimaced, the world spun and colors blurred together.

"Sturgeon, are you all right?" He didn't know who spoke.

Sturgeon blinked, swallowing, and leaned back in the chair. Scayde's head servant walked to him, a fresh mug of water in his hand. "Drink," he said, tipping the mug against Sturgeon's lips. He drank the water, eager to moisten his mouth, which had suddenly gone dry.

"Thank . . . you." Sturgeon took another breath. Slow and steady, he closed his eyes, focused on his breathing, trying to clear the pain he'd experienced.

The head servant nodded, stepped away.

"Sturgeon, are you all right?" the king asked.

"I . . . hope . . . so."

"You are displaying a lot of revolting qualities we see in Duke Velturo," said Duchess Arena. "Are you sure you don't need help?"

"I'm . . . fine." Though he wasn't sure about that. Offering further weakness, however, was a bad idea. Had he been in their shoes, Sturgeon would've called an immediate vote to expel him from his titles due to health concerns. Perhaps some of them were thinking that.

"Back to business, then," the king said. "Harlem can stay in Cyrok, for all I care. The man deserves an extended leave." Meaning the king was still angry over Harlem's prior insults. "Plus, as you said, Arena, he can expunge the refuse. Kill them all!" King Garcovi pounded the table again, knocking over a glass of wine. The cup fell to the floor, shattering. He ignored it while Scayde's head servant hurried to replace beverage.

"I agree. Bring Harlem down a notch." As if Velturo had any right to criticize someone.

"And . . . what of . . . Remeria?" Sturgeon had assumed Remeria would be the primary subject of discussion.

"Let the Vessians kill them," the king said.

The chancellor stepped forward. "That . . . might not be advisable, Your Highness."

"Bertrand, I swear on Mother Avani's ass that if you don't back yourself against the wall, I'll have you flayed. *STOP INTERRUPTING!*" The king slammed his fist on the table again for good measure. *One of these days, he's going to break a bone.*

Sturgeon dabbed at his forehead again. Cold sweat formed, causing him to shiver once more. *What is wrong with me?* His breathing, the pain, his vision. He was old, sure, but this was new. *Perhaps I've picked up a nasty cold.*

"I concur, Your Majesty. It's about time those Remerian rats got their comeuppance. Let them eat dirt flung into the air from Vessian steeds, ah-hah!" Velturo stabbed the air with his pointer finger, emphasizing his point.

Sturgeon's chest tightened, and the lightheaded feeling returned, his vision blurring again, colors bleeding together. "Fuck . . ." Stabbing pain lanced his chest again.

The king clapped his hands. "Sturgeon, damn it, what's wrong? You look awful. If you're going to die, go inside. We have matters of state to discuss and games to watch, and you're distracting."

"Perhaps . . . the cold . . . air . . . is . . ." The stabbing pain in his chest blossomed like shards of knives trying to escape his insides, and his vision faded to black. Sturgeon gasped. He slumped in his chair, falling to the floor. *Why am I losing control?* His head bounced off wooden floorboards. Drool spilled down his cheek amid screams and shouting. He gasped, lifeless eyes ending their stare on the glass half-wall across from him, where the crowd in Buzzard's Bowl cheered. Scayde Haklon had blown the horn already, giving the signal.

The games began.

2

EDELBROCK BRENDIS

Buzzard's Bowl reminded him of his past, most notably, of the Battle of Leeward. Before everything bad happened. Before Edelbrock met his wife, Jaylena. His murdered son Gordane hadn't been born. Perhaps it would've been better if Edelbrock had, like so many of his soldiers, perished during that battle. Then maybe Gordane could've been born to a woman who loved him.

Instead, Edelbrock had survived the Battle of Leeward. And now, he stood on the deck of a giant ship, staring across the water at his enemy—another ship full of rookie gladiators. His ship—he'd named it *Allegiance* in the minutes since climbing aboard—had the rookies from his own House as well as King Mikas Garcovi's. The king, along with a bunch of noblemen, were sitting in the King's Stand, an elevated luxurious spot to observe Buzzard's Bowl's proceedings. Scayde Haklon had tossed Edelbrock's son off its balcony.

His hand clamped tighter around his sword hilt. The battle would start soon—the crowd was growing too impatient. Their thirst for blood disgusted him.

The gladiators were all equipped with a standard set of leather armor, a shield, a sword, and rope with a grappling hook attached. Not long enough to escape Buzzard's Bowl, of course. Not like he'd be able to, anyway. The crowd would probably kill him themselves, so deep was their hatred and bloodlust for the men and women they watched die. Taunts and cheers and chants echoed from the stands. Once, Edelbrock would've given anything to afford a stake in the gladiatorial arena. He wanted nothing more than to raze it to the ground now.

Edelbrock peered across the water at the other ship—in his mind he'd named this one *Vengeance*—and knew there to be three Houses of new gladiators. Two Houses against three. *Fair odds.* But, Edelbrock had learned, nothing in Buzzard's Bowl was fair.

He remembered Marshal Everic's words before Edelbrock boarded *Allegiance.* "You're going to be on that ship," the marshal had said, pointing to the vessel, "and join forces with King Garcovi's House. There's another ship with candidates from the other three Houses. Kill them. If you're wounded and find yourself able—however unlikely—to retreat to this dock, the crowd might grant you your life. If you please them. Best of luck. Oh, and don't fall in the water. It's not safe." Edelbrock didn't know why the water was dangerous, but he preferred avoiding it altogether. He saw what appeared to be constant flashes, like lightning, underwater. Ripples suggested something lurked beneath.

On his right stood Lucky, who gave him a wink; on his left, a silent, stoic Nauc stood, ready to fight.

The Buzzard's Bowl's announcer, using a magical voice enhancer, addressed the crowd. "Ladies and gentlemen, it's that time! The season of games and gambling has begun. Today, we're going to test the new recruits. It's the purge! We'll see who'll have what it takes to survive. Some of these people might become the next Derelict Dagger, the Gored

Bull, or even, dare I say, Flimsy Shirley the Remerian Girly." Edelbrock knew Shirley was the only one of the three still active in Buzzard's Bowl. The other two were either dead or free, he didn't know. The crowd erupted. Various chants of their favorite long-dead gladiator icons echoed around the arena. "That's right, and now we begin!"

The ship lurched; he heard a grinding sound as stern scraped against the dock and then, just like that, *Allegiance* pulled away from the dock at the same time as *Vengeance*. Soon, the two ships began circling Buzzard's Bowl, following the current that guided the ships. All predetermined by the Magicai, at Scayde Haklon's orders, Edelbrock figured, as there wasn't anyone actively steering the ship. Slowly, the ships made smaller circles. Edelbrock saw they were going to converge near the center of Buzzard's Bowl. When that happened, the fighting would begin.

Concerned whispers and demoralized groans echoed around the men. Just like what'd happened at the Battle of Leeward. Except he'd commanded his men to victory and Edelbrock didn't think he could control this. *But I have to try.* Outnumbered, they'd need a plan, a way of cohesion.

He banged the grappling hook—not wanting to weaken the sword—on his shield, hard. Twice.

Some people turned to him. Most didn't.

"Listen up!" Edelbrock used his officer's voice. A few more snapped their heads in his direction. "I know most of you don't care about me or my opinion, but if we want to survive this, we're going to have to work together. As a unit. We're outnumbered, and if we go into this as a pack of confused barbarians, we're going to get slaughtered. Tactics. Tactics and leadership. That's how we'll figure this out. So, everyone who wants a chance to live, anyone who realizes they can't do this alone, step in line. Right here." He pointed at the floorboards in front of him. Nauc and Lucky took a step in that direction. Twelve others joined them.

He noticed the sky darken. Dark gray clouds gathered above them. A cool breeze brushed over him and Edelbrock knew a storm was coming. A moment later and he heard the soft thump of several raindrops spattering on the deck. The weather, it seemed, was a prediction of things to come. Edelbrock took in a long, slow breath to calm himself, then turned and glanced at the other gladiators.

"I don't know when, but I'm sure there'll be a good cause to use these." He lifted the grappling hook, which he'd draped over his shoulder. "When that happens, we need to remain on this ship—*Allegiance*, I call her. That ship we'll call *Vengeance*." A tremendous splash of water cascaded over them, and the ship tilted to one side. Edelbrock grabbed hold of the taffrail and steadied himself. Several others had to pick themselves up off their asses. He stifled a chuckle—there were more serious things at play—and resumed his officer pose. "Focus on repelling anybody attempting to board *Allegiance*. Cut the grappling hook ropes. Don't allow anybody onboard. We'll pair up—watch each other's backs. Henceforth, we'll call ourselves Buzzard's Battalion. Remember that so I can call out to all of you in the middle of chaos." Quick, identifiable names, he'd learned, were so important during battle. Being able to address everyone he commanded in a quick manner was paramount. Edelbrock paired the men, giving Nauc and Lucky the courtesy of working as one. Lightning and thunder punctuated his words, then rain poured from the tortured sky. He doubted it was a natural storm, but something ushered in by the Magicai to give the battle a bit more flair.

Edelbrock found himself with a man from King Garcovi's House. He had big ears and a pointed chin. "What's your name, soldier?"

"Argdis. Used to be a cobbler."

"Well, Argdis, you're a soldier now. And, if you went through the same training I did, you have been for a while."

Argdis snorted, wiping rain from his face. "You might be right. Sounds like you were a soldier before."

"I was," Edelbrock said. Another crash of water slammed into the ship, sending men and women sprawling. One man screamed and plummeted into the arena. Edelbrock stared down, watching the man flail about in the water, shouting for help. Then what looked like a zap of energy or lightning or some other magic, surged in the water by the man and he stopped yelling, and floated on the surface, bobbing with the artificial waves. The energy wasn't from the storm. It had come from underwater.

"The fuck?" Argdis said, next to Edelbrock. "Don't fall in, I guess."

"No."

Vengeance was only a few dozen feet away now. Edelbrock saw gladiators aboard hefting their grappling hooks, getting ready.

"Get ready, Buzzard's Battalion!"

Moments later, the first grappling hook was flung into the distant water. A miss, but it had been close.

Edelbrock looked into the water. A snake wrapped around the floating man's body, twisting around his neck.

Somebody shouted out to nobody in particular, "Eels! There are eels in the water!"

Edelbrock didn't know what an eel was but decided he would do anything in his power to avoid finding out.

Metal crashed and wood splintered as the grappling hooks came. Many of the people on *Allegiance* leaped off, swinging to *Vengeance*. Buzzard's Battalion remained aboard, and Edelbrock became too focused on survival to notice much after that.

He slashed through a pair of grappling hooks before their occupants jumped off *Vengeance*. Perhaps he should've waited for them to start swinging, but Edelbrock knew from experience sometimes waiting for opportunity yielded even worse results.

Argdis plunged his sword into a woman's shoulder, then kicked her in the face. She shouted, lost her grip, and fell overboard, her shrill screams disappearing in the crashing waves.

Another several grappling hooks landed. Edelbrock went to cut them, but a shout from behind warned him of impending danger. He turned, saw one of Buzzard's Battalion getting cut down before the attacker came for Edelbrock.

The world silenced. He didn't hear the cheering and jeering spectators. Sounds of water lapping against the hull and the storm dissipated. The creaking of the ships, smashing of grappling hooks, cries of the dead or wounded, and the clash of metal on metal all muted. He ignored the rainwater dripping down his face. He focused on his movements and thoughts, closing off his surroundings. The attacker surged forward and Edelbrock parried the blow, a familiar ringing climbing his numb forearm. *Parry, parry, block with shield, counterattack, parry, step back.* Edelbrock chanted his moves to himself, remembering his days in the military, using his training to fight smart and wait for an opening. Edelbrock heard a death cry from behind, hoped it was Argdis dispatching somebody, but kept his focus on his opponent.

His opponent snarled and waved his sword back and forth. "I'll cut ye!" The man did a quick double-step forward and lashed at Edelbrock's thigh.

Jumping back, Edelbrock's foot hit something solid and he tumbled backwards, head bouncing off the wooden floorboards, his back arched over someone's body. His vision blackened for a moment and his forehead began pounding. The grappling hook he'd slung over his shoulder had whacked him. "Fuck," he said. He scurried back to his feet, abandoning the damn thing. He saw Argdis finishing the attacker.

Allegiance lurched, and Edelbrock almost lost his footing again. "Fuck," he said, again. He experienced a moment of nausea, forced it down.

The spectators continued cheering and yelling, enjoying the event. Edelbrock grit his teeth and pushed them out of his mind. The King's Stand came into view as *Allegiance* rode another wave. This angered him more, knowing Scayde Haklon was lounging up there, watching him fight, and he looked away.

More gladiators from *Vengeance* had boarded. Argdis engaged one. Nearby, Lucky fought another. Edelbrock gathered himself and rejoined the battle.

A fist smashed into his face, and he lost his grip on the sword. It fell, clattering on the deck and skidding away. A beefy, shirtless man, who'd elected not to wear the provided armor, was pulling back his arm for another punch. Edelbrock ducked, but the punch still clipped him across his temple. Beefy reached out, grabbing Edelbrock by the neck, and dragged him to the edge of the ship.

Edelbrock braced his legs, pulling against the large man, then elbowed him in the gut. Beefy grunted, pinning Edelbrock's arms across his chest. He lifted Edelbrock, slamming him against the taffrail.

Wood scraped against Edelbrock's back. He thrashed in Beefy's arms. Realizing this wasn't accomplishing anything, he took a deep breath and bashed his forehead into his captor's nose. Beefy's nose snapped, blood sprayed, and he released Edelbrock.

Dropping back on *Allegiance's* deck, Edelbrock rolled out of his opponent's reach. He grabbed a sword and surged toward Beefy. Distracted with blood pouring down his face, Beefy didn't react in time. Edelbrock thrust his blade into the man's chest and twisted for maximum effect. Beefy gurgled, then collapsed.

Edelbrock took a moment to recover his breath.

A small black woman appeared in front of him, snarling. If he had a guess, it was a Vessian from the Camel Clans, but he didn't have time to consider it. She lunged, blade slicing through the air at his midriff.

Groaning, he blocked the blow with his shield. He pummeled the woman's face with the hilt of his sword. Blood spurted out her cracked nose, and she hollered what he assumed to be a string of obscenities at him in her native tongue. Their swords clashed once, twice. His fingers went numb from the reverberations, the wet sword hilt slid in his palm. He reinforced his grip.

"I'll kill you," she said.

"I have things to live for."

"Who doesn't?" The woman dropped her shield, gripping her sword two-handed before she leaped. The blade plunged toward his chest.

Edelbrock dove out of the way. *I'm getting too old for this shit.* He regained his footing and heard a loud snap. The woman was screaming and rolling on the ground, holding her leg. It appeared she'd slipped on the wet decking, fallen hard, and broken her shin.

"Tough luck," he said.

"Fuck you!"

And I was going to let you live. His primal, sadistic side took over. Snarling, he slapped her sword from her hand with his, then dropped his own. He picked her up and carried her.

"What are you doing?"

"Giving the people what they want."

"What does that mean?"

"They want a show? I'll give them a fucking show."

She screamed. "Don't! Mercy! Mercy!"

The crowd cheered. Edelbrock tossed the woman into the electrified, eel-infested water. She shrieked before they got her. The crowd's cheering became a sonorous chant. He couldn't make out the words. His breathing raspy, he doubled over, catching his breath. Then, he heard it. The crowd chanted his House leader's name. "Haklon! Haklon!" Edelbrock squinted his eyes, looking at the people in the stands. They pointed in his direction. They stared at him.

Shaking rainwater from his eyes, he turned away from the crowd, ignoring them and focusing on the battle. He blew water from his upper lip, and then a great weight slammed him against the taffrail. The wood cracked, then snapped, and Edelbrock found his upper half dangling over the water, sword tumbling into the water. He pinned his legs against two of the taffrail's support beams, preventing himself from falling. His heart pounded in his chest, and he let slip a panicked shout. His hands scrambled to grab something, anything, so he could hoist himself back up. A blinding flash of lightning caused his vision to blacken, followed by a thunderous crack. The ship lurched and Edelbrock slammed against the hull. His legs strained, and he wondered if they'd snap off, as he dangled like a rag doll.

He popped his ears and blinked several times. Vision returned. Edelbrock's thighs burned from holding his weight. Reaching up to grasp the broken taffrail with his arm, he struggled to haul himself back onto *Allegiance's* deck.

A well-muscled man wearing bronze bracelets—one of House Jaylena's men—lay dazed, blood seeping from a wound on his head. *Was it he who almost got me killed?* Beside the unconscious man was another sword. Edelbrock took it, slit the man's throat, and moved on. He hoped the warrior was one of Jaylena's favorites.

Allegiance tipped back and forth as it circled Buzzard's Bowl's perimeter. The crowd continued chanting for their various House preferences. Edelbrock tuned them out, watching the other ship, *Vengeance*, rebounding off a wall. Wood snapped, and *Vengeance's* motion halted. As *Allegiance* circled the arena and got closer to the other ship, Edelbrock realized they were going to collide.

He ran to the center of the deck, finding a mast to loop his arms and legs around. "We're crashing!" he shouted futilely. Nobody was going to hear him. Another bout of thunder and lightning. The rain-soaked mast chilled him, but he clutched it tight, anyway.

The ship's bow tore into the rear of *Vengeance*. The sound of splintering wood and panicked people bled away as more thunder drowned everything out. *Allegiance* hit resistance from *Vengeance* and the ship slammed to a stop. Edelbrock's face rebounded off the mast, his groin bouncing off the wooden post. Stars erupted, and he lost the strength to grasp the mast.

A pair of men from House Lekhan spied Edelbrock. They didn't seem to find themselves bothered with the current predicament, raising their swords and half-running, half-sliding across the wet deck to get to him.

Allegiance shifted again, and Edelbrock almost lost his footing. He steadied himself, then prepared for the inevitable attack. One of the pair had careened across the deck and fallen through the gap in the taffrail. He'd caught himself, one hand grasping the support beam which had saved Edelbrock. His partner was at his side, trying to haul him back up.

Edelbrock rushed over, dropping his sword on the deck. "No need to die this day," he told the pair.

The one dangling smiled. "Thank you!"

The one hauling his partner said, through gritted teeth, "Help me, then."

Edelbrock reached down, gripping the man's arm, and together, they pulled, hauling him back onto the deck.

"Thank you," the rescued one said again.

"You're welcome," Edelbrock said. "We need—"

The other one lunged at Edelbrock, sword aimed at his neck. Diving away from the attack, Edelbrock fell on his ass. He grasped around for the sword he'd dropped, discovered the blade, and followed it to the hilt. He sprung back to his feet, sword out in front of him. "Devious bastard." He should've known that would happen. He'd seen all the dastardly tactics men used plenty of times in the war.

The man shrugged. "In battle, we must do what's best for ourselves. It's not personal."

The second man—the one Edelbrock helped save—joined his comrade, weapon readied. "This don't feel right, but I guess it's a gonna happen, regardless."

"It doesn't have—" Edelbrock started, but they both charged before he could finish.

He ducked to the side, avoiding one and parrying the other. The one he'd dodged slipped on the deck, sliding out of range—or immediate concern.

Allegiance somehow freed itself from *Vengeance* and was now circling Buzzard's Bowl again. Over his opponent's shoulder, Edelbrock saw *Vengeance* breaking apart, sinking.

He dashed forward, sword nicking his opponent's wrist. The man gasped, dropping his sword, and Edelbrock brought his sword down again, severing the man's arm. The man dropped to his knees, screaming in pain and begging for his life.

"This doesn't feel right, but I guess it's a gonna happen regardless," Edelbrock said, repeating the man's words. He stuck the warrior in the chest. His wound issued a loud squelch when Edelbrock yanked the blade free.

Turning to confront the second man, Edelbrock realized he'd fled. But it didn't matter.

The crowd was cheering again. Chanting various House names. Fighting subsided and Edelbrock heard the blow of a horn, then another. The fight had ended.

Lining up on the *Allegiance's* deck were the survivors of the fight. A cluster of House Haklon gathered together on one side. He checked on them, searching for members of Buzzard's Battalion. Argdis—from the king's House—had survived, along with both Lucky and Nauc. Five others lay dead or were missing. The rest of them nursed wounds. *Could've been worse.*

Then, *Allegiance* stopped moving and waves stopped crashing. A small bump, and *Allegiance* was at the dock. Edelbrock looked out into the water, saw dozens of men and women swimming towards the opposite dock—survivors of *Vengeance.* Some were killed by the electric eels, a few others thrashed around, unable to swim. Many, Edelbrock thought, would reach the dock. Many others would not.

The announcer's voice sounded again. "Congratulations! You've all survived your first event!"

Exhausted, Edelbrock dropped to his knees. He knew this was just the start. He didn't want to consider what was in store for them next.

<hr>

Edelbrock, Lucky, and Nauc returned to their House quarters, and Argdis bade them farewell, then returned to his. Cheers and claps of approval met them, but all Edelbrock wanted was to collapse and sleep for a day. That, however, didn't seem to be an option.

Scayde Haklon, their House owner—and wrecker of Edelbrock's family and life—appeared mere moments after Edelbrock had taken a seat to rest his sore thighs. His yellow cape flourished about his black boots as he paced back and forth in front of Edelbrock, fingers smoothing out his bristling mustache, which reminded Edelbrock of a large caterpillar. His face warped into an arrogant sneer when his eyes caught sight of Edelbrock.

Behind Scayde Haklon, former Marshal of Lochwall—though he'd kept the title for some reason—Everic Deywin stood. The man swished a leaf of skachi in his mouth, an addictive chew, and spat a brownish liquid on the ground. Several other guardsmen accompanied the marshal.

"Did you enjoy your first foray in the arena?" Scayde asked.

Edelbrock clenched his jaw. He wanted to rush the man, kill him, but he wouldn't be able to. Between the marshal and the guards, he wouldn't make it. And he had no weapon.

"Did you enjoy your first foray in the arena, *Ed?*" he asked again.

"No."

"That's too bad. The crowd absolutely adored you. Don't ask me why. You're lucky you're still alive—shit fighter you are. Ain't I right, Everic?"

"Don't know, my lord, can't say I was paying all that much attention," Marshal Deywin said. He spat out a glob of brown juice. Remnants trickled down his chin and he swiped it off with the back of his hand.

"Better things to do," Edelbrock offered.

Scayde sneered at Edelbrock. "Think you're funny? Well, you know what I think's funny? I bed your wife every night. She calls me her husband. She's probably pregnant with my child. Jaylena's so in love with me, that she *killed* your son, after betraying you. You're the one person she *should* have trusted. How, Edelbrock Brendis, do you suppose somebody can hate their husband so much that they allow somebody to murder their only child simply so they don't have to be reminded of their husband's face?"

"Fuck you," Edelbrock said.

"No, Ed, fuck you." Scayde turned to the marshal. "Teach him some humility and respect."

Marshal Deywin tipped his head in deference to the Duke of Lochwall.

With Scayde retreating up the stairs, Marshal Deywin and his men rolled their sleeves up and approached Edelbrock, fists raised. Edelbrock tensed, bracing himself for the blows.

"Knock him senseless, boys," Marshal Deywin said.

The fists slammed into Edelbrock. He dropped to his

knees and blows rained down upon him. Then the kicking started. Edelbrock could only think of his hatred of Scayde and his wife, of how unfair it, how sick it was, that Gordy had died. All for what? For this? A wave of helplessness blanketed his anger. There wasn't much he could do. But someday-

A boot caught him in the forehead, knocking any thoughts from his mind.

He grunted, Edelbrock didn't give Scayde, or the marshal and his men, the satisfaction of making any noise or pleading for them to stop.

Until the marshal retrieved a cudgel.

3

A S H E N H Y R E L

Anepolis, Calrym

"'Never trust anyone, even those you trust,' my father always told me. One of his Five Rules of Survival. I can't imagine that advice becoming any more applicable than now," Ashen said.

"Sound advice, sound advice. I assure you, however, that I'm trustworthy" Jaspard Couliac, a rich nobleman residing in Lochwall, hadn't lied to her before. As far as she could tell. He'd taken her in as an orphan, after all. After she'd admitted she'd stolen from him. Ashen's childhood wasn't ideal—her parents were children themselves when they'd birthed her. They both died when she was young and she'd been forced to survive alone on the streets. However, her father's advice applied to Jaspard just as much as anyone else.

That'd been just over a year ago. Maybe more. Ashen, at the unprepared age of fourteen, was about to attend her first meeting with King Mikas and his dukes and duchesses. Duke Sturgeon Gothal's death from heart failure, while expected, had come earlier than planned, and Jaspard had been able to push her name forward as an obvious replacement—she shared a last name with Duchess Arena Hyrel. Jaspard and Ashen had been discussing potential outcomes, who to distrust, and how to handle various situations. She wasn't sure she understood most of it.

Jaspard popped a sugared honey chew in his mouth—his favorite snack. His dangling mustaches twitched and shook as he moved the candy around with his tongue.

"Dinner's ready," the Couliac house servant, Bethinda, announced from the dining room.

"Well, ain't this a way to spoil a rich man's appetite?" Ashen said to Jaspard, pointing at his mouth.

He glared at her, no doubt about to lecture her on speaking like an urchin. Ashen was supposed to speak proper, always—to prepare for her important meetings and proximity to the king. Instead, Jaspard grinned, then leaned in close to her ear. "Say nothing to Lady Couliac, for my sake."

"I wouldn't dream of it, my lord," Ashen said, offering a slight tilt of her head in deference to him. Just as they'd practiced.

Jaspard beamed, then led them into the dining hall, where the house servant, Bethinda, had already placed steaming plates of food on the long table. He swirled his golden-lined green cloak as he walked for dramatic effect and to elicit a slight giggle from Ashen.

At the foot of the table sat Lady Couliac—Ashen's spot when she wasn't in attendance—Jaspard took his place at the head, which left Ashen square in the middle. The Lady Alora Couliac was Jaspard's sister, and she visited his manor often. As both Jaspard and Alora were hopelessly single, filthy rich, and eternally bored, they made wonderful companions. She wore her hair in elaborate fashions and Ashen had never seen Alora without her extravagant silk clothing or expensive jewelry.

"Lady Hyrel," Alora said, standing, "what a pleasure."

Ashen gave a polite smile. Then, as she'd practiced, turned her face into a sneer. "Why yes, I'm sure it's a pleasure for you, my dear." She placed her hand on her heart. "It seems I've forgotten your name, Lady . . .?"

Alora appeared shocked for a moment and turned to Jaspard. Upon seeing his proud smile, she let out a chuckle. "Jaspard, you put her up to this?"

"She's got to learn the game, Alora. She needs to prepare. Some nobles aren't like you and I."

"Too true," Alora said, returning to her seat.

Ashen found her place, and she practiced eating like a lady of the King's Council. Meaning she didn't eat.

Jaspard and Alora feasted on a delightful meal. Slices of roasted beef; a pitcher of thick gravy made with cream and dotted with mushrooms; stacks of fresh-baked bread and butter; a cauldron of sweet maple and turnip soup; fennel and barley salad with a salted vinegar dressing; and almond pudding.

Ashen's stomach rumbled, but she knew she'd need to get used to it. *Prim and proper, prim and proper. Best not forget or I'll be a squatter.* Deep in her heart, Ashen knew the reason Jaspard let her stay was to fulfill his plans. If she failed, she knew she'd be homeless again. So Ashen dedicated most of her time to practicing proper behavior.

Often, according to Jaspard, the dukes and duchesses of the King's Council had food prepared. Arena Hyrel rarely ate anything, preferring to drink wine. Jaspard thought it'd be good for Ashen to mimic her relative's quirk in this regard—it'd also give an immediate appearance of a life filled with noble influence. Others had developed horrible reputations because of *how* they ate food. Jaspard and Ashen both agreed in order to fit in with the Hyrel familial line, and to avoid any potential disasters, she'd abstain from eating. The first task was to learn discipline, no matter what was served.

When dinner finished, Jaspard wiped his lips and popped another chew into his mouth.

"You're going to get sick one day, Jaspard," his sister said.

"It'll be worth it. These are delicious." Jaspard turned his attention to Ashen. "Aside from staring at the beef and gravy, the slight biting of your lips when I broke into the baked bread, and your tongue darting out of your mouth during almond pudding, you managed yourself nicely. The subtle cues might go unnoticed by some, but other, more observant individuals will pick up on them."

"For the love of Mother Avani, Jaspard, let the child eat," Alora said.

Ashen didn't care if it was for the love of the goddess she'd never thought of, didn't care about proper decorum of Calrym nobility, she just knew her stomach was rumbling.

"Fine, fine. Eat up, Ashen," Jaspard said.

Grateful, Ashen dug in. But not before being reprimanded by Jaspard for the way she held her fork.

Pretending to be something she wasn't irked Ashen. She'd grown up on the streets, murdered her best friend—who'd murdered Ashen's father—scavenged for food, avoided city guards, and had entitled noble women shriek at her. Ashen didn't feel prepared for this.

The next morning, Lady Couliac did Ashen's hair, demonstrating how to plait it. For extra effect, Alora left two smaller braids loose from the plaited hair, which draped off Ashen's forehead and hung below her breasts, so long it had grown.

"This fashion will tantalize the eyes. Women will be jealous, men will be intrigued, and you, Lady Hyrel, will be immediately recognized. Trust me." With such elaborate hairstyles, Ashen doubted anyone knew more than Alora.

Bethinda, the house servant, assisted Ashen into her outfit

—a white underdress; a long-sleeved yellow gown, made of velvet; and a dark blue hooded mantle, where Jaspard had paid a tailor extra to sew a few hidden inside pouches.

"Beautiful," Lady Couliac said, looking Ashen up and down. "You'll be unstoppable."

"I can hardly wait," Ashen said. It wasn't true. She'd repeatedly thought about all the possible ways her mission could go wrong and the many ways she could end up dead. Ashen swallowed, nervous.

"You'll be all right, Ashen. You're young. Nobody is going to suspect a thing."

"Ashen? Alora?" Jaspard's voice came from the front of the house. He'd gone out earlier.

"Ah, he must be back with your gift," Alora said. "Come." She led Ashen through the manor, to the entryway where Ashen had first arrived as an orphan, carrying Jaspard's stolen weapon.

Gift? I certainly don't deserve a gift. If anything, Jaspard had given her enough. He hadn't reported her theft; he hadn't killed her when she returned the sword she'd taken from him, and he'd given her a home. All she needed to do was promise she'd train and work hard to become an excellent lady and he'd secure her a spot on the King's Council. Ashen didn't know how he did it, but Jaspard made good on his promise. He'd appealed to King Mikas's chancellor, proved Ashen's lineage, and once Duke Sturgeon Gothal passed, they reached out and accepted Ashen, though with a clause stating if she wasn't liked, she wouldn't stay. Jaspard gave her a much more notable first name, too: Cithrial. "The name 'Ashen' is much too urban," he'd said.

Jaspard and a stranger sat in the meeting room. Ashen noticed Jaspard wore his decorative rapier beneath his cloak, and his mustache shined with wax.

The stranger looked rather frightening. A jagged scar crossed the top of his bald head. Mean brown eyes peered at her from beneath bushy brown eyebrows, and his lip rose in a sneer above a bulbous chin, presenting a lengthy scar. One of his eyes had a pink splotch of marred flesh surrounding it and, upon second glance, the iris was milky. It appeared as if something had hit him in the face at one point. A long-handled axe leaned against the wall, and an assortment of sheathed blades hung from his body. All of the clothing he wore, she noted, was gold.

"Lady Hyrel, you're looking magnificent," Jaspard said. He stood, and so did the stranger—who bowed in Ashen's direction.

"Milady," the stranger said. His voice was sharp and gruff, like he'd been a drinker much of his life. He cleared his throat.

"A pleasure," Ashen said, giving a ladylike curtsy. *Well, ain't this a sight for the blind?* She immediately felt bad about the thought, given the man's eye.

"Lady Cithrial Hyrel, or shall I say, beginning today, *Duchess* Cithrial Hyrel, allow me to introduce this man, Tallas Taybold. Once known as the Golden Knight." Jaspard paused, glancing at Tallas. "I got that right, yes?"

Tallas dipped his head. "Correct."

"He is a man of few words, but they're the proper ones," Jaspard said.

"It's my pleasure to meet you, Lord Taybold," Ashen said.

"Just Taybold," he said. He cleared his throat again. "Or Tallas."

Ashen smiled. She didn't know what Jaspard, or Tallas, expected from her.

"This man is to be your personal guard," Jaspard said. "I've hired him to protect you. He's the very best, I promise. You'll be expected to have several guards, actually. Tallas will see to that. His job is to make sure you're safe. In fact, he'll be staying with us now. Permanently."

Tallas dipped his head in acknowledgement again.

Ashen didn't know what to think. It hadn't occurred to her she'd have guardsmen. On one hand, she wondered if the man was there to spy on her for Jaspard. On the other, it might be nice to have somebody she could boss around. Aside from being an ugly fellow, he had a mean expression and a grumpy posture. She could tell that although he had a gruff exterior, he was also kindhearted. It was easy for her to recognize the bad men, so many she'd been around during her time on the streets, and much of her analysis was based on their overall demeanor. Tallas acted tough, was probably tough, but he didn't say the tough things bad men often did. He was hiding. "I look forward to our working partnership," she said. Ashen offered the man a smile. He switched his gaze to his feet. She frowned, not sure if she'd offended him.

"Ah, Tallas, my apologies," Jaspard said, gesturing to Lady Couliac. "This is my sister, Lady Alora Couliac. She visits from occasionally and should be free to come and go as she pleases."

Tallas, ever the talker, dipped his head in her direction. "Milady," he said.

"It's wonderful to meet you, Tallas," Lady Couliac said. Even Ashen could tell the woman was trying her best to put on a brave face. "Jaspard said he was bringing back the best, and your reputation precedes you. The Golden Knight? I had no clue he hired somebody of such . . . *talent*." Her lips contorted in a grimace of sorts.

Tallas's eyes narrowed for a moment, but he corrected himself and offered a grim grin in return. "I'm pleased you've heard of me."

"With introductions made, Tallas, I believe you have a crew to get ready? Lady Hyrel has a meeting to attend—and she won't be late on the day King Mikas recognizes her as a duchess of Anepolis!"

A horse-drawn carriage waited outside Jaspard's manor, Tallas's men stood ready. Ashen, having mastered the art of acting noble, knew it was time to figure out if the king would accept her. Time to become Duchess Cithrial Hyrel. She could do it. She knew she could.

Both Jaspard and Alora remained behind, leaving Ashen to ride in the carriage, alone with Tallas Taybold, the former Golden Knight.

Duchess Cithrial wouldn't have talked to him. But, since they weren't yet inside the palace, Ashen thought she'd attempt to learn a few things. Examining the cold-looking man, she realized there wasn't much to discuss. Tallas was busy peering out the window, watching for trouble. His right hand remained loosely gripping the long-handled axe tipped with a spike he laid across his thighs.

"Sir Tallas, what is that weapon called?"

"Tallas," he said, not turning to look at her. "It's a halberd."

"It seems . . . impractical. And I shall call you what I want. Lord Couliac *is* paying you a salary, yes?"

Tallas grunted.

"Perfect. Sir Tallas, how are you to use a weapon like that indoors?"

"I don't," he said. His spare hand patted one of his many blades. "That's why I have these."

"Then why bother carrying that awful thing around? It's enormous. I'd die." Ashen had carried her house on her back for several years—the thought of having to carry around such a large object for no reason seemed odd.

"It frightens people. And I'm good with it."

Ashen raised an eyebrow, then dropped it, remembering he couldn't see her facial expressions. Good practice, anyway. *Well, ain't this a conversation for a tongueless shithead?* She leaned back, crossing her arms in a most unladylike way.

Jaspard's voice echoed in her mind, correcting her posture. She ignored him.

Ashen worried about how she'd be perceived—she was only fourteen. She knew she wouldn't receive much respect. But, then again, she wasn't here for respect. Ashen had a goal. Well, it was more like Jaspard had a goal. She'd do her best to fulfill it, repaying him for taking her in as an orphan. And also, because it felt good belonging somewhere.

Tallas, for once, stopped watching out the window and faced her. "Lord Couliac says you're allowed a single guardsman inside the palace."

"I've been informed."

"Which one would you like it to be?" he asked.

"You're the only one I know, Sir Tallas. You're who Jaspard hired, and therefore, who I would assume he trusts most. I will have Sir Tallas accompany me."

"Very well. But it's just Tallas."

The carriage slowed, and a guardsman opened the door. Tallas hopped out, then offered his hand to her.

Duchess Cithrial took the offered hand, exiting the carriage. "Thank you." She paused, distracted by the marbled palace looming in front of her. Not one to let things go, she offered Tallas a beaming smile—her last action as Ashen—and said, "Thank you, Sir Tallas."

He narrowed his eyes at her but said nothing.

Turning back to the palace, she took a deep breath. Her duty began now.

Duchess Cithrial Hyrel's mission was to murder the nobles. And the king.

4

SERADAL WINTLOCK & VILLIC THE IMBUER

Andora, Remeria

Villic the Imbuer scratched his bald head and squinted at the people standing atop the hill.

"Worried?" the Speaker in his head asked. Speaker was, as far as Villic knew, a god. Though he claimed not to be, Villic was unconvinced. Well, sometimes he was unconvinced. He went back and forth on what he believed. Speaker also gave Villic his newfound powers—the ability to imbue his weapons with unique elements.

"Villic? Pay attention. This is how people die."

I know.

"If you knew, you'd pay attention. Are you worried about the new arrivals?"

Villic looked back at the colorful people on the hill. They had very pale skin, and each one wore a different colored cloak. He saw blue, green, yellow, and one wore gray. "I want a cloak."

"People would notice you."

I don't want a cloak.

People started marching down the hill, in the direction of the camping Camel Clans. Towards Villic's clan, the Splintered Manes. Other men and women formed a perimeter between the Remerian capital, Anepolis, and the approaching strangers. Nobody was allowed in, or out, of the city. At least, that's what the shamans said. And Villic listened to the shamans. Ignoring them would ignore the gods, as shamans were godspeakers. To ignore the gods would invite their displeasure upon you, and since Villic had become an Imbuer, he felt they'd blessed him. He didn't want to lose their favor.

"The gods didn't give you this power. I don't know how many times I have to reiterate that."

Villic didn't know what "reiterate" meant. He also didn't care. Speaker liked to speak too much.

"Villic the Imbuer. Come."

Talking was something Villic wasn't great at. Sometimes, he got so lost in thoughts, he wondered—

"Villic, answer the woman."

What?

"Turn around."

Villic swiveled. One of the clan's shamans waited for him. He didn't know her name. Villic rarely remembered anybody's name.

"She wants you to follow her."

Villic followed as the woman led him away. He wanted to ask her what they were doing, or where they were going. But that'd mean having a conversation with her. Starting one himself. Beads of sweat formed on his forehead. He didn't enjoy talking to normal people, let alone the shamans. Shamans made him nervous. They could, on a whim, decide to banish clan members. Or ask the gods to strike someone down. Not that he thought they would. He was an Imbuer. They needed him. *Don't they?*

"Yes, Villic. They need you."

Villic didn't trust Speaker's word. He trusted Speaker, but not with matters of the gods.

The shaman brought Villic to a circle. All the other shamans and Imbuers surrounded Jedkah, leader of the Splintered Manes. Jedkah frightened Villic even more than the shamans because as leader, he had the final say in everything related to the clan and could banish Villic anytime he wanted. He had a firm voice and had etched and burned various markings and symbols on his body as a sign of strength. The strongest members of a clan often practiced this technique. Villic would never do it, though. He didn't think it proved anything.

Jedkah spoke to the circle. "We don't know what the Hill Strangers want, yet. Mutaz hasn't offered an opinion." *Mutaz, god of war*, Villic recited. If he were to remember what each god represented, he had to rehearse their title. "The shamans have advised me the Hill Strangers are from the north. They shouldn't be here. Their presence is unusual and disturbing. We will have to discuss this with Killiak." *Killiak, lord of lords. Ruler of all gods.* Nobody wanted to upset him.

"*Myths,*" Speaker said.

Why call attention to us? You insult the gods and Killiak, lord of lords, won't forget it.

Speaker didn't respond. Just as well, Villic knew they'd never agree with one another on this topic.

"Prepare for battle, just in case," Jedkah said. He dismissed the circle, but remained with the shamans, pointing at the northern Hill Strangers and talking.

Villic overheard one Imbuer talking to another Imbuer.

"It's not right. We're more powerful than the shamans. Why aren't we allowed to stay?"

"Hush! What if they hear us? You'll anger the gods and invoke their fury!"

"Let them try. We're more powerful than they are."

"You're going to get us killed. Quiet yourself."

Villic shook his head. *Nobody is more powerful than the godspeakers.* He would've reported the offending Imbuers to the shamans, but the shamans were busy. And he wouldn't initiate a conversation either way. *The gods know everything, anyway. No need to inform the shamans.*

"Villic, I think—"

"No, Speaker. Leave me be," Villic said. He knew Speaker wanted to talk more about the gods. He wasn't in the mood for another debate, though.

Silent as usual, Villic made his way to his camel, Dunecrest. He made sure the beast was taken care of, then checked to ensure his scimitar and spear were in good condition. Then Villic sat and waited.

The setting sun created an orange glow in the sky, and though the air cooled a bit, the humid warmth of Remeria was constant. Villic watched the sky, searching for the gods while wondering what would happen next.

It might've been Villic's success during his last battle that made the clan respect him more. It might've been that he was the closest Imbuer, ready and available. Either way, Jedkah, leader of the Splintered Manes approached, a shaman at his side. The same shaman who'd brought him to the circle earlier.

"Villic the Imbuer," Jedkah said, "you're with me. An envoy from the Hill Strangers approaches. You will protect us."

Villic stood, unsure of what to do or say.

"Leave your camel," the shaman said.

Villic growled under his breath. *His name is Dunecrest.*

"Maybe she'd know that if you talked to them. And might I inquire, what is the shaman's name?"

Villic didn't know, and he knew Speaker knew that.

"It's Dashiki Magoro. If you paid more attention when people spoke, you'd remember these things."

I don't like talking. Which wasn't true. Not really. Villic just didn't enjoy talking to people he wasn't close to. And, because of his social anxiety, it was difficult to get close to anyone. He'd had a family he'd been close to. His mother and father. His brother, too. Villic's mother had died of sickness a few years ago. His father and brother had died in a battle against the Plagued Ones, another Camel Clan. Villic didn't possess any grudges against the Plagued Ones—it was just the way of the Camel Clans. He was saddened that he lost the only people he was close to. One day, Flaytz, god of death, would claim his soul and he'd meet up with them again.

"You're standing still, Villic."

Villic blinked. Jedkah and Dashiki stared at him.

"Let's go," Jedkah said, a harsh tone in his voice. If Villic were to take a guess, Jedkah had already said this once.

"He said it once. Twice, actually. The man's patient with you."

Villic ignored Speaker and followed Jedkah and the shaman. Two men waited for them halfway down the hill where the Hill Strangers camped. Both were armed, though neither seemed concerned about Jedkah, Dashiki, and Villic walking their way. As they got closer to the men, Villic saw them in more detail. One was old and wore a gray cloak. The other looked unclean and unwell, and he wore a decorated, stained jacket. He smelled funny, but Villic couldn't place the scent.

"Whiskey. A type of alcohol."

Villic had only had peshi, a drink made from the fermented juices of a type of cactus. It tasted like camel dung, so Villic refused to consume it.

One of the Hill Strangers said something Villic didn't understand.

I'll translate. That one introduced himself as Sir Vecchio Rizurri.

Speaker's translation wasn't needed, though, because Dashiki translated out loud.

"And he is Captain Decklin Hoarst," Dashiki said,

pointing to the other man.

"I am Jedkah, leader of the Splintered Manes. This is Dashiki Magoro, shaman, from the clan Seven Signs. She is aiding me with translations. And that is Villic the Imbuer. He will protect me from anything you try," Jedkah said. Dashiki translated all this back to the Hill Strangers.

Dashiki gestured toward the Remerian capital. "They want safe passage to the city."

Villic scratched his neck. He was getting sick of the bugs.

"Pay attention, Villic."

I am.

"That is not for us to decide. Not without the approval of *all* the Camel Clan leaders," Jedkah said.

"Your eyes were wandering."

"They say that is acceptable and ask that you inquire on their behalf." Dashiki paused a moment. "Jedkah, if I may offer some advice?"

I got distracted.

"No," he said. "What else do they have to say?"

"That's the problem. Watch the people. Listen."

Quiet. But Villic listened to Speaker and turned his attention to the people, again.

Dashiki, looking rather annoyed, turned back to the two men, and said something. She didn't translate. "They say they want to rest. They've had a long journey. Sailed across the world. They want an audience with King Alondo, of Remeria, because their homelands were conquered by Calrym."

Jedkah looked surprised. "We're also an enemy of the Calrites. Tell them that after we kill King Alondo, we mean to do the same to King Mikas."

Dashiki translated, and the two men appeared happier. "They ask that you leave Remeria alone. Remeria is the only faction able to contest Calrym's power."

Jedkah laughed. "They haven't seen our Imbuers in action, yet!"

"I don't think I should tell them that, Jedkah."

"No, no. You're right. Tell them that the Camel Clans are stronger than ever. We will kill King Mikas. But we aren't leaving. And tell them we'll meet with the other clan leaders. Maybe we'll allow a small group to pass and deliver a message to the king, but that is not for me to decide. Inform them the Camel Clans are bringing vengeance on the Remerians because of their allegiance with Calrym, because they've helped keep us in Vessia. Instead of allowing us a small portion of farmable land, they helped kill us. It's time we claim land of our own."

Dashiki translated Jedkah's words to the Hill Strangers.

The old man frowned but nodded. Then the two Hill Strangers retreated to their camp.

"Come, Villic," Jedkah said. "Thank you for being here. If Mutaz, god of war, beckons us, we'll need you. And I have a feeling he's going to be calling upon us soon. First, however, I must meet with the other shamans and leaders."

Villic wouldn't resist a command from the gods. He wasn't that foolish.

Seradal Wintlock was exhausted from travelling. And now, here she was with her companions, trying to think through what they would do next. Her black hair had escaped its binding again from a breeze, and now blew in her face. She gathered it up and bound it, once again.

Cyr Vecchio Rizurri, the Old Vulture, looked rigid and professional when trying to appear relaxed. He sat in the grass atop the hill, watching the Camel Clansmen outside the city. Next to him stood Captain Decklin Hoarst, or Royal, as he preferred to be called, draining his flask. Beads of moisture clung to Royal's wild goatee, which had flecks of gray Sera hadn't noticed before.

Royal smacked his lips, then licked his whiskers, wiping his mouth with the sleeve of his stained captain's jacket. "Think they'll let us in?"

"Impossible to predict, foolish to postulate."

Royal swallowed the last few drops of his drink. "You can't go inside the city," he said.

The Old Vulture frowned for a moment, then turned away from Royal and gazed at Andora. The city, flanked on all sides by Camel Clansmen, rested next to a large river which wound its way through a wide stretch of grasslands. "I know," he said after a moment.

"You're too important out here."

Sera agreed. The Old Vulture was the only remaining member of the leadership they had. King Mikas's army had swept through Cyrok, leaving most of their people dead. Governess Stasia Falconel. Cyr Ilic Strictland. Cyr Ollitha Oxhorn. Somehow, the Old Vulture made it. His title was accurate, at least.

"I know," the Old Vulture said, again. His face still furrowed; it seemed he wasn't happy about the decision.

Quiet fell as everyone thought about this. A shrieking bird caught Sera's attention. To her left she saw a small bird fleeing an eagle. Long talons reached out and plucked the smaller bird midflight and the screeching stopped. The bird either dead or too afraid to make noise. Then the eagle disappeared.

Royal broke the silence. "I'll go, cyr."

Sera gasped. She couldn't help it. "You?"

"What's wrong with me?"

"You'll both go," the Old Vulture said.

"*I'll* go?" Sera asked. Now she really didn't understand what was happening.

"Yes. Both of you."

"Surely there's somebody more suited to the task," Sera said. She didn't hold any rank over anyone other than Royal.

Sera was the newest Falcon Knight in their group, and Royal was the only normal Cyroki military soldier of their group. Everyone else was a Falcon Knight—aside from her page, Renard, who'd insisted on sticking with her. All the Falcon Knights outranked her in tenure.

The Old Vulture rose to his feet. "Captain Decklin Hoarst, though an alcoholic," Royal shrugged, "is wiser than he may appear. I have a hunch he's decent with the sword, though nobody seems to have seen him using it. And you, Cyr Seradal, have suffered, and yet you still persevere. You've maintained composure and have done what's been needed to survive. You're a fighter, and you'll do the best you can."

I abandoned my people. I stole away on a carriage and escaped with my father. He can't possibly think I should be the one for this. She thought of her family, too. How her mother and brother had been slaughtered. How her father's friend, Angazo, had died in battle. Sera knew because of the war—because of everything that kept happening—she continued suppressing her feelings. Her grief. She hadn't mourned properly. Every time she thought of her mother or her brother, she pushed them out of her mind. *Just a little longer.* But she had been thinking that for too long. Nevertheless, more kept happening.

"You're strong, Cyr Seradal. If the Camel Clans allow it, our country needs you to go inside the city and meet with the king. The Falcon Knights need you. *I* need you. It's important trustworthy people enter the city. We need to see what King Alondo's situation is like. We need to learn what's going on here."

"We don't know if we'll be allowed through," Sera said.

"Well," Royal said, straightening the collar to his captain's jacket, "we're about to find out." He pointed down the hill. Three Camel Clansmen stood at the base, looking up at them.

Villic stood to the left and just behind of Jedkah. To the clan leader's right, the shaman Dashiki Magoro. Villic was here to protect, so he crossed his arms and bared his teeth, and watched the trio of Hill Strangers descend towards them.

Am I fierce-looking, Speaker?

"It took us a long time to have this conversation, Villic, but I hope you're aware that I cannot actually see you."

"Huh."

Jedkah cocked his head in Villic's direction. "What? Do you see something wrong?"

Nervous heat flashed across Villic's cheeks and forehead. He swallowed. "No," he said.

Jedkah returned his attention to the Hill Strangers, who were now only a lion's lunge away. Or was it twelve camel strides? Villic didn't know. He couldn't tell distances very well. With Jedkah's focus off Villic, the heat dissipated and he relaxed, letting out a whoosh of air.

"You're hopeless."

When you walked around, you had problems. What were they?

"I didn't have problems. I was flawless. We were the most powerful people who've ever existed."

Sounds like you thought you were better than everyone else. Sounds like you might be a liar. Alhexa, goddess of truth, would frown at you.

"We were. How do you think I'm here? We discovered how to make ourselves immortal."

Only the gods are immortal.

"Then explain how I'm here now."

You'll die one day.

"I don't think you under—"

Quiet, Speaker.

The nice thing about talking to Speaker was that it happened much faster in his head. On the other hand, Speaker was annoying and often wouldn't leave Villic alone.

Once again, the Hill Strangers spoke and Dashiki translated.

"What's your verdict?" the old man asked.

If fighting were to happen, Villic would go after him first. There was a reason he was old, and it wasn't his diet. Villic almost laughed at the idea of food impacting how long you lived. He shook his head. Then stopped and bared his teeth at the three Hill Strangers again. The smelly one ignored him. The pale girl looked confused. He stopped presenting his teeth and closed his mouth, looking down at the ground. Then he realized if they attacked, he wouldn't notice, so Villic stared at the girl's sword, waiting for her to draw it. She didn't.

"The shamans and leaders of the clans wish you no harm. We cannot allow you into the city, though," Jedkah said.

"Just two people, that's all I ask," the old man said.

Dashiki looked at Jedkah, and said in their native tongue, "When I convened with the other shamans, the gods approved of sending a few of them in. The gods are willing to remain neutral with the northerners. For now."

"They don't know that. If we resist a little, they'll feel more obligated towards us. Like we're doing them a favor," Jedkah said.

"Therefore, you're a leader and I speak to the gods," she said.

"Please," the old man said. "Just two?"

Jedkah looked to the sky, as if he was having a secret conversation with the gods. "Just two," he said. "No more."

"Thank you. You've been kind. We assure you we want no fight. Go with peace. These are the two who will enter the city," the old man said, gesturing at the stinky man and the girl.

Jedkah nodded. "You may pass."

That man smells awful.

"At one point in his life he failed something, or somebody. This

is the price he pays."

Villic wondered how true that was.

***

Sera and Royal had passed through the Camel Clan camps. Most ignored the pair as they worked their way through the throng. Upon arriving outside Andora, the Camel Clansmen made a conscious effort to create enough distance between themselves and the gate, allowing the Remerians to feel comfortable letting the pair inside without incident. Several Remerian soldiers immediately escorted her and Royal to King Alondo Sedoa, inside his palace. The king sat in his throne, elevated on a dais, while Atticus Crenshaw, King's Council, hovered behind him. A long table with many chairs sat off to the side—a place to take meals and host meetings, Sera guessed.

"*Sick* is what it is. Sick!" The king slapped the wall. A bang sounded as his arm rebounded, and the man winced. King Alondo Sedoa's face contorted in anger. "It's absurd. A group of knights shows up at *precisely* the moment I need reinforcements. Then they choose to ignore the plague that's been slaughtering Remerians for weeks. It's *sick*." The king bit his lip. Possibly in frustration, possibly to conceal other words he wanted to spew, Sera couldn't tell. "Sick." King Alondo ran a hand over his crownless head.

They'd informed him they weren't looking to aid either side in the conflict.

"Your Majesty, we have guests," Atticus Crenshaw, King's Council, said. He stepped forward and gestured at Sera and Royal, reiterating their position on the situation. "They've come a long way and many of their people lay murdered, staining the Cyroki snow with their blood."

"My apologies," the king said, resuming the circles he'd been pacing. His boots echoed on the marble floor. "It's ironic that we're under siege and under-manned, and you, another armed force, arrives but is unwilling to offer aid. I need to let my temper cool. I'm certainly no King Mikas. He's a raging lunatic." Sera wondered if that was true of King Alondo as well. "Is that a drink, Captain?"

Royal swallowed and held up his flask. "Whiskey, Your Highness." He wiped his face with his stained jacket sleeve. "Want some?" He proffered the drink to the king. Sera swore the man had emptied it earlier.

"Fuck it." King Alondo retrieved the flask and took a heavy mouthful. "Excellent. Thank you, Captain." He handed the flask back.

"Keep it," Royal said, pulling out another and uncorking it. "I'm always well-stocked. I about emptied the tavern in Maceport. Funny name they had: the Winded Man."

The king chuckled, and Atticus pulled a face which resembled amusement.

Sera attempted to refocus the conversation. "We tried to get the Camel Clans to leave Remeria alone, but they're adamant about remaining."

"And why would you care what happens here?" Atticus asked. He pointed the quill he held at Sera. In his other hand, he clutched a stack of parchment filled with words Sera couldn't see well enough to read.

"Calrym almost killed us. The Remerians are the only force powerful enough to aid us," she said.

"There's always the Magicai," Atticus said.

Royal snorted. "They're expensive, and they do nothing for free."

"Help us crush the Camel Clans, and we'll destroy Remeria together," King Alondo said.

Sera tightened her lips. She didn't know what to do and it was her call. The Old Vulture wasn't here.

She opened her mouth to answer when shouts of alarm rang out.

5

DEMRI SLARN

Calrym

Demri swayed in time with his horse. He stared at the back of the only woman he'd ever loved, flanked by two companions. On his left, his life partner, his only friend, Caius. And on his right, one of Myri Celioh's allies.

He and Caius had spent several weeks living in an inn, waiting for the Duke of Lochwall, Scayde Haklon, to secure them passage to the Magicai University of Arcanical Arts —Ashmount. Now, though, he was riding west of Pinecrest, towards a secret Elkavich hideout. Because life was strange that way.

Before climbing atop his gelding, Myri had whispered, "Don't say my name. Please. I'll explain later." Her hand had gently touched his shoulder. She smelled of lavender. Demri couldn't stop smelling her.

They rode. Caius grumbled. Demri smiled. And Myri ignored him and Caius. She kept looking to her left and right, as if she expected pursuers. The man to Demri's right—Myri had called him "A-Sixty"—watched their backs. He picked up on the other names of their companions, too. "A-Eighty-Nine" and "B-Seven". Myri, they called "D-Four".

The horses brought the group to the forest, toward the mountains. As they rode, Demri flicked his eyes at Caius a few times. Every time he glanced over, Caius had his bloodied knife sliding across his fingertips, where his fingernails should be, but they'd been whittled down so they ended far higher where they would normally would, even after trimming.

A few hours into the forest they'd reached their destination. Hidden within dense foliage and a circle of trees entwined with vines, sat a camouflaged building. The insignia of the Elkavich carved in the door—a runic symbol that looked like a triangle tipped on its point, with a line drawn across its center.

Myri hopped off her horse. "A-Eighty-Nine, take care of the horses. A-Sixty, go tell Ced we're back with the prize. B-Seven, take a group of A's with you and make sure our path isn't visible."

They made a similar gesture in Myri's direction—a snap of their fingers with a small flame that puffed out of their hand when they did so.

When it was the three of them, Myri smiled at Demri. She held his gaze with her green eyes, though her face held a pained look. "I'm assuming you know of Scayde Haklon, the Duke of Lochwall?"

Demri nodded. In his peripheral vision, he saw Caius's blade stop flicking across his fingertips—she'd gotten his attention.

"He hired the Elkavich to kill you. Paid us well. When he warned us who we were dealing with, I talked to my superior. Told him you were on the run from Ashmount, and the Magicai. I told him it'd be advantageous to keep you alive. My superior isn't a trusting person and didn't like it. Until I told him we're married. I don't want to kill you, Demri, but you have to play along." *Huh. I'm guessing that's how Scayde knew everything about my past, then.*

It took a moment for her words to register. "M-M-Married?"

Caius laughed. "Funny how things find a way of working out. Isn't that right, Demri?"

Demri glared at Caius and went back to filing his fingers with the knife that was more blood than blade.

"I mean it. The Elkavich take their secrecy seriously. We need to go inside now. Everybody uses a code name here. It's imperative that you don't give up my true name. D-Four is my name, but it's also my rank. I'll explain more later. Come," Myri opened the door. "Welcome to Hidehedge."

Inside, it looked like a well-managed tavern. There were many tables and chairs, all clean, a fully stocked bar complete with glasses and bottles of wine and mead. Demri smelled something cooking in another room, hinting at a kitchen.

"Looks like this place should have a better name than Hidehedge," Caius said. "May I make a suggestion? How about—"

"C-C-Caius. Stop."

A-Sixty entered the room and gave Myri a nod. "Ced's waiting upstairs. But before you go, Disaster wants a word."

Myri nodded and A-Sixty retreated the way he'd entered.

"Disaster is one of the Elkavich leaders," she said. Myri started walking and Demri and Caius fell in line. "There are five leaders, all with monikers, of course. Apocalypse, Bloodbath, Catastrophe, Disaster, and Erasure. They are above everyone." Myri held opened another door for them. They entered a hallway that held several more doors. "The ranking system is simple. 'E' is the highest, 'A' is the lowest. The lower the number you have, the closer you are to the next tier. A-Eighty-Nine is a vetted and trusted newcomer. I'm D-Four, so I've been here a while." She lowered her voice to a whisper. "Inside that door"—she nodded in its direction—"is Disaster. Do not piss him off."

Demri swallowed. He was here. In a place that, until now, he didn't know existed. It was full of people like him. Full of Magicai Ashmount didn't want. These were the illegals, all banded together in a hidden society. All hiding in plain sight, despite their tendency to wear their insignia on their robes. Few knew of the symbol, though rumors had escalated in recent years.

Entering the next room, Demri saw a big sycamore desk. In front of the desk was a row of four plain wooden chairs. Behind the desk sat the man who Demri assumed to be Disaster. He wore a cloth wrapping that concealed his face. His eyes and the top of his head hidden by a fitted hood that looked like it had been made for him. He would be hard to identify. Demri noticed a "D" stitched into the man's robes, below the Elkavich insignia.

"Sit," a deep, monotonous voice said, gesturing at the chairs.

Demri took a seat. *This feels too familiar.* Demri remembered a similar situation with Scayde Haklon. The bastard had tried to pit him against Caius, and then, according to Myri, tried to have him killed. He hoped to get back at the man one day.

Myri placed herself next to Demri. A hand slid onto his thigh, and she looked at him with warmth. His heart thumped. This wasn't real, Demri knew, but the idea that it could be was intoxicating. Still, he had a part to play and he returned her smile,

"D-Four, report," Disaster said.

Her hand stayed on Demri's thigh. "This is my husband, Demri Slarn. Rogue Magicus, apostate, professional evader, and survivalist. He is also the love of my life."

An awkward moment of silence passed. Disaster quirked his head ever-so-slightly, as though to question the validity of the claim. Demri picked up on it, and so did Myri. "Are you —" Disaster said, before stopping.

She leaned over and cupped Demri's cheek, twisting his face to look at hers. Her moist lips found Demri's. For a moment, he froze. Then, either out of desire or because he was acting, or because of natural body reaction, or a combination of all three, he kissed her back. Her lavender scent filled his nostrils. For a moment, their tongues skimmed, and Demri let out a low, unintentional growl.

"Is this . . . professional?" Disaster asked.

Myri pulled back, still smiling, and wiped her lips with her hand. Not the hand which, to Demri's surprise, remained on his thigh. A slight squeeze. He felt himself harden. *Out of all the things I should fear, why am I most frightened of poking her hand?*

"Perhaps not," Myri said. "It's just been a very long time."

"Eighteen years, I recall you saying," Disaster said.

"Yes, eighteen years," Demri said. It'd been the only time he'd seen Myri after he'd fled Ashmount. It was, Demri realized, the only decent memory he had after fleeing Ashmount.

"Continue."

"Scayde Haklon is expecting one of us to return the bodies to his estate outside Lochwall." Myri had removed her hand from Demri's thigh to gesture through her speech. Demri wasn't sure if he was relieved or disappointed. "I assume he'll figure out within a day or two that we've double-crossed him, or he'll assume us dead. Either works with the plan we're forming. It doesn't matter if he finds out. We're hidden, and our plans are already in play."

Disaster nodded, then looked at Caius. "If Demri is a powerful Magicus who might aid us, what can this self-harming fool do, other than cut his fingers?"

Caius looked up from his bloody knife. "I kill people," he said.

"I see."

"I c-can c-c-confirm this. Without C-Caius, I'd have d-died many times over. He's also b-been invaluable t-t-to m-me in innumerable cir-c-c-cumstances."

"He may live, then. For now."

Demri felt Myri's hand return to his thigh. He swallowed, enjoying her warmth.

"D-Four, the only reason I've allowed this to take place is because you are married. It'd be a sad place if the Elkavich, as powerful as we've grown, can't take care of our own members, and those they love. Though, with the limited time we all have left, I'm not sure there was a point to this escapade. However, I'll never claim to be the expert on human psychology or emotional pleasantries." He paused a moment, seeming to consider something, before saying, I want to talk to you alone, now."

"Return to the common room, Demri," Myri said. "Ask for Ced. Somebody will direct you to him. He'll take care of you. Oh, and from now on you'll want to come up with alternative names for yourselves. As unofficial Elkavich members, you won't have a title, but you won't want everyone talking about your true name, particularly if we return to a public place."

C-Eighty, or "Ced" as he preferred being called, was a small, skinny man. Tiny wisps of hair dotted his prepubescent looking face, and he had a high-pitched voice. Nevertheless, everyone treated Ced with respect.

"This here's going to be yer new place of respite," Ced said, waving his hand across two simple beds and a beat-up trunk. He beamed like he was offering them a luxurious room in an expensive resort reserved for nobility. *It's better than most accommodations I've had during my life as a criminal. I can't complain.* Half of the rooms at inns they'd been to had a singular bed infested with bugs and smelled of piss. Caius always volunteered to sleep on the floor. He wouldn't have to do that here. And the room smelled fresh.

"Thank you," Demri said. "I appreciate your p-p-patronage."

"Oh, you've got a bit of a stutter on you," Ced said.

Demri narrowed his eyes at him. He wanted to say something. Berate the man. Insult him. But Demri didn't want to start problems with the Elkavich already. He held his tongue.

"No judgement, no judgement." Ced's excited voice pitched higher and higher—obviously Demri's glare got the message across. "As you can tell, I've got my own voice problems." He cleared his throat, then said in a more controlled— and lower—voice, "If you need anything, I'll be around. 'That's what Ced said, they said.'" He giggled, then mumbled something about how "the other members love to say that" and retreated down the hallway, toward the staircase leading to the main floor.

"He's a character," Caius said. A moment later. "I almost killed him."

"We need to b-b-be c-careful."

"We need names. And you need to stop fawning over that bitch. She's just going to hurt you."

"It's nice that you c-care. B-B-But I am not f-fawning."

Caius quirked a brow but said nothing. He sheathed his bloodied knife and closed the door. "Say what you want, Demri, but we both know you're head over heels in love with that woman. Even I can see that. If she asked you to lick dog shit off a floor, you'd do it."

Demri growled, almost denied it, but said nothing. Caius wasn't wrong.

They shifted to silence, placing their few belongings inside the trunk.

When Myri arrived, Demri and Caius had taken spots on the beds. Caius was filing nonexistent nails and Demri was lost in thought, retreading the twenty years he'd spent fleeing the Magicai. He'd had one goal: survive long enough to find and kill Doram Quandis. And now, at the sudden appearance of Myri Celioh, he'd dropped everything. Ignored that goal. For what? Even he didn't know.

A knock at the door—and the faint smell of lavender—is what snapped him from his thoughts.

"It's me," she said, stepping in. "Did you come up with aliases?"

"No," Caius said.

"Well, you need them. Now."

"Call me Tythus," Caius said.

Demri snorted. Of course Caius would use his actual name because nobody knew it. Everyone thought Tythus Corbéo was long dead.

"I'll be Enebrial," Demri said. Enebrial Hubbart was an author who'd exposed several Magicai lies. He was, in Demri's opinion, the greatest man to ever have existed.

"Very well," Myri said. "Can I speak to Enebrial alone?"

Caius grunted but obeyed, leaving the room.

When they were alone, Myri walked to Demri's bed and sat next to him. The tantalizing scent of lavender stuck in his nostrils.

"I'm sorry about all that," she said. "This must be difficult for you, considering how you used to feel."

"It's okay," Demri started. Then stopped. *Used to feel? She doesn't know?* "I still—"

Myri interrupted. "Don't apologize. It's nice to see you're alive and well. Better off than me, in fact." She laughed, wrinkles creasing her cheeks. *Still so beautiful.* "Fortunately, we won't have to display our affections often. Just when it's in question. I hope we can become friends. It'd make up for what happened at Ashmount."

His heart shattered, his teeth ground, and he took in a slow breath through his nose, calming himself. Fingernails dug into the palms of his hands. He closed his eyes a moment, opened them, and Demri forced a smile. But the truth was, he had a burning desire to incinerate her right then and there.

6

INTERLUDE
THE BLOODY DUCHESS

Remeria

In the march from Rivane to their present location, Mauve Hardeen and her people had seen a lot of changes. The army made up of peasants was led by a man named Godfrey Saint, though everyone now called him Saint Godfrey. The bastard had half a nose and half a desire to lead the group, aptly named the Saintmaritans, after Godfrey. She'd worked her way up the ranks, earned a moniker herself —the Bloody Duchess—and, when the opportunity presented itself, she took control of the group. Saint Godfrey weren't a fool. Before she was about to kill him, he'd demoted himself and pledged his services to her as her second. Except, she didn't want him as her second. But such is life. Saint Godfrey's name had become known in Remeria. Well enough that killing him wouldn't help matters, as it'd give the rest of Remeria hope one of them had perished. It seemed most people not taking part in the rebellion weren't big fans of them. She couldn't blame them.

In her eyes, Mauve Hardeen had died the minute she'd

doused her body in one of her victim's blood, embracing the nickname Saint Godfrey bestowed upon her. The Saintmaritans were a rebellion, of sorts. They'd started in Rivane, made their way through many of the tiny hamlets and villages that dotted the landscape, killed a bunch of people, recruited even more, and now, the Bloody Duchess figured, they nearly had an army. She estimated they had just over four hundred in their merry group, though she couldn't tell and didn't have the patience to count.

The Bloody Duchess pushed her felt hat with the wide brim back to the angle she preferred and grinned. Their destination wasn't too far now. She turned fast enough so the red cape gave a nice twirl. Her left hand—half-hand, really—rested on the hilt of the stiletto she'd commandeered. She glanced down, looking at the reddened, mangled claw. She'd lost the two fingers furthest from her thumb in a brutal battle with her ex-husband. He'd shoved her hand in a cook fire during an argument and she'd taken his life.

Fuckin' Morsen. She wished he still lived so she could kill him all over again. Somehow, the damage Morsen had done to her hand was paying off. People respected her. They cheered whenever she thrust her hand in the air. The Bloody Duchess had decided, long ago, that she wouldn't be afraid of her deformed hand. The pink, scarred skin pulled her remaining two fingers and thumb together in what could only be described as a claw and had limited maneuverability.

She stopped marching, her two captains, Hershen and Althier, close by her side.

"It looks like we're late," the Bloody Duchess said, pointing with her clawed hand.

"Aye, so it does," Hershen said.

"O'er stretches o' landscape, through thick grasslands green, a city o' Remeria sits, an army o' Camel Clans in-between," Captain Althier said. *Ever the fuckin' poet.* Althier had once created a song to inspire the men under Saint Godfrey. Now, wisely, he'd shifted the people into praising her instead.

"Looks like the army circles most o' the city, actually," Captain Hershen said, pointing both hands at either side of the city. *Ever the fuckin' idiot.* Hershen was Saint Godfrey's best ally. She didn't know why she allowed him to keep his station. *Probably cause he follows orders and don't question me.*

"Hush, Hersh, ya fuckin' always statin' the obvious. If I needed that, I'd ask one o' those idiots." She gestured at the Saintmaritans.

"O' course. Me mistake," Hersh said, looking embarrassed. *Good. Fuckin' idiots, the lot o' them.*

There'd been one time, back when she was Mauve, when she would've looked down on this rabble, but that'd been when she was married to Morsen. Back when she was rich and noble. Now, she was just as poor as they were. Though she liked to believe she was smarter. *I'm smarter, damn it. I ain't the Bloody Duchess for nothin'.* She remembered a time when she didn't think in the fake accent she spoke with. Though now the accent wasn't quite fake, was it? *Spend too much time fakin' shit and it becomes a part o' your blood. Oh well, I ain't the Bloody Duchess for nothin'.*

She reached up with her withered hand, crooked fingers aimed at Althier. "Bring me Saint Godfrey. And the quartermaster, Flatchett."

"Anythin' ya say, Bloody Duchess." Althier gave a mock bow and walked into the cluster of Saintmaritans, hunting his quarry.

She snorted, spat a chunk of snot on the ground. Waited for Althier's return while Hersh bumbled and mumbled shit to stir conversation they both knew wouldn't happen.

Saint Godfrey's original vision was they'd come here, to the capital of Remeria, infiltrate the city, and then kill King

Alondo Sedoa. He convinced a good portion of the Saintmaritans they'd share the wealth. Be equal. Right the economic unfairness that'd plagued the country. Take back from the nobility. The Bloody Duchess, however, didn't like the idea of losing control. If they succeeded in their mission, what would that leave her? She didn't know. And she wasn't fooling herself. They wouldn't be able to murder a king, even with three times their number. They'd never be allowed close enough. That was the moment the Bloody Duchess had decided to take control. Saint Godfrey had gotten too ambitious.

Captain Althier's voice halted her thoughts. "I've brought ya a scarred man sportin' a sneer, a half-nosed bastard o' leadership, I hear. Alongside him stands a man who counts hatchets, the quartermaster ya wished for, named Bartlesby Flatchett."

The Bloody Duchess groaned. "Ya gotta stop with that shit."

"My apologies, Bloody Duchess. I thought ya'd appreciate my rhymes. If it irks ya so much, I promise I'll stop. I'll only do it sometimes."

"Leave," she said, her reddened claw raised and trembling. She issued a low, guttural growl, an animalistic action, she knew, but her frustration had reached that point. "Go!"

Althier shrugged. "A'right."

The Bloody Duchess switched her gaze to Saint Godfrey and Bartlesby Flatchett. Half of Saint Godfrey's nose was a jagged, fleshy pulp. It reminded her of her hand. He had a habit of itching it. Probably checking to see if it was still missing. Bartlesby Flatchett was one of the recruits. He wasn't one of the Originals—the members who started in Rivane with Saint Godfrey. The true Saintmaritans. Bartlesby had begged for his life, and they'd let him live. Good thing, too, cause he'd come in handy. He had a good mind for keeping track of their equipment. Bartlesby was the groveling type. Even after the Saintmaritans had murdered his wife and kids, he'd never actively hurt them. He was too weak. *Or smart enough to realize he'd be a dead man if'n he did any betrayin'.*

"What do ya reckon'?" the Bloody Duchess asked Saint Godfrey.

Though he was her second, Saint Godfrey spent little time around her. She knew he resented his overthrowing. He enjoyed being in charge as much as she did. Perhaps more, because he'd never been in charge before, and she'd been a noble in a past life.

"What do ya mean?" Saint Godfrey asked.

She swiveled her claw toward the Camel Clans and Andora. "'Bout them."

"Maybe they'll let us through. We have no quarrel with 'em."

"Oh? Ya think they'll just let us waltz right in? Are ya fuckin' stupid, Godfrey?"

He glared at her. She'd broken a rule they'd established long ago: never use their names, only their titles. A sign of respect. Only she wasn't respecting him anymore, and he knew it. Saint Godfrey didn't respond, just itched at the pulpy side of his nose with his middle finger. She wondered if he did it on purpose or if it was a veiled insult.

"I'm thinkin' we wait 'em out," Saint Godfrey said.

"Waitin' is exactly what I figured ya say. How one man can start from up here," she said, raising her claw above her head, "and find hisself so low"—she squatted, brushing the ground with her claw's fingertips—"is beyond me."

He shrugged. "The people like ya more."

"You're right. I don't need ya anymore."

He raised an eyebrow at that. "No?"

"The Saintmaritans die with ya." The Bloody Duchess drew her stiletto.

"Wait," Godfrey said, holding his hands out in front of him.

"I ain't waitin' on anyone. Not for the Camel Clans, not for me dead husband, and certainly not for no has-been saint." She tilted her head and peered up at Godfrey out of the corner of her eye.

"I gave you—"

"You gave me nothin'!" She drew her stiletto and plunged it deep into Godfrey's stomach.

He let out a gasp, groan, and then gurgle.

She drove the sword in deeper, then raised her claw and poked his pulpy nose. "Ya always were an ugly one, weren'tcha? Ya gave me nothin'. I took what I earned, right as right." She withdrew the sword and gave Godfrey a quick series of stabs. When he collapsed, she drove the stiletto through his eye, letting it go as it twanged back and forth, tip stuck in the dirt beneath his head. "Fucker."

The quartermaster, Bartlesby Flatchett, stood open-mouthed and silent. *Good. Just the way I want ya.*

The Bloody Duchess turned to the Saintmaritans. Those in the front had seen her murder their former leader. The one whose name had started it all. "Saint Godfrey is dead!" Nobody seemed to know what to do or say, so she retrieved her stiletto, wiped it off, and pointed it at the crowd. "The Saintmaritans are no more. Today births a new group. A group named after the rightful leader. The Redclaws!"

A moment of silence. She growled, bent over, and stuck her withered hand into one of Godfrey's wounds. Coated in crimson, she raised it above her head. The Redclaws let out a cheer. "Let it be known that we don't tolerate pretenders, weak-minded individuals, or anyone tellin' us what we should or shain't do." The Redclaws cheered.

Captain Althier, looking ever the fool, stood in the front row, beaming. Then the fucker, smart-like and fast, let out a quick ditty to commemorate the moment, she supposed.

"She's quick, she's fast, she's a bit more'n sly,
Avoid her stiletto's tip, or she'll stab ya in the eye!
She comes with o' bit of'n extravagant outfit, true,
Fancy hat, silver blade, and a cloak that's red'n not blue!
The Redclaws follow at the Bloody Duchess's behest,
Most leaders are fearful, but in this case, consider us impressed!"

The Redclaws cheered. She'd have to show Althier appreciation in the future.

Grinning, the Bloody Duchess sheathed her sword and gestured at them with her claw. "Now get ready for marchin'!" With Saint Godfrey dead, nobody would stand in the way of the success she knew the Redclaws could attain. She beamed, a rush of adrenaline coursing through her body. She trembled with excitement.

She turned to Bartlesby. "I wanted to ask ya 'bout equipment."

He swallowed, nervous. "We have weapons for almost everyone o' us." Bartlesby didn't used to have an accent, much like the Bloody Duchess. She wondered if he was trying his best to fit in now.

"Good," she said. She'd had another reason for bringing him over, but she couldn't think of it now. Godfrey had pissed her off too much. "Make sure everyone's prepared. We're goin' in a minute."

He nodded and disappeared into the crowd.

She remembered Captain Hershen, Godfrey's close ally. Wondered if she should put him down, too. Figured against it. For now, at least. *Should probably make Althier my second. He's worthy o' it.*

She shook her head, then stared at the city surrounded by the Camel Clans. A moment passed, then she ordered the Redclaws forward. When they got closer, she heard the distant shouting and horn-bellowing typical of panicked guards.

"Ain't sure what they're frightened o'," she said out loud, to nobody in particular. "They's already surrounded."

"Yes," Althier said, appearing at her side. He pointed at the city. "Atop a city wall, the guardsmen scurry. When the Redclaws approach, they best close the gates, a hurry."

The Bloody Duchess rolled her eyes.

7

EDELBROCK BRENDIS

"It's time you fulfill additional duties," Savakkis said. Savakkis was a veteran of the House. Bald, like the rest of the House—as was how they identified one another in Buzzard's Bowl. Savakkis looked the part of a gladiator—one ear missing, many scars crisscrossing his pale skin, and his pants bulged from his thick thighs. Each of his four fingers wore a bloody ring. Edelbrock knew they were for beating the new gladiators into submission. There was something about Savakkis that kept Edelbrock's attention. He'd sometimes catch his eyes lingering or his thoughts meandering in Savakkis's direction.

"And what might they be?" Edelbrock asked. He lay in his straw bed, a thin sheet covering his bruised body. Once Scayde Haklon had taken over the Velvet Mother's luxurious House, he'd changed a few things, making them all more uncomfortable. At first, he'd felt guilty, but another gladiator who'd been traded to the Velvet Mother's House from Scayde's original House claimed it was the same there when Scayde owned it.

"A tradition," was all Savakkis said. Edelbrock swore Savakkis's eyes lingered on him.

Groaning, Edelbrock climbed out of bed.

The rest of the House had already gathered. One man held a large pitcher of water. Everyone else clutched food in their hands. Somebody handed Edelbrock a cup filled with various types of cut up fruit. It was, he noticed, rotting.

They exited the House, through a corridor towards the only place they had accessibility outside their compound—a large cage with bars spaced wide enough to easily see the occupants . Future Draftees.

Four dirty people crawled in their direction; hands outstretched. Food was thrown at them and the gladiators laughed and cheered. Edelbrock set his cup on the floor and marched back into the House. A few people noticed and called him back. He ignored them. He remembered all too well the feeling of being locked in that cage and having people torment him. And for what? A bit of amusement? So they could break him? *Fuck them.*

"You left early, didn't even throw anything," Chellie, one of the five brothers and sisters making up the Chell, said. *Well, four, now.* Chellit had died during last season's games. Chellie sighed, taking a seat on a straw bed across from Edelbrock's. She was bald like the rest of them and walked around the compound shirtless. One of her breasts was missing—also from last season's games—and the other bobbed and weaved with her movements. First time he'd seen her, Edelbrock had mistaken her for a man.

"You're torturing them for no reason. How? After being in there myself, I couldn't do that. It was misery."

"They have to be broken," she said. "Believe me. We've done it other ways. If you don't break them, they never conform. Instead of training, instead of realizing they're stuck here . . . they waste their time trying to escape. Escaping from Buzzard's Bowl is impossible."

"So they make an escape attempt or two, then focus on being down here. There's no harm in that. It'd be quicker, too."

"You think any House owner is going to let somebody who tried to escape live? This is how we save their life, Edelbrock."

He wasn't sure he agreed, but it wasn't his call to make.

<hr>

Day two.

Edelbrock's bruised and battered body ached. Now he sat in the waiting room wondering what Buzzard's Bowl was going to look like today. With the first battle over, the first season gladiators would now fight alongside those with more experience. Every day an organizer would deliver an agenda with who was fighting with whom, during each time slot. Today, Edelbrock found himself with Nauc, and two veterans: Coston and Fethric.

Allowed to select their weapons of choice, Nauc picked a long sword, while Edelbrock grabbed a heavy mace. Coston wielded a scythe; Fethric, a scimitar in one hand, a rapier in the other. A black haze obscured their view through the archway into Buzzard's Bowl.

"Don't flake on us," Fethric said to Edelbrock and Nauc.

"Whatever the arena holds, embrace it. Or die," Coston said, though it sounded more like a personal vow, rather than advice to either Edelbrock or Nauc.

Nauc's face remained stoic. "I used to be a soldier. I won't abandon you."

"Live to seek vengeance," Edelbrock said. He thought about impaling Scayde Haklon. About pushing his wife off the King's Stand. He wanted to kill everyone who contributed to his being here.

The fog in the archway changed to a gray haze. Surviving members of the last bout entered. The Chell, who always fought together, returned. Chellie, Chellik, Chellis, and the one-armed Chellin. He noticed they didn't return with the other two gladiators they'd fought with.

Edelbrock glimpsed a flash of foliage before the gray haze returned to black. The Magicai would reset the battleground with whatever crazed concoction Scayde Haklon thought of next. Or, whoever thought these things up. Edelbrock didn't know if it was Scayde, the crowd, or some maniacal genius who lived to torture people.

Minutes slid by and felt like hours.

In front of the group was a huge, open archway. Edelbrock could see the sands of Buzzard's Bowl on the other side, obscured by the fog.

Edelbrock followed Fethric and Coston out the archway. The sound of cheering deafened him, and he saw Fethric and Coston raising their weapons in the air and yelling back.

He found himself standing on a big, stone slab entry platform. A rock walkway led into Buzzard's Bowl from the platform, and crisscrossed the arena, converging into multiple paths each about ten feet wide. Large square pits of bubbling lava filled the space between pathways. Somehow, a cool breeze blew across his skin, and Edelbrock felt little heat from the magma. *More trickery from the Magicai.* Of course, they'd want the gladiators feeling good. Otherwise, the crowd would watch a bunch of people passing out, and that didn't make for an entertaining fight.

Standing across the arena on their own starting platform, Edelbrock saw another group of four. The other Houses weren't in attendance at this battle.

The announcer's voice flowed through the stadium.

"Ladies and gentlemen, here we are, about to observe our first elimination match of the season!" The crowd cheered.

Elimination match meant to the death. The fight wouldn't end until one side perished completely, Edelbrock knew.

Coston looked over his shoulder at Edelbrock, and Nauc —who was standing to Edelbrock's left. "Good luck," he said.

"You, too," Edelbrock and Nauc said at the same time.

The announcer continued. "From the Duke of Lochwall's House—Lord Scayde Haklon—we have the following fighters: new recruits and survivors of the purge, Nauc and Edelbrock!" The announcer paused a moment, allowing the crowd to look them over. "Farmer Fethric will sow the seeds of excitement!" This time, the crowd cheered and Fethric held his scythe up. "And Coston, otherwise known as the Buzzard of Buzzard's Bowl, is here to feed upon the dead!" The cheering escalated.

"They'll face off against Jaylena Brendis's House. I'm sorry, no—Jaylena Haklon's House—my apologies, my lady." Edelbrock clenched his jaw. "In attendance for the good lady's House—new recruits, Barmigus and Hauser!" The crowd stopped cheering to inspect the survivors of the purge. Barmigus and Hauser both wielded basic long swords and shields. "The up-and-comer, shocking everyone in one of the greatest upsets last season, Seeker Korran—watch out for this man's ability to 'seek' an opportunity!" The crowd cheered. Seeker Korran lifted his arms to the crowd, hefting a small hatchet in each hand. "And what would one of these events be without a true Champion of Buzzard's Bowl? A walking bloodbath himself, a bloody torrent of death—am I right? It's Jarvis Bean, otherwise known as Massacre!" The crowd blew up. Screams and cheers were louder than any Edelbrock had ever heard.

Massacre walked to the front of his stone platform and bellowed, raising a massive two-handed great sword above his head.

"TO THE DEATH!" the announcer screamed. *He's more bloodthirsty than half the crowd.*

"You two go that way," Coston said, waving at one of the rock pathways. "Fethric and I will take this route."

"Great," Edelbrock said while the pair of veterans sprinted away.

Nauc readied his sword. "Feels great to be underestimated."

"They're making assumptions. Bad assumptions we're about to prove incorrect."

Nauc shrugged, and they started along the pathway. Jaylena's House decided to tackle in a different manner. One veteran and one recruit were approaching them, while the other pair headed in Fethric and Coston's direction. Edelbrock recognized the veteran as Seeker Korran, with his dual hatchets, and Edelbrock was pretty sure Hauser was the recruit.

As Edelbrock made it further down the stretch, he noticed a few larger squares of rock placed in strategic locations, making what appeared to be small arenas. Both Seeker Korran and Hauser stood on one, waiting. The path Edelbrock and Nauc walked upon led towards them.

To their right, the other group had already engaged. The distinct sound of metal-on-metal clanged through the booming chorus of the crowd's surging cheers.

Parts of the crowd—those closest to Edelbrock and Nauc —began booing and screaming at them. Edelbrock assumed it was because they were walking rather than running to their deaths.

"Let's focus on one at a time," Edelbrock said. "Seeker Korran is going to be more difficult, so I'll try to distract him. You take down Hauser as quick as you can."

"Not a problem," Nauc said.

Seeker Korran and Hauser closed the gap, blocking Edelbrock and Nauc from entering the arena square. If they were to gain entry, they'd need to fight their way through. And in order to do that, they'd have to fight side-by-side on the walkway.

"Careful not to fall in," Nauc said.

Edelbrock grunted. Then the flurry of blows arrived.

Seeker Korran's hatchets slammed into Edelbrock's shield, once, twice, thrice. *Thrice?* The fourth blow came whizzing at his side. Edelbrock swung his broadsword, barely deflecting it. *He's fast.*

Edelbrock took a step back, avoiding two more slashes from the hatchets. On his left, Nauc and Hauser dueled. Glancing in their direction, Edelbrock saw several red gashes on Hauser.

A loud grunt and a hatchet flipping through his vision pulled Edelbrock's attention back to Seeker Korran. He caught sight of Nauc's body slipping beneath the surface of the boiling lava, hatchet handle sticking out his back, and Hauser turning towards Edelbrock. The crowd erupted. A pang of loss reverberated inside Edelbrock. *Well, shit.*

Seeker Korran lunged forward, hatchet slashing.

Stumbling backwards, Edelbrock blocked with his shield. The blade stuck in the wood, and as Seeker Korran wrenched the weapon back, the straps on the shield yanked at Edelbrock's forearm. He fended Seeker Korran off with his sword, and then Hauser arrived.

With the hatchet still embedded in the shield, Seeker Korran was weaponless. Edelbrock feinted, pretending to chop at Hauser's leg. Hauser blocked low, exposing his face. Bashing the shield—and hatchet—into Hauser's face, Edelbrock launched a kick at Hauser's midsection. A loud exhalation exited the gladiator, and Edelbrock brought his broadsword down on his shoulder.

Hauser screamed. Edelbrock bashed him with the shield again and again. Blood spurted from his face. A laceration on his eyebrow ripped open. Several teeth spewed from

Hauser's mouth. Edelbrock smashed and smashed. Again. Again, again! *Die, bastard!* Each connection nudged the gladiator closer to the edge of the rock pathway. Once more, he slammed his shield into the man. Hauser took a step into emptiness, eyes widened, and then he fell. The hissing lava cut his screams short.

Edelbrock turned to Seeker Korran, who held his hands up in surrender. The spectators jeered and yelled at Edelbrock to "finish him!". Sheathing his broadsword, he gripped the handle of the hatchet, and wretched it out of the shield. Seeker Korran turned and ran.

He let him go, turning his sight on the other battle. Edelbrock only saw three figures. Barmigus, the other House Jaylena recruit, lay dead on a walkway. He crossed the miniature rock arena, finding the pathway that led to the battling gladiators.

"Ha, two think they can bring down Jarvis Bean?" Massacre roared, nodding his head in Edelbrock's direction. "Apparently not, because here comes a third!"

Massacre heaved his great sword over his back and brought it down eliciting a guttural cry. Coston crossed his scimitar and rapier to block, but the great blade ripped through the small weapons, cleaving the man near in two. The spectators rose out of their seats, stamping their feet and clapping their hands.

"Kill them all, Massacre!"

"Cleave them in half!"

"Only two left!"

Edelbrock brushed a bead of sweat from his forehead, racing to get to the other arena. He watched Fethric swiping his scythe back and forth, keeping Massacre at bay. Sprinting down the stretch, he arrived at the rock square as Massacre's great sword chopped Fethric's scythe in half. A loud snap silenced the crowd.

Massacre raised his sword for another swipe.

Fethric dropped the useless wooden piece, using the bladed half of the scythe as a sickle. He deflected the next blow, catching the blade inside the curved scythe, and sending Massacre off-balance.

Edelbrock surged forward, already knowing he was too late.

Massacre's knee slammed into Fethric, who doubled over. Then Massacre backhanded Fethric with the pommel of his great sword. Blood ran down his face. Dazed, he was too sluggish to dodge the next attack. The great sword cut a great gash in his side and he dropped, dying.

Edelbrock drowned out the sounds of the crowd with his cry. He made it across the square arena, closed in on Massacre, and drove his sword into the back of the man's thigh, ramming the point into the rock. The stone chipped as the blade scratched, reverberating through Massacre's leg.

Hollering, Massacre tried to swing his sword at Edelbrock, but he couldn't turn around.

He wanted to remove the blade and stab Massacre again, but Edelbrock wasn't sure he'd have enough time. Instead, he did something far more gruesome. Edelbrock shook his shield off his arm then, he grasped his broadsword two-handed, and heaved up. The blade slowly sawed its way further up Massacre's thigh.

Massacre screamed and dropped his huge blade. The massive sword clattered on the pathway and lay forgotten. Thrashing, Massacre tried to grab at Edelbrock's arms.

"I'm sorry," Edelbrock said. And he meant it. He didn't enjoy murdering his opponents, but it was either them or himself.

He grunted, ripping the sword from the man's leg. A chunk of flesh tore from the thigh, leaving a gaping hole behind.

Massacre fell. The crowd cheered and booed and hissed

and screamed. Here was one of their favorites, gone to the grave.

Edelbrock looked down at the man.

"End it," he said.

So, Edelbrock did. He brought the broadsword down on Massacre's neck, severing head from body. The crowd roared.

"FINISH HIM, FINISH HIM!"

I did. Edelbrock looked up at the crowd, noticed they were pointing elsewhere.

Standing at the other end of the small arena, Seeker Korran knelt, hands placed face down on the rock, head exposed. Waiting for his execution.

Edelbrock dropped his sword. He'd had enough. Enough of the killing. Enough pointless slaughter. What was he even doing here? Providing entertainment for bloodthirsty citizens? People who saw him, and the other gladiators, as animals ready to butcher one another? He saw the carnage around him, knew what he'd done, what others had done. *Disgusting.*

He looked up at the crowd, shaking his head, and roared back at them. "No!"

They quieted. He shouted it, again and again, until there was nothing but the sound of his "no's".

"Enough is enough," he shouted. "I am not your toy to experiment with. I am not somebody who's life you can bet on. You do *not* own me! Or him," he pointed at Seeker Korran. "Scayde Haklon has blinded you all. This isn't fun! This isn't right!"

Scayde Haklon's enhanced voice from the King's Stand answered him. "Incorrect, Ed. This is justice! We gather miscreants, criminals, and other men and women of nefarious backgrounds and we remove them from our peaceful society. Answer me this: where would you be had I not discovered your plans? You'd be up in the stands, among your House supporters. You'd be rich. But I didn't let you steal from me, or the citizens of Lochwall. No, I found out your dirty little scheme to steal Trigg Gelbrandy's deed to Buzzard's Bowl. A *beloved* House owner." Edelbrock knew that to be a lie. " You're both pathetic and wrong, Ed. You've always wanted to be part of the nobility, right? Rich? Well-known? I've given you everything you've wanted. The power to stand out. Fame and recognition. A crowd roaring your name. Roar away, citizens. Cheer for the jester of Buzzard's Bowl, the bumbling buffoon of the arena. Cheer for Edelbrock Brendis, the Ass of Lochwall."

The crowd erupted. His legacy created, Edelbrock grit his teeth and glared at the King's Stand. *The Ass of Lochwall? Fine. But be ready when I shit all over you.*

Edelbrock hadn't noticed them before, but when he raised his eyes to look at the King's Stand, he saw them. A swirling group of buzzards, ready for a feast.

8

SERADAL WINTLOCK & VILLIC THE IMBUER

Andora, Remeria

King Alondo and Atticus Crenshaw, King's Council, gave each other worried looks when the alarmed cries began. Moments later, the door burst open, and a frantic soldier stumbled in. "My Lord, I apologize for the intrusion—"

"Out with it, soldier," Atticus said.

"Armed men have arrived."

King Alondo sighed, relieved. "They've been here for quite some time."

The soldier shook his head. "More. Not the Camel Clans."

A barrage of questions came from all of them at once.

"Who?" the king asked.

"From where?" Atticus asked.

"Are they allies?" Sera asked.

Royal took a drink. "Whiskey?" he asked the soldier.

The questions went unanswered because the king decided he didn't want to wait and rushed out. The soldier and Atticus followed, Sera and Royal trailing behind.

"You're an alcoholic," she said.

"You are what you drink."

She sighed. "What's wrong with you?"

"Not enough whiskey," he said, taking another swig. "Want a drink?"

She shook her head and picked up her pace, leaving him standing, flask upended over his mouth.

Outside, after a walk to the nearest entrance, the king climbed the ramparts. Sera followed his entourage and, once atop the wall, had a wide view of the surrounding area. Across the river, Remerian grasslands wound their way into the distance, a dot of dark green at the very cusp of her vision —a jungle, maybe.

They followed the soldier down the wall, so they stood above a gatehouse that manned the drawbridge and had remained raised since the arrival of the Camel Clans. The drawbridge crossed the river, where a group of hundreds of dirty, sick-looking peasants stood, all armed and armored with various incohesive parts. It appeared the Camel Clans had parted to allow them to pass unhindered. Two figures stood in front of the rabble, a man and woman. The woman gave half a wave with a clawed hand, removing a wide brimmed felt hat with her other, bowing her head.

The man cleared his throat, and then said, "'cross the river's depth stands a king amidst his folk, but the Redclaws wonder something—will he listen to this bloke?"

"Ignore me Captain Althier, please," the claw woman said. "He ain't good at conversatin'."

"What do you want?" King Alondo asked.

"Safe passage for me'n mine."

"You're safe. Keep walking," the king said.

Around the Redclaws, the Camel Clans began converging. They held their weapons, hesitant, though didn't make any hostile moves.

The clawed woman pointed her mangled hand at them.

"The Bloody Duchess could help ya with a certain problem, I sees."

"The Bloody Duchess is a criminal," the king said. "We've heard all about your exploits, raiding and destroying good Remerian homes during an invasion."

"We might've done some raidin' and destroyin', true," she said. "But I'd be remiss if ya thought I was a true criminal. I ain't. The Bloody Duchess removed the plague o' the group. Might o' heard o' him yourselves—Saint Godfrey. But like all saints, he's dead 'n gone. It's just me—the Bloody Duchess—now. The Saintmaritans you've likely heard o'. But they're gone, too. Gone with Godfrey. Call ourselves the Redclaws, now."

"What's your real name?" the king asked.

"Ain't so sure it matters, but if it's a name ya want, 'twas Mauve Hardeen. Used to be rich and noble-like. Coulda maybe been your wife in another life." She laughed.

The king didn't laugh back.

"No matter," the Bloody Duchess said. "I'm here. Ya figure out what ya want done with us, then call us back o'er."

"After two midnights pass, beckon with a holler. But don't give the Redclaws commands, we ain't wearin' a collar," the poet, Captain Althier, said. Then he and the Bloody Duchess retreated to the Redclaws.

"What do we do, Your Highness?" Atticus asked.

"Nothing. What can we do? Let the Camel Clans kill them."

They stood in mute silence, wondering what would come next. Except Royal. He took another drink, smacking his lips.

***

Villic relaxed his grip on his spear. The Redclaws, as they called themselves, showed no aggression as they marched away from the river. He was on the other side, with half the other Camel Clansmen, ready to reinforce his people if the Redclaws attacked.

"With a fourth faction thrown into the mix, it seems unlikely fighting won't break out soon."

Villic grunted, ignoring Speaker. Another clansmen looked at Villic, surprised. Villic shifted his gaze to the man's feet, avoiding eye contact. "Not you," he said, mumbling.

"I doubt he understood that."

Villic walked away from the clansmen. When he was alone, he let out a sigh of relief.

"How long is it going to take for you to become capable of talking to others?"

Never.

"That's unhealthy."

It's only unhealthy when I talk to people. My heart wants to give out.

"You'll die of loneliness."

I'll die of talkingness.

"That's not a word."

Quiet yourself and leave me alone.

He wandered to where Dunecrest milled about, munching on grass.

"Dunecrest."

The camel's beady black eye turned in Villic's direction. He kept chewing. *Munch, munch, munch.*

"Hungry? Sick of grass? I'd get sick of grass."

"Do you get sick of your favorite food?"

"I'm talking to Dunecrest, Speaker."

"That doesn't negate my point."

"You know nothing about real life."

"Sometimes you forget that I've already lived my own life."

I didn't forget, I don't care. That was long ago. Before the Camel Clans. Before the gods.

"The gods don't exist—"

"How many times do I have to hear this!"

Startled, Dunecrest trotted off, leaving Villic alone with his thoughts.

"Not alone."

Villic did the only thing he could to get some peace. He lay down under the sun and took a nap.

"You're sure you can't help us, Cyr . . . Seradal, was it?" King Alondo asked.

They'd returned to the king's throne room, though this time, they sat at the table. Everyone was drinking wine, though Royal stuck with whiskey, and Sera had ignored the wine for chilled water.

"We're not looking to kill anyone, Your Highness. The people we came here with . . . we're all that's left. As far as we know, we're the only Cyroki survivors," Sera said. Thoughts of her mother and brother wafted through her mind. She took a moment, inhaled a deep breath, and pushed them out. She needed to focus. "This isn't our fight. If we joined, we could all be killed."

"I understand," King Alondo said. It didn't look like it, though. His face, bright red and fuming, combined with his trembling lip and furrowed brow, told Sera otherwise.

Royal might've been a fool and he might've been an alcoholic, but the man was smart enough to know when to slip into the background. Sera caught his eye, and he nodded, offering an encouraging smile. She wanted to walk over and throttle him, useless as he was.

"Perhaps it's best if you leave the city," Atticus said.

"If the Camel Clans and the Redclaws join up, what happens?" Sera asked, ignoring the King's Council.

"I don't know. It doesn't appear as if they have any Magicai, but their numbers are vast. There are several Magicai here," the king said, glancing at Atticus. "I'm certain we can protect the city. My primary concern is if they're willing to continue the siege until we starve to death. That would take a long time, but with the capital shut down, Remeria would suffer."

"Perhaps a proposal," Royal said. He stepped up to stand next to Sera.

Atticus snorted. "You don't speak for the Falcon Knights, *Captain*." He sneered. "Take a step back and provide the security you're here for."

"Atticus!" the king slammed his fist on the table. "That was, undoubtedly, one of the rudest things I've ever heard!"

The King's Council raised an eyebrow, but otherwise, didn't seem bothered.

"Captain Hoarst is more than capable of speaking on behalf of the Falcon Knights," Sera said. She wasn't sure that was true. Didn't necessarily want an alcoholic thinking he had that kind of power, but she also wanted to hear what he had to say.

"I've served in the Cyroki military for a long time, gentleman," Royal said, unscrewing a flask and taking a sip. He smacked his lips, licked his whiskers, then wiped his mouth with the sleeve of his stained jacket. "I might not hold significant rank, but I know strategy. It might be your advantage to have an ally outside the city. The Falcon Knights could be that ally."

Furious, King Alondo rose from his chair, slapping his cup of wine away. The liquid sprayed the wall; the goblet clattering on the stone floor. "We've been trying to convince *you* of that!"

Royal nodded. "Yes, you have. But I'm proposing something different from what you have in mind. You'd have us join Remeria in a cohesive counterattack. The Falcon Knights are tired, weak, and demoralized. There needs to be an incentive."

Sera saw where Royal was heading. "We could make a

pact to flank any potential attackers, but we can't commit to anything else."

The king, though displeased, nodded. "You help protect the capital. We'll assist you in rebuilding Cyrok."

"I'm not sure we'll be able to rebuild Cyrok," Royal said. "But perhaps a bit of revenge would go a long way."

"A pact to destroy Calrym?" the king asked.

"Yes," Sera said. "Agreed. It's time Calrym knelt for somebody else's whim. The attack on Cyrok was unnecessary and pointless."

Atticus nodded. "Strategically and economically. Which leads me to believe they wanted to line up another advantage. Militarily makes the most sense."

"But why?" King Alondo asked. "What could they possibly gain?"

"A new place to launch ships," Royal said. "Think about it."

"They've been setting themselves up to invade my country this entire time?" A moment passed and King Alondo snarled, throwing another goblet. This one belonged to Atticus. It bounced off the wall with a clang, then skittered across the floor, coming to a stop at Royal's foot. "King Mikas's a liar! He promised to send help, and yet we haven't seen a single Calrite flag, symbol, or message since. He's a liar! Probably laughing at us as we speak. Well, we'll show him! We'll slaughter him and his family and his group of pissant nobles and anyone else foolish enough to let the Camel Clans run rampant! They'll all die—and Calrym will beg to live under Remerian rule!"

Sera didn't want to tell King Alondo she didn't plan on living under Calrym *or* Remerian rule. But, at this point, she went along with it. Revenge tasted better.

9

DEMRI SLARN

Eighteen Years Ago
Zemur, Calrym

The first few years after Demri fled Ashmount, it seemed everyone pursued him. He had to remain hidden, which often meant he holed up in a grimy tavern room while Caius ran errands. It also took those first years for Demri to get used to his injuries caused by Doram Quandis. Every time he walked, burning pain coursed through his legs. Whenever he saw his reflection, or another person caught a glimpse of his face, he was reminded of his scars.

He'd escaped to a town in Calrym, called Zemur. Demri had considered visiting Vessia, the lands of the Camel Clans. He investigated the possibility of checking out Kelm or Argoa, two small towns far into the desert, but realized they'd be too remote. He wanted access to a civilization who didn't believe his powers were gifts bestowed upon him by a large group of gods. *Probably Muscle, god of power or some shit.* He had little knowledge of the Camel Clans, and even less desire to learn anything about them.

While staying in Zemur, Demri had grown accustomed to peering out his window, lusting for freedom. He didn't like being cooped up. *Such is the life of a murderer.* At least, that's what the Magicai were calling him. Murder in the act of self-defense shouldn't count, and everyone he'd killed had tried to kill him. All were Magicai, hired to hunt him down by Ashmount. So far, all had failed.

Peering out the window, Demri caught sight of a familiar figure. Another Magicus snooping around, interviewing random passersby.

Caius was gone—had been all day, would be until late evening at the earliest. Demri had sent him out to purchase supplies so they could leave Zemur behind. *Before this shit happened.* But it was too late. They'd found him.

He grasped the window ledge and hauled himself to a standing position. Demri's legs wobbled and he groaned in pain. It wasn't getting easier. "F-Fuck."

He glanced out the window. It was an Enforcer; he saw one of the Soul Glyphs that allowed the Enforcer access to his Well of power. "Damn. Gods of the desert, b-b-bestow upon me your p-power." He looked up at the ceiling of the inn, holding his hands out, ready to receive. "That's what I thought. B-B-Bastards." Mother Avani remained the only believable goddess, and even she wasn't anything Demri had faith in. Not with everything he'd gone through. A real deity wouldn't allow that injustice to occur.

Wincing, he limped his way out of his room. Demri passed several daytime drunks—he wasn't sure how there could be this many in such a small town—then bumped into a smelly woman wearing little.

"Hey there, wanna go for a—" she cut off when Demri glared at her. His hood had slipped back and exposed his burned face.

"Get out of m-m-my way."

She scrambled away from him, which suited Demri just

fine. He limped out the doorway and into the street. Right into the path of the Magicus. *Perfect.*

The Magicus had bouncy brown hair and bright blue eyes. The only flaw on his face was a crooked nose. He looked rather boyish, but charming, and he flashed Demri a beaming smile. "Excuse me, sir, I'm Magicus Vistario. I wonder if you've seen a man—" Vistario cut himself off. The Magicai were looking for a robed man who walked with a limp and had a burned face. No doubt Vistario figured him out. "Everyone off the street!"

Damn it. He wasn't planning on causing a public disturbance today. He knew he'd have to kill the Magicus. If he tried to flee, the Magicus would kill him. *These Magicai force me into these situations.* Demri, unconcerned for nearby civilians, raised his hand. "Surrender or d-d-die, Vis-t-tario."

The Enforcer chuckled. "I'm several years your senior, Demri."

Demri pushed a significant gust of wind into Vistario and flew back, smashing into a mud-and-wood building. Bits of dirt cascaded on the Enforcer's limp body. He'd been knocked unconscious.

"You're the criminal," a Zemur citizen said.

"And you're next, if you d-d-don't leave m-me alone," Demri said. He pointed his finger at the man.

"Don't hurt me!" The citizen turned and ran.

"Now for the hard p-part," Demri said. He looked down at Vistario. In order to do what he wanted; Demri would have to kneel. *Or flop down on the ground like a fish out of water.* Kneeling hurt his legs so much, it might've been preferable.

He braced himself against the wall of the building, then bent his knees. The closer he got to kneeling, the more his legs trembled until they gave out. He collapsed, falling on top of the Enforcer. "F-Fuck."

Demri brushed some mud off his robes, then rolled Vistario over. He pulled the man's hands behind his back.

Then he . . . then he what? *If luck was a woman, she'd kill me.* He searched for something, anything, to bind Vistario's wrists with.

A woman huddled behind a cart, peeking at him from around the corner.

"Stand," Demri commanded.

The woman stood.

He waved her over. "I won't hurt you."

Nervous, she took two steps in his direction. "I have children," she said.

"Wonderful. They'll see you in a m-m-moment. Your laces."

"What?"

He nodded at her boots. "I need your laces."

"Why?"

"D-Do you want t-to see your children again?"

She blanched, then bent and unstrung both her boots. Tossing the strings to Demri, she took a step back. "P-P-Please don't hurt me."

He smirked. One of his abilities was making other people stutter. "Go. When I d-d-disappear, you can retrieve your laces from this m-m-man. He won't need them anymore."

The woman scampered away.

Demri took the laces and used both to bind Vistario's wrists as tight as he could make them. At the very least, it'd require Vistario attempting to free himself, and by that time, Demri could kill him.

He waited, patient. Demri didn't know how much time— or citizens—passed by.

Vistario coughed, opening his eyes.

"You've b-been b-b-bested, Vistario. Try anything, and I will k-k-kill you. Understand?"

Vistario nodded.

"You're from Ashmount."

Vistario nodded again.

"I'm not f-forcing you to b-b-be quiet."

"My name is Magicus Vistario. I'm an Enforcer, and—"

"Yes, yes. You're here to k-kill m-m-me."

Vistario swallowed. "I'll pretend I never found you."

"You'll d-do what I say."

"And that, yes. Yes, sir." He flashed a grin. "Nobody will know I found you. In fact, I'll tell them you weren't here. Yes, that'll work. I'll throw them off your trail."

"Are you here alone?"

The grin disappeared for a moment, then returned. "Of course! Vistario's a loner, a hunter of solitude. Partners aren't my thing."

"You lie."

Vistario exerted a nervous laugh. "Why would I do that?"

"D-Do you know D-D-Doram Quandis?"

"Yes, he's the one you hated at Ashmount. It's the reason you fled, right? Attacked him."

"He t-tried to m-m-murder m-me."

"Yes, yes, no doubt, no doubt. I never thought for a moment you were in the wrong. No, sir."

Demri sighed. "You'll answer m-my questions with t-true answers."

Vistario swallowed. "Yes."

"D-Doram Quandis."

"He's in hiding! Changed his appearance and everything."

"He's p-pale, t-t-tall, and has squinty eyes."

"Not anymore! He's gone undercover. Still tall, but very tan, like a Qothan. Lot fatter, too."

Demri wasn't sure he believed Vistario. Doram Quandis didn't seem to be the type to go into hiding. *I did survive when a group of Magicai tried to kill me, though.* If that was possible, perhaps Doram had become frightened and paranoid Demri would return to finish the job. Later in life, he'd reflect upon this moment as being the crucial mistake—Vistario had lied about both Doram's appearance and location. Doram Quandis had never left Ashmount, but Demri's hubris led him to believe otherwise.

Vistario's hands tugged at the bindings.

"No," Demri said. He slapped Vistario's cheek. "Try again and d-d-die."

"Yes, sir."

"Are you alone?"

"No."

"More M-Magicai?"

"Yes."

"Who?"

Vistario didn't answer.

"Who?" Demri asked again.

"Another Magicus, yes. Just one, though. She's harmless."

"Who?"

Vistario shook his head.

"Answer, or d-d-die."

"Magicus Myri."

"M-M-Myri?"

"Yes."

Demri curled his lip. She was here. He hadn't seen her since he'd fled Ashmount.

"Thank you," Demri said. Then he held his hand against Vistario's chest.

"No, sir, please, don't kill—"

Demri unleashed a concentrated bolt of power, resembling a flash of lightning. It roared through Vistario's chest, burning flesh and organs. Vistario's eyes rolled back and his head lolled, tongue slipping out his mouth.

Demri let the body collapse to the ground, smoldering. The scent reminded Demri of a nice roast. Hauling himself to his feet—amid much leg pain and trembling—he decided to search for Myri.

Then he slipped on a chunk of wet flesh and had to repeat the process of standing again.

———

Demri found Myri Celioh sitting on a bench outside a diner. She appeared worried, foot tapping on the cobblestone street, eyes darting around. *Must be Vistario is late.*

He decided to return the way he'd come and approach Myri from behind. As he limped down the street towards her, he could feel his heartbeat. *Go away.* He wanted to focus on what needed doing, not be drowned by feelings. Old feelings, at that.

Myri's hair wafted in the breeze, stray blonde hairs whipping behind her back. He swallowed, told himself he wasn't nervous, and limped to the bench, collapsing next to her in what he hoped was a suave and relaxed way, but secretly knew to be opposite. His legs burned—probably from all the kneeling.

"Hello, M-M-Myri," he said.

She gasped and jerked away from him. "What are you doing here?" Her voice sounded shrill and panicked, and if Demri didn't know any better, a bit disgusted. He was used to that, though. He shoved his affection back down into his stomach.

"Surviving," he said.

"There are a lot of people searching for you."

"I know. I've k-k-killed many of them." He paused, wondering if he should ask the next question. Decided to do it, anyway. "Are you going to b-be next?"

"I'm not trying to kill you, Demri."

"Vistario was trying."

"Vistario's dead too, huh?"

He shrugged. "Had it c-coming."

"Indeed." She sounded like she mostly believed him. *No doubt, Vistario was a fool. She's probably glad he's gone.*

They sat in silence for several minutes. As the evening sun dipped lower, more people passed the pair by and entered the diner.

"If you aren't here to k-kill me, why are you here?"

"I wanted to apologize."

"Why?"

"What Doram Quandis did to you was unacceptable. And, if I'm being honest, I took part in it." She turned and looked him in the eyes. "I've been living with the guilt that I didn't stop them. I stood by. After you left Ashmount, so did I. I couldn't be part of an organization which so callously attacked one of their own . . . and for no reason. Now, I'm finding my own path."

Demri didn't expect to ever hear an apology from anyone. Surprised, he didn't know what to say. He opened his mouth to respond but didn't have the words.

"The Magicai aren't going to leave you alone, Demri. You need to remain hidden. Keep moving."

"I know. You c-could c-c-come with me. And C-Caius." *Fucking C's.*

"I have my own journey to take, Demri. Good luck." Myri stood, resting her hand on his shoulder for a moment. "Once again, I'm so sorry." She walked away, disappearing into the crowd.

Demri watched the people walking back and forth as the sun slipped behind buildings. He wondered about future plans. Considered where to go next. He wasn't sure how long he remained on the bench, but at some point, Caius returned.

"What are you doing, Demri? You're supposed to be inside, hiding. There are Magicai around."

"Not anyone who's going to b-bother us."

IO

EDELBROCK BRENDIS

Lochwall, Calrym

The Ass of Lochwall could fortunately still go by "Edelbrock" as nobody in the House went by their legacy outside the fight. Edelbrock washed himself with a basin of dirty water left out after every fight for gladiators to rinse themselves. When he returned to the living quarters, Savakkis informed him of new Draftees arriving later that day. They'd collected ten people. Edelbrock wondered where they came from. He supposed he'd learn soon.

He ate some food, sparred with Lucky, and took a nap, feeling guilty he hadn't thought about Nauc's death. Someone shook him awake after what felt like moments of rest.

"Up and at it, boy," Marshal Deywin said, swishing a clump of skachi in his mouth.

Groaning, Edelbrock got up. "What now?"

"Lord Haklon wants a word."

"Wonderful."

"Mm." The marshal spat a glob of spit on Edelbrock's bed. "Whoops. Sorry about that."

"For a former man of the law, you certainly stopped giving a shit about it."

"Watch your mouth, son."

Scayde Haklon, surrounded by armed men, greeted Edelbrock when they entered the common room. "Ah, everyone give a cheer for the Ass of Lochwall. Welcome, Ed. I've noticed you haven't been connecting with the spirit of Buzzard's Bowl. It's important to this House, and the crowd, that you follow the rules. Otherwise, the crowd becomes unruly. And look at what's happened with Seeker Korran. Nobody respects him anymore. Should've put the dying dog down. Now we have to roll him out, a should-be dead has been. It's disappointing, to say the least."

"I'm not conforming to your sick games, Scayde," Edelbrock said.

The marshal thumped him on the back. "He's a duke. Pay him proper respect."

"No worries, Marshal," Scayde said. "He'll learn his place one of these days. I'm not sure you could do much to him that'd affect him. We've seen he has an iron will. Even when beaten and bruised he seems unaffected. Impressive. I certainly couldn't fight like you did after Marshal Deywin beat me, but you're a stronger man, I suppose. I'm the smarter one. Perhaps if we took away his . . . *luck*. Marshal?"

The marshal nodded to two armed men, and they exited the room.

Scayde smiled at Edelbrock. "You might dislike your new title, but I assure you, the Ass of Lochwall has a certain marketability I hadn't foreseen. The crowd loves you. I've already heard people discussing how they can cheer you on—'take a shit on him, Ass'. 'Just push through it' and, possibly my favorite, 'You've survived prunes, you can do this'. You've become Buzzard's Bowl's toilet overnight. Congratulations, Ed."

Edelbrock heard a loud smack, a scream, and then the marshal's voice. "Get his other arm, Wallace, you idiot."

The marshal returned, leading the other two men who were dragging a semi-conscious Lucky. *Oh shit.*

They dropped Lucky to his knees, then the marshal pulled his head back. "Cut his throat, Lord Haklon?"

"No," Scayde said. He withdrew a small dagger and offered it to Edelbrock. "Take this and kill him."

"I'm not killing him."

"If you don't kill him yourself, things will become much worse," Scayde said. He sneered at Edelbrock, shaking his head in disappointment. "We'll kill more gladiators here. Maybe we'll torture you more. Perhaps I'll exhume little Gordy's body and hang it in Buzzard's Bowl as a reminder. We could use a symbol for our citizens to recognize."

"You wouldn't hang a baby's body for all to see," Edelbrock said, though his words were empty. He wasn't sure what Scayde would do.

"You underestimate how sick the people in the stands are, Ed. Another reminder of a gladiator's tragic backstory displayed for all to see? They'd love it! Here's Edelbrock Brendis, a man who suffered betrayal at the hands of his wife, a man who watched his son die and did nothing to stop it. Perhaps it'd turn the crowd against you—for who could truly tolerate a sick man who doesn't defend his son?" Scayde grinned. "Kill Lucky or your life becomes much worse," he snapped, grin gone, eyes narrowed, the knife still hovering in the air, waiting for Edelbrock to take it.

He took it.

Now's my chance. Guards surrounded Scayde. He'd never make it in time. But the marshal?

Edelbrock lunged for Marshal Deywin's neck. The guard holding Lucky spotted Edelbrock and leaped forward to stop him. The knife plunged into the guard's chest, and he stared, wide-eyed and open-mouthed, at Edelbrock, then sank to the floor.

"YOU'RE DEAD, ED!" Marshal Deywin roared, drawing his sword.

"Stop!" Scayde Haklon said. "Kill him," he pointed at Lucky. "And retrieve my knife."

"He killed Wallace, my lord," Marshal Deywin said.

"I don't give two fucks about Wallace. Wallace is replaceable. My satisfaction at watching the Ass of Lochwall suffer is not."

While Marshal Deywin slit the throat of the half-conscious Lucky, several of Scayde's retinue approached Edelbrock, swords drawn. He tossed the knife on the floor, frustrated he'd failed. And made things worse.

"Bring him to me," Scayde said. He twisted the knife in his hands. It was clear he was contemplating his next move.

Marshal Deywin grabbed Edelbrock from behind and pushed him in Scayde's direction. A kicked to his knee sent him sprawling.

"Why is it that every time we attempt civilized conversation, you act like a feral animal?" Scayde asked. "Perhaps we should send you to join the Camel Clans."

"Do whatever you want," Edelbrock said. "But let's hurry it up. I have a battle to prepare for."

"You don't really have a say, Ed." Scayde knelt in front of Edelbrock, knife held out in front of him. Then, quicker than Edelbrock thought possible, Scayde struck.

Blood, a searing lance of pain and anguish, then a cascade down the left side of his face. He knew his ear was gone. He looked at the floor, saw it laying in a pool of blood.

"That was for insolence," Scayde said. "This is for revenge. Stand him up."

The marshal and another guard lifted him.

Scayde lashed the top of Edelbrock's pants, and they fell to the floor. He cut Edelbrock's shirt off next.

"Hold him still. This requires a delicate touch," Scayde said.

The men holding Edelbrock tightened their grips.

"You won't forget who you belong to, Ed." Scayde walked around to Edelbrock's back and the knife pierced his skin. He screamed as he felt his flesh tearing. The knife carved what felt like a snake, followed by three lines. Scayde repeated the pattern, digging into Edelbrock's neck, his lower back, his shoulders, his thighs, his calves, each ass cheek. The point scraped and poked, ripping Edelbrock's skin, carving the same pattern over and over until he stood in puddles of blood and felt faint.

Then Scayde came back into view. "Now for the front," he said.

Edelbrock grit his teeth and prepared for more pain. The knife dug into his chest, and Scayde drew a large S, followed by a large H. His initials. They were carved into Edelbrock's forehead, his cheeks, his stomach, the fronts of his thighs, even the tops of his feet.

"I apologize, Ed, as I think this might hurt a significant amount more."

A cold hand grasped his cock, holding it up.

"No," Edelbrock said. His eyes widened in horror as the tip of the knife started poking his manhood.

"Yes," Scayde said.

Then the point of the blade scraped across his scrotum and began writing. He screamed; a hand clasped over his mouth. He squirmed, but arms held him.

"Hold still," Scayde said. "Wouldn't want me to slip."

The blade made a series of movements, cutting. Warm flecks of blood spattered Edelbrock's feet. Blood ran down his legs and tears filled his eyes. He couldn't see. His body felt like it was on fire. Scayde slipped and the knife penetrated deeper. Edelbrock's teeth ground into one another. He bit his lip, cut his tongue on a tooth. Agony.

"Halfway," Scayde said, pulling Edelbrock's cock back down so it faced the floor. Then he started carving into the top.

Edelbrock moaned, felt his legs trembling, felt his body weakening. He peeked through slitted eyes, saw the S. H. carved into his chest, rivulets of blood trailing down to his bloody cock, replete with its own signature. S. H. The letters would haunt him forever. He closed his eyes again, dizzy.

A hand patted his cheek. "Done," Scayde said. Then he gave a swift kick with a booted foot into Edelbrock's groin.

"I'm done with the insolence" were the last words he heard.

Edelbrock saw stars and dropped.

Another kick hit him in the head, knocking him out.

II

ASHEN HYREL

Anepolis, Calrym

Since the day she'd bumped into Jaspard on the streets of Anepolis, Ashen had kept a pouch of Black Dust on her. Thieves and urchins often used a combination of black and red pepper, along with a handful of sawdust, a concoction they'd called Black Dust to make quick escapes or distractions, as it caused immediate, uncontrollable sneezing and watering eyes. Today was no exception. Tallas Taybold led the way into the palace and Ashen followed, hand inside one of her mantle's secret pockets, clutching a bag of the concoction.

They followed an intricately patterned carpet, muffling their footsteps. Armed guards stood in corners, outside doorways, and patrolled the halls. Everyone wore expensive clothing, jewelry, weapons. Everything was elaborate and unnecessary. Simple holders for candles lined the walls, the wicks unlit, unused. Instead, monumental chandeliers hung from the ceiling every few feet. Wide corridors went ignored by everyone of importance, because the fancy carpeting only filled the center section. Pages, servants, and professional-looking knights bustled around, running messages, delivering orders, or following their employers.

"Never been inside," Tallas said.

"Me neither."

What would my father think if he could see me now? She recited her father's Five Rules of Survival in her head—if there was a time she needed to recall her roots, now would be it. *Never forgo food because it appears dissatisfying. Starving to death isn't worth it. Never accept a helping hand. You never know who you'll owe and you have nothing to leverage. Never display your belongings, however meager they may seem. Somebody always has less than you. Never assume you're returning to the last place you felt safe. Unforeseen circumstances could mean you won't be able to. Never trust anyone, even those you trust. In matters of life and death, your life is meaningless even from your friend's point of view.* And the sixth rule, one she'd tacked on after her father's death: *Never let them know you're a girl, even after dark. Girls find themselves at the violent hands of angry men.* She'd shorn off her hair as a homeless urchin, to appear as a boy. Ashen didn't miss those times. She also knew she didn't need the rule anymore, but it was part of her creed now.

She took a breath, exhaled, sending Ashen out into the void, and became Duchess Cithrial Hyrel.

"It'd look poor to ask for directions, My Lady," Tallas said.

"Indeed." She straightened her shoulders, walked in the stiff manner of nobility, and offered a condescending glare to any who stared in her direction.

The thumping of the butt of Tallas's halberd on the carpet they strolled on gave a soft echo in the chamber. This attracted further stares.

"Sir Tallas," she said, whispering to avoid further scrutiny. "You're attracting the gaze of the commoners!" If anyone overheard, at least she'd sound like a lady.

"My apologies." The thumping ceased. "My Lady," he

said, after a moment. He caught her gaze, then flicked his eyes and tilted his head ever so slightly ahead of them.

She peered around him, noticing a bedazzled woman. Several shirtless servants followed her, all men, all very muscular. They each wore a sword at their belt. The woman walked as tall and stiff as she could make herself, her chin pointed up, as if she was trying to keep her head above all the riffraff. She turned down a corridor and, after ignoring a greeting from one of the hall guardsmen, disappeared.

"Hyrel," a voice said.

She turned her head, looking for Duchess Arena, but all she saw was a young boy. A page.

"Duchess Cithrial Hyrel?" he asked.

"That is correct," she said.

"I'm sorry. I was supposed to greet you at the entrance, but . . ." he trailed off.

She arched a brow.

The page cleared his throat. "I misunderstood and went to the wrong entrance. It was my mistake, my lady. I'll inform my mistress later of the infraction—she'll see me punished properly. But first, allow me to lead the way to the Great Hall."

"I became lost today," she said. "Perhaps we should place signs." She gave the boy a smile.

He grinned. "Mayhap, but then I'd be out of a job."

"We'll pretend you led me from the entrance." She winked.

The boy smiled wider. "Brilliant. This way, My Lady."

The page led them down the corridor where the woman with many servants had disappeared. At the end, a pair of huge double doors reached from floor to ceiling. Several of the palace's guards stood outside the doors, and a menagerie of other armed men and women huddled in different groups, staring at one another.

"Inside the doors is the Great Hall. Good luck, my lady." The page bowed, then ran off to do his other duties.

"It would appear Lord Couliac's information about only bringing a single guard inside the palace is incorrect," Tallas said.

"I'm sure you'll suffice, Sir Tallas. You have your halberd."

Tallas grunted. "Lady Hyrel, politicians will pretend to be your friend to your face, but in the end, they'll stab you in the back. If there's one thing I know about both politics and war, it's a saying I once heard a man mutter. 'Honorable people die young'."

"What happened to him?"

Tallas frowned, averting his gaze. His milky eye stared off in a different direction. "I killed him. The man was a fool. Stumbled on me when I was unarmed and unarmored. Instead of gutting me, he removed his armor and handed me a sword. Started counting down from five to give us a fair start. On 'three' I stuck my sword in his chest. Honor is for fools and the dead."

Something about the way he wouldn't look at her gave her the impression he was lying, but everyone has their secrets. She nodded rather than confront him. "You did what you had to, as I have done myself." Lowering her voice to a whisper, she said, "And now, I dress myself as a caricature of nobility, in order to further the goals of the unfortunates."

He didn't physically react to her openness. She found out later that Jaspard had informed Tallas of their plans already. "When it comes to politics and power, never underestimate anyone. Especially those of us with the smallest stake in the game, and the largest portion to gain." He offered her a frightening grin, his good eye staring at her, the milky one wobbling in a slightly different direction.

"How'd you become so wise?" she asked.

"I've seen enough to make me a learned man, my lady.

Education can be both taught and read, it's true, but ofttimes the most educated of us all just use our seeing eye."

She wondered if he was making a joke or believed that everyone only saw with one of their eyes. "Wise men are few and far between. I'm glad to have met you, Sir Tallas. But now, I must attend the Council."

She walked towards the doors.

A guardsmen spoke. "Name?"

"Duchess Cithrial Hyrel. Open the door and never question me again unless you relish the idea of spending a night in the prison."

They opened the door and bowed their heads in deference, muttering apologies.

Duchess Cithrial Hyrel entered the chamber. *Prim and proper, prim and proper. Best not forget or I'll be a squatter.*

D uchess Cithrial heard the doors thud closed behind her, but she paid them no mind. In front of her, a table filled much of the room. An array of food graced the tabletop, but didn't catch her attention, either.

Never forgo food because it appears dissatisfying. Starving to death isn't worth it. One of her father's Five Rules of Survival. She needed to forget those rules she followed as an urchin but was finding it difficult.

King Mikas Garcovi sat at the head of the table, jeweled crown glistening. Beside him stood a timid-looking man. All eyes were on her. She noticed the woman she'd seen back in the hallway. She seemed disinterested as she took a sip of wine. Another man gorged himself on food, though it appeared much of it rolled down the front of his belly, rather than ended up in his mouth. Other figures surrounded the table, and she noticed an empty chair. Her spot.

"You must be the new duchess," the timid man said.

"Who else would it be, Bertrand?" King Mikas said. He gestured toward the empty seat. "Please, Duchess . . ."

Bertrand whispered in the king's ear.

The king waved him back. " . . .Hyrel, take a seat. Come, join us."

Duchess Cithrial weaved her way around the table, taking her seat. It saddened her when she noticed she'd be sitting next to the messy eater. *Well, ain't this a place for an earthworm who prefers shit?*

"Mmph," the eater said. "Delicious." He swallowed. "Velturo Ondakka, ah-hah." He let out a strange laugh, then held his hand out to take hers.

She suppressed a grimace, then reached her hand out, despite not wanting to.

"Do not let him touch you," the woman she'd encountered earlier said.

Duchess Cithrial retracted her hand before Velturo could take it.

"He is disgusting, and one as young as yourself should not have to feel so . . . denigrated," the duchess continued. "Apparently, we are related, which is the only reason you have been allowed to attend this council. I am Arena Hyrel, and I must say, I do not recall ever having met you." She clasped her hands together, resting them on the table in front of her. Cithrial noticed the beautiful purple polish on Arena's fingernails.

"You haven't met me. My parents died when I was very young and I found myself in a couple notable households unrelated to the Hyrels. Perhaps someday we can discuss it further," Cithrial said. It wasn't completely true, but it was close enough. It was the story she and Jaspard had agreed to. She fingered the Black Dust in her hidden pocket, a comforting touch. *Prim and proper.* She straightened herself in the chair, holding her chin up more, mimicking the posture of Arena.

"The king would like to remind the prospective duchess that she hasn't yet been offered a permanent title," Bertrand said. "If things don't go well—"

Cithrial didn't know who this Bertrand man was, but he wasn't sitting at the table, which meant he wasn't important. She cut him off. "*If* my lord has something to say about it, I'd much rather discuss it with him, rather than one of his incompetent cronies. Honestly, if we're to take orders from somebody who's not even allowed a chair, I'll leave."

Bertrand flushed. "I'm the king's chancellor!"

Velturo choked on his food. Arena let out a cackle. The king's booming laughter a second later canceled out any other noise.

"She's got the Hyrel blood in her, all right," King Mikas said.

Arena clapped her hands, loud enough to make a noticeable slap, but gentle enough to not even leave a touch of redness. "Spectacular."

Velturo continued choking next to her, spraying breadcrumbs across the community dishes. Cithrial was relieved she'd promised Jaspard she wouldn't eat at these meetings. Any desire to had been swept away.

Another duke spoke. "It's a change of pace having somebody who isn't dying in that chair. We should've replaced Duke Sturgeon years ago."

A glare from Arena silenced the man. "Finding your voice after all these years, Hemmel? Sturgeon dies, the pretty young duchess shows up, and suddenly you can speak? We all know your preferences outside the meeting but seeing as I am not allowed to bring in my servants, I see no reason we should allow you to gawp at the young duchess. Besides, is she not the wrong sex? Last I heard, you were more interested in the little boys at Madam Zeitwitch's."

Duke Hemmel leaned back in his chair. He was, Cithrial guessed, the oldest one in the room. A thin fold of hair crossed his balding pate, and his eyes were too close together. He had full cheeks with thin tufts of hair poking from them and a large chin, making him look like a chipmunk she'd tried unsuccessfully to hunt when she lived on the streets. He even had two large, prominent incisors she glimpsed whenever he opened his mouth. "Let's leave our sexual preferences outside the room, I would think." She disliked Hemmel immediately. His exaggerated pronunciation of "sexual" made him even creepier and more revolting.

"Enough," King Mikas said. "If we had to remove people in here based on their bedroom habits, I'd be alone."

Cithrial wondered if that was the king's bedroom habit but realized voicing the question would be a terrible tactical decision.

"There's more news of Remeria," the king said. He waved Bertrand back over. "Read King Alondo's latest missive."

Bertrand unrolled a parchment and made a show of clearing his throat. He gave an angry stare at Cithrial for a moment, and then read. "To King Mikas Garcovi and his elected councilors—"

"Get to the informational part," the king said, resting his forehead in his hand. Cithrial thought the king was angering.

"Of course, Your Highness," Bertrand said, shifting the parchment in his hands. "A mighty band of rebels has appeared in the east. They're led by a man named Saint Godfrey and have destroyed several towns and villages already. With the Camel Clan threat coming from one side, and this band who call themselves the Saintmaritans, we need your immediate assistance. We fear the Camel Clans will approach Andora soon and have yet to receive aid. It's imperative you consider the possibility of a Vessian invasion in your country soon. If Remeria falls, they'll be in Calrym next.

For Calrym and Remeria to both continue flourishing, we need to halt this threat. Signed, Atticus Crenshaw, King's Council, on behalf of King Alondo Sedoa."

"Why should we give a shit if there's a band of rebels growing in Remeria? Let them wreak havoc for all I care, ah-hah," Velturo said. He took a drink of wine, dribbling a good mouthful's worth down the front of his tunic. "Oh, shit, ah-hah."

"There is nothing we can offer Remeria," Arena said. "Sure, we could send what military we have stationed in Calrym. But that would leave us vulnerable to another attack from elsewhere."

"Elsewhere?" Hemmel asked. "What elsewhere? Vessia is invading Remeria. There isn't another country to worry about. Cyrok is taken care of, and Qothe isn't a worry. The Magicai aren't going to start attacking just anyone. The only thing we need to worry about is a rebellion, but our citizens have never been happier!"

Hemmel reminded Cithrial of Tallas's words, though she changed them so she wouldn't incriminate herself. "When it comes to politics and power, never underestimate anyone. Especially those with the smallest stake in the game and the largest portion to gain."

"Profound," Arena said. She dipped her head in acknowledgement of Cithrial.

"If Harlem were here, he'd say we'd need to help, ah-hah."

"Harlem's busy," the king said.

"We should let the Camel Clans destroy King Alondo. Think about it," Arena said. "We could wait until one side wins, then attack the weakened side. Then we would rule the entire continent."

"A sound plan," Hemmel said.

"Does anyone actually want to attack, ah-hah?"

"Why would we?" Cithrial asked. "Why protect anyone other than ourselves?" *It's what rich people did, anyway.*

"All in favor of protecting ourselves?" Hemmel asked.

Nobody disagreed.

"That settles it," King Mikas said. "Ignore the missive, Bertrand. Sedoa won't be receiving a response."

The King's Council covered a vast array of topics, most of which bored Cithrial. Taxation, local policies, a desire to return to the Duke of Lochwall's estate, and other current affairs of Anepolis. At the end, the king officially bestowed the title of duchess upon her. She was now part of the King's Council.

Cithrial was relieved when the king dismissed them. She exited the Great Hall, after allowing everyone else to precede her, and found Tallas Taybold leaning against the wall, halberd in hand.

"My Lady," he said.

"It's time to leave, Sir Tallas. Bring me to my carriage."

When they exited the palace, Tallas took a deep breath and looked at the sky. Then, he said, "You're a sight for sore eyes. It's oppressive in there."

"Let's return to Lord Couliac's manor."

Regrouping with her entourage, Cithrial and Tallas climbed inside the carriage and began the ride home. Tallas kept peeking out the window.

"We have guards for that," she said.

"I am a guard."

"Other guards."

He turned back to look at her. "I am another guard."

"You know what I mean."

"And you don't know how easy it is to get ambushed."

"The Golden Knight takes his duties seriously."

Tallas grunted.

"No?"

Tallas grunted again.

"Well, ain't this chatter fit for a mute?"

He turned away from her and looked out the window again.

12

INTERLUDE

ALYST GARCOVI & HARLEM MACCARO

Vox, Cyrok

They had nothing exquisite when it came to Cyroki cheeses. Nothing he'd located, anyway. *Depressing.* That was a word which could describe much of the barren lands of Cyrok. Under his leadership, he'd conquered the country, destroyed almost every town, and killed any Cyroki native he'd found. Other than the ones under his employ, though, they'd fucked him. They'd hired Captain Adavir and his men to sow discord in Cyrok. Instead, the bandits had made a mess of things, and accomplished nothing—other than forcing Calrym to invade. *Never trust a ruffian.* If Harlem ever made it back to Calrym, he'd kill the self-titled Captain Blago Adavir himself—the bastard had fled, taking his bandit men, and going . . . somewhere.

King Mikas had sent Duke Harlem Maccaro to oversee the invasion personally. When Harlem's ship arrived, he'd disembarked and caused destruction. With only a small crew left to man the vessel, Harlem pushed further into Cyrok, razing towns and cities. He began in Alekl, followed the roads to Timberglade, and eventually made it to Vox, the capital. He'd broken through the gates, executed the Falcon Knight leader —Ollitha Oxhorn—killing all the citizens afterwards, and burned most of the city to the ground.

The king's nephew, Alyst, had flanked from the east and followed a similar trajectory. Except Alyst had the honor of killing both Governess Stasia Falconel and Sir Ilic Strictland, two notable figureheads. The leader of Harlem's force, the Old Vulture, had escaped. Whispers of Harlem's incompetence wove their way through the ranks. He knew they believed him incompetent he saw the looks on their faces whenever they saw him and their admiration whenever Alyst was around. Alyst's popularity soared, Harlem's plummeted. But Harlem was in charge, and that's just the way things go sometimes. He'd sent a message to King Mikas, requesting to return home. Knowing the group of bastards who helped advise the king, it wouldn't surprise Harlem to hear a strongly worded "no" in the return letter.

Harlem had commandeered an extensive building to use as his personal headquarters. He wasn't sure what the Cyroki had originally used it for—a blacksmith, horse stall, a tannery. Harlem hadn't asked. He'd had his men empty it, then filled it with furniture.

Sergeant Kolb Wickam, the only other current occupant of the building, stoked the fireplace with a poker. During the daytime, most men were out doing various tasks: patrolling; searching; rebuilding; gather food, water, and firewood. "Can't ever shake the chill, my lord," Kolb said.

"No," Harlem said, "you can't."

"Any idea how much longer we're going to be stuck here, my lord? I don't mean to sound disobedient, but it's getting ridiculous. The Cyroki are all dead."

"We must do our best to make sure we've weeded them all out. King Mikas will send for us when it's time to return," Harlem said. He wasn't sure how true that was.

"With all due respect, sir, why not leave now of our own accord?"

"We could, Sergeant Wickam, but there's a very fine chance our bodies would hang from taut ropes if we did. The king is not an even-tempered individual. As somebody who knows King Mikas personally, I suggest we wait for further orders."

Kolb stoked the fire more, enticing more heat to flow into the room. The two sat in silence for a few moments.

"Sir Alyst doesn't think so," Kolb said.

"No?" Harlem sat straighter in his chair. He'd want to pay attention to this and sitting straighter kept him focused.

"He's the king's nephew."

"And? I'm one of the king's dukes."

"No disrespect, sir, but blood is blood."

Harlem considered his daughter Jaylena. She'd been blood, even when she'd married that bastard Edelbrock. He'd rejected the idea she married him. But children are fools, and fools don't listen. He'd still loved her, though Despite her ridiculous decisions, he often remembered her as a child, smiling and happy. Upon reaching womanhood, she changed, became more needy and arrogant. *'Insufferable' might be the right word.* He missed her, regardless. *Perhaps, upon returning to Calrym, we can make amends. Perhaps she'll even see the error of her ways and leave that foolish fop of a husband.*

"You are correct, Sergeant Wickam. There's one minor flaw in your reasoning, however."

Kolb backed away from the fireplace and took a seat opposite Harlem. "What's that?"

"We are not the king's blood."

Kolb frowned, then shrugged. "I hadn't considered that, my lord. I figured if Sir Alyst backed us, the king would, too."

"King Mikas is no fool, and if somebody triggers his temperament, it's impossible to reason with him. If he's angry enough, the mumblings of an inexperienced man like Alyst won't get through. The king has a propensity for killing people unrelated to him when he's upset. Abandoning Cyrok by returning home will not go well. Mark my words."

"You're right, My Lord. We'll remain in Cyrok, do the king's bidding. You are the one in charge, after all."

Yes. I am. But something about Sergeant Wickam's words didn't set well with Harlem.

Alyst Garcovi was more than just a king's nephew. He was a knight and a wooer of women. Most of all, he was a person, not a sacrificial grunt or Lord's plaything. He'd done his job—conquer Cyrok—and near froze to death doing it. And now it was time to return home. The lines of command made it clear, however, this wasn't the current plan. Duke Harlem Maccaro, brownnoser, a man with no agency, and a pathetic weasel who wanted to preserve his status, refused to disobey King Mikas. Alyst had killed Cyr Ilic Strictland in one-on-one combat—with a touch of help from a Magicus—while injured. Afterwards, he'd stabbed Governess Stasia Falconel to death after she surrendered. A highlight in his career.

Calrite soldiers patrolled the area around where Alyst sat. He'd recovered from his injuries, but found he still needed to take it easy. Either he was getting older or the injury on his side had caused more damage than he thought. They had a pair of Healers with them. He could command one of them to fix him up. Since he wasn't dying, however, it wasn't worth the waste of life. *Save it for when I really need it.*

He rested on the stump of a tree, a glowing firepit a foot in front of him. It was so cold the fire wasn't melting the snow around the pit. Alyst shivered, waiting. He could be inside with Duke Harlem, but that bred contempt. Long ago, Alyst had learned, the more you stuck it out with the soldiers, the more they respected you. Once you fell into the trap of ordering everyone around and avoiding the revolting or arduous tasks, you'd lost them.

His foot tapped in the snow, an attempt at increasing his blood flow. A steel sword rested on his thigh, bouncing with the tapping motion. Alyst oiled the blade, a habit he developed when bored.

The sun had long passed its peak and was setting when Sergeant Kolb Wickam returned. He took a seat on one of the other stumps, after Sir Alyst gestured at one.

"What news do you bring?" Alyst asked.

"Sir Alyst, he's not budging. I brought up the points you suggested. Duke Harlem is convinced we must remain here until the king sends for us."

"That could be cycles."

"It's going to be cycles, sir." Kolb stretched his feet out, almost putting them in the fire.

"Put it out and you'll be on patrol for half a cycle," Alyst said.

Kolb retracted his boots a few inches.

"Incompetence should be punishable by death," Kolb said.

"It often is." Alyst thought about the sergeant's words, though. What would his uncle, King Mikas, do if Harlem didn't return? *A Cyroki guerilla group ambushed the good duke while he went for a shit in the woods.* It was plausible. The king had no notion of what was going on. And, with Duke Harlem's death, Alyst figured he could reason his way out of returning to Calrym. "You've given me an idea, Kolb."

"Are we going home, sir?"

"Hopefully sooner than you think."

At night, Duke Harlem dined with Sir Alyst. It was one of the few times Harlem could say he'd see the young knight. The only time Harlem found himself in similar company as the meetings he attended with King Garcovi and the other dukes and duchesses. He missed Duke Sturgeon, the raspy old fool who had outlived many serving members of the King's Council. Harlem consented that he even missed Duke Velturo's messy eating habits. Duchess Arena was another matter, though. Harlem planned to get her title removed. He just needed to figure out how.

"The glazed duck is good," Kolb said. For some reason, Alyst insisted Sergeant Wickam joined them for dinner.

Harlem sat his fork and knife down. "Yes," he said, glancing at the remains of greasy duck swimming in onion sauce. He took a sip of nochi—spiced chocolate ale.

Alyst, sitting across the table, hadn't taken his eyes off Harlem since they'd taken their seats. Harlem noticed Alyst's portion of duck lay soaking in sauce, the compost mix-up of vegetables and vinaigrette was undisturbed, and the roasted rice had a single forkful removed from its pile—still resting on the fork Alyst held in his hand, and had been holding, for at least five minutes.

Harlem switched to the ale sitting beside his nochi, taking a long draught. "Is something the matter, Alyst?" Harlem dabbed at his mouth, wiping excess ale from his lips.

"I've been thinking, my lord," Alyst said. He leaned back in his chair, setting the fork down on his plate.

"What about?" Harlem cut another piece of glazed duck and swirled it around the sauce. He liked a gratuitous amount of sauce, ensuring it covered the entire bite.

Sighing, Alyst leaned further back in his chair. When he spoke, he raised his voice a lot more, so he was almost shouting. "I think it's time we return to Calrym, my lord."

"I would like that myself," Harlem said. He placed the duck in his mouth, and the front door burst open. A retinue of

Calrite soldiers rushed in, swords drawn. Harlem spat his food back onto his plate—an undignified and unacceptable maneuver in most circumstances which he'd never have done —and stood. "What do you," Harlem said through gritted teeth, "think you fools are doing?"

"I'm sorry, my lord," the first one at the door said. "I'm just doing my duty. You're under arrest."

Harlem snorted. "Arrest? You don't control me! Get out of here. Men, arrest this foolish captain!" Harlem pointed at the offending man. The soldiers standing behind him appeared confused.

"No need," Alyst said.

Oh, look, here comes King Alyst to the rescue. Harlem would've rolled his eyes, had he not had half a dozen armed men looking at him. He supposed it was a good thing Alyst had such command over the soldiers, otherwise he'd be in deep shit.

"Captain Dursten," Alyst said, emphasizing the man's name, "is acting on my behalf."

"What!" Harlem swiveled in Alyst's direction. "I'm in command here!"

Alyst shook his head. "So often I find those who command are unfit to rule. It's a sad reality that it comes down to us lesser beings to bring them down a peg. Remove his sword, Captain Dursten."

Dursten, keeping his sword raised and pointed at Harlem's neck, stepped forward and drew Harlem's blade from his belt. "I'm sorry, my lord," he said. At least Dursten had the decency to look apologetic.

"I'll see you hang, Alyst," Harlem said. He wondered if he could make that a reality, considering Alyst's relation to the king.

"I don't think you'll have an opportunity to make that request," Alyst said. "Sergeant Wickam, take the duke next door and lock him up—use as few men as possible. Then prepare a fire. We'll burn the city. Captain Dursten, round the army up and march for the coast. We're returning to Calrym. Don't wait for me, Captain. I want to deal with Duke Harlem's treason myself."

"Sir!" Sergeant Wickam saluted, then selected a couple of soldiers, and they grabbed Harlem.

His hands were yanked behind his back, then cold manacles closed around his wrists. He was a prisoner in his own army.

<hr>

Captain Dursten exited next, bringing the rest of his soldiers with him. They'd leave for the ship docked in Coldridge immediately.

Kolb Wickam remained with him. Alyst would need a few loyal people he could trust, and the sergeant had proven himself.

"What do you intend to do with Duke Harlem?" Kolb asked.

"We can't bring him with us."

"You're going to leave him here? Alive?"

Alyst hadn't thought of that.

"I'm unsure," he said. The prospect of leaving Harlem here, alone, seemed worse than death.

"That'd be a shit way to go."

"He's a shit person."

Kolb nodded. "Bit weak, I'd say."

"Doesn't matter now. We're returning home, where we'll be considered heroes. With Cyrok gone, we can focus our efforts on conquering Remeria."

"Is that the plan, sir?"

"I'm not a part of the planning, Kolb. I bet upon my return, I will be."

"Probably, Sir Alyst. You're a hero. If they don't make you duke, I'd be pretty upset if I was you."

Kolb was right. They *should* make him Duke Alyst Garcovi. Maybe he could be the Duke of Dukes. It'd be nice to be in charge of such a prestigious group. *Ah, the power.* He could taste it.

Alyst walked outside, Kolb following. Already he saw a large gathering of wood stacked in the center of the remaining Vox buildings. They'd preserved a small section of the city and burned the rest. Now it was time to finish the job.

"Sergeant Wickam, please erect a pyre. I've made my decision on what to do with Duke Harlem."

"Yes, sir."

Harlem found himself locked in a small hut. He'd kept it from burning down, in case they had needed to imprison anyone. As luck would have it, they'd never used the building. It was cold, dark, and small. One of his soldiers —he couldn't remember the man's name—had said he thought it might've once been a shed to store gyrfalcons, a native hunting bird the Cyroki often bred.

He shivered, searching for the thin blanket he'd had thrown in here, on the off chance they'd imprison someone. With the level of his anger, the shock of the betrayal, Harlem knew he wouldn't be able to rest. There were no windows, and only a solitary door, which he knew nobody could break down. He'd had it reinforced. He closed his eyes and waited.

Harlem had breached no rules, nor committed any treasonous offence. Which gave him a terrible feeling about what was going to happen to him. Alyst Garcovi was no idiot. He wouldn't betray Harlem without a plan. And, if anyone found out about Alyst's treachery, he'd die himself.

In Harlem's heart, he knew his time was limited. Even if

they offered him a last meal, he'd never again get to taste his favorite cheeses. Shockingly, he realized he cared more about that than seeing his daughter one last time.

———

The soldiers had piled the wood against the back of the building Alyst was keeping Harlem in. The pile collapsed out into the street, where they'd built the pyre.

Sergeant Wickam returned, two other men in tow. One was abnormally short and skinny with a crooked posture, the other one taller and thick, almost like a walking barrel. "These are them you requested, Sir Alyst."

"Names?"

Kolb pointed to the short one. "Tauven Shekt." He shifted his finger to the tall one. "And we just call him 'Thief'. Not because he steals from the army, Sir Alyst, he's just damned good at cards. Formal name is Jafe Valendar."

Tauven and Jafe saluted Alyst.

"Drop the nickname, you're a soldier," Alyst said to Jafe Valendar. The man blushed, and Tauven and Wickam both appeared uncomfortable. *Good. We don't need that juvenile crap in my army.* "You've told them their job, Sergeant Wickam?"

"They're loyal, Sir Alyst. Won't be a problem. With your help, the four of us will be fine."

Alyst nodded. "Round them up. Once the deed is done, I want Tauven and Jafe to bring Harlem. Then we'll catch up with Captain Dursten. I want to leave this freezing hell as soon as possible. Mother Avani herself would forsake this piece of shit."

———

The cold got stronger; Harlem grew weaker. He wasn't sure if fifteen minutes had passed or several hours. The thin blanket wasn't doing a good job, and his shivering had become uncontrollable. He'd underestimated how cold it got without a fire. If he'd imprisoned anybody and didn't improve the heating conditions, they probably would've died before he'd gotten to them. *Is this how everything goes for men in power? Do we think we know best, only to discover we were wrong?* He knew the men would've known the blanket wasn't enough protection, yet nobody said anything.

The door opened. Two men walked in.

"Duke Harlem?" one of them asked in a squeaky voice.

"Yeah."

"You're coming with us," a much lower, gruffer voice said. Shaped like a barrel, the man bent and lifted Harlem up.

"Try anything and die," the squeaky voice said.

Harlem followed the men outside and became even colder. He noticed droplets of fresh blood in the snow leading around the corner of his prison.

The pair forced Harlem in the direction of the bloodstains. Around the corner of the building, his jaw dropped. A huge cascade of wood piled against the back of the prison stretched into the street. Next to the pile, an erected pyre awaited an unfortunate victim—he guessed himself. Laying in the snow, forming a semi-circle around the wood, were half a dozen dead bodies in pools of blood.

Alyst and Sergeant Wickam were wiping off their pink swords in the snow.

"Harlem," Alyst said, giving a polite nod.

The pair of soldiers who'd retrieved Harlem were dragging him towards the pyre.

"Alyst," Harlem said. "How will you live with yourself after this is finished?"

"I'll be fine."

"What about your honor?"

"Honor? I once knew a man who said, 'Honorable people die young'. I've listened to that advice since first hearing it."

The soldiers pushed him against a pole, stringing his hands up behind him. More ropes contained his legs.

"This isn't the way, Alyst," Harlem said. Inside, he was panicking. He didn't want to die. He also knew showing panic wouldn't help anyone. Anybody who displayed panic in his vicinity he discounted as losing their mind.

"I can't go back on it now, Harlem. Imagine what my uncle would do if he found out?" Alyst waved at the dead bodies in front of him. "I can't restore their lives now, either. So, this has to be done."

"Captain Dursten won't allow this!"

"I know. Captain Dursten won't make it back to Calrym either, Harlem. Sergeant Wickam, please start the fire."

"Wait. Kolb, you know you can't do this," Harlem said. He heard his voice's pitch rising. He couldn't help it. "Please, Kolb."

"My apologies, Duke Harlem." Sergeant Wickam started a fire near the wall of the prison building. It would take ages to reach Harlem.

"You're sick," Harlem said. "You're crazy! This isn't right! Let me go! The king appointed *me*!"

"He's right, Sergeant Wickam," Alyst said. "It's not right. It is sick. Start another fire under his feet. It's cold out."

Harlem shifted and squirmed against his bonds. "Kolb, don't. Don't do it, Sergeant." He twisted, turned. The ropes were too many, too tight. There was no breaking free. He felt them rubbing against his wrists, burning them. "Sergeant, please," he said, as Kolb got closer.

Kolb looked him in the eyes. "You should've let us leave." He bent down and started the fire.

It only took a few minutes and Harlem's feet burned. He screamed, he pleaded, he threatened, he begged.

Nobody listened.

Duke Harlem sizzled. His skin pinkened, then reddened, then blackened. He popped, crackled, bubbled, and split.

Pain. Agonizing pain as he cooked alive. Somehow, he lived until the smoke took him. And that took a fair while.

***

Alyst Garcovi, Kolb Wickam, Tauven Shekt, and Jafe Valendar left the burning city of Vox behind. They swore an oath to Alyst not to speak of the truth of what happened, and all planned on murdering and disposing of Captain Dursten's body an hour after leaving Cyrok.

During the two-day trek to Coldridge, they caught up with Captain Dursten and the rest of the men. Instead of waiting until the next morning, Alyst found an opportunity that night. He killed Captain Dursten in his sleep by stabbing him in the neck and used Tauven and Jafe to help drag the man out of camp and bury him beneath a heap of snow.

The second day, Alyst informed the men of Captain Dursten's midnight heart attack—the stress of the campaign had ended his life. Another death attributed to the Cyroki menace. Alyst, backed by stories told by Sergeant Wickam, Tauven, and Jafe, explained the fire burned out of control, and the other soldiers, along with Duke Harlem, became trapped and perished. *A fire taking Duke Harlem's life eliminates my responsibility even more so. The king can't possibly be angry at me for that.* At least, not to *him*. He was the king's nephew. He should be fine. Well, he hoped he'd be fine.

The Calrite army spent a day preparing *The Wet Maiden* for departure.

The following day, Sir Alyst Garcovi stood on the deck of the warship grinning as the wind whipped his hair.

He was heading home. Victorious.

13

SERADAL WINTLOCK & VILLIC THE IMBUER

Andora, Remeria

A shaman woke Villic from his nap and told him a circle had been called. Circles were the meetings in which a clan's leaders and shamans met. Since the birth of Imbuers, it included them, too. This circle included all clans, so Villic stood among a wide group of people. *A lion wouldn't be able to run around us without tiring.* Villic didn't know that for sure. He was terrible at measuring distances.

In the center stood each clan's leader and a shaman spokesperson. Villic recognized his clan leader, Jedkah, and the shaman.

"Dashiki."

Right. I'd forgotten.

"You always do."

He knew other clan leaders, but didn't know their names, though Villic knew enough to place them with their clan.

Surrounding the leaders was a ring of shamans, then the Imbuers formed an outer ring. The Imbuers were the newest rank in the clan, and most numerous, so they weren't as important.

The leader of Seven Signs spoke first, when all had gathered. "Andora continues to strengthen. We don't know if the Hill Strangers or the River Walkers are planning on helping the city. If we continue to wait, who's saying we won't also have to deal with Jungle Hiders or Sky Gliders, too?"

Murmurs passed through the group at the mention of Sky Gliders.

Villic rolled his eyes. *Sky Gliders? Ridiculous.*

The leader of Glory Blades, and rival of the Splintered Manes, spoke next. "We cannot be sure what's coming, but if we are to test our Imbuers, the time is now. Let us see what they can do. Let us break down the walls of Andora and crush everyone inside!"

The leader of Masters of the Lost spoke next. "Are we sure we want to keep attacking? The Remerians are pacified. Let us go crush Calrym next!"

Jedkah laughed at that. "We haven't finished taking our revenge on Remeria, and Masters of the Lost want to run?"

Many others laughed at his comment.

The leader of Masters of the Lost didn't laugh. "We've conquered enough land. We can settle down and live happily!"

"No," the leader of Bride Warriors said. "They will come and kill us all again. It happened in the past. They'll keep murdering us because they think we belong in the desert!"

Leader of the Sharpclaws spoke. "It's time we attack. It's time we take the city for ourselves!"

The leader of the Plagued Ones spoke last. "A majority of us say to attack, the Plagued Ones agree. We crush the Remerians and if the king is smart, he will be forgive us when we hold his life in our hands!"

The shamans agreed, which led to the Imbuers agreeing. A loud cheer went up.

"The gods favor us!" one shaman said. "Tomorrow we'll destroy the Remerians!"

Villic agreed.

The circle dispersed and returned to their respective clans. They spent the night in their camps, had a filling meal, and the following day, Villic joined his clan. The siege began.

———

Atticus had offered Sera and Royal the opportunity to spend the night in the city. At first, she'd declined, but figured a final conversation with King Alondo to iron out the details of their new partnership could be in the Falcon Knight's favor. Before the sun went down, she and Royal had gone to the ramparts facing the hilltop where the other Falcon Knights camped. The Old Vulture had kept his word —they'd had people watching this section of wall and agreed to have her signal them by the end of the day, if all went well—and several people were watching her. She gave them the signal that all was going well—a triple wave—and then she and Royal returned to ground level, where the Remerians provided an entire house for them to stay the night.

A man had cooked them a meal before bidding them a good night and leaving them alone.

"Who's house do you suppose this is?" she asked.

Royal shrugged. "Not a clue. Wonder if they have anything to drink, though." He peered into cabinets.

"I thought you had spare flasks."

"Can't ever have enough spare, though."

"It seems strange they'd have an empty house. I hope we didn't kick somebody out."

"More than likely," Royal said, walking to a chest and popping the lid open, "the man who served us our supper lives here." He rustled a few items around, grunted, then closed the lid. "It seems our homeowners took all the goodies with them."

"Shame," she said. "We need to maintain clear heads, Royal."

"I'm at my clearest when I have whiskey in my system."

She sighed. "I mean it. We don't know what's going to happen with the Camel Clans. Or the Redclaws. What a frightful woman."

"The Bloody Duchess? Interesting name. Makes you wonder what she's after."

"I don't know," she said.

"Probably the same thing everybody wants—acceptance. Power. Money. Everyone's always clamoring for something they don't have. Even the richest of rich folk."

They bid each other good night and went to separate bedrooms. Sera laid in her bed, thinking about her father, Jaidik. Wishing he'd come with the Falcon Knights and understanding why he didn't. Wondering why she went with the Falcon Knights, then understanding why she did. Jaidik grieved the loss of his family, the loss of how things were. Despite Sera feeling similarly, she'd also longed for adventure. She didn't want to stay in Gyrloft forever. She wanted to explore the world. And, truthfully, she felt guilty for abandoning her country, though she knew everyone she left behind had died.

Sera slipped into dreams about her past life. She woke, stiff and exhausted, with vivid memories of her mother and brother. The smell of eggs and bacon grease calmed her.

In the kitchen, the man who'd cooked them supper was laying out a breakfast spread. "Good morning," he said. "The King's Council has asked for you to eat, then meet with him and the king. Rumor says they let in that clawed woman, but Atticus didn't mention her."

"Thank you for your kindness," Sera said.

"But of course. I do as my king commands," the man said, bowing. When he finished plating the food, he gave another gracious bow. "I hope my house has been to your liking.

Enjoy." Then he turned and left before Sera could compose a response.

She ate her food, waited for Royal to stumble out of bed, nursing a hangover despite her requests. After Royal ate a bit of food, then vomited on the poor house owner's floor, they left.

A pair of Remerian soldiers met them outside and escorted them to King Alondo and Atticus Crenshaw and, to Sera's surprise, the Bloody Duchess and her poet were already seated at the king's table. King Alondo sat at the head of the table while Atticus Crenshaw loomed over the king's shoulder.

"Welcome, Cyr Seradal, Captain Hoarst. This is Mauve Hardeen, otherwise known as the Bloody Duchess, and Althier, the poetic one," Atticus said.

Sera and Royal took seats across the table from the Redclaws.

The king wiped a bit of sweat from his forehead. "My men tell me the Camel Clans are acting differently. In fact, they predict an attack today based on their behavior."

"Sounds like ya need the Redclaws, eh?" the Bloody Duchess twisted her claw to point at herself. "O' course, we're gonna need to figure out a stipulation or two, first, I'spect."

"We need everyone we can get. The truth is, the Camel Clans shouldn't be here," Atticus said. "Magicai were sent to halt their progress. The clans don't have access to magic. At least, not trained Magicai. It is possible they harbor a member of the Elkavich or two, but it's unlikely. How they pushed their way through the Magicai we sent is a mystery I'm sure we won't want to solve. They must have some secret power."

"Let's get down to it," the king said. "Cyr Seradal, you and Captain Hoarst are trapped inside the city. The Falcon Knights are behind the Camel Clans. Getting to them is impossible, and I won't let you walk out there and die. I can't risk allowing them a chance inside."

Sera figured that. With the Camel Clans surrounding Andora, they wouldn't raise their gates. And, Sera wondered, would the Camel Clans even let her return to the Falcon Knights?

"What o' the Redclaws? They're all 'cross the river."

"Yes, Bloody Duchess, and we're going to need them to fight. Will they?" Atticus asked.

"They do what me tells 'em to do. I think it sounds like ya mean to let 'em die, though."

"What are you after?" King Alondo asked. "Equality? Your own parcel of land? Power? A title? Money?"

"I want a better life. I used to be a noble, don'tcha know? Lost everythin' o' course. Killed me husband after he burned my hand. Justice. Never liked the prick, anyway. The Redclaws want o' bunch o' shit. Fuck 'em. I want assurances I'll have money, and a bit o' power. Take care o' myself and Althier, and ya got a deal."

"What about you, Althier?" Atticus asked.

"I'm a simple man, from simple means. I'm not lookin' for much, so it seems. A pouch o' coin, a pretty broad. Perhaps o' fancy title complete with a public applaud."

How is he her right-hand man?

"Fine, we'll take care of you both," King Alondo said. "On my honor."

"No offense," the Bloody Duchess said, turning the mangled claw to point at him, "but me issue with the crown is why the Redclaws are here to begin with. Not trustin' royalty an all."

"The Falcon Knights have witnessed this, and so has Atticus, my Council. Either can hold me accountable if I break your trust."

"Fine, I 'cept your offer."

"Thank you," Atticus said. "I believe it'd be prudent to go inform the Redclaws about the plan? We need to be ready."

"Agreed," the Bloody Duchess said. She stood, then walked to Atticus, grinning wild and holding her claw out to him. "Let's put it to the shakes."

Grimacing, Atticus extended his left hand and shook. "This might be the first time I've ever shaken somebody with my left hand before."

"I'm also a right-hander, meself," the Bloody Duchess said.

Atticus held out his right hand. "Then let's do it right." He seemed relieved to not have to touch her mangled claw anymore.

"Sees, that's what ya don't understand. All o' ya use your right hands. And all o' ya lies. Left hand it is. Perhaps it'll make an honest man o' ya. C'mon Althier, let's go up the wall and call o'er to 'em. Hope they's can hear us."

Althier followed the Bloody Duchess out, his poetic words trailing behind him. "A king in despair, a group of bird knights. If you and I are lucky, we'll avoid the biggest fights. Magic known and hidden, steel and blood predicted, death and destruction assured, we coerce Redclaws unbidden. A new alliance found. A true coalition birthed. In moments, our Mother Avani's goals'll be unearthed."

Sera wasn't sure what to make of either the Bloody Duchess or Althier.

"Strange people," Atticus said.

"The Falcon Knights," King Alondo said. "What will they do if the Camel Clans attack and you're still inside the city?"

"I don't know," Sera said. "I can only guess. If the Old Vulture see us joining the fight, I'm sure he'll help."

"We will hide the king for protection," Atticus said, "but you and I will go to the ramparts. Assess the situation. Maybe we can get the Old Vulture's attention? If the Falcon Knights help save the city, we will do whatever we can to aid you."

"If the Falcon Knights help you, we want Calrym to pay," Sera said. "We want help rebuilding Cyrok."

"Nothing would warm my heart more than to see both things come to fruition," King Alondo said. "But first, let us take care of a more immediate issue."

Sera and Atticus shook hands. Taking a cue from the Bloody Duchess, Sera extended her left hand. Atticus snorted but shook it.

<hr>

"*They're onto us.*"

There have always been people up there. Villic watched the patrols on top of the walls. There seemed to be more people than usual, all observing the Camel Clansmen.

"*There wouldn't be that many people there if they didn't know we were about to attack.*"

We won't even be able to get through their walls.

"*Nonsense. You're an Imbuer. There are many, many ways you can breach simple stone. The walls won't be an issue. The issue is going to be getting close enough. This is a capital city. A king's home. There are bound to be more Magicai, too. From what I've learned of these people, they operate in similar ways as the country I'm from—Jedovia. Our people poured most of their resources into protecting our leaders and our mages.*"

Villic checked his spear, his scimitar. Both were in solid condition.

The shamans were praying to the gods. Villic whispered his own prayer to Mutaz, god of war. Then Cocaro, god of luck. Then Carana, goddess of life. "Piss on Flaytz," Villic said, spitting on the ground. Flaytz, god of death, wouldn't take Villic in this battle.

The Camel Clans had formed into seven armies, each a different clan. They'd attack at the same time. Most of the army weren't Imbuers. They'd suppress the soldiers on the walls with arrows, while the Imbuers were to get in close and find ways through. Once the Imbuers breached the city, the rest of the clansmen would ride in.

Villic hopped on Dunecrest. He was ready. Minutes later, horns blared.

He raised his spear and screamed, spurring Dunecrest onwards. Seven armies, seven clans, one united force. Remeria stood no chance.

Atop the city's ramparts, Sera, Royal, and Atticus spotted the Falcon Knights. She waved her sword in the air, then pointed at the Camel Clans. She couldn't tell if they got the meaning, but they'd figured it out soon enough.

"If I don't make it through this," Atticus said, "please protect King Alondo."

"I'll do my best," Sera said.

Royal nodded, taking a swig from a flask. He smacked his lips and wiped his mouth with the stained sleeve of his captain's jacket.

Sera looked down. The Camel Clans had grouped into different armies. She swallowed, nervous, wondering if this was what it was like back in Vox. She'd fled that siege, now she found herself in another. *Hopefully the Camel Clans aren't as brutal as Calrym.* It was a weak hope, but it was all she had. Something in her gut told her the Remerians were losing this fight, and she wasn't sure why. The Remerians stood on walls. The Camel Clans didn't have Magicai. There was no reason they had a chance. Yet, they seemed confident. And they'd made it this far.

Horns blared. She tightened her grip on her sword, wishing she'd brought her shield.

"If anyone makes it up here, Cyr Seradal, it's imperative you keep them away from me," Atticus said.

Men ran past them, reinforcing various positions. Crossbowmen took aim, archers drew bows, runners were already running supplies.

A pair of robed figures approached. "Atticus," a woman's voice. "Sticks here."

A man's voice. "And Zale."

"Good," Atticus said. "Zale, fire. Sticks, lightning. Go slow. I don't want either of you dying from old age if you can help it."

Royal drew his sword, joining Sera. Atticus, Sticks, and Zale moved closer to the edge of the ramparts.

The mounted Camel Clansmen surged forward.

Crossbows twanged; arrows loosed. Camels and men and women collapsed. Another wave, then another, of arrows and bolts. But it wasn't enough. There were too many of them.

<hr>

Camel feet thundered across the plains as the Splintered Manes surged towards Andora's walls. A flash of arrows and bolts peppered the clans. Imbuers raised their weapons in defense. Villic morphed his spear into a stretch of molten flame. He waved it in the air, incinerating projectiles before they could hit their marks. Another wave of projectiles, and Villic saw the shaman, Dashiki Magoro, flop off her camel. Other riders thundered over her dead body, trampling her into the ground.

With a shaman already dead, Villic wondered if the gods favored this attack. If the gods didn't want this, and the godspeakers were dying already, this attack could have disastrous consequences. He looked into the sky, imagining different faces of the gods looking down at them in disapproval, shaking their heads, removing the powers of the Imbuers. He wondered—

"Villic, we're in a battle. Pay attention!"

Villic focused and saw another wave of arrows dipping towards him. Calling upon the power of water, he swiped his spear in the air, drawing a river of water over his head. Any arrows caught in the path followed the stream away. The water dissipated moments after being drawn. He was no Magicus after all, and the gods limited his powers to the weapon he wielded.

Villic turned his attention back to the wall. They'd made it about halfway, he assumed, though he wasn't good with measurements. Seemed they'd already traveled the length of a thousand water buffalo. Could've been ten, though. He didn't know.

An orange glow blinded him. He looked up as a gigantic ball of fire fell from the sky.

———

S era watched the arrows and bolts cascade down among the Camel Clans. She saw flashes of different colors here and there. She couldn't make out what was happening.

Sticks raised his hands and dropped them. A massive fireball formed in the sky and fell. As it picked up momentum, burning droplets of fire trailed behind it, making it look like the sky burned.

"That'll do it," Sticks said.

The fireball crashed to the ground, incinerating half an army—or it should have. The fireball collapsed into two halves. Between the fuming mass, a group of clansmen charged. *No, that's not possible.*

"How?"

"What?"

"They ran right through it!"

Atticus slapped the ramparts. "Impossible! They've got Magicai!"

Moments later, the Camel Clans made it to the base of Andora's walls.

The fireball sped towards the Camel Clans.

Jedkah pulled out a horn, blew a quick burst, waving everyone in.

Villic drove Dunecrest toward the center.

"Imbuers! Imbuers!" Jedkah chanted. When the shaman heard, they picked up the cry.

"Imbuers!"

Villic followed suit. "Imbuers!"

"You are an Imbuer, Villic! They need our help!"

Oh.

The fireball fell closer.

"Water!" one Imbuer shouted.

"Imbuers, form a line in the center. Everyone else, come in close," Jedkah said.

The Splintered Manes hurried to comply. Together, the Imbuers held their spears straight, calling to the power of water. The fireball fell upon the spears, splitting in half. A line of water poured over the clan, shielding most from the burning fragments. Screams from a few unlucky ones were drowned out as the charge resumed.

They reached the base of the wall.

Now what?

"Destruction," Speaker said.

14

DEMRI SLARN

Hidehedge, Calrym

A few days passed without interaction from most of the Elkavich. Ced dropped by to invite the pair to a meal or check in and see if they needed anything. Myri hadn't reappeared. According to Ced, she was a high-ranking member of the organization, and often busy. Demri and Caius spent much of their day sitting on their beds, ignoring each other. They still didn't agree about Myri, and rather than argue, they kept to themselves.

On the third day of their stay, Demri cracked and asked Ced what the plan was.

"Soon," Ced said. "I think Myri'll be wanting to see you again. Spouses shouldn't be apart too long, least that's *my* relationship advice. I might be out of my element, though. Never been married. But whenever I give advice, everyone agrees I'm right. 'That's what Ced said, they said', whenever an issue comes up and somebody quotes me. They always refer to my advice, even though I've never been married. Nope, not even once. Just smart, you see." He tapped his temple with a finger, to emphasize his intelligence.

Another day and a half passed before Myri returned.

A knock on their door. Caius answered. A whispered exchange. Then Myri entered, Caius left. The familiar scent of lavender wafted in with her.

"M-Myri."

"Enebrial."

Coded names even in private, huh? Way to make things impersonal. "D-D-f-four," he said.

She offered a smile. "You're learning. How are you enjoying your time in Hidehedge?"

"It's f-fine."

She walked over, sat aside him on his bed.

"Why d-didn't you turn me in to the M-M-Magicai b-back when we ran into each other in Zemur?"

She arched an eyebrow. "Been thinking?"

He shrugged. "A little."

"It was the least I could do. After what happened at Ashmount, I felt awful. I left as soon as I heard they'd labeled you a criminal. If anyone was the criminal, it was Doram. He couldn't see that, though. Nobody could. I tried to tell the Archmagicus the facts of the situation, but he said it didn't matter what the origin of everything was—you'd researched forbidden material *and* caused a violent battle by escaping."

Demri grunted. He remembered those events well. It was difficult to forget them when every Magicus in the world was hunting you.

"One reason I found myself here was because I questioned the Magicai's rules against researching certain topics. It never made sense that they'd limit what we could do. If there were other possibilities, why would they prevent them? And Enebrial, there are *far* more interesting things you don't yet understand. We'll need to discuss those sometime. In fact, I'll have Ced bring up an old book for you to peruse. There's a lot that Ashmount censored."

Intrigued, Demri wondered what else there could be. *More*

knowledge on how to unlock different schools? Are there other types of magic we don't know about? What could they possibly have hidden? Demri's thirst for information grew.

Myri cleared her throat. "I have news about Ashmount."

Demri snorted. "What?"

"It's gone."

He chuckled.

"I'm serious. We sent people to destroy it. It's . . . gone. Everyone inside is dead. News will begin spreading, soon."

"You c-c-can't be serious. The M-Magicai would never let that happen."

"They're gone," she said.

"How?"

"Three people combined their powers. They consumed their entire Well. An explosion destroyed everything. It's gone. The world doesn't know it yet, but they will. It was our first move. The Elkavich are done hiding, Demri."

"Doram was at Ashmount."

Frowning, Myri shook her head. "No. He has contacts in the Elkavich. They warned him, unfortunately. When he discovered the plan, he found a reason to quit his position as a professor. I don't know where he is now. He's disappeared."

"F-Fuck." For a moment, he'd hoped.

"I'm sorry."

"At least I d-don't have t-t-to worry about being p-pursued."

"This is true. When the Magicai learn of Ashmount's destruction, they won't know what to do. They'll be lost. As new powers surface, they'll be confused. Between the Imbuers and the Elkavich, the Magicai are, as we know it, done."

"What d-do you mean?"

"The Elkavich have vowed to kill every Magicus of Ashmount. We plan on blowing up every major city. Ashmount was a test."

"What? You'll destroy the world."

"The world will recover," she said. Myri stood, hand lingering on his shoulder for a moment. "I'll get you that book."

Demri forgot about his earlier desire to incinerate her.

Ced delivered the book, *The Lost Histories: An Archive After Removal* by Magicus Rensley Hobark, the next day.

Demri found it easier to ignore Caius now that he had material to occupy his time. Caius spent more and more of his day outside of their room, while Demri remained more and more closed off. Hobark had written the book in response to the Magicai's decision to erase all other forms of magic, while also deciding what a Magicus should and shouldn't be able to do. The first few chapters confirmed information Demri already knew—the Magicai could access multiple branches of power and they could access vast amounts of power by working together. There was a lot of corruption within Ashmount's plan to control the Magicai.

He pored through the book for days, leaving only to eat or shit. Myri didn't return. The only company he received was Caius when he turned in for the evening, or Ced when he announced each meal.

The book delved into how one could manifest multiple powers. Ashmount taught that civilians needed to possess something called the Trace to even unlock their powers—this was a lie, meant to keep the Magicai powerful. But Examiners could actually unlock the various Magicai powers for anyone. Hobark wrote if one were an Examiner themselves, they could unlock all of the other branches. *Without* spectacles . . .

While the Magicai plan on using spectacles to "unlock" a Magicai's power, they're wholly symbolic in their usage. Most Examiners wouldn't normally be able to unlock other threads of power because they haven't been trained and don't know what they're searching for. But, if you are one of the Magicai who learned from the original teachings, they'd have taught you how to find these strands. There have been reports that prove this is possible without having Magicai aid. Power manifestation has always been a possibility, though exceedingly rare. Now, with the ban on Magicai research, it's even more unlikely.

Demri knew this. After running into Myri in Zemur, he'd focused more of his time on trying to will new powers into himself. He tried everything. He'd never realized he'd unlocked Examiner powers until one day, he'd killed an Examiner and tried on their spectacles. He'd seen things he'd never imagined—each branch of magic had its own energy, or aura. Demri couldn't explain it, and he'd only seen it a few times. He avoided putting on the spectacles as much as possible. As he completed more research on the Elkavich, he noticed this might not be as rare an occurrence as he thought.

There were other fascinating entries. One discussed a type of magic called "Imbuing".

Imbuing is a long-forgotten magic, which, upon reading several tomes, fascinated me. The people who used to Imbue have been gone for centuries. Most accounts are lost. I read one detailed description, which, though mind-boggling, has piqued my curiosity. According to these now-destroyed scripts, Imbuers are a magic created by intelligent beings many, many civilizations ago. When Imbuing awakens within you, a spirit inhabits your body, sharing your thoughts, conversing with you, and granting access to powers. An Imbuer can only funnel these powers through something they hold. A weapon, or shield. I struggle to wrap my mind around such limited magical functioning, but they were more powerful than I can understand.

Another entry discussed an even older, more primal type of magic. Synthepists.

The Synthepists, or, as I call it, Synthepy, was a type of magic that perished before the dawn of true civilization. For those of the unscholarly types, Synthepy is derived from the term "synthesis", which means a combination of two parts to form a whole. Some primal cave inscriptions and, in later history, early written documentation, mention the rise of odd pairings between man and beast. (It's important to note, upon rereading, a small clarification. Above, when we talk about the ages old Imbuers, I mention intelligent beings. Here, with Synthepy, I mention primal beings. Do not be confused! Imbuing has far older origins and, the ancient civilization long fell to ruins. It's well-known that before our primal history, humanity flourished at least once before, though all knowledge of what it may have been like is lost. The brightest scholars suggest it was very similar to today's world, and I'm inclined to agree). *These pairings of man and beast led to friendly partnerships. According to what I've read, combined with a healthy dose of speculation, these Synthepists were born with the ability to commune with a single animal. They formed a lifelong bond with one another, and if that bond was to shatter, a Synthepist may recover well enough to form a second, though this was, apparently, rare. It's possible Synthepy is the oldest form of magic known—we're unsure when it came into existence—and once it disappeared, it has never resurfaced. Imbuing is confirmed to be older and there are also instances I've found suggesting it might've made a resurgence once or twice. Needless to say, much of what I've written is no more than wildly speculative theories.*

Fascinated, Demri found he couldn't put Hobark's work

down. He continued to delve in, determined to finish the book. Every page was filled with new information, hinting at something that could've been or had existed. Things Demri wondered, wished, and worried about.

Some speculate the world is alive, capable of shaping itself around magic. This idea seems ludicrous, but some of my peers have postulated this theory.

Demri snorted. *Unbelievable.* But was it? He wasn't so sure, upon reflection. Hobark's writing entranced him. He wasn't sure what to believe—and there was no way he could double-check Hobark's work. The man had written these accounts after the Magicai destroyed any remaining knowledge. Even if he was a trustworthy source of information, everything Hobark wrote would come down to how decent his memory was.

He read on.

Philosophically, the Magicai are attempting to control the world. But other types of magic have demonstrated this to be a very poor idea. If we consider past religious magic, we have seen various types fail because of their exclusionary methodologies. Consider the Veckheim, a cult who lived roughly a millennium ago, and all information relating to them has been transcribed through ancient texts taken by the original Magicai. They used what we can only call Veckheimism, an elusive, secret magic, and worshipped a figure known as V. Presumably a god-type individual, or perhaps the originator of the very cult. We're still unsure of how it worked, or what they did. We know it involved a lot of dark practices. As they gained popularity and power, they began tightening their restrictions on who may learn Veckheimism. The cult of Veckheim perished once the powers we know were discovered. At the behest of the Magicai, the cult ceased to exist—in this case, for the better of the realm. Rumors of blood sacrifices and other dark rituals ran rampant for centuries after Veckheimism ended. What's true or false is anyone's guess.

Demri read late into the night and woke early each morning. When he finished Hobark's work, emptiness gripped him, but he felt much fuller in his mind.

Myri returned a day after he'd returned Hobark's book to Ced.

15

ASHEN HYREL

Anepolis, Calrym

There were perks to becoming a Duchess of Calrym. A small portion of Anepolis became hers, with the flick of a hand and a signature. She moved into the manor that had belonged to the former Duke Sturgeon's. Jaspard, Bethinda, and Tallas Taybold moved in, too. There was more than enough room. It almost felt like she had a real family.

"Ah, the Lady Hyrel," Jaspard said one afternoon. His words were slightly slurred, meaning he had one of his sugared honey chews in his mouth.

She cocked her head back and walked past him, as if she were too good to answer.

"You've mastered the art of nobility. For the love of Mother Avani, don't become one of them."

"Ha. Well, ain't you a preacher preaching to a deaf girl?"

"And just when I thought she fooled me, Ashen reveals herself." He stroked his waxed mustache with thumb and forefinger.

"Won't ever be able to hide who I am for long."

"Just long enough to reach our goal, I hope?"

"Course. It's what I promised. And all of them are shitheads."

Chuckling, Jaspard led the pair of them into a glorious den filled with comfortable chairs, a bookshelf, and a wide windowed view of the streets—outside their gated property. He took a seat in a green armchair he'd taken a fancy to.

"That's nobility," Jaspard said.

"It's like I always say," Tallas said. His voice sounding right behind Ashen made her jump. "Honorable people die young. It's the pieces of dung and fungus who cling to life."

"Don't sneak up on me," Ashen said.

"No sneaking. I've been following you since you engaged Lord Couliac in conversation."

Jaspard nodded. "You didn't notice? He was behind you the entire time."

"No," Ashen said. "And I don't like it."

"You might end up changing your mind about that one day," Tallas said. Even in the house, the man clutched his halberd, hauling it around with him. "I'm good at blending in and being there when you need me. As long as the money keeps coming, of course." His gaze shifted to Jaspard.

"No need for concern. With her elevation in rank, we've inherited all the former Duke Sturgeon's holdings. We went from being a minor noble family to being incredibly rich over night! It's magnificent."

"Surely it is," Tallas said.

Ashen heard distant conversation taking place, heading in their direction. The voices got louder, more distinguishable, until she recognized them as belonging to the house servant, Bethinda, and Alora Couliac, Jaspard's sister.

"Lady Couliac is here?" Ashen asked.

"Indeed. I told her to stay in the city until we heard the news. Now that I'm—we're—rich, I'm sure she'll be interested in remaining."

Lady Couliac entered the den, looking fine as ever in her silk clothing and flashy jewels. As usual, she wore an elaborate hairstyle—this time, intricate woven braids tumbled down her shoulders.

Receding footsteps let Ashen know Bethinda was returning to her cooking.

Tallas cleared his throat. "You're a sight for sore eye, my lady."

Lady Couliac gave a polite giggle, no doubt traumatized by the origin of the compliment. "Why, thank you, Sir . . ." *As if she hasn't already met the man.*

"Tallas Taybold."

"Why, thank you, Sir Tallas. You're quite fetching, yourself." As luck would have it, Lady Couliac had flushed. Ashen couldn't believe it.

"Well, ain't this a long-lost lover's reunion in the wrong room?" Ashen said, collapsing into her chair in a very undignified and unladylike manner. She folded her arms and stared at Tallas.

"I have to oil my . . ." Tallas cleared his throat again. " . . .axe," he said, patting his halberd. Red in the face, he strode out of the den.

Lady Couliac sat adjacent to Jaspard, across from Ashen. "Lovely man, Jaspard. You picked the right person to protect Ashen, I'd say. Just enough mix of grit and glory."

"Yes," Jaspard said. He scrunched his face and his finger slipped into his mouth.

"Is something wrong?" Alora asked.

"Nope, got it. Damned candy stuck to my teeth."

Alora rolled her eyes. Ashen laughed.

Both of them glared in Ashen's direction. She stopped laughing. *Prim and proper.* Nevertheless, she felt the need to say something. "I've gotten this far. I think we can stop worrying that I'm going to muck this up."

"A fair point, Lady Hyrel," Jaspard said. "However, now

is the time when you need to truly practice vigilance. The Lady Arena Hyrel is stopping by tonight."

"What?" Ashen said. Panicked, she sat straighter in her chair and uncrossed her legs, running her hands self-consciously through her hair.

"She wants to get to know you better."

Ashen swallowed. She hadn't met members of her own family before. Well, other than meeting Arena at the Great Hall, but that was different. It was professional. Didn't even feel familial.

"Don't get too attached," Jaspard said. "You are, after all, planning on killing her."

<hr>

Duchess Arena Hyrel: pretty, perfect, proper, and powerful.

Because they were operating under the guise of Ashen being a duchess, she sat at the head of the table. To her right sat Jaspard. To her left, Arena Hyrel herself. Next to Jaspard, Alora.

Faint whispers of conversation drifted from a few rooms down—Tallas, a few of his men, and a few of Arena's servants and guardsmen, all socializing.

Bethinda had just delivered their first course. Apparently when dining with the utmost of nobility, one dined in courses. Ashen knew this but had never witnessed it in practice. Jaspard preferred to eat a meal together. "The process of courses," Jaspard had said when educating her on the practices of nobility, "is to draw out the meal. It's less about the food, and more about the conversation being had *around* the food," he'd said, noticing her confusion. "It's about what's taking place around"—he'd made a circle in the air with a finger—"the food. You might dine on fine wine and chocolates but talk about murdering your second cousin who's gotten a little too greedy. Betrayal makes a fine dinner topic. You'll see. The strongest alliances, the best deals all have one thing in common, Ashen. They are done around a dinner table. The food is just a way of having these conversations, without saying you're having them."

"You are much quieter in the presence of family," Arena said, smiling. "Much less abrasive, too."

Ashen took a long, quiet breath, exhaled, became Cithrial. Offering the same type of wide, fake smile Arena was giving, Cithrial let out a polite giggle. "I must admit, watching Bertrand get angry was a highlight of mine."

Arena laughed—Cithrial judged it sincere or very well-acted. "He does not get worked up often, and if he does, it is usually because of the king."

Cithrial swallowed another spoonful of onion soup. Jaspard said it was "important to intersperse conversation with eating" to not give your guest the impression you were using them for anything—even though everyone knew other-wise. "Manners don't usurp the truth," according to Jaspard.

Polite sipping of soup all around the table.

"So," Arena said. "My darling . . . cousin? It is a pleasure to meet you. But excuse me for being rude. I would love to know how we are blood related?"

This was the moment she'd been waiting for. Cithrial had gone over the story Jaspard fabricated hundreds of times. It wasn't far from the truth. It just didn't include Cithrial becoming homeless, or her mother being raped by a random street guard. "My mother's name was Omari Hyrel." Truth.

"She was my cousin," Arena said. "I hardly knew her. Her parents were a disgrace to the family name. Caught stealing money from investors, duped into investing. I believe they operated a textile factory, focused on fabric for the rich. They told everyone they had discovered a new type of fabric which was going to take the city by storm. I cannot remember, as I did not pay them any mind. When the citizens found out they had been robbed, the city caught the pair and hung them. Rather undignified way for Hyrel family to go, but they had pissed off the wrong individuals. I knew they had a daughter, Omari. I had only met her once. When her parents hung, I did not know what happened to Omari. I assumed she went to live with another disgraced Hyrel family member—Shauvona, Shauton? I do not remember their name."

"My mother lived with a minor noble family. Gasteau, I believe, was their name," Cithrial said. False. She turned her head to Jaspard for confirmation.

"Why, yes, the Gasteau's. I knew of them, but they've all been dead for a few years. Nice family . . . I've heard Charlin was a master musician, though I admit, I'd never heard him play. They adopted Omari," Jaspard said. False.

"When the Gasteau family died, my mother claimed their house for herself. She was young." False.

"And what happened?" Arena asked.

They paused to sip at their soup again.

"The city wouldn't let her have it. Omari wasn't a Gasteau." False. "She found herself on the streets, pregnant." Truth.

"Horrifying," Arena said.

"She found shelter with a family who felt bad for the disgraced Hyrels." False. "She got sick." False. "When I was four, she died." Truth. Omari died after being assaulted and murdered by a group of off-duty city guards. "My dad died when I was nine." Truth. "His heart failed." False. He'd died at the hands of a hungry urchin who'd seen her father carrying a heel of bread.

"I am sorry to hear that," Arena said, teary-eyed. Cithrial knew it to be an act. They all did, really. Manners and all, though.

More soup sipping. Bethinda entered, cleared their half-eaten bowls, left.

They sat in silence, dabbing at the corners of their mouths and taking sips of wine.

Bethinda returned with the next course—a roasted and stuffed pheasant. After serving each of them a portion, she dismissed herself again.

"It's a sad tale," Cithrial said, as if they hadn't passed five minutes of silence.

"Yes. It sounds it. But that has not explained how you came to live with Lord Couliac," Arena said.

"I was only nine when my father died. And the kindly man who'd taken us was sick. He let me go and Lord Couliac was gracious enough to take me in."

"Nothing to it, nothing to it," Jaspard said, beaming. "I saw potential in Lady Hyrel the moment I met her. I knew she was destined for wonderful things, wonderful things."

Like killing you, Arena. I'm going to kill you.

She wasn't sure if she wanted to, though. She wasn't a murderer. Well, not really. But she also wouldn't back down from her promises.

"I understand that Lord Couliac," Arena said. "She made a stir in the Great Hall. Impressed some of us, I must say. Nobody expected a child," she turned to Cithrial and offered a patronizing smile meant to be comforting. "No offense, dear," she turned back to Jaspard, "a force to be reckoned with. But she was and, like I have mentioned, some of us found it impressive."

Cithrial returned the compliment. "I can only aspire to be as strong and wise as you, Duchess Hyrel. Your performance, your very ebb and flow is magnificent. An inspiration to any with aspirations of wealth and power. But next to your beauty? No one can match your radiant smile, polished nails, or shining hair." False. Duchess Arena wasn't ugly, but she sure wasn't the prettiest.

Dinner progressed. They discussed Arena's family, boring as it was; different dukes and duchesses, boring as they were;

and potential policies and upcoming debates which may be had at the Council, boring as it was.

When Duchess Arena Hyrel left, Cithrial felt relief, but also successful. Once she had the rest of the dukes and duchesses disarmed in similar ways, perhaps she could accomplish her goal. How that would happen, she didn't know.

16

EDELBROCK BRENDIS

Lochwall, Calrym

He shivered, freezing.

Pain.

So much pain.

He shivered again. *So cold.*

His head was heavy, his chin resting on his chest. He lifted his neck. Skin split, pain screamed across his body. Blood trickled down his back.

Cold metal on his wrists, ankles. His toes scraped a cold, stony floor. It seemed he could barely touch the ground. He wanted to open his eyes, couldn't. Tried again, couldn't.

He stretched his foot to reach the ground better. Wounds tore. He thought better of it. Too much pain. *Help.*

But there would be no help.

He collapsed into unconsciousness.

He awoke, more energized than before. More aware, more awake. *Pain. So much pain.* His body roared. His skin felt like it burned. Ankles and wrists throbbed, head pulsed, cock seared.

A crack of dull light when he squinted open his eye. Opening his eyelid took more force than usual. Something had caked it shut. Dried blood, he guessed. His eyelids opened after several attempts and more peeling than he would've liked.

His head still hung, and he saw his feet. Chains wrapped around his ankles; his toes barely touched the stone floor. He saw a dried puddle of blood, the S.H. carved into his body everywhere. Legs, thighs, stomach. He saw bits of raw flesh sticking to the dried blood in his wounds. Everything was red or pink. He worried about infection. In the army, he'd seen people die from a single small, infected cut.

Groaning, he shifted his position.

Then, to his horror, he heard a door unlock and open.

"I noticed you were awake," a gruff voice said. A familiar voice.

A dark figure appeared; face obscured by shadow. It was dim in the room. *Cell?* Only a bit of torchlight.

Edelbrock knew it was Marshal Deywin.

Spit hit the floor.

"Sorry, Ed. Gotta clean the wounds. Figured we'd wait for you to wake."

The marshal held a bucket, scooped something out, tossed it on Ed.

A fiery pain lanced across his body. Sharp shards of something landed in his wounds. *Fuck!*

He yelled. Tears ran down his cheeks. Another scoop thrown in his face. It landed where his ear had been. Pure agony.

Some spattered his lips. He tasted it. Salt.

The salt burned. He screamed. And screamed more.

Marshal Deywin laughed.

The burning continued.

He woke again to the sound of Marshal Deywin's voice. "Wake up, Ed. Lord Haklon's here."

He lifted his head, grunted. His throat was too dry to say anything. He croaked.

The blurry face of Scayde appeared in his vision. The Duke of Lochwall held a lantern. Light blinded Edelbrock, and he snapped his eyes closed.

"You said you salted him, Marshal?"

"I did, as you commanded."

"You must've heard me wrong. Now we've got to get the salt out or he'll be ruined!"

"My mistake."

Liquid poured over Edelbrock's head. The distinct smell of alcohol met his nose before his wounds flared and burned and his voice awakened. He screamed, and screamed, and screamed, his throat raw.

17

THE SIEGE OF ANDORA

Andora, Remeria

Villic thrust his spear upwards, calling to the power of plants. The spear morphed into a long vine, snagging at the top of the ramparts. Villic didn't have to run, just willed the vines to pull him up. Some Imbuers followed him, while other Imbuers found different ways up and over. Still others went *through* the wall, instead of over it.

Molten blades cut through the stone; others sheared holes into them with weapons shifted into harder materials than rocks.

When Villic was atop the ramparts, a flood of Remerian soldiers greeted him. He threw his spear, calling to the power of lightning when he did. As he let go of the spear, it threw a fork of lightning that burned through a cluster of soldiers. He drew his scimitar and charged the closest soldiers.

"See, Villic! See what we can do? You're becoming a true Imbuer!"

The gods call upon my power.

"There are no gods, just you and I."

Villic dodged an attack, then brought a rock-blade down on the soldier's helm, crushing him. A splintering sound let Villic know he'd broken the man's neck.

The gods flow through me.

He surged forward, to the next enemy.

Sera screamed. The wall shook, chunks fell from it. They went from watching a battle safely to a disaster in moments.

Dust and flashes of colors blurred her vision. When she could see clearly, she saw Zale, one of the Magicai, dead. Sticks, the second one, was hurling lightning at clansmen who'd climbed over the walls. She saw their weapons morph into odd things, like they had the powers of a Magicus.

Confused, she stepped back. "This isn't good, Royal."

"Stay close," Atticus said. "Everyone back. Do it, Sticks."

Sticks stepped forward and, raising her arms, let out a roar. A thunderous boom, followed by another, and another. It took Sera a moment to realize Sticks had called forth an enormous lightning cloud that was zapping crowds of clansmen beneath them. Crashing, jagged lines of lightning tore through the air, smashing through any clansmen who stood together. One bolt landed on the wall, feet away from the group, blowing a dozen of the clansmen off. They screamed as they fell to their deaths.

Behind, Sera heard the rush of footsteps. She turned and found herself face-to-face with a crazed-looking clansmen. He swung his sword, and she stepped back.

The bald man growled, then dodged a swing from Royal.

"Atticus!" she said, hoping he'd rescue them, but it was too late.

The bald man did something with his weapon and before Royal had a chance, a gale of wind blew him off the wall.

Sera took another step back, wanting to avoid the bald man. She bumped into somebody—Sticks.

The woman turned, looked at Sera. Three decades had aged upon her. Sera almost didn't recognize the woman.

"Get behind me," Sticks said.

***

Villic saw the Magicus step in front of the lady warrior. "Get behind me," she said.

"Careful."

I've fought the Magicai one-on-one before.

Villic growled, trying to put fear in the women. It worked. They were nervous.

"That's more likely a result of you having powers than acting like an animal."

Silence yourself, Speaker.

He called to the power of fire, Imbuing his scimitar and leaping towards the robed woman.

She raised her hand, open-palmed, and he bounced off a solid shield.

Purple energy surrounded her and the other woman. She yelled, and Villic saw her skin wrinkle. He called to rock, smashing the shield with his scimitar. It held.

"Go!" the Magicus said to the knight. The knight backed off, but her sense of duty bound her. Or something else. Perhaps the gods told her to stay.

***

Sera stepped back, watching the bald man hammer the shield with his sword.

"Go!" Sticks said, again.

Where's Atticus?

Sticks grunted, and the shield collapsed. She shot a bolt of lightning at the clansmen, but he dove to the side and evaded it.

"Sera!" *Atticus.*

She turned, saw the man running back to her, a decade older.

Her jaw dropped. "You're a Magicus?"

"Of course, I'm a Magicus." He looked insulted. "We're losing. Bad. You need to protect the king. Go."

"But—"

"Don't stand around like a fledgling city guard. Go. Protect the king."

She considered Cyr Ilic Strictland's words he'd used when she trained under him in Cyrok. "A resting knight's a dead knight," he'd said to her.

She went.

Villic stood, back singed by lightning.

"Now there are two of them!"

They grow weak.

"I've got this, Sticks," the newcomer—a man—said. He stepped forward. "Go back to your homeland, marauder."

Villic bared his teeth like a lion. And, like a lion, he leaped.

The Magicus fired a huge blast of fire.

The Bloody Duchess had warned Captain Hershen of the Redclaws about this potential outcome, and upon seeing the battle start, he called the Redclaws to arms.

"Quick, everyone! Across the water and o'er there," he said, pointing at the closest grouping of Camel Clans.

Bartlesby Flatchett, quartermaster, stood next to Captain

Hershen as the Redclaws surged forward. "Not sure I'm keen to follow 'em."

"Not sure I am, either, truth be told," Hersh said.

The pair looked at each other and retreated.

———

Sera ran. She couldn't help in this battle. None of the bladed people could. She wondered if Royal was dead. He *had* to be dead. He'd fallen from the wall.

She dodged, ducked, and weaved around other people, friend and foe alike. *I have to get to King Alondo.*

A huge rumble, and she stumbled, catching herself on the edge of the wall. She kept moving. Screams of the dying, screams of the panicked, screams of those engaged in fighting. Sera heard it all.

In front of her, another battle raged. A Camel Clansmen, her back to Sera, engaged several of the Remerian soldiers. Sera saw her opportunity and, running up behind the woman, Sera drove her sword into the clansmen's back.

Celebratory cheers from the soldiers rang out, and they dispersed to find other targets.

Sera ran on.

———

"To arms!" the Old Vulture said, encouraging the Falcon Knights. "Let's hit them from the rear!"

With two of their own inside the city, nobody raised a complaint.

The Falcon Knights sprinted down the hill, clambering over dead camels and Camel Clansmen alike.

"They're at the wall, pinned," he said. "Let's give them a fight!"

The Falcon Knights, like a hunting bird, dove towards their prey.

Atticus backed up. The mad clansmen had cut through the blast of fire with water, sending one half out towards the grasslands, the other puffing into nonexistence after smashing into a parapet. His breath heavy, he didn't know what to do. He was aging, and these clansmen had the reflexes of warriors, combined with the powers of a Magicus. It was maddening.

He flung his hand, conjuring a blast of air, hoping to sweep the man off the wall. It worked. For a moment.

The bald man caught the edge of the wall with the vine-sword and climbed up and over.

Sticks ran in front of Atticus, fingers shooting lightning. She'd gone full self-immolation. Screaming, she charged, electrifying the stone in front of her, the bald man, and herself.

The bald man dropped to his knees, shouting in pain.

Shouting, Royal fell.

He hadn't realized it until that moment. He didn't want to die. Royal had drunken himself sick countless times, to forget his past. To die. But now, he didn't want to.

Too late.

A loud crunch, then a squish. He screamed, pain shot up his broken leg, but he lived. Something prevented his death. He'd fallen on a dead camel, which had been split open by a Magicus or Camel Clansman, he didn't know.

Thankful to be alive, he took a sip of whiskey.

When he saw a mob of Camel Clansmen approaching, he drank deeper. *Shit's Blessing has found its way to me once again.*

Hersh and Bartlesby stopped, doubled over, lungs heaving. They gasped for air, standing in the middle of the grasslands.

Hersh turned, looked behind him at the walls. Colors flashed.

"Shit. Ya gotta be fuckin' kiddin'," Bartlesby said.

"What?"

Bartlesby pointed.

An enormous blast of stray fire came their way.

They screamed, but it didn't stop the fire.

Scorched earth was all they left behind.

Sera's lungs burned from exertion or fear—she couldn't tell. She looked over her shoulder. A portion of wall she'd just run across crumbled apart. The dead and dying slid into openness, spattering the grounds below.

She found a stairway and ran down, two at a time. Halfway down, the momentum became too much and she slipped, crashing down the next several stairs. Bruised and battered, she hauled herself up.

"Ain't ya the Falcon Knight?"

Sera looked up. The Bloody Duchess reached her mangled claw out to help steady Sera.

Villic shrieked. Lightning coursed through him, burning him alive. Hytrok, god of storms, laughed. Villic became Hytrok, laughing and dying.

The lightning stopped. The female Magicus slumped to her knees. She'd burned herself alive. Or she'd died of old age. It was impossible to tell. Tendrils of smoke rose from her corpse.

"Get up! There's another one!"

Villic saw the man rushing towards him.

S ticks died a fool's death. Atticus ran to finish the job. How one clansmen could cause this much trouble was beyond him. If everyone else was struggling like he was, they were doomed.

His heart beat irregularly. He was growing old. Had to finish the job fast.

Atticus raised his liver-spotted hand. *Odd, to develop liver spots this young.* He knew he wasn't that old. He tried to remember if his father had spots early in life. Couldn't.

The bald man's eyes met his.

The fight resumed.

"I am the Falcon Knight," Sera said. "I need to get to the king."

The poetic one was with the Bloody Duchess. He grabbed Sera, hauling her down the stairs. "Direct us and we'll get you there," he said. It seemed he didn't rhyme in times of turmoil.

Sera sighed, relieved.

It wasn't far.

V illic's head bounced off the stone floor. The Magicus had feinted and surprised him. Instead of blasting him from the front, he'd moved his hands and attacked from above. Fortunately for Villic, a powerful force had crushed him against the wall, but nothing more. Blood ran from the lip he'd bitten.

"Kill him."

Give me darkness.

The bald man had escaped Atticus's attack again. And now, his sword was pure black. Wispy shadows surrounded it; tendrils of smoke followed the blade.

Frightened, Atticus backed up. He wasn't fast enough. The bald man came.

Villic drove his black blade into the Magicus.

The man gurgled. Didn't even yell. A surprised look passed through his eyes, then he disintegrated. His body turned to black smoke, and the smoke dissipated with the wind.

What?

The sword absorbed the man. And Villic felt recharged. Powerful. His wounds healed. He felt stronger.

An explosion knocked him off his feet.

Garv Tixis was his name. Though middle-aged, Garv Tixis looked elderly. He'd used much of his Well already, in defense of the Remerians. But Garv Tixis had a plan.

He reached up, touching the symbol on his cloak—an orange triangle split in half and tipped on its side, point facing east.

Garv Tixis didn't have as much power as he was supposed to. The Elkavich would probably be angry with him, but it didn't matter. He had to do something.

He'd descended the wall, found a gate—broken by the clansmen. Empty of enemies, he walked outside, into the grassy fields littered with dead bodies and living Camel Clansmen. They saw Garv Tixis. It didn't matter. It was too late for them. And him.

Garv Tixis ignited himself, freeing his stored power in a devastating display of self-immolation. He glowed for a moment, and then burned away to ash. The world became orange. Like his insignia.

⸺

The Old Vulture slashed his way through a clansmen. Blood dripped from his sword, spattering the already bloody ground. Somebody had blown a hole through his calf muscle with a rock spear—he could walk, but it was with a heavy limp. He fell to a knee, grunting.

"A resting knight's a dead knight," he said, struggling to stand again.

Corpses of Falcon Knights and Camel Clansmen intermingled with one another. He climbed over a pair of the dead, limping towards the other Falcon Knights.

The Old Vulture noticed a figure walking out the gate. Slow, deliberate.

"Help," he said. The figure didn't notice him.

The Old Vulture stuck his sword in the grass to steady him. A squelching sound made him realize it wasn't grass, but a dead body.

The strange figure ignited in a fiery orange blast.

"Like a bird, we rise at dawn," the Old Vulture said.

And, like dawn, orange consumed him.

J edkah, leader of the Splintered Manes, had lost his spear. A Remerian soldier had knocked his scimitar from his hand. Somehow, a common soldier bested him.

He, along with a group of shamans and other Splintered Manes soldiers, had stormed through a chunk in the wall. The Remerian soldiers had driven them back, and no Imbuers were nearby. They'd ended up further away because of their powers.

Jedkah spat blood out of his mouth. He lay on his back, the Remerian soldier's sword pointed at his neck. The blood trickled down his chin, ran down his neck.

If the Remerian spoke Vessian, Jedkah would've surrendered. He wasn't a fool, knew when he'd lost. The shamans translated for him and he didn't speak a sand grain of the Remerian language.

The soldier said something. Jedkah didn't understand. He lay even more still, if that was possible.

Killiak, lord of lords, return my clan to me.

Tabashi, god of fire, was who answered the call, though.

The Remerian burned in front of Jedkah's eyes.

Then Jedkah, too, burned.

18

INTERLUDE
BLAGO ADAVIR

Anepolis, Calrym

His tongue darted across his mustache, a habit he'd had since he first grew one. He wasn't sure if it was because he liked the feeling, wanted to make sure it was still there, or only did it in times of insecurity —he'd considered all three possibilities at one point or another. Nice thing was, in Calrym, there weren't any ice crystals stuck in it.

Blago Adavir had a habit of surviving. Somehow, some way, whenever something bad happened, he found his way out of it. He hoped today would be another of those days.

Adavir had stolen one of Duke Harlem Maccaro's ships and, bravely, he thought, sailed it back to Calrym with his band of bandits. The moment he disembarked and saw the Calrite soldiers, he conceded he might've made a mistake. That was in the port town of Bryn, though. When he arrived in Anepolis, he knew he'd made a mistake as soon as he saw the palace. He disappeared into the crowd and hid for days in the city, considering his options. But, with Cyrok destroyed, he didn't have many. He was going to come clean.

Which meant owning his betrayal to the very people who'd paid for his services. The Council.

Adavir had little experience with King Mikas, or the Council, just a letter here or there. Heard rumors that crossing them wasn't a good idea. Didn't take a rumor to guess that. Politicians were touchy in the best of times.

He'd run out of money and his bandits had left him. No sense in sticking around for somebody who quit paying them. He would've left, too.

He'd sent a letter along to the chancellor, hoping to secure a personal meeting. His tongue flicked across his mustache again. *Just checking.* Or was it the insecurities popping up? He didn't know.

He swallowed, nervous, licked his mustache, again. It wouldn't make sense for King Mikas to kill him, he reasoned. Blago Adavir knew he had one quality most didn't: he was a bastard. He'd do anything for coin, or to save his life. And few people could say the same. That's what made his services valuable. He could kill an innocent person, children, even. Or gyrfalcons. Adavir had zero qualms about anything, as long as it happened to someone other than himself.

He looked about the city, watching the crowds mingle. He saw assassins under every cloak, behind every corner, hiding behind every stall and building. "Fuck," he said. Because there was no other word for it. And because he liked the word. Probably more the latter than the former.

He leaned against the wall of the palace. Not the best idea. The Calrite guards had already chided him once. They were going easy on him. He was foreign, and they knew he had important business with the king. Whether that ended with his head on a pike wasn't for them to decide though, he conceded, they'd be the ones to carry out the orders had the king made them.

"Captain Adavir, right?"

Adavir turned. The rank wasn't true military, but it's what everyone called him; what the king knew him as. "Yes," he said.

"Chancellor Bertrand has scheduled you for tomorrow's meeting."

"Wonderful," Adavir said. He breathed a sigh of relief. No matter what, the issue would be resolved soon. He'd either be free or dead, and if he was dead, he didn't have much to worry about, now did he? "I'll be back tomorrow."

He went to find himself a cheap inn with cheaper whores. The type who weren't fussy and were apt to give him a disease. He had very little money, and quite possibly, very little life left to live.

Two shit pints of ale, one stench-riddled, squat woman, and a sleepless night later, and Adavir entered the palace the next day. A boy brought him to where he was supposed to be, and he was told to wait in the hallway. Somebody would retrieve him when they were ready.

Armed men filled the hallway. One leaned against a wall, casual, bouncing a halberd off his shoulder. Adavir could see a milky eye, but that didn't make him consider the man any less a threat. If anything, Adavir noted, it made him more of one. Anybody with a single eye assigned to guard duty knows their shit. Or at least know when to run.

Since arriving in Calrym, Adavir had shucked his weapons and hoped for the best. He figured showing up, begging for forgiveness with a sword in his belt, might send the wrong message.

He licked his mustache again. *Damn. It is insecurities.* At least, that's what he thought. Tomorrow it'd be a different reason. If he lived to see tomorrow.

The door opened. A man came out from the Great Hall, meek and foolish, with a goofy grin on his face. One Adavir probably would've pushed to the ground, spat on, and demanded money from, if this was Cyrok. It wasn't, though.

"Captain Blago Adavir?" the man asked, as if Adavir wasn't the only stranger standing in the hall. He could tell it was the chancellor by the pin on his robes. It surprised Adavir to know a man in that position could be so ridiculous.

"Present," he said. Because sometimes it pays to play nice.

"You're wanted."

And, like a prisoner asked to jump off a cliff, Adavir entered the Great Hall where the politicians sat and made life-changing decisions for the people of the world. *A pit full of dead carcasses being circled by hungry gyrfalcons fighting for their offspring's lives.*

"Captain Blago Adavir, from Cyrok, Your Highness," the chancellor said.

Adavir swallowed, glanced around the room. Though large, there wasn't much within it other than a long table, chairs, and several ugly faces staring at him. The king, jewels glittering and taunting Adavir with his crown and rings; a snarky-looking woman; a petulant child; and a slobbering man with food rolling down his front were the standouts. It didn't appear as if he'd have any allies. All looked angry. Or was that the natural face of the politician? He didn't know. He licked his mustache out of familiarity. Or was it insecurities? Who could tell?

"Why are you here?" King Mikas asked.

"To apologize, My Lord. I—"

"You abandoned Harlem, ah-hah," the messy eater said.

"Normally we would not condone that, but seeing as it was Harlem, I can pass," the snarky-looking woman said. *Guess it's not just an appearance.*

"Nonsense," King Mikas said. "Despite your opinions on

Duke Harlem, Arena, how would you feel if this man took off with your ship?"

"To be fair," Adavir said, "Duke Harlem agreed to let me return to Calrym with him."

The king held up a finger. "'With' sounds like the key word."

"Well, yes, perhaps I was a bit hasty . . ." he trailed off, licking his mustache. At that moment, Adavir realized how much he enjoyed being in charge, how much he enjoyed prisoners groveling to him over their lives. He should've stayed in Cyrok.

"It seems," the child said, "he should hang."

Adavir swallowed. He knew this was a possibility. Didn't think a child would be the first to bring it up, though.

A man he hadn't noticed spoke next. "I have a counter-proposal."

"Go on, Hemmel," the king said.

"Madam Zeitwitch is looking for—"

"You are sick," Arena said.

"I am not! Madam Zeitwitch is a friend who's in need."

"She prostitutes children."

Hemmel snorted. "And? Is there a law saying she can't whore out the willing?" Hemmel looked around the table. "No, no, there's not. Nobody's attacking you, Arena, for fucking your servants. What kind of power play is that? We all have our whims and fancies. Until we decide to make it illegal, let's let what happens in the bedroom stay in the bedroom, agreed?"

Nobody said anything.

"Great," Hemmel said. "Now, back to my counterproposal. Madam Zeitwitch is looking for somebody to clean rooms, after, well, you know."

"You want me to clean your sweat and semen up?" Adavir asked, disgusted.

"Until Duke Harlem returns, yes," Hemmel said. "It'll build character."

"He'd just run away," the child said. "It's what I would do in his position."

Hemmel laughed. "You are a smart child, Cithrial."

"Do not get any ideas, Hemmel. She is of my blood," Arena said.

Hemmel, flushing, turned and glared at Arena. "Must I reiterate what we just agreed to?" He slammed his hands on the table, rattling the cutlery. Turning back to the child, and putting on a broad smile, he said, "Madam Zeitwitch ensures her employees don't leave because she hobbles them with a ball and chain. He won't be able to run, and if he tries, she's very cruel. It's one of her best qualities."

"Acceptable," the child said.

"Fine, ah-hah," the slobbering man said.

"Agreed," Arena said.

The king nodded. "Until Harlem returns, you will work for Madam Zeitwitch. Consider it a remedial job."

Madam Zeitwitch's was an establishment which Adavir would have never been able to afford. Everything was an expensive silk, smooth velvet, or lush cushion. Everything was clean, shiny, or, in the case of people, oiled. Even though he wasn't merchandise one could fuck, Madam Zeitwitch required him to be nearly nude. He wore sandals and a small pouch, attached to a string, which held his privates in place and exposed his buttocks. Doing anything was a chore, because during his work hours, oil coated his body, making everything slippery and impossible to grab ahold of.

"It adds to the allure," Madam Zeitwitch said. She, too, was nearly naked, oiled breasts slipping from their thin covering, plunging towards the ground, and swinging back and forth as she gestured and commanded him. "Oops," she'd said, scooping them back into her silk cover.

If Adavir wasn't so disgusted with what he had to clean, he might've found her, and many customers and employees, rather arousing. Two days into the job, however, had tainted his opinion of anything sexual.

"Addy, my boy, come here," Madam Zeitwitch said.

He grumbled. Hated that nickname. Went to lick his mustache, scraped against the stubble that had replaced the glorious hairs. She'd required he shaved it. He hated her for it.

"We have a special guest," she said, beckoning a man forward. It was, much to Adavir's chagrin, Duke Hemmel.

"Well, look who's coming along nicely," Hemmel said, beaming. He'd entered the establishment half-naked himself. Adavir could see Hemmel's manhood pressing against the thin silk covering he wore around his thick thighs.

Adavir nodded.

"Here for the usual, Hemmel, darling?" Madam Zeitwitch asked.

"No, no. I want something a bit different. Something more satisfactory. Something . . . *older*."

Madam Zeitwitch cackled. "Oh, don't mean *me*," she said.

"I don't," Hemmel said, grinning at Adavir. "I want him."

Madam Zeitwitch's face fell, though she recovered nicely. "He's just an employee."

"An employee I found," Hemmel said.

"No," Adavir said. He wouldn't partake in this. Couldn't. He'd kill the man.

"I'll pay four times the going rate for a child, Madam Zeitwitch," Hemmel said, waving one of his guards forward. The guard placed a heavy sack in Zeitwitch's hand. Metallic clinks could be heard.

"No," Adavir said again, louder.

"Take him, enjoy, and don't ruin him," she said in a singsong voice, like she'd said the same line many times before.

"Do I ever ruin the goods?" Hemmel asked. He stepped forward, grabbing Adavir by the hand and dragging him toward one of the private rooms.

"Please don't," he said.

"Consider it punishment for betraying us," Hemmel said.

Adavir felt the metal ring on his left ankle tug at him as he was pulled forward, the scraping of a heavy metal ball following him.

19

EDELBROCK BRENDIS

Lochwall, Calrym

Groaning, Edelbrock opened his eyes. His body ached. He noticed he was lying on a bed and didn't feel any burning. He heard footsteps receding and somebody calling out. Edelbrock awoke.

Then, a handsome face entered view. Strong arms lifted his head. "Have some water," the man said.

A bowl of water held to his mouth, Edelbrock drank until it emptied.

The man, Savakkis, let Edelbrock back down. He trusted Savakkis, leader of their House. Although Savakkis had started out rough, when Edelbrock had first arrived in Buzzard's Bowl, once Edelbrock became an official gladiator, trained and proven capable, Savakkis had become a close friend.

"Where's Scayde?" Edelbrock asked.

"Gone. Marshal Deywin dropped you off, told us to take care of you. You're supposed to fight tomorrow."

Edelbrock moaned in disbelief. "How?"

"I'm not sure. But you're fighting alongside the Chell. They'll take care of you."

"How long was I out?"

"Two days. We thought you weren't returning."

"Same."

"Get some rest, Ass of Lochwall. You're going to need it." Savakkis smiled, and Edelbrock once again swore the man's gaze lingered. He turned his head away, for some reason finding himself nervous.

He forgot about it as soon as he closed his eyes, disappearing into dreams of revenge.

He woke again in the middle of the night with a pressing need to piss. Stiff and battered, his muscles didn't want to work, but he forced himself out of bed anyway. Edelbrock hobbled to the bucket nearby, pulled out his marred cock, and let loose a powerful stream of urine. He felt the jagged cuts where Scayde had scarred him, tender to the touch, and he grit his teeth. When he finished, he collapsed back in bed. Cuts had ripped back open, he felt blood trickling down his skin. It seemed every move he made opened them. He succumbed to exhaustion again.

He rose early in the morning, and Savakkis greeted him. "I wasn't sure if you'd need help to get out of bed," he said.

"I managed in the night." Edelbrock gestured at the bucket of piss.

"We'll take care of that later. While you were away, we received two new gladiators."

Edelbrock grunted, unsure what Savakkis wanted.

"We need to beat them."

"No, we don't."

"It's the way we've always done things, Edelbrock. If we don't, they don't understand how things work. If we don't, they rebel. Rebellion causes trouble. There is no escaping Buzzard's Bowl, except in death. Or, in the rare case, when you're set free."

"Beating does nothing except anger them."

"At first, yes. But what happened to you? The anger didn't remain. It was beat out of you long before you were a gladiator in this House. And that's on purpose. You haven't tried to escape. You've accepted your fate. This is the way it needs to be. There are plenty of examples when the House didn't beat their new recruits. Do you know what happened every time, Edelbrock?"

He shook his head. "No, but I'm guessing it wasn't good."

"You're right. They all died. And do you know how many other gladiators died with them? Hundreds. Because whenever there's a rebellion, Scayde Haklon kills plenty of people who weren't involved to discourage further rebellious behavior. Trust me, Edelbrock, I'd love just as much as you not to hurt any of these people. But if we don't, they'll get themselves killed. And it's likely we'd die, too."

Edelbrock sighed. He didn't like it, but he knew it made sense. He thought back to how he'd been arrested, how he'd vowed revenge. Edelbrock still vowed revenge but wasn't sure he'd ever get it. In fact, thoughts had recurred here and there, but never as strong as they should've been. His resignation was final. Edelbrock knew that without outside help, he would die in Buzzard's Bowl. That was a fact. Scayde Haklon took far too much joy from Edelbrock's torture.

Savakkis beat the prisoners while Edelbrock watched. The man, angry, tried fighting back. Of course, he was malnourished and hadn't the strength. The woman accepted her beating, though cursed Savakkis the entire time.

When they'd left the gladiators alone, Savakkis offered a grim smile. "It won't take long for those two. They're half-broken already. Time for your fight," he said, clapping Edelbrock on the shoulder, then giving it a squeeze.

He winced in pain, then wondered how he was going to fare in battle with such a broken body.

<hr>

Edelbrock considered it a blessing in disguise when he learned that during this battle they weren't being offered armor or shields. It was a single weapon frenzy, any weapon they chose. Edelbrock, knowing his injuries were going to affect him, strode to the rack holding longer weapons. He wanted to have a significant reach. If anyone got close to him, he didn't think he'd be agile enough to win, so stiff were his muscles. He picked a simple spear—light and easy to wield.

Chellie, the sister of the bunch, selected a broadsword; Chellik, a great sword; Chellis, a glaive; and one-armed, Chellin picked a mace. The Chell all fought shirtless, and since Edelbrock's wounds hurt to touch, he followed suit.

"Don't worry, Edelbrock, we've got you," Chellie said.

When the entrance revealed itself, the survivors of the last battle passed them. Three of five returned. Minutes later, it was his group's turn. They entered Buzzard's Bowl, and the crowd cheered, ready for another event.

Edelbrock looked around the arena, attempting to figure out what it was. Tall grasses stretched far above his head, and he couldn't see anything. A slim, empty path weaved its way through the maze.

The announcer introduced the event and gladiators. "Welcome to our next event, ladies and gentlemen! Next up is a maze. Our brave fighters can choose to navigate the paths or sneak and hide among the grasses, but what other twists and turns might this scenario have? You'll have to wait and see! This event comprises five fighters from Scayde Haklon's House, five from King Mikas's, and five from Castede Varono's. It's a last-House-alive-wins scenario. Let's introduce the contestants, shall we?"

Edelbrock tuned out the announcer's words for House Castede's. The crowd's cheering had given him a headache and he touched the side of his head, wincing when his hand brushed the place where his ear had once been.

When the announcer introduced the first name of King Mikas's lineup, Edelbrock remembered him. "And from King Mikas's House, regretfully he hasn't been present since the season's first event. We have none other than the vile, the disgusting, the hated Anditus Roberon . . . otherwise known as Greasy And . . ." the announcer paused.

The crowd chanted back. "Revolting!"

The announcer laughed. "That's right! Greasy And Revolting!"

Anditus Roberon. He'd tried to kill Edelbrock during the pre-season bout Scayde had held for the king before the season started. It was an illegal attack, and Edelbrock was sure Anditus had been reprimanded for it. He wondered how angry Scayde had been since Anditus hadn't been able to finish the job before the match ended. *Or maybe he enjoyed that I nearly died.* It was certainly painful having a sword pierce his back.

"And now, for House Haklon!"

The crowd's roar escalated.

"We have the Chell—the Quintessential Quintuplets themselves. Well, Quadruplets, anyway! Chellie, Broad of the Bowl. Chellik, the Sister's Shield. Chellis the Forgotten Sibling. And Chellin, the Arm of Death! And, last, but definitely not least, I bring to you . . . Edelbrock Brendis, the Ass of Lochwall! Cover your noses, shit's about to get real!"

The crowd cheered even louder, chanting his name. While

the Chell had raised their weapons and given in to the spectators, Edelbrock stared at the tall grass in front of him. He wouldn't give them the show they wanted. The games were sick, the spectators, sicker. *And yet, I don't know that I'd be any different were I offered a place up there now.* Unless Scayde was running the place. He'd try to murder the bastard.

"Kill each other!" the announcer said. The crowd screamed; the battle started.

"Path or grass?" Chellin asked.

"I know it's going to hurt," Edelbrock said. The grass on his wounds wouldn't feel good. "But we need to get into the grass. The path is a walking death trap. We could be ambushed."

The Chell agreed and they crouched, entering the thick grass.

"Seems too simple," one brother said.

"There's gotta be a twist," another brother said.

Without looking at them, it was difficult to tell who was who.

Edelbrock wondered if there was something else to the battle. There were three Houses, which seemed odd. He wondered if the other Houses were told to come after them first. It's what he would do in Scayde's position.

Edelbrock remembered Buzzard's Battalion—what he called the gladiators who followed his orders, and his military mind returned. "Listen up," he said. "I know you've all had success in the arena before, but what are the chances the other two Houses are working together?"

"Unlikely," Chellie said.

"Let me rephrase," he said. Grass crunched and snapped as he took another step. The thick, hard stalks brushed against his skin, irritating him. Crouching had already split the wounds on his back and chest, and thin lines of fresh blood appeared in the S.H. carvings. "What are the chances

Scayde Haklon purposefully outnumbered our House in an event I am partaking in?"

Nobody answered. More grass crunching beneath their boots.

"You might be on to something," Chellie said.

"I think we need to split up, sit, and wait," Edelbrock said. "Make little noise. Perhaps we can ambush some of them. Even if they aren't working together, it's a solid strategy." It might've been selfish—he didn't know if the Houses were actually working together against them—but by splitting them up, he'd have a better chance of others encountering people. Of other people dying. *I need to survive.* Edelbrock needed revenge. And to get revenge, he needed to live.

"Like Buzzard's Battalion," Chellin said.

"Yes," Edelbrock said, surprised. Word had gotten out, it seemed.

They agreed. Chellin and Chellis they took up a spot across the path.

After they'd disappeared, the twist made a grand appearance. A loud growl behind Edelbrock alerted him. He turned, staring into the grass.

A flash of orange and white, followed by a snarl. Then, pouncing out of the grass, a tiger, teeth bared.

"Fuck!" Angling his spear at the beast, Edelbrock stabbed it. His arms jolted back as the tiger slammed into the spear, driving it into its side. It gave a painful roar and leaped back into the grass, disappearing. He knew it hadn't gone far. A blood trail sprinkled across the thatch.

"What just happened?" Chellie asked, hurrying over.

"Tiger."

"Tiger?"

"Tiger. The twist must be tigers."

"Well, shit."

"Quiet. It's still close," he said, searching, but he couldn't see anything. He listened, but only heard the crowd reacting to other things happening elsewhere in the arena.

Chellik crab-walked over. "What's going on?" he asked.

"Tigers," Edelbrock said, head spinning, watching, waiting.

The tiger growled, then sprang from the grass behind Chellik. Its claws sank into the man, and he dove to the ground.

Edelbrock thrust the spear into the tiger's side, while Chellie hacked at its neck with her sword. The tiger ripped at Chellik's back, biting at his neck and head. He drove the spear into the tiger again. The beast yowled, leaping off its prey and turning to face Edelbrock.

Chellik, coated in blood, rose on shaky legs, using his great sword as a crutch.

Growling, the tiger let loose another roar, bloody teeth dripping with saliva.

Edelbrock caught Chellie's eyes, gave her a nod. They attacked together, stabbing and slashing the cat.

Oozing blood, the tiger retreated into the grass. This time for good, it seemed.

"Are you all right?" Chellie asked Chellik.

He waved her away. "Something's happening to the others," he said. "I hear them."

Sure enough, when Edelbrock concentrated, he heard yelling coming from Chellis and Chellin.

"Buzzard's Battalion, attack!" He yelled this both out of adrenaline and a need to let his comrades know reinforcements were coming. Edelbrock charged, leading with his spear in case another tiger lay in wait. After a dozen feet or so, he broke through and found himself on the path. He heard the sounds of metal on metal, the scream of an injured man, and the growling of a tiger.

"I'll go through here," Edelbrock said. "Chellie, take the left flank. Chellik, find your brother's original path and approach from that direction." Not questioning his orders, they moved to fulfill them. Edelbrock, adrenaline pumping through his veins, forgot about pain, and hurried to find the embattled Chell.

He entered a circular area of beaten down grass. Four people and a pair of tigers battled one another. A man screamed, falling, blood spurting from a bite on his neck.

Chellie and Edelbrock attacked a tiger together. Edelbrock rammed the spearpoint into the tiger's head. The point clicked off the skull, and Edelbrock's momentum halted. He tripped and fell. The tiger offered a low growl, then took a step away from them, collapsing itself.

A man with branded cheeks—a House Garcovi fighter—took advantage of Edelbrock's position. A large axe-head came plunging down at Edelbrock's chest.

"Shit," Edelbrock said.

A great sword cleaved the man's head off, and he dropped the axe. The heavy axe landed on Edelbrock—horizontally, Mother Avani be praised—and knocked the wind out of him. He coughed, gasped for oxygen. Chellik nodded at him, then rushed off to fight somebody else.

When Edelbrock recovered his breath, he looked around, saw the dead bodies of Chellin and Chellis. Another House Garcovi gladiator lay close by. The other tiger had been driven off.

Chellik dispatched the third—and last—House Garcovi attacker with a nasty blow to the head with his mace. Which meant there were two more out there, somewhere. One of them being Anditus Roberon.

"Let's get back into the open," Edelbrock said, wheezing. "We can't stay in the grass."

They stumbled back out of the tall grass, injured and cautious. The crowd was cheering at something. Edelbrock was sure he heard some chants of, "rip his head off!"

A tiger howled in pain and the crowd gasped.

"We must head to the center of the maze," Chellie said.

Edelbrock nodded, taking in a deep breath. Many of the S.H. wounds across his body cracked and bled.

Together, Edelbrock, Chellie, and Chellik followed the path at a light jog. They came to a crossroads.

"Which way?" Chellik asked.

The sound of swords clashing came from the west. Edelbrock pointed that way. "If you want to head towards the fighting, we go this way."

"It's the quickest way to get out of here," Chellie said.

Edelbrock nodded. "Then let's go." His eyelids drooped and he let out a yawn. He didn't have the energy for this shit. Muscles protested and his stiff limbs wanted to reject his commands. He pressed forward.

Following the trail, they heard the sounds of fighting getting closer. Turning another corner, and they saw the fight.

Anditus Roberon fought a pair of House Castede gladiators. When he saw Edelbrock and the others, he backed away. The Castede men recognized the issue, too. Killing Roberon would put them at a disadvantage, against Edelbrock and the Chell. Instead of continuing the fight, they turned to face their new opponents.

The Chell charged. Edelbrock followed, but before he'd even engaged anyone, Chellik was on the ground, dying from a mortal wound caused by Roberon, while Chellie was double-teamed by the two Castede fighters.

Edelbrock, feeling stupid, or brave, he wasn't sure, drew his spear back and threw with all his might. The weapon impaled one of the two men attacking Chellie, and he gave out half a yell, then tipped over. The crowd roared.

Edelbrock ran over to Chellik, whose eyes were closed and his breathing shallow.

"Sorry, friend," Edelbrock said. He picked up the heavy great sword and turned to meet the greasy Roberon.

"And so we meet again," Roberon said, twirling his sword.

"You won't kill me," Edelbrock said. He kept staring at Roberon's broken and bulbous nose, wanting to break it again.

Roberon, chuckling, raised his sword. "You admit you lost to me before."

"You cheated."

He shrugged. "I want to survive. It's been my motto since I watched my father hang."

Edelbrock took a step forward. Another step or two and he'd be in range. "I give zero shits about you, or your father," he said, watching Roberon. The man seemed unconcerned. Was it a bluff, or did he have a plan? Or, perhaps, was it false confidence?

"We agree about my father, then," Roberon said. "I'm a bit more biased about myself, though."

Edelbrock didn't care for the conversation. He hurt, and he wanted to end it. He rushed Roberon, slashing at his stomach.

Roberon skipped back, dodging the blow. He danced back another few steps. "I'm happy to wait for our friends to finish," he waved at Chellie and the other gladiator, still fighting.

"You're afraid to fight."

"Fear keeps people alive."

"No," Edelbrock said, realizing something he hadn't known before. "Fear prevents people from living." And, pushing aside any fear he had, Edelbrock sprinted at Roberon, sword raised.

"Well, fuck!" Roberon raised his sword in an attempt to deflect the great sword, but the power of the great sword was too much. He lost his grip. His smaller blade dropped. "Don't kill me." He knelt. The crowd booed.

Edelbrock cleaved the man's head off. It sailed one direction while his body fell in the other. He drove the point of the sword into the path, leaning on it, catching his breath. The crowd was chanting something.

Chellie walked over, blood-covered and smelling of sweat. "My brothers are all dead."

"I'm sorry."

"They live on through me, in victory."

"I suppose they do."

"The crowd chants your name," she said. Edelbrock noticed her watery eyes and a combination of exhaustion and pain pass over her face. He didn't know what to say. Losing family was difficult, he knew that better than anyone. He wanted to offer some sort of reassurance things would be okay, but he knew that would be a lie. Edelbrock would never get over Gordy's death. Would never be able to move on. Instead, he ignored her feelings. Wasn't much he could do about them anyway, and talking about them would likely just upset her more.

It didn't sound like the Ass of Lochwall to him. He listened carefully.

"Bloodlines, bloodlines, bloodlines!" They chanted, over and over.

"Bloodlines?"

"I think," Chellie said, pointing at his chest, "they have a point."

Edelbrock's wounds, bright from leakage, stood out across his body. "I guess Bloodlines is better than the Ass of Lochwall."

"No doubt Scayde won't be happy about the change."

He snorted.

"Grab some glory," Chellie said.

Gripping his hand in hers, she let out a primal scream, raising their arms up. The crowd cheered.

Edelbrock looked up at the King's Stand, ignoring the ever-present buzzards. He saw a distant figure holding the half-glass wall. He couldn't tell who it was from that far away, but he knew. It was Scayde Haklon, staring at him.

Edelbrock let go of Chellie's hand. "There's something I need to do."

Walking across Buzzard's Bowl, he approached the king's stand. He glanced up, confirming the man was Scayde Haklon. Then Edelbrock pulled his trousers down and pissed on the wall beneath the stand.

The crowd laughed and cheered and chanted his name.

For a moment, he smiled at the humiliation. Then Edelbrock wondered what repercussions he'd suffer for that.

20

SERADAL WINTLOCK & VILLIC THE IMBUER

Andora, Remeria

Sera winced, removing bits of rubble from her legs. They'd made it back to the king, but before anyone said anything, an explosion rocked the city and half the palace collapsed.

She heard coughing to her left and moaning on her right. Stretching her legs to test for broken bones, she hauled herself up. Bruised and battered, Sera didn't feel any sign of serious injury.

Dust permeated the air and made it difficult to breathe and see. Blurry rays of penetrated cracks and holes in the collapsed wall.

"What in the name of Mother Avani just happened?" King Alondo asked. His voice sounded muffled, like he was buried. A moment later and the man stumbled into view. She saw him holding a kerchief over his mouth, his jeweled crown was missing.

"I don't know," Sera said.

The sound of shifting rubble came from where Sera had heard moaning.

"I think we should get out o' here," the Bloody Duchess said.

"I've hit my head. It hurts." The poetic soldier's voice—Althier.

"Why don'tcha make a rhyme about it then, for fuck's sake, eh?" the Bloody Duchess asked.

Together, the king and Sera made their way towards the light. The Bloody Duchess and Althier clambered after them. When they reached the wall, Sera could see through the cracks outside. Other buildings had crumbled. Refuse littered the streets. Limbs and bodies and blood mingled among the wreckage. She heard cries of the injured and those searching for survivors. There didn't seem to be a war happening anymore.

Carefully, they removed chunks of the wall until they'd opened a hole large enough to slip through. All four of them climbed out of the collapsed building. A stream of blood coursed down Althier's forehead, dripping down his cheek, while the Bloody Duchess nursed a bruising arm—the one with the claw.

"Everyone all right?" King Alondo asked. He didn't wait for an answer before hurrying down the streets. "Hello? Are there any survivors out there? Atticus? Atticus!"

Navigating through the refuse, they located the stairs that should lead to the wall, except the wall was gone. A gaping hole stretched almost the entire length of the western side of the city.

Spatters of blood coated the remaining rubble, bones and fragments of bodies scattered the area. Outside the city, a massive spread of burned people lay among the charred grasslands.

"What happened?" King Alondo asked. "What fucking happened?"

"Your Highness!" A soldier waved from the top of a destroyed building—a former tannery, if Sera had to guess.

"We've been searching for you." He climbed down from the wreckage and made his way to them. "My Lord, a group of survivors have gathered in the city park. The officers in charge have dispatched runners throughout the city to search for other survivors and lead them back."

"Bring us there," the king said.

She wanted to think Royal was alive but didn't have any hope. He'd fallen from the wall onto the enemy's side. She also wondered what had happened to the Camel Clans and the Redclaws. *Is everyone dead?* And she didn't want to think about what might've befallen the Falcon Knights who'd all been outside, attacking the Camel Clans from behind. *Are they all dead?* Her head was ringing. Dust and rubble. Blood and dead bodies. *Everything we were fighting for is . . . gone.* A cold chill crawled through her. *Now what?*

———

S unlight exploded in Villic's head. A throbbing ache in his temple caused him to wince. He remembered the battle and sprang to his feet; another pulse of pain rocking through him.

"Relax. I haven't heard anything."

Villic saw the man he'd stabbed with the power of darkness, his skin gray and bloodless. He heard nothing alive, saw nothing alive.

"How would you have heard anything? I was out."

"I don't disappear when you disappear, Villic. I don't sleep. Although I can still hear what's going on around you, I can't see, because you close your eyes when you sleep."

"Who doesn't close their eyes when they sleep?" Villic looked down the stone wall, saw it ended in a large hole. Something bad had happened.

"There was a person I once inhabited who . . . you know what,

never mind. You're right. Everyone sleeps with their eyes closed. It is the way."

Villic leaned over the battlements, looked down at the grasslands. Bodies littered the scorched grass. Pieces of stone and limbs and camel carcasses lay in ruin. *Dunecrest.* He saw some camels grazing several hundred feet away and hoped Dunecrest was among them.

"Something bad happened," Villic said. He turned around and looked down the other side of the battlements. Much of the city had crumbled into debris. "Something terrible happened."

"Magicai? Or one of the Imbuers, I wonder."

"Imbuers can't do . . . this, can they?"

"I don't know. I know what I can imbue into your weapons, and I know the limits of the powers I have access to. Who knows if someone else discovered a secret, altered the way of Imbuing. Or, perhaps, they discovered another type of power altogether. It's not out of the realm of possibility. I exist, after all. And I'm unaware of what could happen if an Imbuer did something . . . creative . . . while a Magicai did something, themselves. As it were, I didn't know if the darkness would absorb the Magicai's power, do something good or bad, or fail to have an effect at all. I've never had anybody ask for darkness, though I knew it could theoretically be wielded. Fortunately, it paid off."

"What? You didn't know? You could've gotten me killed! Piss on Flaytz, I knew I shouldn't have trusted you."

"You asked for the power, and I delivered. We didn't have time for a debate about the efficacy of an Imbuer's powers versus a Magicai's."

"May Killiak, Lord of Lords, damn you," he said.

"One of these days you'll be appreciative."

"Sure, Speaker. Sure."

Villic started walking the wall's length, towards the gigantic hole. He didn't see any signs of life. He checked each body he passed, but they were dead. It appeared most of them had died before the explosion. As he got closer to the hole, the bodies got blacker and blacker, until he found several piles of ashes he assumed were former people.

A jagged stone edge threatened to collapse under Villic's weight when he reached the hole. He peered through and saw more bodies, and further down the grasslands, the destroyed remnants of the gate. He saw no Imbuers. No Falcon Knights. No Remerian soldiers. Everything was . . . gone.

"Now what?"

"I don't know." He didn't have a leader. Nobody was telling him what to do. Villic had no direction. For as long as he could remember, he'd always had somebody to tell him what to do, some goal to attain. His parents, until they had died. After that, he listened to Jedkah and the shamans. When Villic had once found himself separated from the Splintered Manes, he had a single goal—return to them and find out what to do next. But he didn't know where they were. *Or if they even are.*

"I don't know what to do."

A stranger's voice called from far away. He didn't understand the words, but Speaker translated for him. "Hey, you on the wall! The battle's over. Come down!"

Villic found a man standing atop a collapsed building, waving to him. Using his spear, he called to the power of vines, and lowered himself from the wall to the ground. He had to use the power of vines twice more to climb high piles of junk and buildings. When he made it to the soldier, the man was quaking in fear.

"He's nervous. You're an Imbuer. As far as he knows, you're about to kill him."

Villic lowered the spear. "I'm not going to hurt you."

The soldier, who didn't speak Vessian, closed his eyes and raised his hands.

Villic heard more shouting, then saw a group of Remerian soldiers heading in his direction, weapons raised.

I don't want to kill them.

"You might have to."

Sera leaned against a fountain filled with clear, bubbling water. The delightful sound of trickling streams was hypnotizing. She studied the destroyed city, and tension filled her. *What's going to happen next?* They'd searched for Royal in the city park, intact after the explosion, but didn't find him. He was, like so many others, missing or dead. Now, she stood near King Alondo. The king seemed wary to allow her out of his sight, and she didn't blame him. She wouldn't want to be left alone with the two rebels, the Bloody Duchess and Captain Althier around, either. Perhaps they'd consider this an opportune time to murder the king. So, instead of doing what she wanted to do, she remained out of duty and loyalty. And a bit of guilt for abandoning the Cyroki leadership during the Calrite invasion.

"My lord, we've found another survivor," a soldier said, rushing to the king.

King Alondo had commandeered a remaining chair from an injured woman. Sera didn't think this right, but it wasn't her place to say anything. These weren't her people. King Alondo wouldn't listen to her. The injured woman had limped off and now sat in the park's grass, bleeding. King Alondo was, as was customary for him, pacing. He'd hardly sat in the chair at all.

"Who did you find?" the king asked, eager. He'd been searching for Atticus.

"A Camel Clansman. One of the powerful ones, I think. He understands our language."

"What! Kill them!"

"He's not being hostile, Your Highness. He surrendered," the man said. "We have him in custody, but I didn't want to bring him to you unless you wanted to see him. He can't speak our language, though, so communication is difficult. I'm unsure if we still have a translator."

"Have you found any of the Magicai?" the king asked.

"A few, My Lord. Not many, though. They're searching for other survivors. A couple of Enforcers. No Collectors or Healers."

King Alondo sighed. "Bring the Camel Clansman. I'll judge him appropriately."

"Yes, Your Highness," the soldier said, saluting.

"At this point, we might not want to kill them," Sera said. "With all the forces destroyed . . . we'll need anyone we can get."

"You're not wrong, Cyr Seradal. But we can't have a raving lunatic walking around murdering those who remain, either. We'll see how this Camel Clansmen acts."

"*They're bringing you to the king.*"

I'm not sure if that's good or bad.

"*Just listen to me, and you'll be fine.*"

I can't communicate with them. Villic followed an armed group of Remerian soldiers towards a bright clearing in the dull city. Citizens and soldiers alike lounged upon patches of green grass, some of them very injured. A stone object sat in the middle of one patch of grass, water raining from it. *What is that?*

"*That's called a 'fountain'.*"

It creates water?

"*No. It's decorative.*"

Villic didn't understand water being decorative, but he didn't have time to ask questions. Now, he stood before a pacing man. A woman leaned against the fountain, watching him, one hand resting on her sword. The Remerians had taken Villic's spear and scimitar, and he felt fear at being unable to protect himself.

"We've seen that woman before. The Camel Clans let her enter the city before the fighting started."

Villic didn't remember her, but that wasn't unusual. She had very dark hair and very pale skin and a very mean look on her face, Villic thought. But Villic often thought everyone looked mean.

The king stopped his pacing and glared at Villic. Speaker translated his words. "You murdered my people, blew open my wall, and now you're here? For what? To kill me?"

Villic shook his head.

"You need to speak to them. Listen to what I say. Tell them that the Camel Clans are missing and you're looking for your people. You mean them no harm."

"Jedkah and the shamans are missing. We don't want to hurt you."

The king stared at him and shook his head.

"You need to speak their language. Follow the sounds I make. Ready?"

Villic tried to follow Speaker's guide. "Cuhmul Cland mizzing. Luke for peeples. I meano arm."

The king moved to the woman and spoke in hushed whispers for a moment. He didn't look pleased.

The king gestured at the girl. "This is Sir Seradal Wintlock, from the north. A country called Cyrok, not sure if you've ever heard of it."

Villic nodded. He'd heard of it but knew nothing about the lands. The Camel Clans didn't care about Cyrok. They hadn't attacked them or prevented the Camel Clans from having better lands to live on.

"Sir Seradal is going to care for you. She'll make sure you're fed and watered and have a place to sleep. Any developments regarding your people will be relayed to you as soon as we find anything. Until then, you aren't allowed your weapons, and if you do anything anyone even suspects as hostile, I'll make sure you hang. Do you understand?"

Villic nodded.

King Alondo addressed Sir Seradal next, but loud enough Speaker could still translate. "I'm going to go with my men. See how things are out . . . there," he said, waving at the city. "Monitor the Bloody Duchess and Captain Althier. And keep an eye on this freak," he said, pointing at Villic. Then he left with the soldiers who'd escorted Villic there.

Villic swallowed, looking down at the ground, avoiding Sir Seradal's gaze.

"Careful, Villic. We need her to trust us. Don't act odd."

I'm not acting odd.

"You're staring at her feet."

And so he was.

21

ASHEN HYREL

Anepolis, Calrym

Tallas Taybold escorted her through the palace, as was routine. Now that she'd become a recognizable figure, her title made official, people greeted her with polite nods or smiles, or dodged out of her way as she strode through the corridors.

"You have garnered respect," Tallas said, walking behind her.

"Indeed."

Outside the Great Hall, Arena Hyrel and her guards weren't moving. Arena's stern and impatient expression told Cithrial something was annoying her. When Arena noticed her, she offered a forced smile, but it was clear something was annoying her.

In front of Duchess Arena, Duke Hemmel crouched over a figure in chains, leaning against the entry doors to the Great Hall. The pair of king's guards seemed unsure what to do. They kept trying to remove the man by force, but Duke Hemmel was blocking them.

"No, no, no," Hemmel said. "I paid good money to rent

him for the day, and he's not even mine. If you break him, I'll have to pay for him. And if *you're* the ones who did it, I'll require King Mikas cover the costs. Doubtful he'd be pleased with either of you. Now stand aside, stand aside." Hemmel turned back to the man on the ground. "Get up. I said . . . get up. Stand, damn it. You're making us look like fools!" He yanked on the chains that looped around the man's ankles. "Get up or I'll pay Madam Zeitwitch to hang you."

The man stood, and Hemmel pulled him away from the doors. He handed the chain to one of his guards, and the man collapsed back to the floor, hiding his tear-stricken and reddened face in his hands. "If he does anything foolish, kill him. I'll reimburse Madam Zeitwitch if need be." Hemmel turned back to the man on the ground. "Be good, Adavir, and perhaps I'll feed you before our last romp together." Laughing, Hemmel directed his attention to Arena and Cithrial. "My apologies for keeping you in the hallway like a pair of uncivilized, poverty-stricken urchins. It's poor practice to bring your playthings to work. I know, I know, I'll do better. If you start bringing your servants to work, Arena, perhaps we could have a group session after meetings? No?" He laughed again, then entered the Great Hall.

You are a bastard.

As a former urchin herself, she found her distaste for Hemmel increasing.

"Repulsive. I am not sure which I dislike more—Hemmel or Velturo. I am not sure why Hemmel has become so vocal suddenly, either. He used to be quiet," Arena said. "Do yourself a favor, Lady Hyrel, and keep a respectful distance away from either of those pigs."

"I planned on it."

"Good." Arena lifted her chin and walked past the guards. They opened the door for her and she entered the Great Hall, Cithrial close behind.

Before stepping through the doors, Cithrial glanced down

at the poor man who'd returned from Cyrok. He was half-naked and blotchy-eyed. Whatever Hemmel was doing seemed to take a toll on the man she recognized as Captain Blago Adavir.

Inside the Great Hall, Cithrial noted an uncomfortable ambiance. King Mikas's reddened face twitched and contorted in anger, while his chancellor, Bertrand, trembled in what she assumed was fear. Silence hung in the air, except for Velturo's silverware clinking as he crammed food into his mouth. She took her seat, and, as she was last in, expected somebody to speak after she sat. Nobody did.

Her hand reached into the secret pocket of her mantle and she fondled the pouch of Black Dust hidden within.

The king cleared his throat and she, along with the others, turned her attention in his direction.

"We've received devastating news. Bertrand?"

"An official missive arrived today from a Qothan politician—yes, they exist, though there are few. They all reside in Sultiva—it's the only place of civilization outside the University of Arcanical Arts. Not that—"

"Bertrand!" King Mikas backhanded Bertrand's thigh. "We don't need your endless prattle. Read the fucking note. For the love of Mother Avani herself, *stop* talking!"

Bertrand muttered an apology. "From the official delegation of the—"

"Bertrand!"

"Yes, we can skip the introductions, my apologies. Dearest King Mikas and his surrounding councilmen," Bertrand said, his eyes narrowing. "Should read 'members of the King's Council', but I digress."

The king cleared his throat again.

"My apologies, Your Highness. Continuing . . . A grand travesty has graced the Qothan nation—one of which the world of Cedain has likely not yet seen. I write this with the gravest and most sorrowful heart, for information of this magnitude so rarely occurs and, when it does, it's even rarer that it affects the entire world. As Calrym is the foremost nation in employing the Magicai, it brings me even further pain to deliver this news. The University of Arcanical Arts—otherwise known as Ashmount—is no more. It is alleged a magical experiment went wrong. Another theory is that saboteurs attacked and blew up the building. Whatever the cause, pillars of smoke and fire graced the skies for days. The influential school is leveled. Gone, completely and utterly. It appears all Magicai present were incinerated. This is a shocking loss to any living Magicai, Qothe, and the rest of the world. We have nothing but the deepest regrets. Any help you can afford would be especially helpful. Please send any available funds, donations, resources to—"

"Yes, yes, quiet yourself. We're not sending anything," King Mikas said.

That's not right. They need help. "Certainly, we could send them something," Cithrial said.

"Are you willing to make a contribution solely out of your own holdings, Duchess Cithrial?" Hemmel asked.

"Could we not pool our resources?" she asked.

"No, no, definitely not, ah-hah." Velturo laughed, food dribbling down his chin. He scrambled to wipe it up, dropped the cloth, and food spattered on his lap.

"Do roses blossom in the spring?" Arena asked, folding her arms, and looking at Cithrial disapprovingly.

"No, thank you for the offer though, Duchess Cithrial," Hemmel said, holding his hand up, signaling her to stop.

King Mikas leaned forward, taking a deep drink from his goblet of wine. "I think we're all in agreement we don't want to spend our hard-earned money."

Cithrial nodded. "I'll concede to your expertise."

Everyone's expressions relaxed when they realized nobody would further advocate for them to relinquish their funds.

"This presents another issue though, ah-hah." Velturo didn't mention what it was, though. He became enraptured with a glazed pastry he'd dropped on the table.

"The Magicai," Arena said, picking up where Velturo left off, "are a rare commodity now. And without leadership. It is worth noting any local Magicai should be scooped up, paid well, and kept inside the city. They are a precious resource in a world where there won't be a large supply to draw from anymore. We will want to capitalize on the ones in Calrym. Whoever controls the most Magicai will rule the world."

"It's true," Hemmel said. "We'll want to prioritize hiring Magicai. Each of us should commit to personally staffing several if they're available. Spread the costs around. I'm sure I can locate and support half a dozen, at least. If you're unable to afford a Magicus, send them to me. We must work together." Cithrial heard the hinted implication—those who controlled the most Magicai controlled the city—and Hemmel wanted to have the most.

"I am sure we will do just fine hiring the Magicai we find, Hemmel," Arena said.

"We need to secure Lochwall's power, and more importantly, Calrym's," Cithrial said. She didn't believe it, but figured it sounded good.

Hemmel nodded, Arena gave a thin smile, and Velturo choked out a "Yes, ah-hah!".

"Then the business with Qothe and the University of Arcanical Arts is complete," King Mikas said.

We didn't do anything. But she knew that was normal. The dukes and duchesses and the king seemed unable to want to do anything other than meet and yell and sit on their riches, while pretending they were the force of good Calrym thrived upon.

A shen left the Great Hall, stepping around the chained Blago Adavir, and regrouped with Tallas. She remained silent—angry and thoughtful about the response to the tragedy in Qothe. Tallas seemed to sense this and didn't make any noise other than the butt of his halberd thumping on the carpet as they walked to her carriage.

They made the ride back to her manor in silence, as well, Tallas uttering a mere, "my lady," when helping her in and out of the carriage.

She wasn't sure who to trust. One of her father's Five Rules of Survival popped into her head. *Never trust anyone, even those you trust. In matters of life and death, your life is meaningless even from your friend's point of view.* Ashen trusted Jaspard if she continued to do what he wanted. She trusted Tallas if he continued to get paid. There were no friends, no family. Growing up homeless, she had too much to worry about with taking care of herself. Once her parents died, it became too dangerous to search out companionship. Everything was a risk as a vulnerable child with nothing to trade or barter, or the strength to hold on to it even if she had something.

"Ah, the Lady Hyrel returns," Jaspard said. She realized she'd walked into the den—Jaspard's favorite room—without noticing she'd even entered the manor. "How was it today?"

Sitting in her preferred armchair, she explained what they'd discussed, how things resolved, and her feelings about much of it.

"I understand your attachment to helping those who are beneath us, but it's not your job to fix the world. If you try to do that with everyone, you'll never be able to help yourself," he said. "Do you recall when I allowed you to stay with me?"

"Of course." It was the happiest day of her life, even if he'd told her she'd have to murder people to live with him.

"I opened my door to you, a stranger. I let you live with me. I helped you. How many others would've done the same?

Not many, I wager. But it made a difference. You've had a much better life. I've had a much better life by having you here. We've become a family. If you can make a difference in at least one person's life, you've succeeded." He smiled at her, then placed one of his sugared honey chews into his mouth. "Delicious," he said. "Never underestimate the things that bring you pleasure. Life's far too short, and the things you enjoy hardly last longer than a few moments when compared to all the boring or horrible things one must experience." He retrieved another piece of candy and proffered it to her. "Honey chew?"

"All right." She eagerly popped it in her mouth, and a rush of sweetness greeted her mouth, saliva swam across her tongue. "Delightful," she said.

"How are things with Tallas Taybold?"

"Wonderful. Where did you find him? And why did you decide to trust him, of all people?"

"Splendid questions," he said, the clink of candy-on-teeth as he shifted the chew in his mouth. "I found him in a bar providing security. He seemed unhappy, underpaid, and bored. Knowing I needed to procure a guard, I struck up a conversation with him. I figured he'd know where to find such people. I don't think I got further than, 'do you know where to find a good bodyguard' before he'd told the bar's owner he quit. We had drinks in a different bar and I learned about his background." He laughed. "When I discovered he was the original Golden Knight, I knew he was trustworthy and skilled. He sold his services at a bargain of a price. I think he wanted something to do. Tallas became much more interested when he found out it was a young girl he was protecting—no, not like that, have a little faith in me, please —but in a guardian-type way. Perhaps he has a daughter of his own, or somebody he considered as such. Or maybe he never had children and always wanted a daughter. Or, quite possibly, I am looking too far into it." She doubted that.

Jaspard was good at understanding people and how they work.

"I wonder what happened."

"Well, Lady Hyrel," Tallas said from the den's entryway. "It's a story. I'll tell you if you're interested."

"Please," Jaspard said, motioning at an empty chair, "come sit."

"Well, ain't this a surprise fit for a suspecting crowd?"

22

DEMRI SLARN

Hidehedge, Calrym

Demri was sitting in his bed when Myri returned, staring at the wall. He couldn't stop thinking about ancient powers. How useful and interesting they'd be. She entered without knocking and flung herself on Caius's bed. Demri immediately picked up her lavender aroma.

"Things are progressing faster than we thought, Demri," she said. *No code name. A slip? Feeling friendlier? Or, perhaps, she's distressed.*

"Why?"

"A-Twenty-Three has detonated."

"I'm not sure that m-makes sense to m-m-me."

"One of our agents consumed his Well, blew himself up. Took a good chunk of the Remerian capital with him."

"Andora?"

"Besieged by the Camel Clans, we can only guess the infiltrator decided it was necessary to eliminate a threat. Something strange occurred, though."

"How d-do you know?"

"We have many ways of keeping track of our agents, Demri. I can't share specifics, but if somebody detonates, the leadership knows it."

"T-Tell me how."

Demri waited, silent. She looked like she was thinking, and he didn't want to interrupt her.

"I don't know how. I'm not them. If I knew, I still wouldn't tell you. There are countless possibilities we could speculate upon, but that's not why I'm here. We need to discuss what he did." Demri didn't find that comforting at all. Secrets were what brought the Magicai down. The Elkavich weren't seeming all that much different to him. "He destroyed less than a quarter of the city. Which means we either vastly overestimated how much damage one of us can do when we free ourselves or he'd had much less power. If he had less power, that means he wasted it fighting. That would make more sense." She sat, lips pursed, staring at the same wall Demri had been staring at before she entered. He wondered how they knew such specific information already. Andora was not close by. She was biting her lip in concentration. Demri had an overwhelming urge to approach her but didn't. "He was to be our anchor—the person responsible for bringing in other Elkavich members under-cover, so when the time came, they'd have enough people."

"Your p-plan was to b-blow up the entire city?"

"Well, not anytime soon."

"Not soon?"

"We have a lot to discuss, Demri. Much of it is secrets of the Elkavich. I shouldn't have allowed you to read Hobark's book."

"It was fascinating."

"Yes, I'm sure you enjoyed it. Remarkable what the Magicai removed from history, isn't it? Makes you wonder how much they removed that *wasn't* recorded. I'm sure there's plenty."

"I'm not going to t-tell anyone anything."

"I know. You won't be allowed to leave the Elkavich, Demri. You're stuck in Hidehedge."

"Stuck?"

"You can't believe the leaders would allow you entry and then allow you to go free without becoming a member, would you?"

"Why did you bring me here, M-M-Myri?"

She frowned, biting her lip again. Her eyes met his.

He might've bit his lip, too.

"Because I owed you, Demri. The Magicai wouldn't stop coming after you."

"You destroyed Ashmount. I should b-b-be safe now."

"But now you need to worry about the Elkavich."

He raised a brow. Wanted her to elaborate. She didn't.

"I have bad news, Demri." She let out a long breath, like she'd been holding back something. "Promise me you won't act on it."

"Act on what?"

"What I tell you. Promise you'll be good."

"I'll b-be good."

"Promise, Demri. If you do anything, and I truly mean anything, wrong, the Elkavich will kill you."

"I p-promise."

"Okay. I'm sorry Demri, I'm really sorry." Her eyes met the floor. "One of our most prestigious agents is returning to Hidehedge tomorrow."

Demri shrugged. She couldn't see him do it, though.

"I didn't know," she said. "I didn't know until today."

"Say it."

"E-Two. The only rank higher is—"

"E-One, yes, I know. Then the leaders with the end of times names."

"E-Two was working abroad. When warned about

impending disaster, E-Two fled and is returning here." She looked up at him. "E-Two is Doram Quandis."

Fire burned his heart. Demri had only kept promises to one person: Caius. He figured it wouldn't matter if he broke this one.

"You knew he was p-p-part of this organization and you lied to me about not knowing where he is?"

"I didn't know where he was, Demri. And him being part of the Elkavich or not wasn't relevant."

"I'm going t-to k-kill him."

"Demri, you can't hurt him."

"He'll k-k-kill me."

"He can't. Disaster offered you sanctuary. He won't revert the decision. Doram can't do anything about it."

"I'll k-kill him."

"I'll kill you, if you do," she said.

He saw her expression. Stoic, serious. She meant it.

"I wouldn't want to, but I'd have to." Myri stood. "I need to check in with the leaders. They're all here, and they're expecting me and other high ranking Elkavich members. Don't be stupid. Revenge can wait." She walked to him, let her hand linger on his knee for a moment, then exited his room.

He snarled, gritting his teeth. His hands clenched and he wanted to bring Hidehedge and all its inhabitants into his inferno. But Doram wasn't even there so he'd have to wait a day, first.

———

Caius returned that evening. Demri had spent hours stewing over what he'd say or do when Doram Quandis arrived. It was, Demri knew, time to have a serious conversation with his friend.

As had become routine, Caius walked in, said nothing,

and laid on his bed. A moment later, he turned to Demri. "Who fucked up my bed?"

"Her."

Caius knew who that was. Grunted, turned back on his bed, staring at the ceiling.

"We need t-to t-t-talk."

"I'm listening."

"I'm sorry, C-C-Caius."

"For?"

"Not listening." Demri informed him of all that he discussed with Myri.

"I told you not to trust the cunt. Not even going to allow you revenge on the person who's caused all this trouble? What kind of sick person does that? The man tried to have you killed, got you expelled from school, and because of both those actions, the Magicai have chased you for two decades. Chased *us* for two decades." He pulled out his knife and started filing his nails.

"You're not wrong," Demri said. "B-But I need to p-play along."

"Of course you need to play along. I need to play along. It's all we do, Demri."

"We'll f-find a way to k-kill him."

"We better," Caius said, wincing as he poked a finger.

"You need a b-b-better habit."

"You need a better habit."

"I d-don't have habits."

"Myri is your habit."

Demri withheld a response. Caius was right. Demri decided he needed to break his habit.

With their friendship repaired, Caius didn't abandon Demri to his thoughts as he'd been doing.

"Where have you b-been going during the d-d-day?"

"While you've been in your head, I've been scouting. Checking this place out. Meeting different people. Learning about the Elkavich. For a secret organization, they're not very good at keeping secrets."

"That's b-because we're not allowed to leave."

"I know. You said that yesterday. Do you know why the Elkavich symbol looks like a triangle?"

"No," Demri said. The insignia never made sense to him.

"It's a reference to the person who founded the Elkavich. Becciana Elkavich. She's dead now, but they respect her, I guess." Caius's knife was back in his hands, filing away. "After Becciana died, they created a symbol in her honor. An orange 'E'. Not discreet enough, so somebody altered it. They pulled the ends of the E together, meeting the middle prong. Forming the triangle that's cut in half. Strange, but I guess it's a way for them to honor her."

"And you just f-found that out?"

"I asked Ced."

"I see."

"Speaking of," Caius said, quirking his head toward the door, "I think I hear him coming."

Sure enough, Ced's customary knock sounded. Then he opened the door.

"It's time for the midday meal, my friends. Glad to see you've reconciled, oh yes. Glad to see it, indeed. And we have a new arrival downstairs! One of our most respected members. You should meet him. Lovely man, I tell you, lovely man, indeed. One day he might actually know me by name —Ced, I mean—instead of C-Eighty. Everyone knows me by 'Ced', except the people who matter most." He turned to leave, closing the door behind him. They heard his rambling as he retreated down the hall. "Ah well, what can one do except try their best to be noticed? Most people notice me, I've noticed. Ha, what a saying. Soon they'll be saying something, followed by, 'notice me, I've noticed is something Ced said'!"

"T-T-Time to greet the m-man who's eluded us for t-two d-d-decades."

Caius wiped his bloody knife on his trousers. They left the room together.

They took seats at one of the many tables in the dining hall, one nearest a corner of the room. The Elkavich arrived in twos and threes, taking their places. Five masked people sat at a large, round table in the center. Apocalypse, Bloodbath, Catastrophe, Disaster, and the current leader of the Elkavich, Erasure. Each had the first letter of their name stitched into their robes, to identify who each one was. Demri saw no sign of Doram Quandis.

A woman who introduced herself as an A-something—he didn't pay her any mind—served them a plate of food each. Demri, not hungry, hardly looked at it. Caius dove in, shoveling runny eggs into his mouth.

And then he entered. Tall, pale, and his signature squinty eyes—just as Demri remembered from twenty years ago, at Ashmount. A far cry from how he'd been described by Magicus Vistario eighteen years ago. The Elkavich leaders waved Doram over, and he took a seat with them. So consumed by hatred and rage, Demri didn't notice Myri approach until she placed a hand on his shoulder.

"My dear husband, Enebrial," she said. Myri leaned down, placing a kiss on his lips. Before he could react, she'd withdrawn, sitting in an adjacent chair.

"D-D-D-Four," Demri said. The intoxicating scent of lavender drifted into his nose.

"I'm glad to see you haven't leaped from your chair in an attempt to kill him."

"He just walked in," Caius said, wiping egg from the corner of his mouth. "Give him a minute to contemplate the best course of action. He'll be up in a moment." He winked at Demri.

Demri ignored him and watched Doram. The Magicus had taken a seat on the table of Elkavich leaders. If Doram moved his head to his right, just a little, their eyes would meet. Demri waited.

Caius and Myri said things, but Demri had closed them out. *Look at me. Know you're about to die. LOOK. AT. ME!*

Seconds felt like minutes, while minutes felt like hours. But the moment came.

Doram Quandis met Demri Slarn's eyes. A look of quickly concealed surprise passed across his face before he grinned. He even gave a slight nod.

Demri consumed a Soul Glyph.

23

INTERLUDE
THE GOLDEN KNIGHT

Four Years Ago
Largos, Calrym

The Golden Knight had the best weaponry provided to him, courtesy of King Mikas's treasury. He had the strongest, thickest armor, plated in gold, provided to him, courtesy of King Mikas's treasury. His reputation as one of the most feared fighters was spread, far and wide, courtesy of King Mikas's treasury. One moment, the Golden Knight had been a master ruffian, outwitting regular guardsmen and stealing valuables from merchant caravans; the next, he'd come under the employment of the King's Guard, his appearance and reputation created by some fancy person he couldn't remember the name of. All in the name of inducing fear in the minds of any individual considering treasonous acts against the king.

"The Golden Knight" title came both from his armor, and in his mind, as well as the fact he'd stolen plenty of gold from the king, though nobody knew about the latter. Tall tales were told about his honor, how he'd regularly protected the weak, saved the innocent, and vanquished any who opposed the

Garcovian line. It was lies, but only a year into service, the fables melted away into glorious truths. Stories of his exploits traveled far and wide. Everyone wondered who the Golden Knight truly was, for when he'd taken up the helmet, his sponsor had made but one request: never disclose his identity. If the Golden Knight was present, people behaved.

He'd protected ludicrous amounts of the king's money, assassinated the most dangerous of the king's enemies, and trained even the weakest of soldiers into a formidable power. The Golden Knight was both legend and skill.

But with legend and skill, jealousy and hatred rise. And he was no exception.

He'd survived plenty of assassinations targeted at himself, avoided the life-threatening mistakes of envious colleagues and cohorts who desired the Golden Knight's title, and suffered plenty of ridicule from many of the king's political allies—an attack aimed at discrediting him, and removing him from the king's service. After all, nobody wanted to have the second-best soldier.

The Golden Knight wasn't the only legend. Delicourt Ramses, Khlaux Corbéo, and the Watchtower of Calrym—a man named Zervan who was taller than anyone else by a full foot—were all prominent guardsmen serving either King Mikas, or a duke or duchess. They expressed their disdain for the Golden Knight, publicly and frequently. And, as fate would have it, they often accompanied him on various tasks the king sent him on. Just like this one.

Sweat dripped down his face. A bead slid down his eyebrow, hung there for a moment, then trickled into his eye. The salt burned. Others were around, though, and he'd made a vow to never lift his visor or remove his helm in front of anyone.

One foot fell in front of the other. Marching, he led the caravan of carts full of luxurious goods down the road, towards Largos, which he could see in the distance. A cool breeze slipped beneath his golden chain mail. He felt good. Other than his head, which roasted inside the helmet. The king had commissioned an armorer to custom craft a helm which hid the Golden Knight's face, aside from an empty strip that exposed his eyes and the bridge of his nose. He paused, taking a deep breath. Carts passed him, though he didn't worry. He could still see the Largos guardsmen and knew they were safe.

"The Golden Knight must be an old man, if a little heat is going to slow him down." That would've been Delicourt Ramses speaking. He was the loudest of the trio, always quipping and jeering at the Golden Knight.

He turned, saw Delicourt approaching. On the other side of the road, Khlaux and the Watchtower loomed. They'd also stopped walking and stared in the Golden Knight's direction.

"Let's turn this shipment in, get paid, and go our separate ways," the Golden Knight said. It was like this every time. He tried to remain silent, polite. They never let him go without getting a couple of good jabs in. They coveted his armor, his title, and the favor the king showed him.

"You're always wanting to abandon us," Delicourt said. He was now only a few feet away, waving his halberd at the Golden Knight. "I often wonder if we got off on the wrong foot, you and me. I think we could've been friends."

"In another life, perhaps," the Golden Knight said. His hand fell to the hilt of his two-handed sword.

The last of the carts rolled by. The Golden Knight gave a reassuring nod to its driver, who looked concerned. He'd handled Delicourt and the other two before. Now would be no different.

Khlaux with his sword drawn, and the Watchtower hefting a great two-handed mace crossed the dirt road, flanking Delicourt.

"It's time the identity of the Golden Knight is known," Delicourt said.

"I don't think the king would appreciate that."

"The king?" Delicourt spat. "The king doesn't give a fuck about you. He just wants the reputation. The Golden Knight could be anyone."

"Let's just get paid," the Golden Knight said. He turned back towards Largos, knowing they wouldn't do anything. They couldn't, regardless of what they said—the king would have them hanged. *A good meal, and some ale, would help—*

Something smashed into his back, rattling the chain mail, and he stumbled forward. The Golden Knight swiveled, drawing his sword. He felt his back bruising already.

Delicourt Ramses swung the halberd once, twice. The Golden Knight blocked the first blow, but the second scraped across his chain mail, emptying his lungs of air. Gasping, he retreated a step.

The Watchtower charged, two-handed mace held above his head.

Fuck. His armor wouldn't protect against that.

Khlaux was circling around to get behind the Golden Knight.

"Is this honorable?" the Golden Knight asked. He knew they wouldn't answer. Knew they knew it wasn't honorable. It wasn't. It was just like the times he had to put down a stray dog in the city during one of his patrols. Something that just had to happen. He should've known, though. The Golden Knight spent his life watching honorable people die young— he'd killed several of them, though with honor, of course.

He dodged the charging Watchtower, parried another assault from Delicourt, then felt Khlaux's sword bouncing off his helm. He fell to a knee but regained his footing and, with the fury built from half a decade of these men harassing him, surged at Delicourt. The halberd, being longer, hit his armor three times before he closed the distance.

The Golden Knight drove his sword into Delicourt's thigh. Delicourt screamed, dropped his halberd, and fell backwards.

And then the Watchtower of Calrym returned.

As the Golden Knight turned to face his next attacker, the mace smashed into his helm. The metal squealed and buckled under the pressure. Before the Golden Knight could regain his bearings, the mace hit him again in the helm. Sharp edges of the broken helm dug into his cheek and lip, ripping away skin. Dazed, he fell to a knee. The mace hit him again. The helm flung from his head.

"Wait," the Golden Knight said.

The Watchtower didn't wait. The mace hit him in the face, and the Golden Knight's skull cracked. He fell.

The pain was so great the Golden Knight remembered little. A fragmented memory.

Delicourt limping over and proclaiming the Golden Knight dead.

The removal of his armor.

The approaching Largos guard inquiring about what happened.

He next remembered waking in the middle of the night. At first, he thought he'd lost his vision. It wasn't until he moved his head and saw the bright moonlight above that he realized it was nighttime. He groaned. Passed out.

He remembered nothing until he found himself laying in an infirmary, naked. He learned he'd been there for many days, in and out of consciousness. His caretaker explained he'd almost died. When he questioned her about the knights, she said, "The Golden Knight and the Watchtower have left."

"Delicourt Ramses?"

"He's being treated for his wounds."

Four days after that and Delicourt died from infection. It was a small recompense for losing everything.

When they discharged Tallas Taybold, he remained in Largos. He had nothing. No money and no prospects. He had to pick up a basic job doing basic duties and tried to ignore the stares at his face, the questions about his recent wounds.

Tallas earned enough to buy basic equipment—a sword, some leathers—and returned to the work he did best: killing. He joined a mercenary company, stuck with them until they died off, or quit, which didn't last long. They weren't very good.

When he had enough money, around four years after the attack, Tallas returned to Lochwall, though he never went to the king. He'd seen the Golden Knight and the Watchtower roaming around. Clearly, the king had moved on. And nobody likes the past coming back to haunt them.

Which was exactly why Tallas Taybold had done nothing. Until Jaspard Couliac walked into the bar where he worked as security and hired him. When he learned what he'd be doing, Tallas became enthusiastic about his new occupation. He might get a chance to take down the Golden Knight or the Watchtower. Hopefully, both.

24

DEMRI SLARN

Hidehedge, Calrym

Anger and a lust for vengeance coursed through Demri's blood when his eyes met Doram's. A jet of fire blasted from the palm of his hand, sizzling towards Doram Quandis and the five Elkavich leaders. But fate, like anything else, is a fickle bitch. Or, perhaps, Caius was.

A fist slammed into Demri's chest and he doubled over. His hand jolted, the torrent of flames falling short of Doram, searing the wooden floor.

Several of the Elkavich launched water at Demri and the floor. One made it rain; another sent a wave cascading over Demri, Caius, and Myri, while yet another sprayed the fire with two water streams. Meanwhile, Myri had projected a protective barrier around the trio.

"What in the name of Avani are you doing, Demri?" she glared at him, face flushed. "We had an agreement!"

Demri narrowed his eyes.

"Calm down, calm down," Erasure said. "Everyone stop. Let's not destroy Hidehedge." He directed his gaze to Demri.

"And if you do anything foolish like that again, I'll make sure you regret it."

You've invited poison into your organization. Demri clenched his jaw, said nothing.

The Elkavich leaders approached the shield.

"Release it, D-Four," Erasure said.

Myri lowered her hand and the shield faded.

Disaster shook his head, his hood threatening to fall. He tugged it forward. "My apologies. She vouched for him and I allowed his entry. We must banish him."

"He tried to kill one of us," Apocalypse said. "This must not go unpunished."

"It won't, but let's not be hasty in deciding his fate," Erasure said. The other four masked leaders bowed their heads in deference. "E-Two, what do you have to say on the matter? Is this not the man you were discussing a moment ago?"

Doram nodded. "I figured he'd try something. He did the same when we attended Ashmount. Sorry little shit, he—"

"Liar," Demri said, through gritted teeth.

The congregation turned towards Demri.

"He couldn't follow rules then and it's clear he can't follow them now. He's a mess," Doram said.

"So you would recommend removing him from Hidehedge?" Erasure asked.

Doram shook his head. "No, I have a suggestion, but we'd best discuss it in private."

"Take the Magicus to a cell," Erasure said. "You"—he pointed at Caius—"will remain here. If the Magicus tries anything, kill him. If you try anything"—he swiveled his forefinger at Myri—"I will also kill her."

A group of the Elkavich, led by Ced, escorted Demri away from the dining hall. Doram offered a sadistic smile as Demri passed him.

"Caught us an important one, boys. Remain vigilant and

don't let him escape," Ced said. He laughed. "Oh yes, they'll say, 'Ced wouldn't let us slack off, no sir, not one bit.' Then I'll say, 'quiet down, and pay attention. He's dangerous!' and they'll tell their friends, they will, they'll say, 'quiet down, and pay attention, Ced said.' I imagine they'd remember me quite well—I think I'm fairly memorable, don'tcha think? Only C-Eighty now but give me a year or two and I'll have an end-of-time name myself. What'll it be, you ask? Not sure, but I was thinking of calling myself 'Calamity'. That way, I could be 'Calamity Ced', ha!"

"Quiet," one of the Elkavich said.

"Yes, sir, D-Sixty." He quieted the rest of the way.

The cell was a plain room with typical bars and a cot with a nice blanket. An empty bucket rested on the cold stone floor. When Demri entered, the door closed, and the lock clicked. Demri almost laughed at that—a lock wouldn't keep him in there. He sat on the bed while the one Ced had called D-Sixty kneeled at a contraption opposite the cell. D-Sixty flipped a lid, poured a Collector's vial into a small tube, and then a dome switched on, encasing the cell. The same type of protection which kept the Buzzard's Bowls prisoners in captivity, or protected Ashmount. Demri couldn't free himself.

Well, fuck.

He spent his time lying in bed, staring at the ceiling. Nobody visited him the rest of the day or that night. He didn't receive food or water. *Fuck Caius.* He'd punched him. Stopped him from killing Doram Quandis. *Fuck Myri.* She hadn't helped, either. And she couldn't see how he felt— he would not open up to her again, though. *Fuck the Elkavich.* They'd let his nemesis into Hidehedge and expected Demri to do nothing about it. They didn't see Doram for the monster he was. *Fuck Doram.* Doram Quandis, walking monster. The man who'd ruined Demri's life. He would trade his own life to kill the bastard. And now, Doram Quandis was close.

So. Damn. Close.

They left Demri alone and with his thoughts, hungry and angry, thirsty and hateful.

<hr>

The sound of scraping shook Demri from his dreams of murdering a pleading Doram Quandis. He saw Ced using a pole to push a tray of food under the cell door, allowing him to remain outside the protective shield.

Ced nodded but left as soon as the tray was inside the cell. He said nothing, which was out of character, though Demri appreciated it.

He ate his food, too busy considering how to convince the Elkavich to kill Doram for him to realize what he consumed. Also on the tray was a glass of water. He drank greedily , glad to have moistened his throat.

Demri spent more time laying on the bed, staring at the ceiling. It wasn't too bad. For somebody who'd spent most of his time on the run, he'd stared at enough ceilings, laid in enough beds. It was almost a welcome experience.

The Elkavich leaders, along with Doram, Myri, and Caius, all showed up a few hours later.

"We've decided your fate," Erasure said, while Bloodbath unlocked the cell and Disaster disarmed the shield.

Demri noticed a grim expression on both Myri's and Caius's faces.

Catastrophe entered the cell, along with a nameless man. He gestured at the him. "This is E-Ten. He's going to perform a procedure on you. You will not resist. If you do, they die." He nodded at Myri and Caius. "We're doing something you've likely not heard about, a practice long forgotten. Or, perhaps, suppressed by the Magicai."

E-Ten approached the bed.

"Remain lying," Catastrophe said. "This was a power the Glyphists used to learn. As you're a former student of Ashmount, I don't need to explain all the inner workings of a Glyphist. But like they're able to connect your lifeforce to a Soul Glyph, they're able to sever the connection to your Soul Glyphs. You will be rendered powerless until we deem it necessary."

Demri wanted to resist. He also didn't want to get either of the people he cared about killed. He'd played the waiting game before. Now it was time to do so again. "Fine," he said, sighing. It wasn't like he had a choice. Demri knew he was a prisoner now.

E-Ten leaned down, a Soulpen in hand, and touched it to Demri's skin. He felt nothing, but he watched as the various Soul Glyphs on his arms faded away and, he presumed, the rest across his body did, too.

"Done," E-Ten said.

"Thank you, E-Ten. You are free to leave," Erasure said.

After E-Ten left, Doram stepped forward. "I seem to remember you being in a different physicality when you departed Ashmount, Demri. We've discussed this, and it seems only fair to remedy your current predicament."

"Wait," Demri said, but before the word had left his mouth, a blast of fire seared his face, burning him. He screamed, then the familiar crunch of his legs shattering. The pain, he realized, was much worse than he remembered.

"We're meant to wear the scars of our past," Doram said.

Through teary eyes, Demri saw the demoralized expression on Caius's face before he lost consciousness.

25

SERADAL WINTLOCK & VILLIC THE IMBUER

Andora, Remeria

The next few days Sera spent watching over Villic the Imbuer, who behaved well and did nothing to draw her suspicion. He followed her commands with zero protest. Every day, the Remerians discovered more survivors. The remnants of the Redclaws trickled into the broken city. A group of Falcon Knights, including her page, Renard, had also been found. When a search party ventured outside the walls, they found Royal, badly wounded but somehow alive.

When Sera visited him, he had a shattered leg and was babbling in a drunken, incoherent state. After seeing Royal taken care of, she left him to his whiskey and promised to replenish his cache as soon as she located more. Villic the Imbuer tagged along wherever she went, though he remained quiet unless she pursued conversation—and even then, said little. When Sera wasn't checking with Royal or King Mikas, she and Villic helped the Remerians.

King Mikas had enlisted near everyone to clear rubble, search for survivors, rebuild whatever they could, and secure and patrol the city—in case of a Calrym invasion. Many of the

Magicai had died, so the king ordered all of this done with manual labor, unless a Magicus advised against it. It was important to conserve their powers, though Villic the Imbuer could often aid them. Only two Healers survived the attack, and they dedicated themselves to helping the injured, though under King Mikas's instructions, only prevented important people from dying; and even then, they weren't to be completely fixed.

The Bloody Duchess volunteered the Redclaws to assist in all these duties, though she didn't contribute herself, Sera noticed. The Falcon Knights helped, under the guidance of Sera. With no true leadership available, everyone turned to Sera because she was the one King Mikas kept informed. Renard, her page, had become her personal runner, delivering messages back and forth between various groups of citizens and military alike. By the end of the day, the boy was exhausted. Though Renard wasn't aware of it, she'd secretly gotten the king to approve double rations for him.

Nobody knew what happened with the remnants of the Camel Clans. Nobody had witnessed their escape or destruction. Most the people on the wall nearest the attack had died or were severely injured. Villic the Imbuer didn't offer any insight on what had happened, either. He claimed he didn't know. Sera wasn't sure if she believed him, but the man was so difficult to talk to, she didn't bother pressing him for more information. The only signs of the Camel Clans were a few stray camels grazing out in the fields. Villic the Imbuer approached her, and, struggling through the words of her language, asked if he could take care of the camels. She knew he formed the words through communication with the entity inside his head. How all of that worked, she couldn't comprehend, but she didn't need to, nor cared to. There were far too many other things she needed to focus on. She obliged his request, though she didn't allow him outside the city without an escort containing at least one Magicus. Sera didn't think it necessary, but she didn't want to risk the king's wrath if the man escaped.

I just want to rest. To mourn. To grieve. Sera's days were too busy, full of orders received and orders to give. She didn't think about her mother or her brother. She didn't think of her father. Only what needed to be done. Day after day.

Tired, she just wanted some rest.

V illic the Imbuer, along with a regiment of Remerian soldiers and a Magicus, walked through the hole in Andora's western wall. A small group of Falcon Knights accompanied them to recover supplies they'd left in their camp on the hilltop.

"I'm not sure why you have such an attachment to that camel."

Dunecrest is my best friend. And if we leave the camels out here, they'll leave.

"What are you going to do with an army of camels, Villic? The Remerians will use them for food if the situation gets dire enough."

Hiking across the grasslands towards the camels, Villic waved at the men escorting him to stop. They did, though many of them had nocked bows, in case he tried fleeing. He was happy to see more camels out here than he thought there'd been. At least twenty.

Sir Seradal wouldn't let that happen. She's been nice.

"She's nice until you get in her way. Then what? Look inside historical account and you'll see mounds of evidence suggesting nobody ever takes good care of a prisoner, no matter the situation. As soon as they don't need you anymore, they won't bother to keep you alive."

Villic ignored Speaker and started corralling the camels together, looping reins provided by the Remerians around the camel necks. He'd bring them back to the city, where Sera had pledged they'd find a place to keep them safe. He checked each camel to see if it was Dunecrest. At regular intervals, he'd bring small groups of them back to the Remerian soldiers, who took their reins and waited for Villic to finish his work. After the second group, Villic gathered, he spotted Dunecrest.

"Dunecrest! Thank you Carana, goddess of life."

He ran over and hugged the camel, feeling Dunecrest's soft hair against his cheek. The camel snorted. "I've missed you. It's felt like an entire journey between oases since I've seen you." Villic wasn't sure if it was anywhere close to that long. Or perhaps it was longer. Distances and time were things he never figured out.

After Villic's reunion with Dunecrest, he finished corralling all the camels. Then he helped the Remerians file them into an empty stable in the city.

"You're to return to Sir Seradal," a Remerian soldier said, through Speaker's translation.

Villic nodded, avoiding the man's eyes. He found the ground to be rather fascinating.

"Did you hear me, savage?" the soldier asked.

Villic nodded again. "Yeth," he said, trying to mimic the language.

"Why they haven't executed you is beyond me. You killed a lot of good men."

"Time to leave, Villic. If you hang around, they're likely to rile themselves up and start beating you."

Villic turned and left, restraining his urge to run. When he was outside the stable, he did run, weaving in and out of Remerian soldiers and citizens. He didn't rest until he'd made it to the fountain Sir Seradal often stayed near. He realized upon reaching his destination that several soldiers had followed him and were now doubled over, panting from their exertion.

"They're keeping a close eye on you, it seems."

"Villic the Imbuer," she said, offering a smile.

"Don't believe the smile. It's forced."

She's being nice.

"She's pretending to be nice."

"Did you retrieve the camels?"

He nodded.

"Did you find more of the Camel Clansmen?"

He shook his head.

"I wonder where they are."

Villic wondered the same.

26

DEMRI SLARN

Hidehedge, Calrym

Agony and anger.

27

EDELBROCK BRENDIS

The other gladiators laughed when Chellie related Edelbrock's victory in the arena—by pissing in Scayde Haklon's direction. There was no love lost for their House owner.

Savakkis took Edelbrock aside, into one of the empty sleeping quarters. "I've heard you've done well in keeping people alive as much as you can. People speak of something called Buzzard's Battalion?"

"Just a name I've used to communicate with others in the heat of battle."

"Why?"

"In battle, nobody has time to decipher anything vague," Edelbrock said. "I learned this during the campaign defending against the Vessian Incursion."

"You were there? Brave man," Savakkis said. Edelbrock was certain Savakkis knew this already. They'd talked plenty since Edelbrock's arrival and his military background was no secret. Why then, was he was he asking about things he already knew about?

Edelbrock's palms were sweating. He swallowed, nervous. *Why does this man make me so weak?* "I was."

"We should use the name, even when you're not out there. Keep things unified. I'll bring it to everyone's attention later."

Edelbrock swallowed again, unsure of what to say. Savakkis arched a brow, waiting for a reaction.

He was saved from providing a reply when Marshal Deywin's voice rang out through the compound. "Edelbrock Brendis, you're wanted."

"Shit. More torture," Edelbrock said. He knew he was going to have to pay for his stunt on the field. He didn't think it'd occur this quickly, though.

Together, they left the sleeping quarters and in the middle of the gladiators, Marshal Deywin and five men stood. There was no sign of Scayde Haklon.

"Ed," the marshal said, spitting a glob of skachi juice on the ground. "Lord Haklon sent me down here. Seems your first lessons haven't stuck." He lifted a knife in the air. "Apparently," he addressed the crowded room, "carving the lord's name into Ed's skin hasn't had the effect we thought it would. Neither did the ear removal. Seems like when somebody isn't listening, take both ears, I suppose. Our mistake."

There were six people including the marshal compared to a room of, well, Edelbrock didn't know the exact number of gladiators—he didn't keep count, but of enough. *Why are we allowing this?* He caught Chellie's eyes. She nodded. He didn't know why. Behind him, he felt Savakkis's hand graze his back. It gave Edelbrock a surge of confidence.

"Enough stalling, Edelbrock. It's time to meet your fate," Marshal Deywin said.

"If you knew anything about fate," Edelbrock said, "you'd recognize when yours was about to turn." He was done. Done being tortured. Done being tormented. Done waiting to die.

The marshal and his men chuckled.

"You know what?" Marshal Deywin asked, spitting another glob on a gladiator's foot. "I think it's time to reunite Lord Ed here with his son." He drew his sword, and his men followed suit.

Edelbrock didn't want to die, but perhaps dying now wouldn't be so bad. End the anticipation. Quit the torture. No more fighting in Buzzard's Bowl.

The marshal took a step forward.

Edelbrock sighed, closed his eyes, and prepared for death. It didn't come.

"Move," Marshal Deywin said, after a few moments.

Opening his eyes, Edelbrock saw the gladiators standing in front of Marshal Deywin, separating him from Edelbrock.

"Move," he said again.

"If you want Edelbrock, come through us," one gladiator said. Edelbrock recognized him as someone he fought alongside on the ship.

"How about you leave Edelbrock alone and go tell that cunt of a duke we're done," Chellie said.

The marshal shook his head. "Is the life of one idiot worth sacrificing your own? Think about it. Plenty of you might survive the games, get released."

Savakkis's voice rang out behind Edelbrock with a bitter truth. "Nobody has ever been released in this House, Marshal."

"Nobody else needs to get hurt," the marshal said. "Just give us Ed. We'll sort out the release later."

"So you can forget about it?" Chellie asked. "What if none of us want to fight no more?"

"Stand aside or die."

Edelbrock didn't see what incited the melee. Somebody did something, somewhere and then it was six people fending off a crowd. The marshal and his men cut down several of the gladiators, but they were quickly overrun. Some gladiators rushed to block the stairs so nobody could escape, while others removed the soldiers' weapons. Edelbrock got hold of the marshal's hand, twisting it until he let go of his sword.

The gladiators forced the soldiers into the sleeping quarters Edelbrock and Savakkis had come from.

"Now what?" Savakkis asked.

"I have a score to settle." Edelbrock followed the soldiers into their sleeping quarters. Savakkis and many gladiators filed in after him.

Marshal Deywin and his men stood against the wall furthest from the door. Armed gladiators held the soldiers' weapons at their throats, daring them to move.

"Apparently," Edelbrock said, "we'll need to carve a name into the marshal's body. And since he doesn't listen to my warnings about fate, we'll need to take *both* ears. I wouldn't want to ignore the good man's advice."

Cheers from the gladiators, and Edelbrock saw the marshal contemplating resistance, then realizing the futility of the situation. Marshal Deywin's head slumped in defeat. He knew what was coming. Edelbrock knew what was coming. Too often in tales he'd heard and the books he'd read, when justice was available, people ignored it. Edelbrock wasn't trying to be a better person. He'd never considered himself a good person. Revenge wouldn't bring back his son, but it'd sure ease the burden he carried.

"Remove the marshal's clothes," Edelbrock said.

"Is this a good idea, Edelbrock?" Savakkis asked.

"You figure out what to do with the others, but I need to do this. My vote is to kill them all."

Savakkis frowned, seeming to consider Edelbrock's words. "If they leave, they're going to join whatever retribution comes our way. And I don't think allowing them to walk out of here alive will go over well. Either way, Scayde is going to be angered."

"Fine," Edelbrock said, hardly listening. He didn't care about them. His focus was on the marshal.

"Kill everyone except Marshal Deywin," Savakkis said.

The guards pleaded for their lives, but the gladiators, in possession of weapons previously used against them, didn't care. They drove them into the guards, and after a few cries of pain, they were dead. Blood soaked the floor and the killers, but nobody cared. In Buzzard's Bowl, they'd become used to the smell and sight of gore.

"Hold him down," Edelbrock said. The gladiators did. He traded the marshal's sword for a knife a gladiator had.

"This isn't a smart idea, Ed." Savakkis whispered. "Going down a dark path can lead to unfortunate side effects. Trauma. And think about everyone else. They might look at you differently. Right now, you're a man of respect. Don't ruin your reputation." For a moment, Edelbrock focused on the hot breath of the man, but he refocused, returning to his anger and lust for revenge.

"Maybe it's not a smart idea, but it'll sure feel good." He didn't give a damn about his reputation, or what anybody else thought. This was his moment. And, until anyone had to watch a group of people stand idly by as somebody threw their child off a balcony, it was none of their concern.

"Maybe you should think—"

Edelbrock was done thinking.

He forgot about taking the marshal's ears in the heat of the moment, and rammed the blade into Marshal Deywin's stomach, twisting the hilt as he did. Marshal Deywin gasped, inhaled, and then sputtered.

Edelbrock waited, wanting to carve *his* initials on the man, but Everic continued to choke and cough, and a spray of skachi juice coated Edelbrock's face. Wiping it off, he saw the marshal's face turning pink, then red, as he continued coughing. Edelbrock withdrew his sword.

When the marshal's face purpled and he started convulsing, Edelbrock pushed him to the ground and pounded his chest. "Breathe, damn it."

He hit the bastard's chest with his fist, again and again. With each hit, Ed knocked spittle and skachi out of the marshal's mouth.

Then Marshal Deywin's body sagged and was still. Edelbrock kept hitting. *Don't ruin this. You don't get to die this way.*

There was no reaction. The marshal wasn't breathing. *"FUCK!"* He hit harder. More and more. He hit until the man's ribs snapped.

"He's gone, Edelbrock," Savakkis said.

And so he was. Marshal Everic Deywin had choked to death on skachi. But it didn't keep Edelbrock from hitting him.

28

DEMRI SLARN

Hidehedge, Calrym

He spent much of the first Cycle of Spring in a bed, again. People came, went, and he ignored them all. Demri ate and slept, pissed and wept, drank and shit, and suffered under a constant painful fit. Time dragged. Slow. So slow.

29

INTERLUDE
KHLAUX CORBÉO

Calrym

Khlaux Corbéo, better known as the Golden Knight nowadays, rode his stallion at the head of the small band of soldiers he commanded. At his right, the Watchtower of Calrym loomed. The giant man was at least a head taller than anyone Khlaux had ever known.

King Mikas had commanded them to watch Remeria, see if the Camel Clans invaded, and report back any information. They'd done that, and after Khlaux had sent someone to relay the news to the king, they'd pressed into Remeria—even though this would keep Khlaux away from the king longer. He felt it was his duty to investigate. As the Golden Knight, he needed to be near the king, to protect him. They went slow, not wanting to attract the attention of the invaders, and remained several days behind. Destroyed villages and dead bodies were all the Camel Clans left behind. It sickened Khlaux. If he had a larger force, he might've disobeyed orders and launched an attack.

One thing bothered him, though. Each of the destroyed

villages contained hints of magic, and Khlaux knew the small villages couldn't afford to staff Magicai defenders. Which meant something was happening with the Camel Clans. Something dangerous. They'd followed the Camel Clans, watched them surround the capital, and then they left. It was worse than King Mikas would've believed. Khlaux needed to bring His Majesty this news, and it was far past his expected arrival time—the detour they'd taken in following the Camel Clans had delayed his return. He felt good, knowing his gut had been correct. Khlaux was glad the Camel Clans hadn't noticed him or his men, though. Otherwise, he knew they'd be dead. He didn't have any Magicai under his command, and fighting against whatever magic the Camel Clans had would be suicidal.

With the sun out and riding in the spring, Khlaux wanted nothing more than to remove his helm. The humid forest, though shielding them from the sun's light, held the heat like an oven. His face was overheating, but as the Golden Knight, he needed to remain anonymous. It was the rule. The only people who knew his true identity were King Mikas and the Watchtower of Calrym—and he only knew because he was there the day Khlaux had earned the armor. The Watchtower had actually earned it but didn't want the armor. Or the title. Khlaux was fortunate he'd befriended Zervan long ago. The investment had paid off.

As a member of the Corbéo family, Khlaux had seen the highs and the lows of respect and success. The Corbéos had been one of the wealthier and prestigious families in Lochwall at one point, but they'd fallen into obscurity. Khlaux, looking to restore some honor to the family name, joined the Calrite army. Because of his skill and noble heritage, they'd selected him to serve as one of King Mikas's guards. Now, he was one of the king's favored guards, and rarely left his side. Yet, he felt wrong about being sent to Remeria. It seemed foolhardy to send both him and the

Watchtower. *Perhaps the king just wanted to ensure accurate information.*

He knew it was unlikely he'd ever learn the truth. The king trusted him but didn't tell Khlaux everything. Nor did he expect the king to. He was, at the end of a day, a glorified guard, a knight of the country, a man entrusted to carry out the king's will and not argue his commands.

"What do you think's going to happen when we return, sir?" the Watchtower asked. He only called Khlaux "sir" in front of others, where they'd consider it inappropriate if he didn't.

"I expect a lot of talking, Zervan," he said, laughing. If he could count on anything, it'd be the dukes and duchesses talking endlessly over matters instead of acting upon the information. "Perhaps they'll wash our hair in buckets of gold and send hoards of beautiful women—men for you—to our houses. I'd be quite partial to a feast or two, as well."

"Good food is always reward enough when out in the field too long," the Watchtower said. "If you opened yourself, you might find grimier sex more intriguing."

Khlaux snorted. "You're interesting enough already, Zervan. I don't need to fuck you to make it more so."

"Suit yourself, sir." The Watchtower saluted. "But I'll respectfully disagree. I'd counter your point by asking how many tavern wenches became more interesting inside the bedroom?"

Khlaux assented, chuckling. "Fair enough. It's amazing what some of them hide under those clothes."

Now it was the Watchtower's turn to laugh. "I'd say the same for men, though sometimes you find yourself surprised at what's lacking."

Khlaux shook his head. "You'd think discovering a small package would be a blessing."

"For some, perhaps. But I like a good fight in the bedroom."

Khlaux choked on his laughter.

Riding on in silence, his face continued to drip. He slid his helm up, took a quick sip of water, and continued. They had almost three weeks of riding ahead of them.

The start of the Second Cycle of Spring came and went, and after their near three-week ride, they entered the capital, exhausted and ready to report to the king. Khlaux dismissed the rest of the unit, and he, along with the Watchtower of Calrym, trudged through the palace halls with heavy footsteps, searching for King Mikas. After inquiring, a page informed them he was in the Great Hall, holding council. Khlaux should've known that. The King's Council took place at the same time. Yawning, he realized he was travel weary.

They turned into the passage leading to the Great Hall. Lurking in a corner was a face Khlaux didn't think he'd ever see again: the former Golden Knight. Khlaux didn't remember the man's name but, as he studied Khlaux with his one working eye. A chill ran down Khlaux's spine. The Watchtower stiffened next to him, and he knew the man had also noticed.

"The Golden Knight returns from hard work," the former Golden Knight said, offering a polite nod.

Khlaux said nothing, just plowed through the other guards posted outside the Great Hall. The pair flanking the doorway inside opened the doors for the Golden Knight and the Watchtower, paying them proper deference.

How can he not be dead? The Watchtower had smashed his face in. He knew the former Golden Knight would be out for revenge.

The king and the dukes and duchesses turned to look at

him, many with annoyed expressions. He knew they didn't like being interrupted.

"My right hand," King Mikas said, "And Zervan, the Watchtower of Calrym." His face narrowed. "You're late."

Pushing thoughts of the former Golden Knight out of his mind, the real Golden Knight gave his report.

2ND CYCLE OF SPRING

232ND REIGN OF GARCOVI

30

INTERLUDE
UVA THE SHAMAN

Remeria

Spring blossomed and the vibrant colors of Remeria flourished. *It make Uva the Shaman sick.* Uva the Shaman missed Vessia, the desert, the way of life for the Camel Clans. Here, in Remeria, everything became worse. *It make the Plagued Ones look weak.* The Camel Clans, after the massive explosion which destroyed much of the Remerian capital, had fled. Not worth sticking around if random explosions can eradicate half a population. Of the Splintered Manes and Seven Signs clans, there were no more. Poof. Gone in an instant. Most of the clans had suffered. Most of the Vessian people were gone. It seemed a significant portion of the Imbuers died, which severed much of their power. *It make the gods seem foolish and wrong.*

Uva the Shaman's job was to interpret the will of the gods and goddesses and Killiak, lord of lords. She and any other shamans she'd talked to wondered if they'd screwed something up. It didn't seem right—discovering such power to watch it all burn away. As if Tabashi, god of fire, decided he'd had enough of his own people.

The Camel Clans had made camp in the jungle west of Andora and had been there for three weeks. Scouts patrolled the edge of the forest, watching for fleeing strays and riding out to greet them, returning them to the encampment. As far as Uva the Shaman was aware, most of the surviving members of the Camel Clans had found their way in the right direction. She estimated that in the battle and the resulting explosion, they'd lost around thirty percent of their forces. Most who survived the battle hadn't suffered injuries. Those who were, had either been taken captive or died in the explosion. There were a few who needed a couple of days, and they'd be able to ride again.

Uva the Shaman, waiting inside a clearing they'd created, watched as the shamans and Imbuers formed a circle around her and the other important shamans and leaders of the clans. She picked at a dirty fingernail, flicking bits of black into the foliage.

"Are all present?" she asked. A scent of sweat and dirt met her nose. She snapped her head, sending her braids over her shoulder. The smell increased for a moment, then disappeared when her hair landed on her back. She needed a good washing.

When nobody answered Uva the Shaman, she knew all had arrived. "Good," she said. Her tongue met resistance in one of her teeth and she took a moment to pick and prod at whatever was caught. When that didn't work, she picked at the gap with her fingernail, drawing out a bit of—she peered at it closer, her eyes were failing—gristle. She popped it back in her mouth, swallowing. "Let us begin." She spat—some of the dirt from her fingernail had found its way into her mouth. "The Camel Clans have taken heavy losses, but we've also crippled Remeria. Our vows have been fulfilled."

Nods, smiles, and cheers answered her. Uva the Shaman grinned herself, though she'd often been told her smile was more of a grimace. "It make us look strong," she said, grinning wider. The cheers increased. She had to encourage the clans, encourage the people, otherwise they'd feel incapable of doing what needed doing. "It make us victors. But," she said, holding a finger up and pointing at the sky. Everyone looked up, including Uva the Shaman. Green treetops blocked their view. She snorted, spat in disgust. "Though the trees block the view of the gods, they still watch over us. The leaves part for the eyes of the gods, don't you worry. Nothing goes unseen. Underground, underwater, undertree, under *nothing*. The gods watch, and judge, and offer their favor . . ." she looked around at them, before continuing. "Or their displeasure."

Murmurs among her audience. The leader of Glory Blades gave her a pointed look but said nothing. Uva the Shaman ignored them. Shamans interpreted the gods. No leader could influence the shamans. It was the other way around. And that's why the leader of Glory Blades spoke not. Those who disbelieved the shamans would find themselves cast out of the Camel Clans or, for more serious infractions, dead.

"Remeria is not a worry anymore. Their power is gone, their military broken, their people worried. It make me happy." The other shamans nodded at this. "We lose lots, yes. Flaytz greets many people in death. But our brothers and sisters will not go unforgotten. We have new tasks now. The Camel Clans must remain united, must leave Remeria. We'll return to farm and settle these lands. But we must also ride towards the other country who've attacked us in the past. Our other rival, Calrym." Uva the Shaman shivered, a thrill of the gods making its way down her body. "We'll make them pay. We promised the gods we would. Calrym will fall like Remeria, and the Camel Clans will start being recognized as a true people. The shamans have discussed things, yes. Calrym and Remeria will be told what to do, yes. They will feel what it's like to have somebody's boot stamp on their head. The Camel Clans will rise to victory again!"

Uva the Shaman sneered and stomped her foot once, twice. The circle followed suit, stomping their feet in disgust, pounding the Remerian soil beneath their heels.

"The gods have spoken, and it make me happy," Uva the Shaman said, raising her hands above her. She looked up in the sky's direction, seeing only trees, but knowing the gods watched her. "Though many are injured and need rest, we ride when all are able. We ride to crush Remeria for Killiak, lord of lords!"

Everyone cheered. The will of the gods felt good.

31

ASHEN HYREL

Anepolis, Calrym

Mid-spring meant more of the same for Ashen. One cycle rolled into another, and she didn't have time to notice. The continued regular meetings with the King's Council; time spent inside her manor, resting and socializing with Jaspard, Alora, and Tallas Taybold; and at night, she returned to her urchin past, donning a black suit and disappearing into the night, scouting the homes of the other dukes and duchesses, hoping to discover any information which might help her.

After weeks of espionage, she'd investigated Dukes Hemmel and Velturo, and Duchess Arena, and nobody had discovered Ashen. If they had noticed her, she'd have appeared an urchin wishing for a better life.

Duke Hemmel brought home a new sex partner every night—several of whom Ashen recognized as urchins she used to see around the city's streets. Hemmel didn't hide his enjoyment of younger boys, often leaving his windows wide open. She'd watched him sodomize several—the sounds of a dying cow coming from his throat. She always left before he finished,

One night, she felt brave, and stayed later, to see what he did after. The results horrified her. Ashen witnessed Hemmel contort in ecstasy as he emptied himself, then flung the boy to the floor. Then, still naked, he stormed out of the room. Torn between what she should do and what she wanted to do—she wanted to rescue the boy—her thoughts became interrupted when the naked Hemmel returned, armed with a long carving knife. He took great pleasure in torturing the boy, carving him like a bird. When the screaming finally stopped, Ashen knew Hemmel had finished the job. Retching, she fled. She found out the next night this wasn't a onetime affair. Ashen wished she could aid the young children Hemmel raped and murdered, but there wasn't much she could do other than kill him. Which was already her plan.

Duke Velturo had a few surprises Ashen was unaware of. Aside from being a disgusting slob, she learned he also had a horrible home life. She overheard him arguing with his wife about their two children. Velturo also argued with her about her brother. Sometimes Velturo argued with his wife's brother. Then he'd gorge himself on food while his wife fucked her brother in the next room. Velturo ignored his rude children and struggled to maintain a grip on his sanity. Sometimes he'd rage and throw things against the wall. Sometimes he'd yell and scream—though nobody took him seriously. And sometimes he'd sit at the table, crying as he shoveled food into his mouth. She had to admit she felt sorry for him.

Duchess Arena's secret was also in the open: she was closer to her servants than most people were. Arena had gratuitous and frequent sex with a different servant every night. It seemed she maintained a schedule and had enough attractive housekeepers to spend each day of the week with a different one. There was, however, one man she treated differently than the others. And nobody, as far as Ashen knew, had a clue Arena had such a close relationship with one of them.

Arena's routine, much like Velturo's and Hemmel's, was to come home and unwind. After dinner, she picked the day's servant and lead them to her bedroom where she had them perform extended oral sex on her. Then, once Arena was ready she had the man climb atop her and thrust himself into her. She clutched his shoulders, wrapping her arms around his back, her quivering legs folding themselves around his ass. Duke Hemmel's dying cow sounds were, much to Ashen's surprise, nothing compared to the whimpering and slobbering that came from Arena's mouth. Once Arena had her fill, she pushed the man off her and told them to finish themselves off elsewhere. Ashen had only seen one person fail to last long enough to please Arena, and she'd ordered him whipped.

After sex, Arena expelled the man from her room and another servant would enter and climb into bed with her. They would sleep, his arms cradling her. Ashen had seen the pair wake in the middle of the night and have a much more intimate and mutually beneficial sex. Then they'd go back to sleep, holding one another like a married couple. This man, Ashen noticed, never fucked Arena for the first time on any given day but slept with her every night.

Armed with this information, Ashen reported it to Jaspard, and they sat on it, wondering if they could use it to their advantage.

***

During one of the King's Council meetings, Cithrial tried her best to suppress a yawn, failed, and covered her mouth politely, restraining any sound. Tears formed and she blinked several times, hoping to forgo the need to wipe them, as that would be most unladylike. It worked. She attributed her exhaustion to her near nightly forays into the dark, spying on the other dukes and duchesses. Ignoring her companions, her mind wandered, lusting for sleep. Then, at a peculiar time of the meeting, the doors opened.

Surprised, Cithrial looked over as two men entered. One was, she knew, the Golden Knight. The man who'd taken Tallas Taybold's previous position or, perhaps, a different person, wearing the same armor. The king named the second man—an imposing man of considerable height—as Zervan, the Watchtower of Calrym.

After the exchange of pleasantries and introductions, the Golden Knight launched into his report of the invasion in Remeria.

"Something's wrong," the Golden Knight said. He seemed hesitant to continue. "The Camel Clans have something, or someone. Magicai. Many of them. Or"—he swallowed, the sound audible even from behind the helm—"they have magic themselves."

The king's booming laughter drowned out the laughter from everyone else.

Cithrial smiled but didn't laugh. She had no reason to. She'd learned about the world from Jaspard to prepare for this moment and didn't understand why the Camel Clans couldn't have access to magic. Everyone else did.

"Impossible," Arena said.

"Preposterous," Hemmel said.

"Incon—" Velturo coughed, took a sip of wine, swallowed. "Inconceivable, ah-hah!"

Cithrial kept quiet, observing everyone. Thinking. She wasn't sure how she felt about the situation. On one hand, it wasn't good the Remerians were being invaded. On the other, it meant she didn't have to worry about Calrym being attacked.

The Golden Knight shook his head while the Watchtower's face slid into a grimace.

"It's true," the Golden Knight said. "We saw many villages destroyed. The telltale signs of magical destruction were everywhere. Even in the smallest village, Your Highness. The Magicai don't get hired to protect small hamlets full of farmers. Nobody has the money for that."

"Perhaps King Alondo stationed Magicai throughout the country when he learned of the impending attack," King Mikas said.

"Would you do that, Your Highness?" the Watchtower asked. "Or would you utilize the Magicai in a more strategic way?"

The king's eyes narrowed at the Watchtower. "You forget yourself, Zervan."

The Watchtower bowed.

"But I also agree," the king said. "It wouldn't make sense if Sedoa didn't surround himself with the very best protection, which would mean bringing all the Magicai to Andora. It's the safest plan. The best walls, the most military, the likeliest target. Where else would he hold out? Camels aren't charging through those walls, and as far as I'm aware, the Camel Clans don't have the ability, or knowledge, to create siege engines."

"That's not all, Your Highness," the Golden Knight said. "We followed the trail of destruction left in the wake of the Camel Clans. We ended up outside Andora. They're under siege, surrounded by the Camel Clans. Your Highness, the casualties suffered by the Camel Clans were minimal, which shouldn't have been the case. There was a battle in one of the smaller towns. We found many dead Magicai, Your Highness. They killed *Magicai*. Confirmed. I saw the bodies myself."

Murmurs passed through the room.

"We've been betrayed," Hemmel said. "The Magicai must be working with the enemy. It's the only option."

"We can't have been betrayed," Cithrial said. "Unless the Magicai are people hired by Calrym, they don't work for us. They follow their own rules and laws, and none of them are to protect the people of Calrym."

"She has a point," Arena said. "I think something is amiss, though. The Magicai would not join an attack against Remeria. Aside from Calrym, Remeria spends the highest amount on hiring the Magicai services. If anything, the Magicai would protect the Remerians, not aid in annihilating the country. Perhaps the Golden Knight was onto something. Perhaps the Camel Clans have their own magic." Arena frowned, seeming unsure, then transitioned into a sneer. No doubt the thought of the Camel Clans having power she didn't have access to upset her.

Velturo let the rest of a mouthful of food dribble out of his mouth, back onto his plate. He sat back, like nothing revolting had occurred. "There is another option, ah-hah." He paused, ensuring he had the attention of everyone in the room.

"Don't keep us waiting, Velturo. If this is the first useful thing you have to mention, I'd prefer to hear it fast," King Mikas said.

"Yes, my lord. Have you heard of the Elkavich? They're a rogue group of Magicai who—"

"Damn it, Velturo," King Mikas slammed his fist on the table.

"Ah-hah," Velturo said, because he couldn't let himself talk without finishing it with a stupid laugh.

Hemmel cleared his throat. "While I share the same dubious thoughts you, Your Highness, I cannot help but wonder if Velturo is onto something. What if the Elkavich are riding with the Camel Clans? Yes, yes, I know they're just a myth," he waved away the king's scowl. "It is, however, possible they exist, since the Magicai do. It's a possibility we must, at least, entertain. For the people, and for the country."

"If there is a group of underground Magicai," Cithrial said, "we could be fucked." *Not very prim and proper, but . . . it gets the point across.*

"Indeed, ah-hah."

"Certainly," Hemmel said.

"It is a possibility," Arena said. She took the smallest sip of wine anyone could've taken.

"We need to consider our response," Chancellor Bertrand said, who'd remained silent until that moment. He folded out of the shadows like an assassin, taking advantage of the moment. Except he wouldn't be capable of murdering a fly. "Whatever you decide, my lord, I'll draft and send over."

"Sedoa's surrounded, you damn fool," King Mikas said, backhanding Bertrand. "Are you daft? Who's going to get the message through? And what are you intending to write? 'Sorry, Sedoa, we can't walk over there, but here's a piece of kindling to help keep the city warm'?"

"No, my lord," Bertrand said.

"Right. Get back in the corner and keep quiet. I need to maintain a cool head and you *never fucking help.*"

"My lord," Bertrand said, bowing, and retreating into shadows.

"If I may, my lord?" the Golden Knight asked.

King Mikas nodded.

"We need to shore up our defenses in the east. I can send Captain—"

"No," King Mikas said. "The east doesn't matter. If the Camel Clans are coming, they're coming. Let the east rot. We'll take care of ourselves."

"And what of Lochwall? Our friend, Duke Scayde Haklon?" Arena asked.

"Does anybody actually like Scayde?" King Mikas asked.

"No," Hemmel said.

"Absolutely not, ah-hah."

"And here I was, thinking I was alone in finding the man repulsive," Arena said.

Cithrial leaned forward, wondering how many people she was about to upset. "I don't know the Duke of Lochwall. But I know we have a duty to protect innocent people. It's why we're here. You may complain or bitch about the money. It might even be inconvenient but if the eastern side of Calrym is destroyed, what, pray tell, do you think we'll have to rule over?"

"Ourselves," Hemmel said, snorting in disgust.

Arena offered a small smile in Cithrial's direction, as if she were comforting a child. "Do we care about ruling? Let us take solace in saving our money. We can go elsewhere and spend it. I am sure we could pool our funds and purchase the entirety of Qothe."

"Fuck the citizens, ah-hah."

"But we have—" Cithrial said, interrupted by the door opening yet again.

Another armed and armored man entered, this time followed by sounds of shock and gasps.

"What are you doing here, Alyst?" King Mikas asked, face reddening.

"Relax, my dear uncle, relax," the man said. A condescending look flashed across his face, then he grinned. "Cyrok is destroyed. We return victorious."

"Where's Harlem?" Hemmel asked.

"Oh," Alyst said. "He didn't make it. Harlem's dead. As per his orders, we burned the capital of Cyrok down. Somehow, Duke Harlem got caught in the inferno. We searched for two entire days, but we found no sign of him. He's ashes, My Lord."

"Well, fuck," Arena said.

"Never liked him, anyway," Hemmel said.

"Poor soul, ah-hah." A clatter came when Velturo dropped

a fork. Cithrial felt gravy splatter her shoes. "Terribly sorry, Cithrial, terribly sorry, ah-hah!"

Cithrial glared at Velturo. "You will pay for replacements."

"But of course! Wouldn't accept any other outcome, ah-hah."

"Enough," King Mikas said, slamming his hand on the table. "My nephew Alyst brings us wonderful news. He also disappoints me greatly. You ignored my orders. You left Cyrok. *Why*, damn it?"

"With Duke Harlem's death, I thought I should deliver the news. Personally," Alyst said. He bowed, hand crossing his heart. A particularly graceful and polite maneuver meant to be extra respectful.

"Straighten yourself up, you damn fool." The king, though red-faced, didn't seem as angry as he should have. "It works out, it seems. You're to lead the defenses in the east. The Camel Clans are going to be invading at some point, we believe." *That was a sudden change. He must want Alyst gone.*

"What?" Alyst's face betrayed his surprise. *Are you wanting a medal for success in the north? No. You're about to return to the field, where a soldier belongs.* She could tell he fancied a better option for king than Mikas Garcovi.

"The Golden Knight will catch you up," King Mikas said. "Do you have men you trust? I want you to only assign officers you trust with your life. Promote people if you have to. This is serious. No room for error, Alyst. Or I swear to Mother Avani, I'll fucking hang you. No more ignoring orders. Clear?"

Alyst nodded. "Yes, Your Highness. Sergeant Kolb Wickam proved himself in the north. Another pair of men, Tauven Shekt and Jafe Valendar, would be solid candidates, too."

"Fine. You're to leave before the end of the cycle but you'll also retrieve Blago Adavir from Madam Zeitwitch. Speak to

Hemmel about it. I think we're all weary enough from a hard day's work." King Mikas addressed the dukes and duchesses next. "Any opposition from you lot, or should we end this early? I want to get home."

It might've been the fastest agreement Cithrial ever witnessed in the King's Council.

32

DEMRI SLARN

Hidehedge, Calrym

The second Cycle of Spring brought fresh pain.

Demri gritted his teeth and, upon trembling legs, stood. He needed to use the bed for support, needed to suppress the urge to scream, to moan, to curse the gods. *Fuck.*

Face scarring, legs throbbing, jaw aching from clamping his teeth all day, Demri took a step. Bolts of fierce torture crawled up his healing bones. Memories of happiness flashed through his mind. Nightmares caused by two decades' worth of struggle, pain, and difficulty surfaced. *Fuck.*

"You're not ready," Caius said. "Get back in the bed."

"F-F-Fuck you."

He took another step. A crashing wave of torment drowned out his consciousness. When he opened his eyes, Caius was setting Demri back on the bed.

"Rest, you stubborn shit," he said. "You'll walk again."

Demri grunted. Before Caius finished pulling the blanket over Demri, he lost himself to sleep, forgetting about his pain, for a moment.

S ince Demri didn't have any Soul Glyphs and was now crippled again, he posed a minor threat to the Elkavich. They'd relocated him to the room he and Caius had been staying in following Doram's attack. When he woke, Doram loomed over him.

"I was hoping we could have a discussion," Doram said.

He wanted to roll over and ignore the man, but the action would prove too painful, if not impossible.

"Do you remember Magicus Vistario?" Doram asked. "Why did you kill him?"

"I k-killed everyone who c-came after m-m-me."

"You didn't kill Myri."

Demri swallowed as Doram arched a brow. "She wasn't a threat," Demri said.

"No, she wasn't. Something I lament. I regret how that relationship fell out of my control. Truly," Doram said. Leaning over, he rested a hand on Demri's shoulder. "She could've made a wonderful wife. But alas, I let her go. Perhaps I'll work on rectifying that error I made so many years ago. Regardless, Vistario was a good man. Incompetent, but good. You could have eluded him easily. It's why I pushed him to go with Myri. I figured you'd leave the pair of them alone."

Demri pushed the hand off. "F-F-Fuck you." He wanted to spit at the man. He wanted a fair fight—they both knew Demri would destroy him if it ever happened. Instead, he asked a question he'd wanted to know the answer to. "Why lie about your appearance?"

Doram shrugged. "I figured if you were searching for the wrong person, you'd find yourself occupied for a long time— call it punishment. It seemed like if you went around killing people, the world would revolt against you, you'd have nowhere to go. I must admit, it surprised me that I delayed you for so long. It surprised me even further how many people you slaughtered. Any time a stranger showed up at Ashmount, I thought it would be you. Turned out you kept me in a perpetual state of disappointment. They say some people never change. I didn't use to believe that, but now I do."

"I will k-kill you."

"I find it unlikely. While I'm here, nobody is going to allow you access to your Soul Glyphs, and I hardly need to run to outpace you. You've learned your place, and I will leave you alone. I just wanted to inquire about Vistario." Doram marched out of the room, pausing in the doorway to address somebody else. "You may reenter, although I think he'll be grumpy for the rest of the day."

Caius entered the room and closed the door behind him as he returned to his post on the bed across from Demri's, bloody knife in hand, filing away.

"I will k-k-kill him."

"Sometime, yes. But not today," Caius said.

No. Not today. But I will kill him. And when I do, he'll suffer. I promise that much, at least.

A waft of lavender brought Demri out of his sleep. It was mid-afternoon, and he was napping. Confined to a bed, he slept when he became tired, then slept more because he was bored. He'd exhausted plenty of books Caius fetched him, ran through countless scenarios on how to enact his revenge on Doram, and reminisced about the meager time he'd had recently with working legs. Opening his eyes—the one scarred by fire took a moment to work—he spotted Myri standing over him.

"I'm leaving," she said.

"What?" Without Myri's presence, there was nobody who

would protect him. Nobody that would give him a voice. The Elkavich didn't trust him, he was certain of that. The only reason they'd allowed him to stay in Hidehedge was because Myri claimed Demri was her husband. Now he was injured and offered no benefit. The Elkavich wouldn't let him go. He wondered if they'd kill him instead.

"I am to journey to Lochwall to ensure our agents have been able to infiltrate the city. If they have, we're proceeding with the plan."

"And that's t-to d-d-destroy the city?"

"Yes."

"There are many p-p-potential allies in B-Buzzard's B-B-Bowl. If you are p-patient, we could gather them."

"We don't need allies when the world is going to burn."

"Grim way of thinking," Demri said.

"Life is grim, Demri." She reached down, fingers brushing his arm. "I'll return. And when I do, we need to talk."

About what?

She offered a smile, eyes narrowed in thought, cheeks tightened. Her mind was, Demri noticed, elsewhere.

What else is there to talk about? These thoughts kept him occupied every day she was gone.

33

SERADAL WINTLOCK & VILLIC THE IMBUER

Andora, Remeria

Weeks of rebuilding the city passed. They patched holes in the wall, though a large stretch of missing wall remained. They didn't have the stone to replace it yet. The season grew warmer, and Sera became more uncomfortable. Some days were stifling—and it wasn't yet summer.

Renard, Sera's page, had run himself ragged. He was transitioning from boy to man. His muscles had toned, and he had grown half a foot taller. He proudly told all who listened about the first few hairs sprouting out of his upper lip and cheeks.

"Cyr Seradal," Renard said, approaching her. As was her custom, she sat beside the fountain. It had become her command station, where she ordered the Falcon Knights and the city's guards and volunteers. The Redclaws took their orders from the Bloody Duchess—who, in turn, took hers from Sera—and the Magicai took their orders from King Alondo himself. The king had given her temporary jurisdiction over everyone, which she found strange—this wasn't her homeland, and she knew nothing of Remerian buildings, cities, or customs. If she had a question, however, there were plenty of people who willingly answered. She just kept things organized. "King Alondo has requested your presence."

"Regarding what?"

"He didn't say. The Bloody Duchess is there. And a Magicus. And Royal, though he's in a bed."

"They brought in a bed?"

"Royal can't walk yet." Renard shrugged.

"Thank you, Renard. Keep everything moving here."

"Yes, cyr," he said, saluting.

Rolling her eyes, Sera made her way across the city's center, crossing several streets—one of which was repaired and boasted new cobblestones—before entering the king's building. There was no official name for it, though some called it the King's Lodge. They hadn't rebuilt the king's original throne room, and King Alondo had requested they don't bother with it until the rest of Andora had been repaired.

"Cyr Seradal," King Alondo said, "be welcome." He waved her in, smiling. She noticed he seemed happy, and that concerned her. While the king wasn't an angry person, she hadn't seen him express this type of levity and found the emotion rather out of character. "Sit."

A half circle of chairs faced the king's throne, while Royal lounged in a bed that had been placed off to the side, facing the king. Royal sipped from a flask, nodding to Sera.

She took the only open chair. On her left sat the Bloody Duchess and the poetic man, Captain Althier. To her right, a Magicus whose name she didn't know and Villic the Imbuer —which was strange because the king hadn't included him in meetings before, unless he was at Sera's side. In fact, she wondered why Villic the Imbuer was there at all. He was supposed to be rebuilding a tannery.

"Thanks to all of you, Andora's restoration has been

progressing in a timely fashion," the king said. "But your services are, in that capacity, no longer needed. Something more important has come up." King Alondo took a moment to hold each of their gazes. "Calrym never came to our aid. It's clear they're hoping the Camel Clans wipe us out."

The door opened, interrupting the meeting. A boy ran to them, sweating and struggling to catch his breath. "News, my lord. Apologies." The boy bowed, his matted hair flopping around as he did. "Word has come from Maceport, Your Highness. The University of Arcanical Arts is gone. Destroyed. All inhabitants are dead."

"What?" the Magicus said, standing. "Impossible!"

"It's not, sir," the boy said, shaking his head. "It's gone. A Magicus told me, himself. All the leaders are gone with it."

"If that's the case," the Magicus said, "Calrym will rule the world."

Sera clutched her knees. "We can't allow that." *They'll kill us all.* Some thoughts need to be spoken. "They'll kill us all."

Nobody disagreed.

<hr>

Villic listened to Speaker translate, but still found it difficult to keep up with the conversation. It sounded like they were angry at the Calrym country.

"They'll kill us all," Sir Seradal said.

Why?

"I think the implication is that without the Magicai to balance the power, Calrym will be insurmountable."

In what?

"It's like not being able to get on top of your camel because it stands too tall."

Villic snorted, almost laughed. Not being able to mount a camel? *People are crazy.*

"Never mind."

"We need to do something soon, before Calrym learns of this news and makes a move against Remeria," King Alondo said. He appeared tired, slouching in his chair.

"So what're we doin', Your Highness?" The Bloody Duchess lifted her claw in the air. "Don'tcha think attackin' would make a good plan afore they send o'er their forces?"

"We have little choice," Royal said. He sipped from his flask. *Like a nursing child.*

"Alcohol has that effect on some people, Villic. They become reliant. It ruins them."

Royal held up his flask. "Anyone else want to erase memories and slip into a glorious slumber aside me? No?"

What?

"Alcohol dilutes the memory, making you forget things. For a time."

Seems like a terrible idea. Villic recalled the foul taste of peshi and had zero desire to try other alcohols.

"It generally is, Villic."

Everyone ignored Royal.

"War brings even the most incompatible family together: father, brother, and son. Best prepare to lose many o' families before the bloody battle is won," Captain Althier said.

"And what of the remaining Camel Clans?" Sir Seradal asked. "If you send an army, they may return."

"What do you think, Villic? Will the Camel Clans return?"

No. If they haven't attacked by now, the godspeakers have new orders.

"Return to your homeland?"

Not this early. Unless they're all dead.

"Then they may ride for Remeria."

I don't know. I'm not a shaman. Killiak, lord of lords, doesn't speak through me.

"Perhaps he should. Tell them your thoughts."

Villic the Imbuer had picked up a few words here and

there during his time rebuilding the city, but he still didn't find the king's tongue comfortable. *No.*

"They haven't returned yet," King Alondo said. "I'm inclined to believe they've fled." The king turned his attention to Villic. "What say you?"

"Tell him what you told me."

"Orders," Villic said.

Everyone's expression shifted.

"That's confusion. Elaborate. Tell them what about the orders, Villic. They didn't hear what you told me, remember."

Villic nodded, until Speaker reminded him nobody else heard what Speaker was saying. "They will have new orders. We don't retreat from battle."

The king nodded. "Good. Let's then consider what we'll do about the impending Calrite threat. We'll need more soldiers."

"The Redclaws'll fight," the Bloody Duchess said. "But if we fight, you'll owe me."

"And what does the Bloody Duchess want?" the king asked her.

She thrust her claw into her chest. "Same thing I said before. Equality. The Redclaws want equality."

"Citizens want to live comfortably fed, watered, and at peace. Unfortunately, they're ignored while nobility grows obese."

King Alondo made a constipated face at Captain Althier.

"That's a glare. He's angry."

The silent Magicus stood. "How, my lord, are we to fight Calrym? We have limited Magicai. We know they have plenty."

The king started pacing, restless. It was as if Carana, goddess of life, had renewed his stamina. "I don't know. If we combine Remerian forces with the Redclaws and Falcon Knights, we have a significant—and competent—military force. We need something to combat the Magicai."

"And who's leading this force?" Royal asked. "Surely the king must remain behind." He sipped from his drink again. His ugly tongue wormed its way around his beard. Villic thought the man looked like a physical representation of Flaytz, god of death: smelly and dirty and evil.

"I can't leave Andora, no," the king said, shaking his head. "There's only one option for leading the army. Sir Seradal, of course."

Sir Seradal gasped. "I couldn't, possibly. I have no experience!"

"You've done well at delegating the reconstruction efforts of the Andora," the king said.

"Aye, and the Redclaws don't hate ya," the Bloody Duchess said.

Royal took another drink before speaking. "The Falcon Knights look upon you with favor."

"Sir Seradal controls a hidden beast indeed, the man who hasn't yet spoken."

Who?

"He's talking about you, Villic."

All eyes turned to Villic. He flushed and stared at the ground. His hand twitched.

"We can't allow him to live," the Magicus said.

"No," Sir Seradal said, "we can't kill him."

The king sat back in his chair. His lip twitched. "It's unwise to keep him here, though."

"You can't let them keep talking, Villic, or they'll decide to kill you."

They can't. I've been good!

"Say that, then."

"I no do bad," Villic said.

Everyone looked at him. He found the floor to be a blessing sent by the gods. After a moment, Villic glanced up and they had turned their attention elsewhere.

The king laughed; others followed. "He speaks the truth," King Alondo said.

Why laugh?

"You spoke the truth. They weren't expecting it."

Villic doesn't lie.

"I meant they weren't expecting you to speak at all."

Villic scratched his bald head, watching them. He didn't know what else to do.

"He speaks the truth," King Alondo said.

She half-listened. Sera couldn't get over what she'd just heard. They wanted *her* to lead the army? It didn't make sense. Sera had led nothing her entire life. She didn't have experience. Didn't have the knowledge. She'd watched some great people lead, sure. But she had done no leading herself. When the Old Vulture had perished, there was no leader. No second-in-command to step up. People had deferred to her, only because the Old Vulture had trusted her a few times.

"We can dispatch our forces, but if we run into the Camel Clans, they'll fight us. Even if we win the battle, we'll lose too many. Calrym is unassailable," the Magicus said.

The king punched his fist into his palm. "We need to try, damn it. I won't let Mikas Garcovi think that just because the University of Arcanical Arts is destroyed, he's elected as leader of Cedain. I won't."

"We'll bring Villic the Imbuer with us," Sera said. *He listens to me. I can make this work.*

"And how'll that help ya? How'll that help *us*?" the Bloody Duchess asked.

"Running into the Camel Clans is dangerous at best. Communication, discussion, a parley is all we need. I think taking one who speaks their language is victory guaranteed."

"It's a risk," King Alondo said.

Villic shook his head. Sera could tell he wanted to speak but was too shy or couldn't find the words. "What is it, Villic the Imbuer?"

His eyes widened when he noticed she looked at him and he averted eye contact. *Such a strange man.* He shook his head again, rocking on his feet. *He doesn't want to speak, but he needs to. We need him to.*

"Villic, we need to know," she said.

He mumbled something. Nobody could hear him.

"What?" Royal asked.

"Speak up, lad," the Magicus said.

His voice got louder but trailed off. "Godspeakers don't listen Villic . . ."

"It's okay," she said. "We need you there to speak on behalf of our intentions. And, if they're willing, convince them to ride to Remeria with us."

Villic shook his head. "No. No. No."

Why is he so afraid of people?

"No, no, no," Villic said. *This is too hard. Mephino, god of courage, help.*

"Just speak."

It's hard. The godspeakers wouldn't listen to me even if I went with Sir Seradal.

"You're going with Sir Seradal, otherwise, you're likely to hang here."

Perhaps it is destined. Flaytz, god of death, calls.

"Piss on Flaytz! You can still live."

Speaker used a Camel Clan curse. Villic's eyes widened. *You are changing.*

"I am merely adapting to my situation. Tell them you're going."

"I go," Villic said. "Not sure can I help."

"Can you fight the Magicai?" the Magicus asked.

Villic nodded.

"Then you'll do great," he said.

Villic stared at the ground, wiped sweat from his forehead. He wanted to go outside.

"Sir Seradal, you and the Bloody Duchess will take command of the Remerian army and march for Calrym in a few days' time," the king said. "Villic will be under your charge, though I admit I am hesitant about the prospect of you traveling with somebody who contributed to all this." He waved his arm around the building.

Nothing wrong with this building. It's better than any tent.

"He doesn't mean the building. He means the entire city. The city you've been helping rebuild after . . . destroying."

Yes.

"I think that's all for this meeting, then," the king said.

Dismissed, Villic stood, allowing everyone to file out before him. Then, when the way was clear, he exited, alone and happy. Nobody bothered him.

"Villic," Sir Seradal said, waiting outside for him.

May Killiak damn you. He grit his teeth, looked at the sky. The sun burned his eyes, but it was better than looking at Sir Seradal's face.

"I hope we can make use of the camels you rounded up?"

Villic nodded.

"Wonderful. I'll see you later."

He let out a relieved sigh as she marched away.

"You're awful with figures of authority. Actually, you're awful with everyone."

Silence yourself, Speaker.

34

EDELBROCK BRENDIS

Lochwall, Calrym

The spring bloodshed had, for the moment, ended. Events at Buzzard's Bowl went on standby. After Marshal Deywin's death, Scayde shut down the tournament. The other gladiators lauded Edelbrock as a hero. Rations halted, but they had enough food to get them through several weeks, although they rationed—and because of the starvation they'd all been through to get where they were, they weren't too affected by it. Weeks crawled by. No games, no fighting, no death. No word from Scayde, no soldiers, no more visits from anyone to antagonize, torture, or humiliate Edelbrock. Nothing.

It was—Edelbrock noted the irony—the happiest he'd been since his last night with Trigg Gelbrandy, when he was sure he'd just become one of the richest people in Lochwall.

They received no news from Scayde or anyone else—zero indication of what was happening or why they'd been ignored or when to expect the games to resume. They'd dragged the bodies of the soldiers, and Marshal Deywin, as close as they could to the compound's entrance, and guards had removed them. None of the gladiators had seen or heard anything since.

As the second Cycle of Spring began, Edelbrock wondered if that season of Buzzard's Bowl would ever resume, or if Scayde had cancelled it.

The gladiators trained until their food got so low, they realized they'd need to conserve energy, and still no food arrived. And then they ran out of food altogether.

Weakened, they remained in their beds for most of the day.

"Why do you think they're starving us? They haven't given any indication of what they want," Edelbrock said. It was a conversation he'd had with Savakkis at least ten times since Scayde halted the seasonal competition.

Savakkis rolled over to face Edelbrock. "It makes no sense. If they want something particular, they should've delivered their demands."

Like all the men, Savakkis slept naked. Edelbrock found his eyes drifting down the bronze skin, matted with scars, toned muscles, and in Edelbrock's opinion, meeting near physical perfection. Then he caught himself and returned his gaze to Savakkis's face.

It wasn't the first time Edelbrock caught himself examining Savakkis. He wondered why. Edelbrock had been with Trigg before—but that was business. Or was it? He'd always found Trigg Gelbrandy handsome, but figured it was a respectable handsome. Admiration, rather than lust. Admittedly, he did enjoy the passionate part of their relationship, but Edelbrock figured it was because of his marriage, and the thrill of doing something bad.

"What was that?" Savakkis asked. He stood, pulled on a pair of the gladiator trousers they all wore, and cocked his head, listening.

Edelbrock heard it, too. It sounded like the heavy boot-steps of marching soldiers.

"House Haklon, attend me!" The voice Edelbrock recognized as Tanibris—Scayde Haklon's head servant.

"Let's hear their demands, then," Savakkis said.

Edelbrock threw on his clothes, then followed Savakkis and the other gladiators out of the sleeping quarters. Tanibris posed in front of a group of armed soldiers—swords out—hands clasped behind his back. His thin lips grimaced as he surveyed the gladiators filing in.

When they'd lined up in several rows, Tanibris's monotonous voice broke the silence. "Mmm . . . Lord Haklon, Duke of Lochwall, hopes you've enjoyed the reprieve from fighting in Buzzard's Bowl. After the good marshal's untimely death, Lord Haklon commanded the season to halt. If it were up to me, I'd have you all killed. Lord Haklon is a better man, however, and desires the season to continue. He is mournful over his favorite employee. Expect further ramifications. A fresh delivery of food and water will find its way here later this afternoon, as we know you've been out for a while." He caught the look of a gladiator. "Yes, we keep track of your supplies. The Lord is no fool. The season resumes tomorrow. Anyone who cannot take part —injuries or other ailments included—will be put to the sword."

Tanibris turned and, after the soldiers parted, strode back the way he'd come, his guards backing away from the gladiators, swords raised, readying themselves as if in battle.

"Ramifications?" Chellie asked, then laughed. "We're all fucked."

Murmurs of agreement passed through the crowd.

That night, they received instructions. Edelbrock would fight with Savakkis and Chellie. The House feasted on the fresh food and, spirits rejuvenated, broke into groups to laugh, wrestle, spar, or discuss the following strategies for the continuation of the season.

"Come with me," Savakkis said to Edelbrock.

Intrigued, Edelbrock followed Savakkis into one of the sleeping quarters, finding it empty.

"We have much to consider, Edelbrock." Savakkis sat on a bed. Edelbrock's eyes traced the man's muscular chest, wondering what it would be like to—

"Edelbrock?"

He snapped his eyes to Savakkis.

"Are you okay?" he asked.

Edelbrock nodded. His gaze drifted across Savakkis's wounds—they now shared missing ears, Edelbrock's lost in torture, and Savakkis's lost in the arena.

"I'm fine," Edelbrock answered. Something about the man made him nervous. He wasn't sure if it was because Savakkis was the leader of the gladiators in House Haklon or something . . . more. Savakkis was an intimidating, but handsome, man. Outside of Buzzard's Bowl, without all the scars, Edelbrock assumed he would've been popular with the women. He noticed growth happening in his own trousers.

"If you like men, just say something," Savakkis said, laughing. "How many times are you going to be caught staring and not acting? Plenty of us have lain with a man or two in here. There aren't many women forced to fight in Buzzard's Bowl, so options become limited."

Edelbrock cleared his throat. "You've been with a man?" He sat on the bed adjacent to Savakkis's. He wondered what it'd be like to be with a man here. With Trigg, it had been a secret. They'd completed their acts in the privacy of a bedroom. Here, in Buzzard's Bowl, there wasn't much privacy. Anybody could enter the sleeping quarters at any moment. And Edelbrock wasn't even sure if he liked men. He'd done what he'd had to do with Trigg to get what he needed. But he had enjoyed it. Probably more than he'd like to admit. The thought of doing anything similar with Savakkis almost made Edelbrock squirm—in a good way.

"Most of us have. You haven't? I figured by now you might've. Buzzard's Bowl can get lonely, and people are often here far too long—if they live, that is. We need some way of relieving stress. Why not do it with somebody who understands a man's body? Once we get out of here, well, *if* we get out of here, most men agree that whatever happened inside the Bowl stays here. There are few exceptions, but they enjoyed their male counterparts even before coming here."

"I was with a man once before." Edelbrock told Savakkis about everything that happened to him. He told of his plans to enact his revenge on Scayde, his former wife, Tanibris, and Chardaine—the barrister from Roachford and Singleton's law practice.

The evening wore on, and nobody entered the room, being occupied with their last night of freedom from Buzzard's Bowl. By the time it had darkened, Savakkis had moved to Edelbrock's bed. They sat and talked the hours away. They discussed the arena and various battles Savakkis had fought in the past. Of Edelbrock's experiences in the military, how he'd met Jaylena, their marriage, and his appointment to nobility by King Mikas Garcovi. They spoke of what they'd want to do if they ever freed themselves of the gladiator life —Edelbrock of revenge, and Savakkis of settling down and living a simple life, a life of a farmer with a lover, and perhaps some children.

And then, out of nowhere, a hand gripped Edelbrock's thigh.

"We may only have the one night," Savakkis said, leaning closer to Edelbrock and lowering his voice to a whisper. "Are you interested in making the most out of an unpleasant situation?" He exhaled, and a warm breath teased Edelbrock's ear. The hand on Edelbrock's thigh tightened for a moment, sliding up his leg. A stray finger brushed his hardening manhood.

A monster took hold. With the prospect of death in the morning, he surged forward, pressing his lips against Savakkis's. In seconds, they were naked, kissing and fondling. Warm, sweaty hands groped each other in the darkness.

Their lips met again, warm tongues entangling. And then Savakkis pulled away, lips trailing down Edelbrock's neck, then his chest. Edelbrock shivered with anticipation, knowing full well where this was heading. A fleeting thought of Trigg and how he'd never turned him on in the same way entered his mind, but then his trousers were yanked down and his cock met the wet warmth of a mouth. He squirmed and moaned while Savakkis's head bobbed between his thighs, tongue working its way around his manhood.

He remembered when Jaylena would give him similar pleasures, and how she hated doing so. It had been so long since he'd felt good. He couldn't help himself. Edelbrock grasped the back of Savakkis's head and pushed it down, just liked he'd done with Jaylena. Edelbrock groaned in pleasure, his cock sliding into Savakkis's throat.

Savakkis choked, gagged, and Edelbrock's hips did the rest of the work. He thrust himself deeper and deeper. Hands clamped down on Edelbrock's thighs, squeezing them, urging Edelbrock on. He closed his eyes, bit his bottom lip, thrust farther.

He stiffened, shuddered, and his semen spilled into Savakkis. "Ah, fuck." His hand slipped from the Savakkis's head.

Gurgling, gagging, and sputtering, Savakkis removed himself. "You're a selfish prick." He coughed, a tear trailing down his cheek.

Jaylena had never appreciated that, either. He'd used to think it was Jaylena unwilling to cooperate. It occurred to him then that perhaps when Trigg had done it to Edelbrock; it had been rude, though it hadn't bothered him. Now he felt ashamed about doing it to both Jaylena and Savakkis. "Sorry," he said, though it came out as a breathless whisper. *By Avani's blessing, that was good, though.*

"I'll see you tomorrow. Get some rest." Savakkis stormed out of the sleeping quarters.

"I'm sorry," Edelbrock said, louder.

Spent and too exhausted to care about hurt feelings, Edelbrock didn't pursue him and realized he should've. It was, he considered, before falling asleep, another of his faults.

The following morning, Edelbrock woke, cleaned himself, ate, and waited for the day to pass—the event he'd fight in wasn't until the afternoon. He did some exercise, practicing with a few weapons he felt most uncomfortable with; he found the flail and scythe to be almost unwieldable. Edelbrock and Savakkis avoided one another.

"You ready to fight?" Chellie asked. As always, she was shirtless. Her small breast bobbed and bounced as she walked closer, a ragged scar where the other one had been.

"I think so."

"I've been considering the words Tanibris left us with. About how we were going to face some sort of punishment. I think that's going to happen during our fight. It only makes sense—why else would they group you and Savakkis together? And why do I have to be dragged into it?" She smiled, shaking her head when he went to answer. "I don't mind. I'd rather fight to the end with Bloodlines and the Savage," she said.

In truth, Edelbrock had forgotten all about Tanibris and his parting words. "I've given it a lot of thought, but I can't reason what it'd be. Other than a fixed battle."

"That's what I think, the bloody cunt." She spat to show her disdain for their House leader. "One day, we'll hang the man by his balls."

"They'd just rip off," he said, though he appreciated the gesture.

He grimaced. During the Battle of Leeward, he'd witnessed some of his men try this tactic on a traitor who'd broke ranks. It didn't work the way they wanted—and was more than a little bloody. After their failed attempt, they hanged him the proper way. That method was tried and true for a reason.

Chellie sparred with Edelbrock for a few hours, and then Savakkis came to collect them.

Time to return to battle.

35

ASHEN HYREL AND TALLAS TAYBOLD

Anepolis, Calrym

"We need to form a plan," Jaspard said. "If what you say is true, and the Camel Clans threaten Calrym, we're in trouble. And, without the University of Arcanical Art's presence, the leadership will scramble to attain the services of any Magicai they can muster. If they're surrounded by Enforcers, we won't be able to act. I hate to say it, Ashen, but it's time."

As had become the norm, they sat in the den. Jaspard in his favorite chair, Ashen in hers. Tallas Taybold loomed in a corner, halberd clutched in his hands, silent.

Jaspard sighed as his hand reached into a pocket, searched for a moment, then he pulled it out. He sighed again. *Must be out of his sugared honey chews.* "You're certain you can't slip poison into their food?"

"I could slip poison into Velturo's food. Maybe. There's no way I could get to anyone else's without being noticed. Even if I got there first, it wouldn't matter. The guards—"

"Yes, the guards," Jaspard said. "The guards are vigilant

and don't allow anyone inside alone to avoid this. So, poison Velturo and cause a distraction."

"And then what?" Ashen asked. "Run around the table and drip poison into everyone else's food? Nobody eats. It's rare when I see anyone drinking. Arena drinks wine, sometimes. I don't think I can kill them all myself." *And would I if I could?* She didn't know—they were all terrible people, so she figured somebody should.

The sound of the halberd's butt thumping on the floor, followed by Tallas's voice. "I may have an idea."

Tallas glanced out the window of the carriage, hands clutching the halberd on his lap, palms sweaty. He was nervous, but why? Was it because they'd planned the murder of several dukes and duchesses? The murder of a king? Perhaps. Fighting didn't make him nervous. The punishment for being caught murdering a king? *That* made him nervous.

Escorting Duchess Cithrial had become a contract he'd taken more seriously than any other—even his duties as the Golden Knight. There was something about her he admired. Something he enjoyed and he felt responsible for her. If she was in power, he thought the world might be a better place. *But would she take power?* He didn't know what she'd do once they'd killed the king and the dukes and duchesses. Would the city allow them to live?

The carriage halted. They'd reached the palace. He hopped out, held his hand out to receive Duchess Cithrial, helped her down, then turned and led the way inside. This time, a retinue of guards attended them.

As he led her towards the Great Hall, Tallas felt the sack of Black Dust thumping against his back every other step.

"Thank you, Tallas," Cithrial said. She left her retinue in the hallway, and the door guards allowed her entry into the Great Hall, bowing to her. Inside, the king whispered to Chancellor Bertrand while Velturo shoveled food into his mouth and Arena lounged in her chair, bored. Hemmel's gaze latched onto her, as was often the case.

Smiling, Cithrial took her normal route to her chair on the other side of the long table. She slipped her hand up the sleeve of her velvet gown, uncorking the small vial strapped to her wrist. Keeping her hand upright, she glided over to Hemmel. *No.* She couldn't do it. Not yet. She pressed the cork back into the small vial, made her way to her seat, nerves getting the best of her. *I can't.*

Tallas Taybold tapped his finger on the halberd's hilt. He kept meeting the eyes of the other guards who were all waiting for the same thing he was: commotion inside the Great Hall. Time stretched on.

The commotion never came.

At the end of the meeting, Cithrial stood, and feeling guilty, exited the Great Hall, where Tallas Taybold and his men greeted her. She noticed confusion flash across the man's face. She'd have to explain, of course. *Explain what?* She was too nervous to do what she'd promised Jaspard? He'd be fuming. *Speaking of Jaspard . . .*

Strangely, Jaspard Couliac, followed by a group of armed men, were marching down the hallway in her direction. He wore a beaming smile.

"Lady Hyrel," Jaspard said when he closed the distance, smile dissipating. "I presume all went well?"

"No," she said. It was all she could get out.

Jaspard's lip quivered. "I see." He turned on his heel and marched out of the palace without another word.

Tallas Taybold hopped into the carriage, closing the door behind him. They rode in silence. When they reached the manor, he opened the door, assisted Duchess Cithrial out of the carriage, then followed her inside. The scent of pastries Bethinda, the house servant, was baking, assaulted him.

"Why did you not proceed with the plan?" Jaspard's angry voice said. Tallas couldn't see the man yet.

Turning the corner, he followed Duchess Cithrial—*no, Ashen, now that we've returned*—into the den.

"I couldn't execute the plan," she said. "There wasn't an opportunity."

Jaspard shook his head. "Next time," was all he said. He shoved his hand into his pocket, pulled out a sugared honey chew, and thrust it into his mouth, glaring at Ashen the entire time.

"Yes, next time," she said. "I promise."

"You owe me," Jaspard said. "I saved you. We made a family together. I—"

"I'm well aware," she said. Ashen sounded exhausted. And, by Tallas's assumption, she deserved to be. She was a child, after all, but he couldn't help feeling like her guardian, even without the money.

Watching Jaspard and Ashen argue was difficult for Tallas. Jaspard paid him, but his duty was the protection of Ashen. Should he have to pick a side, he wasn't sure where to go. *I like Ashen, but she doesn't have the money.* And money was required to live. He decided he'd follow Jaspard, should the need to pick a side arise.

W*ell, ain't this a mess dirty enough for hired help?*
Ashen lay in bed, wondering what to do. She'd made a promise, and she didn't want to break it. She would have to complete the mission during the next meeting. *I won't ruin this.* Jaspard had saved her life, had taken her in. It was time to pay her debt.

A couple of tense days passed. Tallas Taybold shadowed Ashen, waiting for the next opportunity. His men were eager to act. Tallas had informed them of the plan, of course, and it irritated them it hadn't proceeded. Tallas wasn't sure he shared their proclivity. In his professional opinion, taking out the leaders of the city—the country, actually—would lead to more death and problems. And who would rise to power? Anything could happen, and that's what concerned him. Sometimes the bastard you knew was a safer bet than the bastard you didn't. And, Tallas admitted, King Mikas Garcovi was far from the worst person, although Tallas himself couldn't stand the king. A king's selfishness and lack of understanding what his own citizens wanted or needed wasn't anywhere near as bad as somebody who consistently harmed their own subjects.

D uchess Cithrial exited the familiar carriage, taking Tallas Taybold's hand. Her retinue followed her. She had left the vial of poison at home. Jaspard would get what he wanted, but she'd accomplish it her way. And, truthfully, she didn't think she could slip the poison into anyone's food or drink without being noticed. There were too many eyes.

Instead of creating commotion by murdering somebody, she'd utilize her knowledge.

"My lady," Tallas said, "we will await you here, if you need anything." He'd had a long talk with her regarding the need to follow through on this plot. Today. No doubt he'd been parroting his employer's words rather than giving her his own. Though he said one thing of note, "Honorable people die young. If you don't act, somebody else will, and you'll find your body missing its head."

She nodded. "Thank you, Tallas." She could hear the implication in his voice—don't fuck this up. *I'll try not to.* Nervous, she strode through the doors. *Prim and proper, prim and proper. Best not forget or I'll be a squatter.* She reminded herself of her past, and her time spent living on the streets. Her confidence returned. If there was one thing she didn't want to relive, it was her life of poverty and neglect. She'd do what she had to.

Tallas took stock of the other men in the hallway, the ones who weren't his. He leaned against the wall, counting. *Seven, eight, nine, plus the king's two door guards . . .* He was fortunate the Golden Knight and the Watchtower of Calrym were missing. Either of them would put up a much stronger fight than anyone else here. Sighing, he removed the large sack he carried, laying it on the ground.

And then the noise he was waiting for, followed by a muffled scream, "Guards!". Tallas nodded to his men, and they pulled their hoods up and placed handkerchiefs over their mouths and nose.

With one hand, Tallas threw the large sack of Black Dust into the air, then closed his eyes.

"The Golden Knight and the Watchtower of Calrym have taken a considerable force and marched east. They—"

"I'm sorry," Cithrial interrupted Chancellor Bertrand. "We know this. There are other important things we need to discuss. Things of a more immediate concern."

Everyone turned to look at her.

"This is both unusual and frightening behavior from you," Arena said.

"What could a child have to report?" Hemmel asked.

"Mmm," was all Velturo managed. He was digging into lamb root pie with a fork.

"What information do you have?" King Mikas asked. He was, Cithrial noted, intrigued. He twisted a gem on one of his fingers, around and around, watching her.

Cithrial straightened in the chair. She needed to appear serious and authoritative, and since she wasn't yet an adult, she knew this was going to be difficult. "There is a spy among you."

The laughter drowned out any other words she might've said.

"Preposterous," Hemmel said, "we're *all* spying on each other!"

"It would seem that Lady Hyrel is as juvenile as she appears," Arena said.

"Foolish! Simply—ah shit, dropped it again, ah-hah." Velturo started mopping up lamb root pie from his lap.

"Is that all, Lady Hyrel?" King Mikas asked.

"No," she said, shaking her head. "I know far more about some of you than I care to admit." Cithrial placed a piece of parchment on the table. "An anonymous letter." *Written by Jaspard.* "It was dropped off two days ago and addressed to me."

They looked unconvinced. Cithrial decided she needed to hit them harder, shock them.

"Hemmel collects urchins off the street, returns to his

manor, sodomizes them, and butchers them. Velturo's wife is more in love with her brother than Velturo and fucks him regularly while Velturo cries and eats himself to death in the kitchen. Arena doesn't just have sex with her servants, she's in love with a particular servant and sleeps with him every night."

A moment of silence and then pandemonium.

"I knew Velturo was lurking outside my manor," Hemmel said.

"Revolting. You kidnap little boys on the street and then *murder* them, Hemmel?" Arena asked.

"Arena has always had a problem with her servants. She cares more for them than for anything else, ah-hah."

"You're all broken, sick, and twisted," King Mikas said. "We know this. Please, let's move on to important things." His face was reddening in anger and was directing an icy glare in Ashen's direction.

"Wait," Hemmel said. "Who's turning us against one another?" He looked at one of the silent dukes, who attended the meetings for posterity, but never contributed. "You weren't mentioned, Meeks. Are you trying to elevate your position? Are you trying to curry more favor?"

Arena sneered at another duke across the table from her. "I have had my eye on you for a while, Odar."

Velturo had turned to a duchess. "I saw you outside my window a cycle ago, Rensla, ah-hah."

And, while everyone was arguing, Cithrial took out a small knife and flung it into Velturo's lap. The handle bounced off his gut, and when he realized what had happened, he'd drawn his own knife and stood.

"I saw that, Hemmel ah-hah!"

"What are you talking about? I did nothing."

More knives appeared.

"*GUARDS!*" Bertrand screamed.

It was the signal Tallas Taybold was waiting for.

Black Dust flung into the air. The combination of black and red pepper and sawdust coated the hallway and all occupants. Tallas Taybold and his men had crouched and protected their faces, though, and held position for a few moments. Then, when the cries of surprise diminished and shifted into the sneezing and complaints of eyes burning, Tallas and his men rose.

In moments, the guards and the king's soldiers guarding the doors, lay in a pool of blood and bodily muck.

"Hold the hall," Tallas said. Halberd in hand, he navigated over the dead bodies and crashed through the doors.

Chaos blossomed.

The dukes and duchesses lunged at each other, stabbing with the knives none of them should have had. King Mikas and Chancellor Bertrand huddled in a corner, slinking away from the commotion towards the exit.

With Cithrial dead and forgotten, Ashen flung herself under the table. She retrieved the pouch of Black Dust she carried on her, gripping it in her right hand, ready to fling it at anyone who approached her with a knife. The duke, named Meeks, slipped under the table, knife in hand.

"Just looking for refuge," Meeks said, noticing Ashen. But something about his face said otherwise, and when he got closer, she crushed the pouch into his face. "You bitch, you've blinded me!" He dropped the knife, digging at his eyes with his hands.

The doors crashed open. Ashen saw a pair of booted footsteps and a familiar thumping noise. The haft of a halberd.

Tallas Taybold closed the doors behind him. Although he didn't have to worry about anyone escaping—he had six men in the hallway—he bolted the doors to slow anybody who tried and prevent unknowns from entering.

Cowering to his left, the king hurried over. "Thank Mother Avani, it's chaos! You've saved me—you will be rewarded."

Tallas looked into the king's eyes. "Do you not recognize me, Your Highness?"

"Should I?"

"I served you for four years as the original Golden Knight, so I would think you would."

The king's jaw dropped. "You look different."

"I'm missing an eye, thanks to my replacement."

The king swallowed. Shouts and cries continued.

If Tallas had still been the Golden Knight, he might've charged into the frenzy in a wild search to ensure his charge was safe. He wasn't the Golden Knight anymore, though.

"I'm glad you're safe," King Mikas said.

Chancellor Bertrand stepped in front of the king. "Let us through or find yourself at the mercy—"

Tallas grunted as the halberd chopped through Chancellor Bertrand's throat. Blood and chunks of bone spattered the king's face, and the chancellor collapsed.

"He was unarmed!" King Mikas held his hands up. "*I'm* unarmed! Where is your honor? You are supposed to protect your liege. I'll pay you thrice what I did before—just let me go and we won't have to think about this ever again."

"Honor?" Tallas laughed, pointing to his scarred eye. "I tried that, once. Honorable people die young. I have, however, been fortunate enough to receive a second chance at life." The halberd swung a second time.

King Mikas's head bounced off the floor with a thump. Like the butt of a halberd. Despite Tallas's reservations about removing King Mikas from his position, it felt good in the moment. It felt right.

Tallas turned to the dukes and duchesses who had stopped fighting and stared at him. He gripped the halberd in his hands and stepped forward. There were more people to depose.

Velturo's body collapsed by his chair, empty eyes staring at Ashen. She looked back at Meeks, who had recovered from the Black Dust and was now scrambling towards her. With a mighty shout and thrust, she plunged the knife into his face. He went limp.

Tallas swiped his halberd through another man—Odar was his name, if Tallas's memory served. The momentum of Odar's fall tore the halberd from Tallas's grip, and he landed in a pool of his spilled gore.

Drawing a sword, Tallas stepped over Odar, boot slipping on a thread of intestine. Regaining his balance, he stumbled to the next closest person—a duchess.

She screamed. He didn't care and drove the sword into her stomach, giving it a quick twist. He kicked her in the chest, pushing her off the blade. She fell to the ground with a moan, and he dispatched her with another quick jab to the throat. He knew her to be Duchess Rensla.

"What is it you want, good knight?" Duchess Arena asked, holding out her polished hands. *Rich people don't have a clue.* "We have all the money you could imagine and enough power to grant you whatever you want."

"Yes," Tallas said, stepping closer. "That's part of the problem." He drove his sword through her chest. She stared at him, unflinching.

"You have made . . ." she said, gurgling. She coughed, a line of blood ran down her pale, smooth neck. " . . . a grievous error."

"No," he said. But he needn't have bothered. She died before she hit the floor.

***

Ashen scurried out from under the table and received a better look at the carnage. Bodies leaking blood. Entrails and gore splattering the table, the chairs, the wall, the doors, and Tallas.

One last man stood: Duke Hemmel.

"Please, sir," he said, retreating as far as he could, back now pressed against a wall. "Let me live."

"So you can murder more children?" Ashen asked, seething.

"What's it matter to you, my lady? They are nobodies, children plucked from the streets. Urchins sapping the city of its resources. Their deaths affect nobody. *They* are nobody."

"*I* was an urchin."

Hemmel swallowed. "Oh."

"Lady Hyrel?" Tallas asked, gesturing at Hemmel, sword raised and ready to strike.

"Kill him," she said.

Hemmel's screams, like the others, faded when the sword connected with his flesh.

***

Tallas wiped the blade on Duke Hemmel's ripped tunic, then sheathed the blade. "A wild success," he said. He then began the task of wrenching the halberd from Odar's corpse. A slurping, cracking noise issued as the blade freed itself from Odar's flesh.

"Now what?" Cithrial asked. *Ashen. The facade is over now.*

"There is a plan," Tallas said. A knock came on the doors.

"What plan?" Ashen asked.

Tallas unbolted the door, pushing it open.

Jaspard Couliac entered, a large retinue of armed men following.

"Stand down, usurpers," Jaspard said. The soldiers, swords drawn, marched into the Great Hall. "Put your weapons down, Tallas. You've done enough." A disgusted look crossed his face as Jaspard glanced around at the carnage.

"My lord," Tallas said. "We've succeeded."

"Excuse me? I wasn't involved in this!" Jaspard turned to a man on his right. "See, Captain, they've lost their minds. Arrest them, immediately."

The guard captain nodded. "Take them into custody. Try not to kill them, but if they do anything hostile, put them down."

Tallas shook his head. He dropped the halberd, held his hands up. "When it comes to politics and power, underestimate no one. Especially those of us with the smallest stake in the game and the largest portion to gain."

"Wise words, Tallas," Jaspard said. "I'll remember that when I'm in power. But at the moment, it's time you quiet yourselves and come peacefully."

"What are you doing?" Ashen asked. *We planned this together. And now he seeks to betray us? Why?*

"I am only protecting the citizens of Calrym, Lady Hyrel."

"My name is Ashen."

"I can't say I much care," Jaspard said.

The soldiers reached her, and manacles closed around her wrists. A similar set clamped over Tallas's wrists, though they fitted him with a ball and chain around his ankle.

"Bring them to the prison, where they'll stand trial for murder, treason, and attempting to usurp the crown," Jaspard said. "And someone send word to Alyst Garcovi. He's next in line for the throne. I assume he'll want to hang these two before being crowned."

Ashen struggled to free her hands, but the manacles were tight. "You're a bastard and a traitor," she said.

The ball and chain scraped against the floor as the soldiers forced Tallas forward. "Most men are." Jaspard smiled.

The ball and chain scraped the edge of the door as the man Cithrial called "Tallas" was dragged out, Duchess Cithrial following. With the soldiers escorting the prisoner out of the Great Hall,, only one man remained: Jaspard.

He paced. "Couldn't have gone better," he said. Jaspard took a seat at the head of the table, where King Mikas used to sit. "Is this what success feels like?" Jaspard stood, hitting the table with his hand. "Yes, yes, I think it's exactly what it feels like." He walked over to the king's body, kneeling, he plucked a gem from the king's hand. "Perfection." Jaspard left the Great Hall.

From beneath the table, Velturo quivered.

36

DEMRI SLARN

Hidehedge, Calrym

Demri forced himself to walk. He needed Caius to assist him, and he often couldn't make it more than three or four steps, but he wanted to be able to walk soon. Needed to. Not a day passed when Demri didn't think about Myri and her parting words: they'd talk when she returned. He both dreaded and looked forward to it.

"Demri," Caius said one evening. "You're getting stronger."

Demri had been so preoccupied with his mind, he hadn't realized he'd made it across the room. "Good." When Doram had broken Demri's legs, the weakened bones had broken in the same place as before—he could feel it. Though a Healer had mended him, it seemed his bones hadn't been completely healed. Whether that was because the Healer hadn't wanted to use his life to do so, or a permanent side effect of having healed after two decades of dealing with it, Demri didn't know.

"We need to b-b-be prepared to leave Hidehedge at a m-m-moment's notice."

"I agree. It makes me nervous, being around all these Magicai while you're powerless."

"P-Powerless? I could—"

"No, Demri, you can't. Be realistic."

Demri grumbled but conceded. Caius was right. He was disabled. Again. And even if he wasn't, it's not like he'd ever trained with a weapon—and even if he had, he didn't have a weapon handy.

"What's the plan?" Caius asked.

"The p-plan?" He turned towards his bed while Caius laid a hand on his shoulder to balance him.

"You always have a plan, Demri."

It was true. "We need to leave this p-p-place."

"I agree, but go where? And what about Myri?"

"We need to f-follow her to Lochwall." Demri took a few wobbly steps.

"Demri, you need to forget about that woman. We should get as far away from Hidehedge, Myri, and any Elkavich as possible. You said it yourself—they're planning to destroy the world. We can't be a part of that."

"Why?" Demri asked. He didn't disagree with Caius's reasoning, but he wanted a solid answer. "What else have we to live f-f-for?"

"Each other. Life. Revenge. Myri?"

"What's the p-point in living for M-M-Myri if I'm t-to stay away from her?"

Caius shrugged. "You're a smart man. You'd figure it out."

"You're useless." He reached his bed and Caius helped him lie down.

Caius shrugged again. He seemed uncomfortable. It was rare when they talked about these things. He twiddled his fingers and stuck them in his pocket. *Strange, you'd think he'd resort to filing his fingers.* Perhaps he was too uncomfortable for even that.

"Demri, I've always been honest with you."

"Except about your entire p-p-past."

"Are omissions lying?"

Demri waved him off. "I'm kidding."

"We should prepare to leave. Ced will help."

"They won't let us."

"They might, Demri. We're a nuisance to them."

"Nuisances are generally discarded."

"Let me talk to Ced. See what he says?"

Demri rolled his eyes. "I c-c-can't wait to see what Ced said."

"I hate you," Caius said, exiting the room.

<hr>

The rest of the day slipped by, and Caius didn't return. Demri hadn't heard from anyone. He was growing concerned when the door to the room opened, and inside walked not Caius.

A masked man with the letter E stitched on his clothing entered. *Erasure.* The leader of the Elkavich.

"Magicus Demri Slarn," he said, taking a seat at the end of Demri's bed. He was careful not to bump Demri's legs.

"Erasure."

"I hear you want to leave Hidehedge, abandoning your wife?"

"It's not that I—"

"I know you'd never abandon somebody you weren't married to."

"B-B-But—"

"Doram said there was no way she'd marry you—and I trust Doram." *Bastard. I could marry her. I just haven't had the proper amount of . . . time with her.* "Nobody spilled your secrets. You don't have to kill your man, Caius." *But I would like to kill you.* "Why do you want to leave?"

"The Elkavich d-d-don't seem to be happy with my p-presence. And D-Doram is not f-fond of m-me." Demri said Doram's name on purpose, instead of his Elkavich name, E-Four. He wanted people to know Doram's name. Perhaps somebody out there held an equal grudge against him, as Demri did. Perhaps somebody might murder the man. *No, that's my job.* And he meant it. He wanted to be the one to kill Doram. The revenge would feel *right*. Just. Proper.

"We can't allow you to leave. Not a free man, anyway."

"You're implying we c-can leave, though."

"You can," Erasure said. The masked face turned to stare at Demri's face. "You need to join us. Become a member of the Elkavich."

"And serve D-Doram."

"You'll have to use the proper codenames. Disobeying is grounds for punishment." Erasure's hand wafted over Demri's broken legs. "And we have punished you enough. Don't make us continue."

"You d-don't have to c-c-continue. Just let me and C-Caius go."

"Once you are inducted as an official member of the Elkavich, you may go. Until then, you remain."

"Why?"

"Because you know where Hidehedge is. We can't allow people to walk around, giving people reasons to investigate. There are already too many tales about the Elkavich floating around out there. Imagine if people had a location to search— we'd have thousands of people milling about. Some wanting to join, some wanting to murder us. Some wanting to extract information, while others would want—"

"Yes, I get it. Fine, I'll join."

Erasure chuckled. "I knew you'd see reason."

"C-Can't say I had m-much choice."

"No, I don't suppose you can." He held his hand out to Demri. "It takes but a moment."

Demri arched a brow, confused. He grasped Erasure's hand. Erasure's grip tightened, then Demri felt a slight shock. He retracted his hand, pained. Glancing at it, he saw a small red mark on his palm—the symbol of the Elkavich. "What was that?" he asked, surprised.

"I should've warned you about the pain, sorry. The mark will allow us to track you if need be. The redness will disappear momentarily." Demri almost laughed. He knew the tracking was a lie meant coerce him into submission. "You and Caius can leave tomorrow. I'll make sure you have a proper code name before you go. And Demri?"

"Yes, Erasure?"

"If I hear you say anybody else's true name again, I'll kill you myself."

"I understand."

Erasure stood. "And one more thing. If you think about crossing us, I'll take away that which you care most about."

"What?"

"If you and Caius run away, I'll kill her. And before I kill her, I'll tell her why I'm killing her. Because *you* betrayed her by not following my orders."

Demri nodded. "Understood." *Asshole.* He looked at his palm again and the red Elkavich symbol had already almost disappeared.

"Good. Your first task is to meet with D-Four in Lochwall. She'll catch you up on the situation."

"P-P-Perfect."

<hr>

The next morning, Demri—with Caius's help—ambled out of bed and down the stairs to eat. It hurt, but it wasn't unbearable. Demri could deal with some pain. He'd been in pain most of his life.

Ced approached them, grinning ear to ear. He carried two plates of food, set one in front of each Demri and Caius. "Word's come down from the top," he said, sitting across from Demri. "I'm to accompany you to Lochwall! We're going to be a traveling group. A whimsical troupe! Ah, to be on the road again. It's been far too long. I can't wait!"

"This is . . . unexpected," Demri said.

"Most gifts are," Ced said.

Caius picked up his fork, stabbing into a sausage. "Are they?" he asked.

"Well, that's what I've always heard. Anyway, on account of your legs, we've procured a wagon to hitch to a horse. It'll be a mite bumpy, but you won't have to walk or straddle a stallion yourself." Ced's gaze swiveled to Caius. "Though, no doubt you've had practice." He laughed, slapping the table like he'd told the world's grandest joke. "Avani save me." He wiped his eyes. "I'll go prepare travel supplies. You two eat up! Oh, and Demri, Erasure gave me your new nickname. You're B-Fifty-Nine." Ced nodded, extricating himself from the table.

"B?" Caius said. "Aren't you supposed to start at A?"

"P-Perhaps Erasure is b-being cour-t-t-teous."

"Maybe. Seems odd, though."

"The As are just p-people b-b-being t-tested or are untrusted. We've b-been here awhile."

"True," Caius said. He dropped the fork and started filing his fingers.

Once Demri had his fill, Caius helped him shuffle outside, where Ced waited with two horses attached to a wagon; two others tied to nearby trees. "In here, B-Fifty-Nine. I already packed the wagon with plenty of food and water. We'll head to Lochwall and be there quick as a snap." He snapped his fingers to demonstrate.

Ced and Caius each took one of the tethered horses, and then they were off, riding and rolling in the city's direction.

"We're going to avoid Pinecrest," Ced called out to Demri. "Erasure doesn't want us spotted exiting the trees. It'd look strange. Should only take two days or so."

Demri nodded, and grimaced as the wagon climbed, then fell over a tree root. The jolt sent shock waves through his legs. It'd be a long ride.

When his injuries weren't pained by the lurches and bouncing of the wagon, Demri thought about the choice he made to join the Elkavich. He found it strange there was no initiation, no ceremony, nothing to commemorate. Perhaps it was a way to speed things along. Perhaps it was all a ruse to get Demri to believe he was part of the group—though that made little sense. If anything, the procedure did the opposite. *Maybe it was Erasure's way of allowing me to leave without feeling guilty about it. Maybe Erasure was doing me a favor.*

The two days of travel reminded him of many days in the past when he'd had to make special accommodations because of his ruined legs. He was lucky to have Caius back then. *I'm lucky to have him now.*

He wished he'd asked Erasure to restore his Well, but he knew the answer would be no. If Erasure wanted Demri to have access to his powers, he would've seen to it.

When the horizon berthed the city of Lochwall, Demri's heart fluttered. When Scayde Haklon's compound, and Buzzard's Bowl, floated into vision, Demri's nerves twitched.

37

EDELBROCK BRENDIS

This time, there wasn't a choice of weapons. Each had only a single club to fight with.

"This is going to get brutal," Savakkis said, hefting the small log in his hands.

They'd already entered Buzzard's Bowl and could hear cheering, though they couldn't see much—only dots of sky and the crowd. They had entered a small, roofed box with no windows, the only light coming from a few holes punched into the roof, providing a limited view of the spectators.

"What's taking so long?" Chellie asked.

Anxiety chilled his blood. He clutched the club in sweaty palms, wondering what might be on the horizon. Scayde had promised retribution through Tanibris. Edelbrock didn't doubt there'd be some hint of that showing itself today.

Then the announcer of Buzzard's Bowl started talking. "Let's welcome our next event . . . this one is special! Lord Haklon's House has volunteered to kick off a series of what we're calling Extreme Events." *There it is.* He knew this would be how Scayde punished them. "Lord Haklon has offered his

House up to take part in unbalanced battles, where his gladiators must overcome impossible odds." The crowd cheered.

"We're dead," Chellie said.

Edelbrock agreed. "It's not sounding great."

The announcer continued. "For today's bout, three members—some of House Haklon's finest—are tasked with navigating a series of corridors, each with their own hazards. If any survive, they will battle six warriors from House Garcovi. These warriors, having been graded as lesser warriors, are all armed with sword and shield, while House Haklon possesses a single club each. With an uphill battle to climb, will we see one of our favored warriors fall? Fighting for House Haklon, we have Chellie—the Chosen Chell!" The announcer waited a moment for the cheers to die down. "And next, we have Edelbrock, the Ass of Lochwall who reformed his image and became Bloodlines!" Louder cheers. "And finally, the leader of House Haklon himself, Savakkis the Savage!" The crowd roared and the box's wall dropped.

A corridor led out of the box and turned to the left a few dozen feet away.

"Careful, there's got to be something amiss," Savakkis said. "I'll take the lead."

"No," Edelbrock said. "Let me." *I owe him this much.*

Chellie stepped forward, glancing at the stone pathway which ended just outside the box. "I'm just as capable as either of you."

"I'm the senior member here, and *I* will take charge." His eyes narrowed, waiting for either of them to issue a challenge. When none came, he exited the box, stepping on the first stone slab of the path. If there was one thing Edelbrock had learned in life, it was that you didn't argue with the chain of command.

Edelbrock and Chellie followed Savakkis, who took careful, deliberate steps. They each examined every inch of the wall and path before taking another step while the crowd spectated from above, staring at them through the open top. The walls reached at least twenty feet, so vaulting over them would be difficult and potentially hazardous. *And who knows what's on the other side?*

Halfway down the hallway and nothing happened.

"What is this, a trick?" Savakkis asked.

"It wouldn't be beyond Scayde to humiliate us," Chellie said.

Edelbrock, behind the pair, shook his head, though neither saw. "Scayde's too sadistic. If he says there are going to be ramifications, it's going to be something awful. Don't be fooled."

Just as Edelbrock finished speaking, the stone slab Savakkis stepped on plummeted. Chellie grabbed his arm, yanking him back. The crowd gasped.

Edelbrock sidled to the edge of the pit and, peering into it, saw dozens of spikes set roughly eight feet below.

Breathing a sigh of relief, Savakkis nodded his thanks to Chellie, then hopped over the pit. At the end of the hallway, the path forced them to take a left turn.

Before Edelbrock finished turning the corner, he heard a scream. He slowed his pace and saw Chellie and Savakkis crouching against opposite sides of the corridor. Trailing down the middle of the stone floor was a line of clear liquid. Both had red marks marring their skin, and Chellie's club was charred black.

Grimacing, Savakkis returned to his feet. "Skip the first stone or watch the middle. Something sprayed from the floor, and it burns. Bad." He grimaced, and Edelbrock saw Savakkis nursing his forearm.

Edelbrock pressed his back against the wall, side-stepping and following Savakkis. On the opposite wall, Chellie mimicked them. He kept his eyes on his feet, glancing up to check on the other two every few steps. Halfway down the length of the hallway he heard grinding, then a grunt, then the tear of flesh and a gasp from the spectators. Edelbrock snapped his gaze to Savakkis, then to Chellie. Chellie grasped a large spike that had bored through her back, penetrating her stomach. Her stomach and intestines lay splattered on the ground, trailing back to her open wound. A rib jutted from where the spike had split it from its cage, and blood burbled from her mouth. She seemed like she was trying to talk, but all Edelbrock heard her say was, "Scayde . . . cunt," and then she gasped, going limp.

"Shit," Savakkis said. He stepped away from the wall, and Edelbrock followed. "We're doomed."

"No." Edelbrock refused to believe that. "We can live. We just need to be smarter. I can't imagine we're supposed to die this way." He thought of his revenge. *For Gordy.*

"There isn't a greater plan, Edelbrock. Sometimes people just die. Weren't you in the military?"

"Yes."

"Then you know."

Edelbrock sighed. It was true. Often there wasn't a glorious send off. Sometimes people just died of food poisoning or dysentery. He knew somebody who'd died of a bug bite that got infected. *Good soldier, him.*

"If anything happens," Edelbrock said, "it's been a pleasure knowing you, Savakkis. And I apologize for what happened last night."

"I return the sentiment, and you're forgiven. In the heat of the moment, we often become overzealous."

"Let's finish this."

They proceeded down the hallway, rounding the corner—this time to the right—and by Edelbrock's best guess, towards the center of Buzzard's Bowl. He saw a wooden door at the end of the corridor.

Savakkis pointed at it. "We're almost out of here."

"And then we just need to beat a two-to-six disadvantage."

"Simple," Savakkis said, grinning.

With Savakkis walking down the left side of the hall, and Edelbrock on the right they got one third of the way to the door when a line of stone sank into the ground, activating something followed by the sound of flowing liquid.

A stream of water sprayed crossed the corridor in front of the door. Then another, and another. New ones activated faster than he could track.

"Acid," Savakkis said.

"Oh." Edelbrock was certain it'd been water.

They glanced at each other and, saying nothing, surged in the door's direction. The longer they waited, the more streams they'd have to avoid or pass through. When they reached the halfway point between their position and the door, Edelbrock passed through the first stream. He tried shielding himself with his shoulder and back, hunching to protect his arms and face. The acid soaked his back, dripping down his body, filled his boots, but he felt nothing. He sprinted faster, passing through another stream, then another. He jumped over a fourth, ducked a fifth, then fell into a sixth spray. That's when the burning started.

The acid bit at his skin, burning flesh. Edelbrock grit his teeth, returned to his feet, and kept running. He heard screaming—though whether it was himself, Savakkis, or both of them, he didn't know.

They collided into the door, smashing through the wood like a battering ram.

Spilling out into a sandy arena, Edelbrock rolled his body back and forth. The sand didn't seem to help, and his body kept burning. He ripped his clothes off, kicked his feet out of his boots, and the crowd jeered and hooted. He used the clothing to wipe as much liquid off as he could. Though his raw skin hurt and burned, he felt immediate relief.

Edelbrock realized there should be six people trying to kill him. He glanced around and didn't see anyone, other than

Savakkis, who was rubbing his body with sand. Edelbrock followed suit, and found it seemed to work better than the clothing. A column of stone stairs climbed up. Following the stairs, Edelbrock craned his neck to see the top. They led to a wide stone platform that stretched across most of Buzzard's Bowl—even above the top level of spectators—then another set of stairs led back down.

"What—" he said. Edelbrock couldn't find more words.

Savakkis, also naked, walked to Edelbrock. Relief crossed his face, though bright pink and red burns patched his skin and blisters were already appearing. Edelbrock knew his body must look similar and, in combination with all the scars from Scayde's carvings, he probably looked worse.

"We're lucky we live," Savakkis said. He gestured to the stairs. "Looks like we need to climb."

Edelbrock agreed.

Together they climbed. When they got halfway up, Edelbrock turned around and sat and caught his breath. Savakkis followed suit.

"There's no wall or railings up there," Edelbrock said. It was just a flat platform, wide enough for two people to lie down.

"Careful footing. We might not have to worry about being flanked."

"Only a fool is putting themselves closer to the edge of that. One wrong step and you're done."

The spectators, silent, watched eagerly. After a few more breaths, Edelbrock clutched his club in one hand and pushed himself up from the stone stairs with the other. Determined, he lurched up the stairs, Savakkis two stairs ahead of him.

Darkness swept over the arena and a cool breeze chilled them, bringing relief.

Savakkis pointed at his groin. "Change in weather is going to make it easier to protect our manhood, eh?"

Edelbrock snorted. A light drizzle started, and the wind picked up.

He felt like it was threatening to blow him off the stairs, so he hunched lower, centering himself. The rain became stronger. A crack of lightning, followed by booming thunder.

Savakkis smacked the stairs with his club. "This can't be real."

"I doubt it is," Edelbrock said. "The Magicai set these up and the crowds enjoy danger, or at least, the illusion of it."

No sooner had he said it and a bolt of lightning crashed into the raised platform.

"I don't think they do illusions," Savakkis said.

"No. I merely meant that the weather wasn't natural."

Savakkis grunted.

They crested the stairs, finding themselves on the flat stone walkway. Six people stood in two rows of three, facing Edelbrock and Savakkis. Each had a sword and shield and wore leather armor. A black scorch mark marred the stone a few feet in front of Edelbrock.

"Together?" Savakkis asked.

"Together."

They lunged toward their opponents.

Edelbrock's club smashed against a shield and surprise washed over him when he realized it was Argdis—a soldier he'd met and fought with aboard *Allegiance*, the ship he'd named in the first event of the season.

His surprise wiped away as two more opponents closed the gap. Edelbrock retreated. He didn't know how this was going to work, having no shield, no armor, and only a club.

The rain made the stones slick beneath his bare feet, which meant it'd be even worse for the ones in boots.

Another jagged line of lightning flashed, crashing into the walkway. One man shut his eyes and screamed. Edelbrock dashed in, cracking the man in the head. Although helmeted, his limp body dropped. Edelbrock assumed he was unconscious. Edelbrock nudged the man's body with his foot, sliding him over the wet edge of the platform, preventing any future threat.

"Mother Avani, help me," Edelbrock said, though no god or goddess had ever intervened to assist him. In fact, if there was a deity up in the sky, Edelbrock figured they probably found his misfortune humorous.

Argdis raised his shield and pointed his sword at Edelbrock. "I'm sorry it's come to this, but it's the nature of the arena. It's either you or me."

Edelbrock hard feet slapping water. He glanced at Savakkis and the trio he was fighting. Savakkis sprinted through them, running towards the other end of the platform. The three bewildered gladiators took a moment to gather themselves before charging him.

"Lay your sword down," Edelbrock said. "It doesn't have to be like this."

"If I don't fight, they'll execute me."

"We need to make a stand sometime. How else are we to get out of this shit hole?"

Argdis frowned, shrugged. "The only way out of here is at the behest of our House leader. You're not fighting your way through the Magicai, the guards, or the walls."

"We already took out plenty of their guards," Edelbrock said. He walked in a circle, keeping Argdis and the other fighter in front of him. "Marshal Deywin is dead."

"Everyone knows that. It's why we've been on lockdown. Good job, but it changes nothing. There will always be replacement soldiers."

"Buzzard's Battalion," Edelbrock said. He didn't think he could convince Argdis of anything. He was simply stalling for time, trying to gather his strength.

"Buzzard's Battalion helped us in the first battle. Make no mistake, I appreciated what you did. You kept us calm and capable, and I believe that without leadership, without something to focus on, I would've died on that ship. But you know what'll happen if I don't kill you. Scayde will ask the crowd and the crowd will vote for my execution. And either you, or a guard, will have to come up here and lop my head off."

"It's true," Edelbrock said. He bent his knees, got ready.

"So, as you know—"

Edelbrock sprang, slamming into Argdis. The man stumbled, and Edelbrock brought the club up into the second gladiator's thigh. A loud snap, and he shrieked.

Edelbrock retreated, examining his club—it was intact. With the man's thigh shattered he collapsed to the stone and crawled away.

At the other end of the walkway, Savakkis stopped running, and his three pursuers surrounded him. He engaged one, driving him back towards the edge, but when the second man's sword flashed at Savakkis's neck, he blocked with the club. The sword embedded itself, and both weapons fell from their owner's grips.

Savakkis looked in Edelbrock's direction. "Win this fight, Edelbrock!"

Savakkis roared, then charged and rammed into a gladiator, taking them both over the edge of the walkway. The spectators, who'd been cheering went quiet, then groaned a second later. Edelbrock's heart lurched, knowing his friend had died.

One against three.

The crackle of booming thunder and the flash of another jolt of lightning. Blinded for a moment, Edelbrock blinked away blotchy vision.

Argdis had regrouped with the two men Savakkis left behind.

Moans came from the man with the broken thigh, who kept crawling away. Edelbrock traded his club for the sword and shield left behind.

"Jennis, right, Leslien, left," Argdis said.

The gladiators branched out to flanking positions while Argdis strode down the middle.

"You're going to let him place you closer to the edge?" Edelbrock asked. "Typical commanding mistake—forcing your men to do something you won't."

Jennis stopped walking. He—no, *she*, her hair was bound in a tail, Edelbrock realized upon closer inspection—looked at Leslien. "He ain't wrong," she said.

Leslien spat on the stone. "I don't care how we does it, but less kill 'em."

"But it's not fair we're closest to the edge," Jennis said.

Leslien shrugged. "Damn it, who cares? Now we's arguin' and for what purpose? He's distracting everyone. Why? Less kill him."

"Enough!" Argdis said, thrusting his sword above his head. "Just take the center, Jennis. I'll switch. It doesn't matter how it's done, as long as he's-"

Yet another crackle of lighting and thunderous boom. Edelbrock ducked, closing his eyes. When he opened them, Argdis lie on the ground, smoking. *Finally, some divine intervention. Thank you, Mother Avani.*

"I'll take center, you take left," Jennis said.

"Weren't your just complaining 'bout that fucker's directions?" Leslien asked, pointing at Argdis's body.

"Ya never did have a large set of balls," Jennis said. "Fine, you take center, Les. I got me a set of giant bear testicles right here."

"I'm fine right here," he said. "Stop changing yer lunatic plans. And there's only two of us, there ain't no center, you stupid cow."

"Oh, so *now* you have a set of balls. Ridiculous."

"You two should get married," Edelbrock said. They reminded him of Jaylena.

"Excuse me?" Leslien asked, looking sick. "Not my type."

"Quickest way to make a man's balls disappear is to

mention marriage," Jennis said. "I wouldn't marry this fool, anyway."

Thinking about Jaylena, his eyes flickered to the King's Stand. He saw Scayde and Jaylena, watching. He snarled. Anger burned in his blood and he attacked. Sword met sword, then shield, then flesh. Edelbrock slashed and stabbed, hacked and thrust, battered and bashed Leslien. He had to stop to fend off Jennis, who'd taken a moment to move against him.

Jennis flailed the sword like a madman, it bounced off Edelbrock's shield once, then again. The third strike Edelbrock thrust his shield against the blow, and the sword spun out of her grip.

"Oh," she said.

He jabbed the blade into her neck.

Clutching the wound, Jennis gurgled as blood streamed down her arm and chest.

"I yield!" Leslien said. He dropped the sword and shield, falling to his knees.

Thunder and lightning crashed and flickered. The crowd started chanting. At first Edelbrock only heard his name being called, but he heard a secondary cry urging him to kill Leslien.

Edelbrock approached Leslien. "I gave you a chance earlier," he said.

"I yielded!"

"KILL HIM! KILL HIM! BLOODLINES, BLOODLINES!" the chants from the spectators filled Edelbrock's ears.

"If I don't kill you, they'll kill me."

He took the man's head off.

38

SERADAL WINTLOCK & VILLIC THE IMBUER

Andora, Remeria

Cyr Patrika Jorst was a fine soldier—more experienced than Sera, more likeable and wiser than Sera, and more respected and sociable than Sera. Long, flowing locks of blond hair dropped past the woman's shoulders; cold blue eyes stared from a pale but slender face. Though she was an upstanding and diligent soldier, she always seemed relaxed, even now, with her hands folded into one another as she stood in front of Sera, one leg crooked. Any of the now-dead leaders of the Falcon Knights would've reprimanded her posture. Patrika was a Hawk, and a green cloak signifying this draped behind her.

Sera's page, Renard, had brought Patrika to Sera, unsummoned.

"Cyr Patrika Jorst," Sera said. She wondered why the Hawk had come.

"Cyr Seradal Wintlock," Jorst nodded, bowing her head in respect. As a Hawk, she had no reason to show deference to any Falcon unless the Falcon became leader of the Avian Knights.

The two women stared at each other for a moment. Renard twiddled his fingers, uncomfortable. *Awkward. The situation is awkward.*

Sera cleared her throat just as Jorst began to speak. They both smiled at one another, waiting for the other to continue.

"Go ahead—" Jorst began just as Sera said, "My apologies."

They smiled again, offering a polite laugh. *There must be a word that means so much more than "awkward".* Sera held her hand out, palm up, gesturing for Jorst to begin. After all, Sera only wanted to ask why the woman was here. They'd never spoken before, other than polite greetings and small talk.

"The Falcon Knights have been speaking with one another," Jorst said.

Sera raised a brow at that. Talking behind her back didn't sound good.

Jorst continued. "We've all agreed you should continue leading us. Although you're younger than some, relatively inexperienced, and haven't been part of the Avian Knights for long, you've shown yourself a capable leader. You've proven you can direct groups, navigate politics, and make informed decisions."

Sera swallowed. This was unexpected. She was waiting for Jorst to reprimand her for taking over the Falcon Knights —though Sera hadn't wanted to find herself in command of anything. It had just happened. The Old Vulture had sent her into Andora, and then she'd fallen in with a king. From there, it just seemed natural. She passed on the information she learned, and people listened to her.

Jorst brushed a loose lock of hair back over her ear.

"I appreciate that," Sera said. And she did. She just wasn't sure it was the right decision. "But I think there are better options to lead."

"You've done well, and everyone supports you, cyr."

Sera laughed. "Please, don't. You're a Hawk. I'm . . . Sera."

"You shouldn't doubt yourself, Cyr Seradal," Renard said. When he realized he'd interrupted a conversation between two Falcon Knights, his eyes bulged, and his ears reddened. "My apologies, cyrs!"

"Your page, while brave—and possibly a bit rude—is correct," Jorst said. "You've impressed the Falcon Knights."

"I can't lead them alone, Cyr Patrika."

"Then appoint leadership accordingly. No leader leads the leaderless alone."

"There is already an established hierarchy," Sera said. Most were Falcons, though there were plenty of Hawks and some Grouses. The Old Vulture was the last of the Vultures, though.

"And when someone rises to a leadership role, they select their own ring of leaders, usurping the normal ranks," Jorst said. "You've understandably overlooked this . . . so many have died since the invasion in Cyrok and we've replaced none."

"Royal would be an excellent adviser."

Jorst nodded. "As long as he stays off the drink."

"He can't do that." Sera grinned, thinking about how grumpy the man would become. "I would also need somebody who knows the Falcon Knights. Someone I could trust."

"I'm confident it won't be too difficult for you to find that someone. Thanks for accepting the position, Cyr Seradal." Jorst saluted.

"I haven't accepted, though," Sera said. "I'm sure there are better candidates."

"There aren't," Jorst said.

What do I do?

V illic ran his hand down Dunecrest's snout. The camel was inside a stable, sectioned off from each other camel. It was a horrible cage, Villic thought. Sera assured him it was temporary. If it wasn't, Villic would've freed them. Camels needed the open desert or fields. It wasn't natural to trap them. *Just like the camels, I am also trapped.* He'd be free soon, too, if the current plan was to continue. *Soon, I'll be riding again.*

It was his job to make sure the camels were all ready to leave in a few days.

Dunecrest snorted, then went back to chewing.

"Soon we'll be traveling again, Dunecrest."

Dark black eyes stared at Villic. As usual, the camel didn't seem to care one way or the other about anything Villic said.

"Glad to have you at my side," Villic said, patting Dunecrest's head.

"He doesn't understand you."

Yes, he does.

"Animals can't understand us."

You must've had a sorry life when you were a person, Speaker.

"Actually, I think I had a pretty fulfilling life. I, along with plenty of others, helped to create wonderful magic, whereupon we could create a way to live on for—"

Stop.

Speaker stopped. Dunecrest snorted. Villic smiled. All was well. Killiak, lord of lords, had stepped in and saved Villic from the people.

"Villic," Speaker started to say something, but stopped. Villic pretended not to hear.

He fed and watered the other camels, then enjoyed the rest of his day. After agreeing to accompany Cyr Seradal, she'd provided him more freedom than before. It was nice to be alone and relax. In the afternoon, he fed and watered the camels again, then slept outside the stable, under the stars for the first time since entering the city.

Sera had dismissed Cyr Patrika Jorst so she could think. Her thoughts, however, didn't remain on the Falcon Knights, becoming their leader, or who she'd rely on to help her. Instead, they meandered to her family. She wondered what her father, Jaidik, was doing and how he was. When she thought of her family, she remembered her mother and her brother, the war, the people she'd abandoned, and all the unnecessary bloodshed. All of it for . . . what? They still didn't know. It would be the first question she'd ask King Mikas Garcovi if she ever met the man face-to-face.

She decided she would take the rest of the day and focus on herself. Not on King Alondo Sedoa or his city, Andora. Not on Cyr Patrika Jorst and the Falcon Knights.

Sera took the day to properly mourn. To cry, to feel, to *remember*.

When the tears came, she locked the door and didn't answer when people called. She realized she wouldn't be able to talk with any clarity, even if she wanted to.

But that's okay. I need this.

She'd spend the day and night crying. Then, like the Falcon Knights said, like a bird, she'd rise with dawn.

"Villic? Villic the Imbuer?"

A foot tapped his side. Villic stirred.

A Remerian soldier stood over him. "Villic the Imbuer?" he asked.

Villic sat up, nodded. He saw more armed soldiers behind the one who'd woken him.

"Sir Seradal, Sir Patrika, and Captain Hoarst request your presence."

Villic nodded again, then stood. He stretched, yawned, and drank from his waterskin.

"They request your presence *now*," the soldier said.

"Okay," Villic said, wincing. He didn't mean to offend.

"If you'll just—"

But Villic was already sprinting away, leaving the soldiers by the stable.

It occurred to him when he was back in the more compacted buildings, he didn't know where Sir Seradal was.

"Try the King's Lodge? Or perhaps the fountain?"

Despite Speaker's protests that he wasn't a god, Villic had a hard time believing it. He followed Speaker's advice, and by the grace of Cocaro, god of luck, Sir Seradal was by the fountain. Sir Patrika, and Royal who was lying in a bed, were close by. Sir Seradal's page, Renard, was also there. For some reason, Villic didn't mind the boy, compared to other people.

Breathing hard and sweating from exertion, he slowed to a walk and gathered himself.

"Villic the Imbuer," Sir Seradal said.

He turned his gaze to the ground.

"Remember to speak."

"Sir Seradal," he said.

"I've—against my better judgement—accepted a role as temporary leader of the Falcon Knights. Royal and Sir Patrika will be my closest advisers."

Villic nodded along with her words, watching the grass grow beneath his feet. *Grass grows so slow. Why? How does it replace itself fast enough for camels to eat it?*

"Villic."

He looked at Sir Seradal. She watched him like he was a lion eating a bush.

"She's waiting for an answer."

She didn't ask a question!

S era sighed. Talking to Villic the Imbuer was difficult. He often seemed absent, or maybe he was purposefully not paying attention to her. *Maybe he's trying to upset me.*

He looked up from the ground—finally—and stared at her, openmouthed, like a child who'd just gotten caught stealing a treat. She closed her eyes and took a deep breath. She'd need to repeat herself.

"You've worked with us well," she said. "There's potential we'll encounter the Camel Clans when we leave. Nobody knows for sure where they've gone. You've picked up our language, know our plans, and you know the Camel Clans." Sera paused, watching his face. He'd looked back down again. When he returned his gaze, she continued. "I want you to join Cyr Patrika and Royal as one of my core advisers."

Cyr Patrika gasped while Royal choked on his whiskey.

"S he wants you to advise her?"
Mephino, god of courage, help.
"Answer her."

Villic swallowed. A bead of sweat trailed down his temple, then ran down his cheek. "What I would do?" He still found the king's tongue difficult.

"You're doing better."

"You'd advise me on what the Camel Clan response would be to our plans. You'd translate for me if we encounter them, and hopefully establish a working relationship between the Falcon Knights and the Camel Clans."

"This is a positive arrangement, Villic."

I don't have the power to speak for the gods!

"You wouldn't be speaking for them. You'd be informing Sir Seradal what you think the Camel Clans might do."

They do what the gods tell them!

"All you need to do is speculate. Accept the position. Trust me."

Villic didn't trust Speaker, although Speaker often turned out to be right. And he'd always helped Villic. But Speaker often ignored the gods and Villic didn't like that. If he was caught speaking for the gods, the shamans would kill him. Or Killiak, lord of lords, would kill Villic himself.

"I do it," Villic said.

Sir Seradal smiled. "Wonderful. King Alondo is going to want to have a proper meeting with us tomorrow."

Royal sighed. "I wish they'd stop moving me everywhere. Why can't people come to me? That used to be a thing, right?"

Sir Patrika laughed. "This keeps you on your toes—pardon the expression. If you were to remain locked inside a room, you'd be a constant drunk."

"And what's wrong with that, Patrika?" he asked.

"Nobody would come to your room again."

Sir Seradal, Sir Patrika, and Royal laughed.

I don't get it.

"You never do."

When Speaker explained the joke, Villic still didn't find it funny.

39

DEMRI SLARN

Ced led them into Lochwall. The stench of civilization permeated Demri's nose. The last time he was here, Caius had become the Velvet Mother and Demri had learned Scayde Haklon was a very knowledgeable and powerful person.

The cobblestone streets paved a smoother ride, and, after the ruts and bumps of the last two days, Demri leaned back and relaxed. He'd lost access to his Well, all Soul Glyphs removed from his body. He had no way of defending himself. And yet he felt at ease. Content. Perhaps it was knowing he couldn't defend himself, even if he wanted to. Demri had to accept whatever the fates had in store for him. Except he didn't believe in fate, only an individual's actions. He'd have to be a bit more careful than usual, that's all.

He gazed at the bright sky, wondering what they were going to learn from Myri about the current situation. He also wondered when they'd be having that conversation she'd promised.

The sounds of children shouting, people talking, dogs

barking, horse hooves clomping, and the squeak of the wagon's wheels sapped any enjoyment out of the moment.

At some point, the wagon halted.

"We're here," Ced said.

Demri didn't bother moving. They had to hitch the horses up and do nine hundred other things before helping him out of the wagon. He learned his lesson about hoping they'd help him out quickly the first night and nobody aided him for at least an hour. Closing his eyes, he shifted, getting more comfortable.

"Demri," Caius said. "Are you taking a nap, or do you want to get out now?"

Of fucking course.

Demri groaned, pushing himself back into a sitting position. The wagon had stopped outside an inn—The Night Mare. A sign outside the building had the head of a black horse engraved on it, with the inn's name stenciled in an arch over the horse.

"Not an appropriate name for an inn," Demri said. "And you should stick to c-c-calling me m-my c-codename."

Caius shrugged, uncaring. "It's not a very popular place . . . Ced said."

Demri sighed. "I hope you f-fall off a cliff, you b-bastard. Get me out of this f-f-fucking thing."

Chuckling, Caius helped haul Demri out the back of the wagon. When Demri was on his feet, he grimaced. Though his bones had healed, there was still a substantial amount of pain whenever he stood and walking was worse.

After grunting through the dozen steps it took to get inside The Night Mare, Caius rested a hand on Demri's back. "Don't be afraid to ask for help," he said.

Demri glared at his companion, but inside, he was grateful for the man. He knew that despite his looks, Caius would know Demri appreciated him and his actions. And, despite his looks, Caius's hand remained on his back.

Ced came loping over like he was a child in a field. "Got us a room!"

"One room?" Demri asked.

"It's all we need, B-Fifty-Nine. Gotta remain discreet!"

"It's not d-discreet if you c-c-call it out."

Ced beamed. "Perhaps not! D-Four is staying in the room next to ours. We need to report in—let her know we're here. I'm sure she'll be glad for the backup."

"No doubt she can't wait to see you," Caius said.

"I'll unlock the room. Meet you there." Ced held the key up like it was a prize, winked, then half-walked, half-hopped away.

Caius, Demri noticed, held his knife in his hand. However, he had nothing to file since his other hand was still steadying Demri and he slipped the knife back into his belt.

"Let's go f-find D-D-D-F-Four."

"Let's hope you don't have to say that too often."

"F-Fuck you."

M yri wasn't in her room, which meant Demri and Caius had ended up trapped in a room with Ced. This was an unusual experience for them—they didn't generally have to share a room with other people overnight, and Demri found it most uncomfortable, considering Ced was the third person.

Time drifted at an unbearably slow rate. Because of his injuries, Demri was in bed. As Ced prattled on and Caius filed his nails, giving noncommittal grunts and one-word answers, Demri found it harder to keep his eyes open. He slipped into sleep.

Dreams. He didn't dream often, but when he did, they were shit. He lay in bed, injured, and Myri was there. She offered a seductive grin. The lavender aroma turned him on and he closed his eyes, breathing it in. Before he'd opened his eyes, she'd climbed on top of him and he felt himself entering her. She wiggled back and forth and he grunted, enjoying the warmth. When he looked down at her, a wide smile on his face, he saw Doram Quandis staring back, cock in his mouth. Doram's eyes turned red, and he opened his mouth wider—wider than any person could. Long, jagged teeth lined his gums. His jaw started clamping shut and before Demri felt pain, somebody was shaking him awake.

"She's back," Caius said. After a moment of staring at Demri, he said, "You feeling all right? I'm sure she wouldn't mind coming here."

"I'm not incapable," Demri snapped.

"Right. Well, let's get you out of bed."

"I'm also not a child, C-C-Caius."

Caius smiled. Demri resisted the urge to slap him.

He could get out of bed by himself. However, he was unsteady when doing so. Rather than risk further injury—he didn't want to break one of his legs for a third time—Caius offered assistance.

When they entered Myri's room, he noticed the lavender, which reminded him of his dream. Or nightmare. He realized he was in The Night Mare and cursed Mother Avani under his breath. *I hope you're amused.*

Myri and Ced were already in conversation.

"Everyone is in place and ready to go, then?" Ced asked.

"Yes. We have a member of the Elkavich in each district of Lochwall, to maximize effect." *They're going to blow up Lochwall.*

"And Buzzard's Bowl? You're going to k-k-kill all those p-prisoners?"

"Nobody lives," she said. "That's our task."

What? They can't be serious. That stunned Demri. He knew the gladiators were just prisoners, waiting to be free.

Ced swallowed, nodding. "Then it's time."

A sad smile passed over her face, and her eyes glossed over for a moment. "Not quite for either of us, but soon." She turned to Demri. "I'm glad to see you"—then glanced at Caius—"and you, too." She returned her gaze to Demri. "Please, sit." She waved at the bed.

"I'll stand," Demri said. He felt Caius's hand still on his back. He was always in pain, but he wasn't *always* wobbling.

Myri smiled again, though Demri thought he noticed a bit more warmth in it this time. He felt his heart offer an unwanted pang. *Stop it, fool.*

"So, you're going to b-b-blow yourself up? Really? For what?"

"Aren't you one of us now?" Ced asked. "You should at least know the Elkavich agenda."

"We know it," Caius said. "You plan on blowing up the world."

"We plan on beginning anew," Ced said.

Demri just frowned.

With a great sigh, Myri fell back onto the bed. It was, Demri thought, the oddest thing he'd ever seen her do. "You don't understand," she said. "It's about rooting out the corruption of the Magicai."

"How many p-p-people need to d-die to d-d-do that?"

"How many people have you killed trying to find Doram?" she asked.

"That's d-different."

"Is it? Different motivations, perhaps." Myri sat up in the bed, swinging her feet onto the floor. "Same result. Many people end up dead to further your goal."

"My goal isn't d-destroying the world."

"Neither is mine. We want to destroy the major cities, eradicating the Magicai teachings."

"So that you can t-t-teach Elkavich t-teachings. What will change?"

"Everyone"—Myri spread her hands out to gesture at the

room—"will have the same level of knowledge. No more lies, no more secrets. Imagine a world where we could use all its resources, study every avenue of magic. You already read Hobark's *The Lost Histories: An Archive After Removal.* Imagine if we had ways to access those other powers, ways to study them. It'd change the world."

"Still, destroying the world? It seems a little extreme," Caius said.

Myri shook her head. "Radical change is always extreme. Demri, you can't be thinking of defending everyone who's come after you. The Magicai are not your friends. The citizens aren't, either. Everyone wants you dead."

"I'm not arguing that," Demri said. "I don't c-care if they d-die . . . I doubt you're okay with it, though." His right leg throbbed from leaning on it too much and he grimaced, almost losing his balance. Caius steadied him.

"It's the only way our voices can be heard," she said.

She was right. Nobody even believed in the Elkavich. And if the citizens learned the Magicai had been lying this entire time, they'd likely not believe that, either. But was blowing up every civilized area the answer? He didn't think so. The problem was, he didn't care enough to stop the Elkavich. Demri just didn't want Myri to be one who ended up combusting.

"I'm not okay with it." Myri stood and began pacing around Ced in a circle. "But I do think it's the only way to rid ourselves of the Magicai. And if we don't get a vast majority of them, Ashmount will continue elsewhere, the teachings will go on, and people will continue to be abused. And people like us, Demri? They'll hunt us. Kill us for asking *questions.* To hide their secrets. To prevent real learning."

"I know," Demri said. For too long, the corrupt Magicai had led them like sheep to a slaughterhouse. They murdered prospective students, assigned the ones they accepted whatever school of magic they desired—without taking that student's opinion into account, and lied to maintain control. The Magicai had manipulated and ruined society and exposing them wouldn't work. The Elkavich had been trying for centuries. *But is this the way? Is eradicating a world the way to repair the damage that had been done?* The answer was clearly no, but Demri didn't have an alternative solution. And he didn't care about finding one. The only person he had a debt to was Caius. Everyone else could die for all he cared. *Except Myri.*

"I d-don't have an issue with this p-p-plan. I think it would be p-pertinent to c-consider other options, though. In Lochwall, that is."

"Such as?" Ced asked. He folded his arms and stared at Demri suspiciously.

"There is an army of gladiators imprisoned in B-Buzzard's B-B-Bowl. If we freed them, the Elkavich would grow in p-power overnight."

"How many fighters?" Myri asked.

"Hundreds," Caius said. His hand still rested on Demri's back.

Myri quirked a brow. "What would the plan be to free them?"

"I d-don't think it'd be hard. Walk in and free the f-fuckers. We've been there b-b-before. They have security, but they'd never expect an actual attack. And, if we d-d-did it d-during one of their games? We could k-kill any Magicai before they realized it," Demri said.

40

INTERLUDE

KOLB WICKAM

Calrym

Trudging across the Calrym countryside made for a boring march. *Not as bad as the ice and snow of Cyrok, though.* Kolb Wickam had seen his fair share of shit, and this wasn't it. In front of him, Alyst Garcovi spoke with the Golden Knight and the Watchtower of Calrym. That pathetic bandit, Blago Adavir, kept trying to insert himself into their conversations, although they were ignoring him. *Good.* It made Sergeant Wickam sick to think of them cavorting with a man who'd abandoned them. A man who'd stolen one of their ships and fled. If it was up to Sergeant Wickam, Adavir would hang from a tree.

Flanking Wickam's sides, Tauven Shekt and Jafe Valendar marched. The three had gotten close—nothing bonded a crew more than a secret murder, though they had a nearly unbreakable bond, and if Wickam had to, he wouldn't sacrifice his life to rescue either of them. The cold-blooded and calculated killing of Duke Harlem Maccaro wasn't something that could ever be known or they'd all die, but otherwise, Wickam didn't feel any true affinity for either Tauven Shekt or Jafe Valendar.

Alyst was insistent on reaching the Elderspikes passage before much of summer passed. This was easy, because summer was still two weeks away, and it took less than two to reach their destination. Alyst, however, seemed to forget this and continued marching them later and later each day.

Tauven, shaped like a barrel and with a gruff, low voice, said, "Every day we go later and later. It's becoming unnecessary." Wickam noticed Tauven spoke loudly on purpose. Alyst was only a few dozen feet in front of them.

The tall, squeaky voiced one, Jafe, followed suit. "My legs ache, my back aches, my head aches. My balls ache! I need a piss."

Alyst halted, swiveled to face them. "Sergeant Wickam, is there a problem in the ranks?"

"No sir," Wickam said, snapping a salute.

"I've been hearing murmurs of dissatisfaction in the ranks, Kolb."

"The men are exhausted, sir," Wickam said. He bit his tongue after finishing the words, pain to reprimand himself for being so stupid—Alyst was in charge and an unsympathetic man to the plights of his soldiers.

"I don't care if they're exhausted, Sergeant Wickam," Alyst said. "I didn't ask."

"Yes, sir." *Dick.* Alyst Garcovi was always a dick, though. *Runs in the family.*

Alyst turned back around and kept marching. Wickam assumed in two minutes' time, Alyst would call a halt. The bastard liked to do that—get angry over information and ignore it, then decide to act on it later as if he'd not snapped at somebody earlier for bringing it to his attention.

Wickam gave Tauven a chastising look, but Tauven just grinned back.

Being an officer with none of the benefits or power of being a high-ranking officer was pointless.

"We'll rest here for the night," Alyst said.

Wickam rolled his eyes while Tauven and Jafe suppressed laughs.

One positive thing about the rank of sergeant was Wickam controlled when soldiers took guard shifts. Although they were in their own country, they weren't taking any chances. No reports of a Camel Clan or Remerian invasion had reached their ears, but that didn't mean it wasn't happening. And there was always the odd group of brave bandits who would see them as a rich source of resources.

Wickam always took a shift for himself—the first shift, usually. As Sergeant there had to be *some* perks and getting a full block of sleep was one of them. And, because he'd felt spiteful, he'd put both Tauven and Jafe on second shift. *Serves the pair of them for making me look like a fool.*

It was the beginning of Wickam's shift and most men were sleeping. He could hear quieted whispers from those Wickam had selected to do regular patrols, and Alyst was discussing something with the Golden Knight and the Watchtower of Calrym. Much to his chagrin, Wickam noticed Adavir was in the conversation as well.

Blago Adavir—bandit, pillager, murderer. A ne'er do well who abandoned the Calrite army and fled back to Calrym by stealing one of their ships. *Why is he favored over me?* Wickam couldn't understand it. No, he wouldn't understand it, even if there was a plausible reason. Adavir was an utter shit, a stain on old underwear that hadn't been changed throughout a long, sweaty military campaign. Wickam knew voicing this wouldn't change anything, so he held his opinion. Sir Alyst Garcovi wouldn't alter his orders or plans based on Sergeant Wickam's thoughts.

It was their fourth night on the road, and Wickam had spoken with Alyst. He didn't feel neglected or ignored. He didn't have a need to constantly be coddled. It'd just be nice if Adavir—a mere bandit from Cyrok—wasn't favored over Wickam, an officer in the Remerian military serving under the Garcovi family rule.

He heard a clomping in the distance. *Horse.* They'd been marching without horses, as there were hundreds of men in the unit dispatched by the king and there was no reason for horses—they had plenty of time to reach their destination—aside from the two or three they'd brought for messengers. Nobody should be on one now, though, or Sergeant Wickam would know about it. He rested his hand on the hilt of his sword, wondering who it could be. The hooves sounded as if from a single horse, so it wasn't an army. Still, it paid to be prudent.

Wickam walked over to a duo on patrol. "Look alive, men. We don't know who's approaching." A pair of lights bobbed in the distance. "Hold your lantern higher, Rickets."

Rickets obliged, aiming the light down the road toward the noise of the approaching horse.

"I don't see anything," Rickets said. "You sure he's coming from this way?"

Wickam sighed. "You can't see the lights in the distance? Use your damn ears, son." Sometimes, Wickam thought the average soldier was a decent fellow, just trying to do the best to serve his country. Other times, he was knew there were some duds in the mix.

"Me mam always said my vision was poor," Rickets said.

"No shit."

Wickam could now make out the horse, illuminated by a pair of lanterns hanging at each of its sides. A minute later, the rider pulled back on the reins, bringing the horse to a stop in front of Wickam and the two patrolmen. Wickam stepped closer, analyzing the rider. A Calrite messenger, all right.

"Sir, is this Sir Alyst Garcovi's detachment?" the rider asked.

"It is. I'm Sergeant Kolb Wickam. What's your name, son?"

"Folks just call me 'Whisper', Sergeant."

"Funny name."

The rider shrugged, hopping down from the horse. The boy was humorless. He handed the reins to Rickets. "I have vital news for My Lord Alyst Garcovi."

"Would you like some food?"

The rider—a boy no older than seventeen—gave Wickam a withering stare. "Nothing is more important than the tragedy I have to relay. I bring dire news."

Wickam raised a brow at that. Messengers were never unnecessarily grim, so the news must be bad. "This way, *Whisper*." He couldn't get over how stupid the younger generation was. *Whisper? Who calls themself Whisper?* "Come on."

"Nothing has ever been more urgent," Whisper said.

That concerned Wickam even more. He quickened his pace.

"Sir," Wickam called out to Alyst. "Messenger from . . ." it occurred to Wickam he hadn't asked where Whisper hailed from.

"The capital," Whisper said.

Alyst and his companions stood. "What is it?"

"A great tragedy has occurred, my lord," Whisper said. The boy looked on the verge of tears. "A nobleman named Jaspard Couliac sent me. A massacre has transpired. Sir, the major nobility in Lochwall are gone. The dukes and duchesses, murdered. Your uncle, King Mikas, too."

"What?"

"How?"

"Madness."

Wickam's jaw dropped.

"It's true, my lord," Whisper said. "Lord Couliac has recalled you to the city—he's currently running things—to claim the throne as the closest surviving relative to the king.

A great coup has happened. A madman entered the Great Hall and slaughtered everyone. I came as quick as I could, but it took a while for Lord Couliac to organize. The city's been in chaos. The event occurred over a week and a half ago."

"Who could've done such a thing?" the Golden Knight asked.

"A man they're calling the Butcher of Anepolis, Tallas Taybold. Aided by one Duchess Cithrial Hyrel. Please, Your Highness, you must make haste," Whisper said.

The Golden Knight made what Wickam thought was a gasp but didn't speak.

"Sergeant Wickam," Alyst said, "you're in charge of the legion. Hold the eastern front and if an attack occurs, send word."

"Yes, sir," Wickam said, saluting. Then, worried he'd addressed the man improperly, "My lord," and bowed.

Alyst didn't notice as he continued issuing orders. "Tauven, Jafe, you're to serve as Sergeant Wickam's new officers." *Well, shit.* "And you three are with me." He gestured at the trio he'd been sitting with all night. "Sorry, boy," Alyst said to Whisper, "but I need to commandeer your horse."

"Of course, Your Highness," Whisper said.

"Stick with Alyst. If he needs a messenger, you're the man for the job. Kolb," Alyst said, turning back to Wickam. "Make a stop at Lochwall and purchase horses for the army. I want you to make haste." He tossed Wickam a pouch of coin. "If you need more, feel free to spend the men's wages. I'll reimburse them upon their return. This is of the utmost importance, Sergeant."

"Yes, my lord," Wickam said, saluting.

Alyst was already walking towards the horses. "We ride!"

And just like that, Alyst, the Golden Knight, the Watchtower of Calrym, and Blago Adavir were gone. A few problems solved, but many, many more gained.

Sergeant Kolb Wickam wasn't meant to lead an army. Unless directed to lead a smaller group of men in battle, there was always another officer to report to. Not anymore. Wickam was out of his area of expertise.

He'd named both Tauven and Jafe as corporals, though they were little help. Both of them were efficient killers, but not leaders. They were, Wickam thought, trustworthy, though.

Three days after Alyst and his entourage departed, Wickam and his men reached Lochwall. They spent a day in the city, restocking some supplies and purchasing horses. Then they were off again.

Rickets, the idiot soldier, decided he'd become "helpful" and tailed Wickam everywhere he went. Wickam wasn't sure if this was because Rickets felt some a duty or obligation to Wickam, or maybe he was licking Wickam's ass, looking for a promotion. Either way, Wickam was getting sick of him.

"Me mam always said, 'if you don't eat in the morn, by afternoon you'll wish ye hadn't been born'," Rickets said one morning. "Noticed you hadn't scoffed anything down, sir." He proffered a slab of cheese and a chunk of rye bread they'd purchased in Lochwall to Wickam.

Wickam begrudgingly took the food and restrained himself from reprimanding the soldier. His mam wasn't wrong. Gnawing on the rye bread and interspersing it with bits of pungent cheese, Wickam felt a little better. The fact was, he'd forgotten to eat. Too much on his mind, too many things to do. He needed to have a talk with Tauven and Jafe about personal responsibility and hope they'd help more. Each followed orders well but took no initiative.

Damp, trampled grass and clumps of mud squished beneath his boots as Wickam pushed his way through the row of marching soldiers ahead of him. He reached Tauven and Jafe, who walked alongside one another.

"Corporal Shekt, Corporal Valendar," Wickam said.

"Sir," they both said.

"We've got about another week of this." Wickam glanced down at a splash from one of his boots. He'd stepped into a murky puddle of water. "Damn it." It'd rained the day they'd spent in Lochwall, and though Wickam thought it lucky then, he was now considering otherwise. "This is horrible."

"Getting worse too, sir," Jafe's squeaky voice said. "Further we get from Lochwall, muddier and wetter it gets."

"Let's pray to Mother Avani it gets better sooner rather than later," Wickam said. He wasn't the most pious man, but he believed in the good Mother. *How else would these fools get through life if not for some guidance?* He thought of people like Rickets in particular. How the man had gotten to be a soldier was beyond Wickam's comprehension.

"Aye, hope the bitch dries it up," Tauven said.

"Corporal!" Wickam snapped. "Do *not* insult Mother Avani while we're on campaign together! Do you understand me?" He didn't care if people believed or not, but he couldn't abide blatant disrespect. There was too much at stake for them to be cursing gods and finding themselves cursed in return because of it.

"Yes, sir."

"We've been through too much," Wickam said. Then realized no speech would work as well as his thoughts. "There's too much at stake to allow you to curse gods and finding ourselves cursed because of it."

"Yes, sir." Tauven's grin said otherwise though.

"Damn it, Corporal, keep the rear moving."

"Yes, sir." Tauven saluted and stopped marching, waiting for the line of soldiers to pass.

"Fucking idiot," Wickam said.

"Aye."

"One more week."

"Aye."

"Damn it, Corporal Valendar, go head the front."

"Yes, sir," Jafe said, double-timing it to pass the line of soldiers ahead of them.

Wickam sighed. Once they'd reached their destination and were on the lookout for invading forces, things would be much easier to manage.

"Sir," the voice of Rickets said from behind Wickam. "Don't forget to hydrate or you'll die." He offered his water-skin to the sergeant.

Wickam inhaled, then expelled a huge breath of air. *Keep calm. You're in charge. Avani help me see my way through this.* She, of course, decided not to help.

They had to march through a forest which stretched across the eastern portion of Calrym, often walking their horses through crowded areas. Old dirt and muddy trails weaved their way through a mix of tall, thick trees, both deciduous and coniferous. Although it wasn't mud season anymore, it seemed it'd rained several days before they'd entered the forest, and the sloppy paths slurped and sucked at their boots. A comfortable breeze wafted through the leaves, and the trees blocked a good portion of the sun's heat.

After the first few days of trekking through the forest, the men started complaining and Wickam harbored the same sentiment, though he didn't voice it. The bugs were out in force—mosquitoes, fleas, ticks. The mud reeked, and their boots and socks remained damp.

Sergeant Wickam led the army, Rickets and Whisper close behind. The messenger had experience as a tracker. "Comes in handy if you're about to run into an enemy," Whisper had explained. Wickam didn't doubt that. The last thing a messenger would want is to fall into captivity.

Whisper would often scout ahead of the main force, checking for signs of the enemy, though Wickam expected none. Still, it was better safe than sorry.

"Sergeant Wickam," Whisper's voice said from up ahead during the afternoon of the seventh day of traversing the forest. "I've spotted fields."

Thank the Mother. Wickam rushed forward, rounding a bend in the mud, and saw Whisper trudging back down the road. "How much further?" Wickam asked.

"A dozen feet or so that way," Whisper said, gesturing over his shoulder with a thumb.

"Rickets," Wickam said against his better judgement, but it was the first name to pop into his head—an indication that Rickets' idiocy had wormed its way further into Wickam's mind. He sighed.

Rickets hurried up the line, dodging a pair of soldiers who'd overtaken him on the road. "Yes, sir?"

"Spread the word—we're clear of the woods."

A few of the soldiers heard, and they issued a meek cheer.

Wickam and Whisper hurried down the road, exiting the forest into the field. Wickam took a deep breath of fresh air. It breathed similar to the air inside the forest but felt liberating for some reason. "Free," he said.

"Aye, Sergeant."

"Been a week now, Whisper," Wickam said.

"Aye."

"I wonder if Sir Alyst made it safely back to Lochwall. Perhaps he's king now."

"For the good of the realm, I hope so, Sergeant." Whisper smiled.

Wickam knew the truth. In leadership and luxury, laborers had no luck. Nobody cared if Alyst became king or not. Either way, they'd be called upon to fight the country's wars and get paid the same amount they were getting paid in times of peace.

"All hail the king," Wickam said. Whisper smiled more at that.

The soldiers of Wickam's army stormed out of the woods, flowing into the fields like herds of deer. Wickam spied his two corporals milling about and, as suspected, doing the bare minimum.

"Corporals Shekt and Valendar," Wickam called to them. "We'll break for the night. You're in charge of guard shifts. I expect each of you to join the men you select on one of their shifts."

"Yes, sir," they both said.

"*Different* shifts from one another, you hear me?"

"Yes, sir," they both said with less enthusiasm.

Wickam shook his head. *Why'd everyone competent leave me here alone?*

Sergeant Kolb Wickam had been resolute in his militaristic standards. He wanted all to see him as an exemplary example. He prided himself on somebody dedicated to the cause, despite the shit conditions and shittier pay. But there was something about the entire experience he enjoyed. Wickam was, simply put, just meant to be in the army. Since becoming a sergeant, Wickam took a night off from doing patrols. He realized he was too stressed, too exhausted, and getting too old for sleepless nights. And, he figured, he deserved a break.

When he woke the following day—the first day of summer—he felt refreshed, rejuvenated and whole. Wickam stood, stretched, and prepared for the morning's march in good spirits. He noticed his good mood transferred to the surrounding men, and by the time they were up and walking, everyone had a smile on their face. He even noticed several plumes of black smoke in the distance, though he didn't let it affect his mood. Out here there was little reason for the smoke. They weren't near any major settlements, and there weren't any battles going on that Wickam was aware of.

"Heading to the Elderspikes, right Sergeant?" Whisper asked.

"Yes, Whisper, we need to get to the pass."

"Might want to alter course a tad more north. It'll be a few hours quicker."

"You know better than I. Lead on." Wickam had a shoddy map and little directional sense. Whisper had to make his way in the world alone and had proven skills. If there was one thing Wickam knew to do, it was to listen to those who had expertise in things he didn't. Something plenty of leaders often failed to do. Something that often irritated Wickam.

The army followed Whisper northeast. They crossed field after field after field. In late spring and early summer, the sun rose high and remained high, beating down on them, and it wasn't past morning before they all had beads of sweat running down their faces. There was little shade, as only a tree or shrub dotted the landscape.

"Remember to hydrate, sir," Rickets said.

Wickam rolled his eyes, then, realizing he was thirsty, took a drink from his waterskin.

A small hill prevented Wickam's view of the mountains for a moment, and when he crested the hill, his heart stopped.

"Oh, fuck," he said.

Below, hundreds of men and women were already mounted on camels, facing Wickam's direction.

"Oh fuck," he said, again. He didn't know what to do. The Camel Clans were waiting for them.

His hands clenched the reins of his mount, and, shaking, he looked over his shoulder at his fellow soldiers. *We're fucked.* A droplet of sweat slid down his face and his men stared at him, stared at the nomads, stared at the ground. He swallowed, nervous. Swallowed a second time, in an attempt to calm his nerves. It didn't work.

Then he heard a battle cry. The camels surged forward. *Fuck. FUCK!*

"To arms!" Sergeant Wickam screamed.

41

ASHEN HYREL

Anepolis, Calrym

It was a constant battle between shivering and just feeling a dull, icy cold. The dungeon had little warmth and the small, ragged blanket didn't help. It wasn't the first time Ashen wished for another human's presence—perhaps Tallas, as he was in the cell across from her—to press against. The guards had stripped her of her clothes and gave her a thin overshirt that draped past her knees. Duchess Cithrial Hyrel, in one fell swoop, died the moment Ashen removed her fancy clothing, and now she felt returned to her urchin past.

Silence. Incredible silence. Sometimes she'd hear somebody cough or shift in their cell or whisper to an adjacent cellmate. Otherwise, quiet permeated the damp dark.

She repeated the Five Rules of Survival her father had taught her.

Never forgo food because it appears dissatisfying. Starving to death isn't worth it. The jail's food was awful, but she needed to eat. And, if she was being honest, she'd eaten far worse food when she lived on the streets. Compared to then, the food was rather luxurious. She had been spoiled by the last few cycles.

Never accept a helping hand. You never know who you'll owe, and you have nothing to leverage. She shouldn't have trusted Jaspard when he offered to take her in. She didn't have leverage. Ashen allowed him to use her, then when she'd done what he'd needed, he threw her in a cell. She never should have broken the rule.

Never display your belongings, however meager they may seem. Somebody always has less than you. Ashen still didn't have a problem here. Anything she'd owned after entering Jaspard's home had never actually been hers. She'd known that. Didn't mind it, either.

Never assume you're returning to the last place you felt safe. Unforeseen circumstances could mean you won't be able to. Until a few days ago, Ashen felt safe at Duke Sturgeon's manor. Before then, she'd felt safe at Jaspard's manor. And now she wouldn't be returning to either house.

Never trust anyone, even those you trust. In matters of life and death, your life is meaningless even from your friend's point of view. Why she ever trusted Jaspard was beyond her. Every time she rehearsed this rule, she felt ill. She'd neglected the most important street rule she learned: don't trust anyone. And she'd broken it.

Never let them know you're a girl, even after dark. Girls find themselves at the violent hands of angry men and never leave them unscathed. The sixth rule—one she'd added herself, though she figured it was time to remove it. On the streets as a young girl, things had been different. She was older now. Ashen was smarter, better able to navigate life. She could return to the Five Rules of Survival without the addendum. It felt wrong to have a rule her father hadn't put on the list, though it had kept her safe.

The bed, a stone slab with old hay sprinkled atop it and a sheet thrown over that, did little to combat the cold. She adjusted the musty blanket she curled up with to warm herself as best she could. Then Ashen returned to shivering.

She wasn't sure how many days she spent in the cell—there was no sunlight to gauge time. Two or three weeks, maybe. Deep in sleep, she woke to the sound of a rusty hinge squeaking as the cell door opened. Rising from her slumber, she spotted a cloaked figure hunched in the doorway, a small candle the only source of light.

A raspy voice spoke, "Come, Ashen. Quick." Before she could do anything, the figure turned and, with a loud creak breaking up the silence again, they opened Tallas's cell. "Tallas," the voice caught in the mysterious person's throat for a moment, "quick, you must leave."

"Who are you?" Ashen asked, stepping into the hall. It felt like a cool breeze was drifting down the corridor and goose pimples spread across her body. She regretted not taking the moldy blanket with her, but she wouldn't willingly return to the cell while she stood free.

"Nobody," the voice said. Ashen believed them. They smelled bad, they sounded awful, they couldn't be anyone of noteworthiness. "Come."

The candle provided enough light where Ashen could see Tallas's face. He gave her a confused smile, his one good eye staring at her, the milky one offput by a fraction.

"Let's not wait around," he said.

They followed the mysterious one past the cells, where people reached their hands through the bars. "Let me out," "it hurts," and "kill me, now," they said. Ashen could see open sores and wounds on several of their arms and wondered if she were in their position if she'd want to die, too. She settled on yes. She didn't want to suffer in a cell for the rest of her days.

"No," the raspy one said, swatting a prisoner's hands with a switch, which shut the prisoners up and returned them to their misery inside their cells.

They led Ashen and Tallas through the jail, upstairs, and into a small room. Ashen, astonished, saw that inside the room was all of Tallas's equipment resting on a small table. Their rescuer pushed Ashen towards a small bundle of items resting inside a small chest aside the table that, she assumed, were for her.

"What's happening?" she asked.

The raspy one just pushed her again.

A full set of clothes, a traveling cloak, a new—and expensive—dagger complete with a sheath, a leather belt with plenty of storage space, and two pouches of Black Dust perched atop the folded clothing, waited for her. Ashen dressed—Tallas turned around and stood in the doorway, blocking the raspy one's view—and when she slipped her arm into the sleeve of the traveling cloak, a small scroll dropped to the floor. Curious, she retrieved it and slipped it into a pocket. There wasn't enough light to read it and she wasn't about to ask for the candle.

Once Ashen finished dressing, Tallas took his turn gearing up. He had all his previous weapons—including the halberd, stained red from the massacre.

"Follow me," the raspy one said. They brought Ashen and Tallas to a door, opened the door, and a gust of fresh air blew into the jail. "Go."

"Go?" Tallas asked. "What's the catch? Who do we owe?"

"I know nothing," the raspy one said. "Go."

Ashen, though bewildered, wasn't hesitating. She rushed outside before the opportunity slipped away. Tallas followed her and the door slammed shut behind them. The sound of a bolt slamming home dissuaded her from interrogating the figure who'd freed them.

"We need to disappear," Tallas said.

"I have something." Ashen retrieved the scroll. In the brighter daylight, she saw a plain wax seal held it together. Unrolling it, she held the letter up for both of them to read.

To the venerable woman whom this note is destined to reach,

It is unfortunate that you found yourself wrapped up in something so dramatic. I grieve over the fact that I couldn't protect you, though I admit I've always put myself higher on the list of things to care about. You have a fine companion, provided he doesn't leave you behind. Something tells me he won't, despite his desire for money and hard jobs. I am offering you an unpaid job, but one of the most difficult. I am sorry I couldn't lift you to greater heights or restore your familial link. You are, and will forever have to be, one of many Anepolis urchins.

If you come to my home or inquire about anything that has transpired—if I'm to encounter you at all—I will, however sad and unfortunate the circumstances are, be forced to have you arrested and returned to the jail to await the justice of the future king.

I wish you the best,

There was no signature, but she saw a sugared honey chew attached to the parchment with a glob of wax.

Tallas finished reading and snorted.

"Well, ain't this a prick of a bastard with a flaccid apology?" Ashen said. No reason to hide her accent anymore.

Tallas laughed. "You're the vilest child I've ever met."

"Ain't met too many urchins, huh?"

"Most urchins I met were dead ones," he said.

"Fair enough. You're too scary to rob."

"Let's go. Our good lord even deemed me worthy of keeping my coin," Tallas said, producing a bulging pouch. "A couple of horses and we can be well on our way out of this shithole."

Ashen nodded. She wasn't sure where they were headed, but she knew she wanted to be far away from Anepolis and Jaspard Couliac.

Riding a horse was a tricky thing, but after a few passes around the stables, Ashen thought she figured it out. It wasn't difficult. Hold the reins for dear life, squeeze the beast with your thighs, and don't let your head tip too far in either direction.

"Aye, you've got it, missy," the stable hand said.

"Just don't fall off. It's a long way down," she said to herself. She'd avoided looking at the ground but took a glance. *Well, ain't this a simple way to crack a foolish head open?* Despite the betrayal of Jaspard—she admitted it hurt but pushed it aside; she'd felt worse before—she felt free. No longer concerned about her accent, the way she acted, the plans Jaspard expected her to complete.

Tallas paid the stable hand and mounted his midnight black mare. "Ready?" he asked her.

She swallowed. "No," she said.

"Good." He brought his mare alongside hers, taking the lead on her reins. "I'll guide you out of the city. Then you can practice outside Anepolis with ease and freedom."

Ashen crouched down, hugging the white horse beneath her. It wasn't the most comfortable position, but she didn't want to fall, and swaying back and forth made her nervous. Her horse, she'd been told, was a mare. Ashen named her Rooftop.

Tallas led them through the cobblestone streets, passing hundreds of citizens and Calrite guardsmen. When they reached the gates, they passed through unhindered. And then, after a half hour of navigating the busy city, they were outside. Free. Into the grasslands.

Relieved, she sat straighter in the saddle. Tallas rode a few feet ahead, still guiding Rooftop.

"Where are we going?" she asked. Ashen didn't care where they went. She'd never been to another city before. Or town, or village. Or anywhere other than the immediate surroundings of Anepolis.

"To a place of opportunity."

"Where's that?"

"Have you ever heard of Lochwall?"

42

EDELBROCK BRENDIS

Everyone was dying. The Chell, gone. Savakkis, dead. Anyone he'd socialized with had been murdered. There were other gladiators. Edelbrock knew their names. Most of them, anyway. He didn't care to get to know the people, though. In times of war, it wasn't worth it. Too many people died. And Buzzard's Bowl had just as many casualties.

The Extreme Events continued, and Edelbrock was involved in every single one. He knew Scayde wanted him dead, but also figured Scayde wanted Edelbrock to die inside the arena, under the watchful eyes of an enthralled audience. Edelbrock was determined not to give Scayde that satisfaction.

He survived. He'd battled his way through four Extreme Events.

In the first one, Edelbrock and a group of his House had to swim through a long maze, depleting their strength. Carnivorous fish nipped at their bodies as they went, injuring them along the way. When they reached a landmark, they had to fight through double their number.

The second event seemed like Scayde's most obvious attempt to kill Edelbrock. He was alone, in an empty arena, only sand. Then a fighter charged out of House Castede's entrance to Buzzard's Bowl. He had a duel, won. Then another came from House Jaylena. He fought a duel, won. He repeated this, one from each of the four opposing Houses. Twice. Eight people dead at Edelbrock's hand. He still wasn't sure how he'd survived.

The third event placed Edelbrock and five others on a series of ever-shrinking platforms. Instead of battling other gladiators, he was fighting to stay out of the boiling water that surrounded them. Only Edelbrock and one other gladiator maintained their balance and remained on the platform which shrunk to a single hand's width. The others fell into the water and burned to death.

The fourth event, inspired by the third, was a hazardous obstacle course, broken up with checkpoints. At each checkpoint, gladiators had to be killed. The obstacles ranged from a simple spiked fence they had to climb over, to pits of lava they had to leap across, the pits spaced far enough apart most of them had difficulty making the leap. Edelbrock was lucky somebody had jumped before him and made it across. If he hadn't had somebody there to help pull him over the ledge, Edelbrock would've fallen to his death.

Since the death of Savakkis, Edelbrock had replaced him as leader of the House. He wasn't sure what his responsibilities were. Wasn't sure why he was a leader at all. He didn't care about the position, didn't want it, didn't deserve it. But everyone looked up to him, so he continued to train them under Buzzard's Battalion. Perhaps coming up with a name for them furthered the notion he was a leader.

Despite all the scrapes and cuts and bruises and blisters, Edelbrock lived. And now, he was waiting for the next of the

Extreme Events to begin. He wondered if he was going to have to take part in these events with overwhelming odds until he died. He was sore, depleted, tired, and bruised. Edelbrock couldn't attribute his survival to anything other than fate. His fate, he believed, was revenge. To secure justice for Gordy's death. To kill everyone responsible for Edelbrock's betrayal—the barrister Chardaine, Jaylena, and Scayde. He'd almost forgotten the insufferable servant, Tanibris.

The archway leading into Buzzard's Bowl opened. Edelbrock and the seven others tasked with fighting with him walked into the arena. Today, Edelbrock had chosen a normal broadsword and shield. One of his favorites.

His foot squelched in watery mud. A mucky mess stretched across the arena, to a long platform where dozens of gladiators waited. And the bastards were dry. Edelbrock took another step, and the bog deepened. "I don't like this," he said. The murky water smelled awful and black flies buzzed by his ear and bounced off his face.

"Gross," somebody said.

The arena's announcer came on and started introducing the fighters of House Haklon. Edelbrock didn't bother listening. He spotted something in the middle of the green tinged water. "What is that?" he asked. "There's something in the water."

He took another step, which required effort to pry his foot from the sucking mud, and the water rose above his shins.

"This is awful," somebody else said.

The announcer started listing off their opponents. Edelbrock caught three names of the dozens who were called out, "Seeker Korran", which Edelbrock recognized as the man who fought with two hatchets, and "Flimsy Shirley the Remerian Girly", a legend of Buzzard's Bowl who often battled with both a flail and mace—further proof Scayde was doing his best to ensure Edelbrock's death, and "Call Me

Freshly", an ugly fuck who stood at the front of the gathered gladiators, thrusting a pair of meaty fists gripping a long lance into the air.

The crowd cheered and chanted their favorite names. Edelbrock heard more than a few "Bloodlines" in the mix.

"What are we going to do, Edelbrock? There's too many on that platform. We'll never get out of this swamp."

"We'll split into two parties of four," Edelbrock said. "If we attack on two separate flanks, they'll be—"

A loud splash interrupted him.

"Did you hear that?"

"What?"

"Shh, quiet."

Another splash from the opposite direction.

The crowd gasped and shouted and cheered. Edelbrock couldn't understand anything they were saying but pushed them out of his mind. He glanced around, ignoring the King's Stand as his gaze swiveled in that direction. No use staring at the idiots up there. Too much of a distraction, too much anger.

Edelbrock stared at the ripples in the bog. Something was swimming in lazy circles.

"Shit, what's that?" Edelbrock said, pointing in the thing's direction.

Something green showed itself for a moment.

"Scales?"

"Looked like a frog."

"Big frog, you idiot."

"That weren't no frog, that were a lizard."

"Have you ever seen a lizard?"

"No."

"Then how do you know?"

"I read about 'em."

"You haven't read shit."

More squelching as the party of eight reached water at the height of their stomachs. Soon they'd have to swim.

Two more splashes, then a pair of light green eyes rose from the water, followed by a scaled snout. The beast opened its mouth and displayed an array of teeth.

"It's a shark!"

"No, it's not. That's a crocodile."

"A what?"

"It doesn't matter!" Edelbrock said, interrupting the argument. "Look at that thing. It could bite us in half."

"Crocodiles pull their prey underwater and drown them."

"Keep an eye out," Edelbrock said. "Let's try not to draw attention to ourselves. Slow and steady. No splashing, yeah?"

"Aye."

"Yes, sir."

"Sounds good, Commander."

Slow, steady, purposeful, Edelbrock lowered himself into the swamp and swam, quiet and steady. He took great care to not raise his arms above the water and cause a splash, though it was difficult swimming with sword and shield in hand.

But all his attempts at being careful didn't matter.

The crowd screamed, and two things happened.

A gladiator behind Edelbrock screamed and then vanished underwater. Edelbrock turned to help him, but red smeared the already cloudy water and he couldn't see his companion. Then, feet away, the crocodile's body resurfaced for a moment, thrashing in a barrel roll, returning underwater, keeping the bloody carcass of the fighter from getting any air.

A sudden boom sounded in his eardrums. A shockwave of water rippled through the arena, and Edelbrock found himself tossed about, rolling underwater, spitting, and sputtering, and gasping for air. His hands clawed the water, trying to turn his body upright. When the wave halted, he thrashed out of the water, taking a deep breath, and regaining his senses. A cloud of dust wafted down from what Edelbrock assumed was the origin of the explosion.

The people in the stands screamed, but it wasn't one of excitement. It was a scream Edelbrock knew to be panic. Fear. He rolled onto his back, floating in the water, and saw a chunk of the stands collapsing, murky swamp draining through the hole in the arena. Citizens jumped from the collapsing stands into the bog. More screams, another thunderous boom, and a second hole appeared closer to Edelbrock.

"What's happening?"

The Magicai who observed the battles of Buzzard's Bowl —and no doubt controlled the arena's environment—used various means to come down from their observatory pillars. One leaped and used a blast of wind to slow his fall. Another conjured steps to run down. Edelbrock counted six of the Buzzard's Bowl Magicai rushing toward the hole in the wall.

"Quick," Edelbrock said. "Now's our time."

"For what?"

"To get the fuck out of here," he said.

43

DEMRI SLARN

Lochwall, Calrym

When Demri explained his plan, Myri agreed to it. The Buzzard's Bowl gladiators were of a potential value to the Elkavich, it seemed. She'd gone to make the appropriate plans with the other Elkavich agents. Ced, having disagreed with Demri's plans, tagged along with her.

Now Demri waited in his room, Caius picking his fingertips with his knife.

To be of use, Demri needed help. He wasn't sure if Myri would oblige, though. He'd need his Soul Glyphs replenished. And some healing. He couldn't be hobbling around if they were about to attack Scayde Haklon.

When Myri returned, Ced wasn't with her. "Ced's carrying out my orders so he won't annoy us," she said, unprompted.

Demri went right to what he'd been pondering. "I need m-my ability replenished. M-M-My Well restored. P-Perhaps a little healing, too." He gestured at his legs. "Otherwise, I won't b-b-be m-much help."

"Tythus," Myri said, using his codename, "would you mind bringing me a glass of wine?"

"Not a problem," he said. He caught Demri's eye, winked, and exited. She hadn't ordered anyone to bring her anything since they met in Pinecrest.

"Demri," she said, sitting on his bed.

He felt his heart surge whenever she said his name and ignored the assigned Elkavich letter and numbers. "M-Myri."

"I can replenish your Soul Glyphs, but we can't waste anyone's power on healing you. If I do that, you can't make me regret it. You must follow my orders."

"I will." He wished she'd have him healed, but he wasn't expecting her to waste her years on him.

"Demri, I mean it. If you don't, they'll have us both killed."

"I know. If I don't d-do what I'm told, Erasure said he'd have you k-k-killed. I d-don't intend on allowing that to happen."

She frowned. He wondered if she believed him. Or perhaps she was considering if Erasure had lied to Demri. Demri wondered about that, too. He didn't think so, though. Erasure didn't seem the type to toss about empty threats. And people in command of secret societies didn't seem the type to not follow through on matters of security.

"I'll have Ced restore your Soul Glyphs when he returns," Myri said.

"Him? Really?"

"You'll take who I offer."

"He's just such a . . ."

"I know," Myri said. They both laughed. She looked at him and glanced away.

Demri swallowed, nervous. *Why must everything be so diffi-*

cult? So awkward? He couldn't figure out why it was awkward, but it always went that way.

"We need to have that talk," she said.

Demri's heart surged. He heard it beating against his ribs. His temples pulsed. Blood surged through his veins—that happened all the time, but for some reason, he felt it now.

"I know you love me," she said.

Demri swallowed, wanting to deny it, realizing that doing so would make the situation both more awkward and foolish. They both knew the truth.

She glanced at his face again, looked away. "I can see it." Her face flushed and her foot started tapping on the floor.

"I—" he started, but she held up her hand.

"Let me finish." She swallowed. He could see she was just as nervous as he was. "It's been uncomfortable since I told the Elkavich we were married. I didn't think it'd matter as much as it has, and I fear . . ." she trailed off, glancing at him again. "I fear you're going to take this the wrong way."

Oh. Fuck.

"I'm not interested, Demri. I never have been. Leading you on was wrong, even if it was to save your life. I appreciate everything you've done. Truly I do, but I don't want you to have the wrong idea."

I'd kill you if I could. I'd tear your head from your neck and toss your lifeless body in a river. After everything we've gone through, everything I've done to be near you, everything I've . . . his thoughts trailed off. It hurt. He loved her, wanted her to love him. Demri knew she didn't owe him anything. It didn't stop him from having those thoughts about wanting to kill her, though. Instead of voicing his thoughts Demri smiled. "I know. I haven't thought about you recently, d-don't worry. I'm not obsessed." *But I am intoxicated by your mere presence.* It sickened him to know somebody held such power over him, somebody who'd treated him so badly in the past. *Why do I allow this to happen?* He'd never actually hurt her, but the pain she caused him made him *want* to harm her. He suppressed his feelings, both good and bad.

She winced, then smiled. "I'm glad we got this out of the way." She placed a hand on Demri's. "If you need anything, let me know." Her fingertips trailed across the back of his hand as she turned and left.

I hate you.

But it was really the opposite.

Ced replaced the Soul Glyphs on Demri's body and ignored Demri's inquiries about healing his legs.

"It won't t-take m-much off your life."

Ced's high-pitched voice grated on Demri's hearing. "That it'll take anything at all ain't right. An Elkavich's power can't be a wasted, no. There is a finite amount of us and a grand plan at stake. Wasting it, and rendering ourselves old and sapped, ain't gonna further the cause, nope." He giggled. "I like yer enthusiasm, though."

Asshole. If I could burn your balls without pissing Myri off, I would. If I could rip your tongue out so you'd stop running your mouth for a day, it'd almost be worth the trouble. I would— Demri cut himself off. *What's wrong with me?* He'd gotten too angry. Perhaps "angry" was the wrong word. Demri had been angry before. He'd made a conscious decision to kill everyone in a tavern, once. He'd tortured and murdered plenty of innocent people. He could deal with anger, make rational decisions. Some might argue those weren't rational decisions, but most hadn't dealt with Doram Quandis.

"Good as new!" Ced said, patting Demri's shoulder. "Except for yer legs, of course. Hope you heal quick an all. Gotta see D-Four. Make sure I know the orders for later!" Giggling, Ced left the room.

"F-F-Fuck!"

Caius, who'd been leaning against the opposite wall, filing away, stared in Demri's direction. "You done?"

"Get me out of this shit hole."

Caius shook his head. "I thought you were gonna say 'nightmare'."

"F-Fuck you, C-C-Caius."

O utside The Night Mare, Demri, with Caius's help, hobbled to the wagon. A moment later, Myri and Ced followed.

"We was looking for you," Ced said.

"We're ready t-t-to go."

Ced nodded. "Everyone'll be in position, B-Fifty-Nine."

Demri rolled his eyes. The codenames irritated him the more he heard them. With Myri taking their other horse, Caius hopped into the wagon with Demri.

They traveled through Lochwall, out the gates, and followed the road towards Scayde Haklon's estate.

Demri noticed the vast stone walls surrounding the compound. "That's going to t-t-take some work t-to get through."

"Not a concern," Myri said from her horse. "We have somebody on the inside."

Sure enough, when the horses and wagon approached the gate, they were waved through without issue by a hooded woman who gave Myri a nod. Other guards ignored the wagon and seemed to defer to the Elkavich insurgent.

The compound was much emptier than the last time Demri had been inside it. Aside from the guards manning the walls, nobody was walking around. He heard sounds coming from the huge gladiator arena and realized it was cheering.

"Brings back memories," Caius said.

"Of what?"

"Being the Velvet Mother. Having power and money. I miss those days."

"They weren't so long ago," Demri said.

"Speaks to how much power and money corrupts, I suppose."

Demri snorted. "It was nice having the money and p-power. For a few days, anyway," he said, with a short laugh.

Caius's response was a remorseful sigh.

Myri and Ced led them around Buzzard's Bowl to the rear, where the view from the compound's entrance was obstructed.

Three people sat, backs against the building, waiting. When the horses stopped and Myri and Ced dismounted, the three stood.

"Is it time, D-Four?" one asked.

Myri nodded. "Let's do it."

The trio turned to Buzzard's Bowl, holding their hands out, and the wall exploded.

44

THE BATTLE OF BUZZARD'S BOWL

Crispen hated the codenames of the Elkavich but adored their plan of resetting the world. He had always been great at tolerating things he didn't like in order to get the things he did. In the current situation, he found the yelling and screaming and shouting and pleading and begging from the dying citizens to be rather grating. *Why don't you die faster?*

He consumed a Soul Glyph, blowing open a second hole in the wall. More yelling and screaming and shouting and pleading and begging ensued. "Ugh. Disgusting." Nothing bothered Crispen more than somebody who couldn't take care of themselves. *Tolerance.* He took a deep breath. The stench of stagnant water infected the air and he choked. "What in the name of Mother Avani is that shit smell?"

Crispen had tolerance. He just didn't have more of it left.

He held his hand out, open-palmed, and sprayed the dying civilians with a scorching blast of fire. Those who hadn't drowned, been crushed to death, eaten by crocodiles, or killed by the retaliation of the Magicai, burned and sizzled and popped.

Crispen laughed. Sometimes it was good to enjoy the little things.

A moment later, another section of wall blasted apart and crushed Crispen to death.

Magicus Hexlow grimaced. He'd sacrificed countless civilians in order to crush a single attacker. But these attackers were also Magicai and confirmed kills were necessary. The citizens were in full panic and Hexlow needed to protect them. Well, no, he wanted to protect them. He *needed* to protect the people in the King's Stand.

A louder scream echoed to Hexlow's left. He swiveled, boots splashing in the mucky water. A woman thrashed in the water, in the grip of a crocodile. *Nobody of importance.* The crocodile had just begun its death spin, anyway. Saving the woman would be near impossible.

He scanned the water, watching as the gladiators on the platform helped their opponents up. *Such a quick alliance. Will it last?* Hexlow didn't think so. Not important, though. He watched for more of the enemy Magicai. "Where are they?"

They'd come in through two blasted holes, but Hexlow had lost them in the menagerie of rubble, citizens, crocodiles, and swamp. He thought he saw one, went to kill them, realized it was just Magicus Barklod, retracted his hand. "Where are they?" he said.

Then Hexlow's face was ripped off.

Demri and Caius had slid into the water. With all the people flailing about, it became easy to disappear.

They'd swam away from the commotion near the hole. His foot got stuck in the mud again and he couldn't pull himself out without causing agonizing pain.

"Stuck," Demri said.

Caius yanked him out.

"Thank you, C-Caius." The deeper they went, the easier it was to navigate. Fewer people, fewer waves, fewer enemies. Both the crocodiles and the Magicai had turned their focus to the breach in Buzzard's Bowl.

"Not much further."

Their destination was the gladiators huddled on the center platform.

Demri saw a Magicus on the other side of the arena raise a hand. A portion of the stands exploded, collapsing on one of the Elkavich.

"You b-bastard," Demri muttered. He consumed a Soul Glyph, drawing power from his Well. For a moment, he savored the feeling with closed eyes. Then he let loose, flinging a razor-sharp spike of ice at the Magicus. The man took a step back and for a moment, Demri thought he was going to miss. The spike sheared through the man's head, separating it in two, and he sank into the bog.

"Smells like shit in here," Caius said.

"P-Probably is."

A flash of orange and then fire was everywhere. Smoke began billowing into the air, darkening the arena.

"Demri, on your left!"

He listened to Caius and found himself looking into two reptilian eyes. Then an enormous mouth opened, and rows of jagged teeth lunged at Demri.

"Fuck!" Scayde Haklon threw his glass of wine over the glass half-wall in the King's Stand. "Fuck!" He punched a pillar which supported the ceiling of the stand. "Fuck!" A hand touched his shoulder and he turned and punched that, too. His servant, Tanibris, fell backwards, cupping a bloody nose. "Don't touch me!"

He raged, he snarled. He hated everyone and everything. "Who the fuck is attacking us?" He grabbed his wife's empty glass, smashed it on the ground. "Fuck!"

"We should leave," Jaylena said.

She was right. It wasn't safe to remain in the King's Stand when Magicai were slinging their shit everywhere. *Fuck!*

<hr>

Magicus Barklod spotted a pair of the feral Magicai. He consumed multiple Soul Glyphs, felt his skin stretching, wrinkles forming, felt hair sprouting. He wasn't about to die without bringing these bastards down with him. Barklod neglected to consider everyone he was about to kill: the innocents. Battle frenzy corrupted his mind, and he charged through the swamp towards the breach. He didn't notice the severed leg bump against his thighs as he half-ran, half-swam towards the commotion.

An enormous ball of flame grew in the sky. The power was too much. If he didn't release it now, he'd have to keep consuming his Well to feed it, and then he'd risk immolation.

Barklod let the inferno drop. The ball of fire crashed into a crowd of fleeing civilians, immediately killing them. Barklod hadn't paid attention. He'd dropped the ball on one of the Magicai. Grinning, he searched for another target. Barklod turned in time to spot the spinning hatchet catch him in the chest. He choked, blood spilled from his mouth, and he keeled over. A crocodile made a quick meal out of him.

<hr>

Seeker Korran only had one hatchet left. He looked for another target, saw a crocodile surging towards a pair of people in the bog. One of them a Magicus he'd seen kill another Magicai. Grunting, he took aim and made another powerful throw. The hatchet spun end over end and hit its mark. The crocodile snarled, dove beneath the water, and disappeared. One of the two men in the water retrieved his hatchet and continued swimming towards the platform.

Captain Jin Whiskey was, despite his parents' sense of humor, a serious man with no time for laughter. He was in charge of local security for Buzzard's Bowl and he didn't know how things had gone so wrong.

"Quick, quick, quick!" Whiskey said, leading a regiment of soldiers towards the gladiator arena. Something bad had happened. Something terrible. Something, Whiskey thought, he should've been able to prevent.

Citizens of Lochwall streamed out of a massive hole in Buzzard's Bowl. A river of murky water came with them. Along with an awful smell.

"Ignore the citizens. They're safe," Whiskey said. "Into the arena. Prevent the gladiators from escaping. Kill them all if you have to. Don't disappoint the Mother, men. She's watching us today!"

The soldiers roared, charging through the throngs of confused, injured, and disjointed civilians. Into battle.

Edelbrock had reached the platform where the other gladiators had been early in the battle. Seeker Korran helped him up, and then Edelbrock helped the five other House Haklon gladiators onto the dock. Where the missing sixth one was, Edelbrock didn't know.

It soon became apparent there wasn't much Edelbrock could do to contribute to the battle. Not much any of them could do. This was a fight between Magicai, it seemed. Whoever had attacked Buzzard's Bowl, he hoped they won.

He watched two factions of Magicai square off, flinging their power at one another. Fire and ice collided, freezing and burning. He saw one of the Buzzard's Bowl Magicai incinerate in a burst of flame and a puff of smoke.

"Weapons ready!" Flimsy Shirley the Remerian Girly said, raising her mace to point at a group of armed men charging into the arena.

Edelbrock walked to the front of the crowd of gladiators, stepping in-between Seeker Korran and Call Me Freshly—a name he'd have to inquire over if they both lived.

"Don't let them onto the platform," Edelbrock said. "Buzzard's Battalion!" he raised his voice to be heard over the sounds of screaming citizens, splashing water, Magicai, and crocodiles flailing about. "Form a perimeter!"

Demri and Caius separated. Caius swam towards the platform to deliver the hatchet to their savior and help stand against the incoming rush of soldiers. Demri would swim across the bog and confront the Magicai.

Being in deeper water allowed him to take pressure off his legs. In the bog, Demri could float, move, and use his powers —without, he hoped, being seen. He pushed his concerns about crocodiles from his mind.

A Magicus stopped firing blasts of flame across the water, and instead, was now pushing the water and its inhabitants— people and crocodile alike—towards Myri. The greenish-brown water rose in waves, and Demri saw a person's hand reaching, struggling to pull themselves above water. Then the water crashed over Myri, knocking her down, and the strug-gling person disappeared. A dazed crocodile landed only a few feet from her. The water flowed from the hole in Buzzard's Bowl, draining the arena. Demri felt his foot brush the muddy bottom. Swimming wasn't an option any longer.

Already, the Magicus was sending another wave in her direction, which would push the crocodile closer.

Demri spied a floating hatchet behind the Magicus. Instead of pushing air, he pulled it, sending the hatchet spin-ning. The blade cleaved through the Magicus with the force of a tornado. He exploded in a burst of gore.

Caius delivered the hatchet to the man who'd thrown it.

"Thank you," he said.

"No, thank you."

The charging soldiers reached the platform. One of the men, Caius presumed he was in charge, shouted orders. "Storm the platform! Crossbowmen, ready, aim—"

Crossbowmen? Caius dove to the floor.

"Fire!"

Bolts whizzed above and around him, and the screams of the injured and dying rang out.

"Charge! Crossbowmen, reload!"

Caius needed to kill him first. He drew his favorite pair of knives.

Ced hung back on purpose. Myri had given him alternative orders. He was still outside Buzzard's Bowl, slinking around the perimeter, watching the stairs which led up to the King's Stand, waiting for someone to come down. Whoever it was, Myri wanted them dead. The hole leading into the arena was on the opposite side of where Ced was, meaning he was isolated, as everyone—soldiers, fleeing citizens, and Magicai—were over there.

"Fuck!" he heard somebody yell, followed by the sounds of people descending the stairs. Ced saw an angry man in a yellow cape—the owner of Buzzard's Bowl, if their intelligence was correct—flanked by a group of guardsmen and companions.

Ced drew his hand back and launched his attack.

Captain Jin Whiskey commanded another volley of bolts fired. They tore through the rebellious curs, cutting down their ranks.

"Load!" he ordered. His voice was growing hoarse and he cleared his throat.

Good men charged the gladiators, were cut down, and killed.

They were fortunate the water levels were so low, or it would've slowed them. There wasn't enough water for either people or crocodiles to hide, and Whiskey saw several of the reptiles tearing through corpses. Civilian corpses. Innocent people killed . . . for what? A rebellion? An attack from gladiators? None of it made sense to Whiskey. *How'd they blow a hole in the wall?*

"Fire!"

Another barrage tore through the gladiators. Whiskey smirked—that annoying girl, the skinny one who'd become famous—had two bolts in her chest, and she lay in the mud, bleeding out. Flimsy Shirley the Remerian Girly was her name. *Even legends are mortal.*

"Load! Second charge!"

His repelled men surged toward the gladiators again.

Scayde Haklon felt a fist slam into his face as somebody tackled him, and he hit the ground, stunned. His head exploded in pain and he moaned. Something was pinning him down. He grunted, opened his eyes, saw black. Blinked, cleared his vision, and shoved the oppressive pressure off his back. It was a body. His head servant. Bloody bits of Tanibris littered the grass and whatever had blown him up had injured plenty of Scayde's companions. His wife, Jaylena, lay a few feet away, clearly injured but not dead.

Several of his Magicai guards had spread out and were looking in the same direction.

"Fuck," he said, drawing his sword and returning to his feet.

"Yer dead," a Magicus said, giggling. He said it with confidence, though he was alone and Scayde had at least three healthy Magicai guards with him.

"What did I do?" Scayde wanted to know. He'd never seen this man before.

The Magicus paused, seemed uncertain. When he opened his mouth to respond, Scayde's guards acted, blasting the man with three different attacks. One, a bolt of power which resembled lightning, another a cone of ice shards, and the other ripped the earth up on either side of the Magicus, squishing him like a bug beneath a shoe.

Scayde was livid. "You didn't let him speak!" He rarely had an issue remaining composed, but today wasn't a normal day. He vented again. "Fuck!"

Ced felt a blast of power course down his body, stunning him for a moment, then a cluster of shards of ice peppered his body. Slicing, cutting, piercing, stabbing, he groaned, screamed, and watched as two pillars of earth rose from the ground on either side of him. He panicked for a moment, before realizing he needed to shield. He threw a bubble of protection around himself just as the pillars met, crushing against one another. Darkness. Silence.

He took a breath, calmed himself down, winced from the wounds he'd suffered. Ced knew oxygen was running out, he'd have to dig his way out—but not too quickly, lest he alarm the enemy who'd almost killed him. Instead of using magic, he sank his hands into the earth and started clawing his way out.

***

A wave of water swept Myri off her feet. She spluttered, coughing mud from mouth. She stood, winced, and realized one of her toes were broken. On a normal day, she'd wait for the toe to heal, but it hurt and was distracting her. She reached within the chamber housing her Healer powers and sacrificed the small amount of life it cost to reset the bone, wincing again as she did so.

The second wave lost most of its power when the Magicai directing it exploded from a hatchet, which tore through him at impossible speeds.

Myri switched her focus from her Healer chamber to her Enforcer chamber.

She watched screaming citizens crowding the stands, trying to flee, causing more carnage instead. Myri learned long ago that anytime tragedy struck, people—and crowds more often than not—turned into fools. *They're all going to die one way or another.* Soon.

Glancing around the arena, searching for Magicai, she saw the gladiators clashing with Scayde's guards. Crossbowmen kept firing into the gladiators. Myri swept her hand like she was backhanding somebody who'd tried to fondle her, then grinned as she found her next quarry.

"Fire!"

The gladiators had changed tactics, and were now in the bog, fighting among Whiskey's men. One had even made a pass at Whiskey himself, but the captain wasn't bad with a sword, and sliced the man's arm off.

Bolts passed by Whiskey, mostly hitting the gladiators. Far more gladiators had died than Whiskey's men.

Catastrophe struck as he finished the thought. Men screamed and Whiskey felt the force of something brushing past his back. He swiveled round and more than half the crossbowmen lay sliced in two, an open-mouthed crocodile still soaring mid-air, teeth cleaving through Whiskey's men.

"Bless the tits on Mother Avani," Whiskey said, open-mouthed.

Call Me Freshly drove his lance into a woman's chest. A plume of blood spewed as her sternum shattered. She grunted, and the light faded from her eyes. He placed a boot on her stomach, pried the lance out, thrust into another charging soldier. There was no end of them. Freshly took a moment and glanced at the hole in the arena—more of Scayde's guards were entering.

Freshly took a moment to stretch, cracked his neck. Fighting was a young man's game and Freshly was getting old, or as Freshly called it, stale.

A flying crocodile ripped through the back line, eviscerating crossbowmen. Limbs, guts, and crossbows entangled, and then the crocodile dropped. It looked like the thing's mouth was broken open. *Somebody needs to put the poor thing out of its misery.* Freshly had always liked animals. They made him happy and—

"Fire!"

"Ah, shit," Freshly tried to say, but only issued a gurgle. He'd gotten distracted.

Blood trickled down his chest and he dropped the lance. His hands reached up, grasping the bolt lodged in his throat.

"Help," he gurgled. Freshly choked, wheezed, collapsed, and fighters trampled his face underwater, though he'd already drowned from the blood when that occurred.

Caius ducked another barrage of the crossbow bolts. He threw a knife; it bounced off a man's forehead. *Knives.* One day, he'd learn to wield a sword.

He drew another knife to replace the one he'd thrown, then launched himself into the melee. Caius stabbed a man in the shin, who was battling an earless gladiator covered in scars. The gladiator finished the man off, nodded to Caius, and found a new target.

Some of these men had once belonged to Caius. Fighting people who belonged to Scayde elevated his adrenaline. It was revenge. Caius would take from Scayde what he'd lost. And, he hoped, that would also mean deposing the man from his station. He fought on.

"Drop bows! To swords!"

Whiskey figured the orders were fruitless—most of the crossbowmen had died or were already using swords. He saw the gladiators were driving a wedge through the center of the remaining guards.

"To me! Rally to me!"

A man with two knives danced through the battle, stabbing, slashing, and slaughtering Whiskey's men, all the while his eyes met Whiskey's. It was then the captain knew the man's target.

Whiskey reached behind his back, touched the handle of the loaded hand crossbow he kept for emergencies. This constituted one.

<hr>

Magicus Kaylan drew up her sleeves. She was short, and her arms were shorter, which meant her sleeves often drifted past her fingertips. Not particularly useful when fighting a battle. Because she was short, instead of descending into the bog like everyone else, she'd remained in the stands, raining death down on anyone she confirmed was an enemy.

"Come on, you civilian-murdering catastrophe-causing shit-spewing entitled fucks! Die!" She always laughed. Some thought Kaylan crazy, others understood she had a different way. She was also great at blowing people up. Kaylan saw an intruder hiding, crouching in the water alone.

One thing which Kaylan wasn't good at was restraint. Instead of ending the man's life, she triple-ended the man's life. She used the water to pull the man down, drowning him —and while he floundered, she conjured a ball of fire and before that had hit him, she blasted a long, jagged bolt of energy at him. Drowned, incinerated, and electrocuted, the corpse floated in the water.

Giddy, she turned, saw another lone man nearby. Another Magicai.

"I'll get you too, you limping ugly turd with the burned face. Why'd your mother even consider keeping you? Haven't done a damn thing because you're a worthless Magicus with zero prospects, no money, and nobody loves ya!

Haha!" She laughed, then a civilian shoved past her, and she wobbled, then lost her balance and fell.

"Ouch!" Kaylan had smacked her knee, bumped her head, and was certain the rude man had bruised her arm. "Come back here, you pussy-whipped dick-licking dog-fucker! Haha!" She stood, saw the man running across the stands. "Nobody hurts me. *NOBODY!*" Kaylan loosed a shard of ice at the fleeing man. It impaled him and he collapsed. "That'll teach you and your liver-spotted bumps-and-fungus-covered shriveled cock! Haha!"

There was a reason Kaylan looked seventy but was only nineteen. She had no restraint.

The hatchet cleaved through a neck, then another person's wrist on the return swing. Seeker Korran gripped the axe with both hands, chopping at the enemy like he was cutting wood for his pa back in the tiny hamlet where he'd been born.

He pursued the raging man with two knives—the one who'd returned the hatchet—watching his back, killing anybody foolish enough to get in Seeker Korran's way. The captain had stopped issuing orders. Instead, he braced himself, sword drawn in his right hand, left hand behind him like he was getting ready to fence in a fancy competition. *Damn fool.* They never promoted people who deserved promotions—in business, military, anything. It was all about how much money you had or worth you brought to the people with money.

He shoved a soldier out of the way and another gladiator finished the soldier off. The man with two knives stumbled out of the melee.

Whiskey faced the knife-wielder, sword ready. His left hand brushed the hand crossbow, and he gripped the handle, unhooking it from his belt.

"It'd be best if you surrender now," Whiskey said.

"Knives are sometimes scarier than they appear."

"I've seen what you can do. You're talented. Don't waste the talent, son. Step down."

The man snarled. Whiskey watched his fingers, saw a twitch. It was all he needed. He whipped the hand crossbow around, pointed it at the knife-wielder, and fired.

Magicus was in the stands, raining her fury down on the Elkavich. Demri thought it looked like an old lady. And, unless he was mistaken, she was the last remaining Magicus working for Scayde in Buzzard's Bowl. The magic had lessened, with only an occasional attack.

The bog's water level had lowered so much, the water didn't pass Demri's lower thigh, which made swimming difficult. Mud sucked at his feet, and each step was an agonizing slurp as he tugged and pulled at weakened bones and nerves.

"C-C-Caius," he said, out of habit. But Caius wasn't there to help. They'd split up.

Groaning, he yanked on his leg. It didn't budge and Demri found himself stuck.

The Magicus in the stands noticed him.

"Forward, go forward!" Edelbrock drove his sword through somebody's back, ripping out an organ. He shook the light pink meat off his blade.

They were winning. Once they killed or routed the

soldiers, the way to freedom was clear. And Buzzard's Battalion was winning.

He caught a spear being thrust at his face with his shield, shoved the man back. Stumbling, the soldier fell into the mud. A great sword chopped him in half and its owner nodded to Edelbrock before throwing himself back into the fray.

Edelbrock searched for the captain commanding the legion, but he'd lost him amid the chaos. Now, he focused on escaping Buzzard's Bowl. He realized this to be a selfish goal —he should return and free the other gladiators. But revenge was on his mind. Edelbrock wanted to find Scayde.

***

Caius twitched, restraining the urge to throw a knife. The captain had noticed, though, and drew a hand crossbow. Everything slowed to a crawl. Caius couldn't move; couldn't react. The twang of the shot, the pointed bolt shooting through the air at him, the pain as metal met flesh. The bolt tore through his stomach, lodging itself halfway through his body.

Caius gasped, dropping one of his knives and gripping the shaft to steady it. Blood spilled down his hand. He stumbled back, taking a knee.

***

Kaylan giggled, watching the Magicus struggle in the mud. She toyed with him, first sending a wave of water over his head, then another, and another, and another. Sputtering, he couldn't get his bearings to attack her. "Not much like the slimy-scaled mud-loving fish-pretender you're attempting to be, I think! Haha!" She sent another wave, then another. Then, because she felt cruel, she reached below the water, forming a large amount of mud into a column. She toppled it onto the Magicus's head. "Haha, eat that!"

***

Demri's eyes, nose, and mouth filled with stinking, stagnant, and revolting mud. He coughed, retched, and near puked. He couldn't see, couldn't breathe. Demri realized he was going to die. What he couldn't figure out was why the Magicus hadn't finished him.

***

Captain Jin Whiskey felt bad about the hand crossbow, but he wasn't taking chances on a madman like that. He carried two spare bolts for the contraption and reloaded it. It wasn't a weapon he used unless he had to. Hooking it back onto his belt, Whiskey saw a new opponent arrive. This grasped a hatchet in two hands.

"Plenty of your kin have fallen at my command," Whiskey said. "Surrender or perish like they have."

"Seeker Korran bends the knee to no man."

Whiskey arched a brow. "Weren't you just fighting in the arena at the behest of Lord Haklon?"

Seeker Korran snarled and charged Whiskey. Hatchet met sword and Whiskey retreated a couple steps, putting space between them.

"Quick to anger, quicker to make a mistake," Whiskey said.

"The only mistake I've made is not ending your life sooner." He swung the hatchet with both hands.

Whiskey blocked, letting the hatchet hook the sword. Entangled, the two weapons pulled against one another.

Seeker Korran snarled. "I'm going to kill you!"

For the second time that day, Whiskey felt the need to use

his hand crossbow. He wouldn't have the presence of mind to pull the trigger, though.

S eeker Korran couldn't have been happier. The captain had fallen for his trap, left hand reaching behind his back to grab the hand crossbow Seeker Korran had watched him reload.

Seeker Korran let go of his hatchet and slipped inside the sword's range. He slammed his forehead into the captain's nose, shattering it, and launched the captain off his feet. Seeker Korran kicked the man in the face, rolled him over, and pried his hand crossbow free. Somehow, he hadn't shot it.

Seeker Korran placed the hand crossbow against the captain's right eye.

"Mercy," the man said.

"Aye." Seeker Korran pulled the trigger.

M yri saw Demri pummeled by mud and the crazed old lady in the stands. She consumed more of her Well, felt her hair lengthen, skin sag, tits droop, eyes weaken, but she pushed the bitch off the stands. The Magicus fell, a shrill scream echoing out over the arena. No, not a scream, a laugh.

The Magicus drew the water from the bog, forming a ramp she slid down. At the bottom, the old lady stood— though now hunched—and started cackling.

Myri fired a cluster of mud she formed into hard rocks from the bog. The old lady blocked them by creating a force shield. The Magicus then collapsed, unmoving. Myri assumed she'd aged out.

She looked over at Demri, who was scraping shit off his

face. Then Caius, who was lying in the mud. She went to Caius first.

Kneeling beside the man, blood leaking down his front, Myri examined the wound. A gut wound. Notorious for killing the strongest of warriors. And Myri didn't doubt Caius was one of the strongest. She also knew she couldn't let the man die. He was Demri's only friend, ally, and assistant. She frowned, not wanting to consume more of her precious life. But she owed Demri this much, at least. She yanked the bolt out of Caius's stomach, and he lurched, groaning.

She accessed the Healer chamber and transferred her life into him. Enough to jumpstart the healing process and close the wound, but it wouldn't erase most of the injury or pain. Myri couldn't afford to do more.

"You'll live," she said.

He grunted.

———

Demri used bog water to wash the mud from his face, but that didn't fix the problem. He had to conjure some fresh water onto his face and age a few hours to do so. But he could see now.

Myri approached, looking grim and several years older, but still as beautiful as ever.

"Demri."

"M-Myri."

"Caius is all right."

"Of c-course he is."

"He almost died."

Demri struggled to his feet. Myri held a hand to help, but Demri would be damned if he'd take it. Not from her.

"Took a crossbow bolt to the stomach. I healed him. Partially."

"Thank you." He wobbled, wincing from the stiffness in

his legs.

Myri stabilized him. "We need to go."

"None of this was worth it if you d-d-don't free the other p-prisoners."

"The gladiators will do it. Come." She led him to where the gladiators were gathered, where Caius, supported by another man, stood.

Caius grimaced upon seeing Demri. "Now we're both disabled."

"Finally, you f-feel my p-p-pain."

Caius snorted.

The man supporting Caius had one ear and scars criss-crossing his skin. "I know you," he said.

"You do?"

"Yes. You were with the Velvet Mother when you visited us. I recognize your voice."

"You're holding the Velvet M-Mother up right now."

Surprised, he glanced at Caius.

"It's true," Caius said, nodding.

"Why are you here?"

"It's a long story. We'll t-t-tell you on our way out," Demri said. "Get some of your f-f-friends and free the others. We d-don't have long."

"I'm Edelbrock Brendis."

"I'm D-Demri, that's C-C-Caius. Get moving." Demri realized he shouldn't have given their true names to a stranger, but he'd forgotten about the stupid Elkavich nicknames.

Edelbrock frowned, looked like he was about to say something and thought better of it, then marched away. He started issuing commands to the others like a military commander.

"Any minute now, the city is going to explode," Myri said.

Buzzards had already landed on corpses and were filling their stomachs with decaying flesh. A few were ripping chunks from a badly injured man. His pained screams faded as they abandoned Buzzard's Bowl.

45

SERADAL WINTLOCK & VILLIC THE IMBUER

Andora, Remeria

King Alondo had delayed the meeting for a few days, giving Sera more time to reflect upon, and properly mourn, the loss of her family and homeland. She remained locked in her room, despite Cyr Patrika Jorst's attempts to coax her outside. Sera knew she was about to take charge of the Falcon Knights, about to lead an army into Calrym. In doing so, however, she'd be expected to take on a lot of responsibility and would be under constant pressure and stress. She needed to clear her mind and prepare herself. Cyr Patrika could lead the Falcon Knights in the interim. Other than Cyr Patrika, nobody bothered Sera—something she was thankful for—and attributed this to Cyr Patrika, who'd posted a pair of sentries outside Sera's door, under instructions to turn away visitors.

Sera longed for the Cyroki landscape, the friendly gyrfalcons her family and village raised, the crisp and early snowy mornings, the ocean's breeze when she brought a gyrfalcon out hunting. She missed the happiness, the stability and comfort of having a home. All that had changed.

She sipped water throughout the days, picked at her food, and slept—a lot. The reprieve did her well, and after two days of uninterrupted rest, she felt leagues better.

On the morning of the fourth day, Cyr Patrika knocked on her door.

"Yes?" Sera asked. The thuds on the door had woken her.

"Cyr Seradal, it's Cyr Patrika Jorst," she said, as if Sera wouldn't recognize her by her first name, or her voice. "King Alondo requests your presence in one hour's time. He's given orders to prepare to march. This afternoon, we leave for Calrym." The knight sounded wary, almost unsure if she should bother Sera.

"Thank you, Cyr Patrika. I'll be in attendance."

"Wonderful news, cyr," Cyr Patrika said, sounding as if a weight had been lifted off her. "I'll inform the officers, ready the soldiers, and ensure we have appropriate supplies."

Sera climbed out of bed, washed, got dressed, and ate breakfast and packed her gear. Then, for the first time in three days, she left her room.

They'd taken to calling him "Sir Villic" and though it felt odd and an insult to the gods, Villic was glad they'd begun accepting him more. Speaker had informed him this was good. That they trusted Villic to help them.

Villic wasn't sure what his goal was. He didn't care about the Remerians, the Redclaws, the Magicai, or the Falcon Knights. He didn't care about the Camel Clans much, either, except forsaking them would anger Killiak, lord of lords, and the other gods. And Villic didn't anger any god on purpose. He wasn't stupid.

He stood behind Sir Seradal, Sir Patrika to his left. On his right, Royal lay in bed. The Bloody Duchess and the poetic man who traveled with her were across the room, next to one of the Magicai, who's name Villic didn't know. They circled King Alondo, who paced back and forth, back and forth. It made Villic dizzy. *Why do that?*

"Some people pace when they're stressed or thinking."

Nobody in the Camel Clans does that.

"Nobody in the Camel Clans thinks."

Villic curled his lip. Every time he thought Speaker was finally getting it, he said something like that.

"This afternoon, Sir Seradal will take a majority of our forces and march towards Calrym," King Alondo said. "Our alliance between Remeria and Cyrok will hold until Calrym is subdued. All who participate shall be rewarded. Sir Seradal and the Falcon Knights will earn Remeria's support in rebuilding Cyrok. The Bloody Duchess and the Redclaws will earn the equality they want. Remeria will provide a remote location for a new University of Arcanical Arts so the Magicai can return to education. And Villic," the king turned to Villic.

Villic flushed, stared at the ceiling, just above the Bloody Duchess's head.

"Villic will attempt to secure the alliance of the Camel Clans. In return, Remeria and the Camel Clans will divide Calrym in half—the western half being allocated to the Camel Clans. No more shall you be relegated to the desert."

Villic liked the desert. But he also knew the reason they had gone to war with Calrym and Remeria was over their better land. And the fact they kept rejecting the Camel Clan presence in their countries. The deal was a good one. He wasn't sure what the godspeakers would think about it, though. He also wasn't sure who to bring the offer to. With Jedkah, former leader of the Splintered Manes, dead, Villic wasn't sure who was leading the clan anymore. Or if the Splintered Manes even existed anymore.

"Does this sound fair?" King Alondo asked.

"It does," Sir Seradal said.

Royal took a noisy sip from a bottle before saying, "Cheers."

Villic saw the Bloody Duchess and her man nodding in his peripheral vision.

"It's good," the Magicus said.

Silence. Villic felt eyes on him. He needed to say something.

Swallowing, he lowered his gaze, saw too many people staring at him.

"Are these terms acceptable?" King Alondo asked.

Villic tried speaking, but his throat was dry and his mind stopped working. He nodded.

"Good," the king said. "For the benefit of all nations, for the betterment of Cedain, you ride to victory in the evening and will crush the Calrite dogs!"

People cheered their assent and Villic nodded, feeling a trickle of sweat dripping down his side.

———

They loaded the horses and camels with supplies and important people. Sera had her own horse, though she felt more comfortable walking. Cyr Patrika was a natural horse rider, though, and kept sauntering up and down the lines, keeping the army moving. Renard, Sera's page, stayed at her side. As did Villic, who never said anything. She'd started calling him "Cyr Villic" in order to help make him feel more comfortable. Perhaps he'd start saying more. She knew family was important, and she was hoping to, if not create a family, create the illusion of one. At the end of everything, family was what mattered.

The Magicus who tagged along was the only Magicus with them. She didn't know his name. Sera had the distinct feeling the man enjoyed remaining elusive. She wished she knew why he was here. Was it to spy on her? Or make sure she was keeping her promises to King Alondo? Or maybe the Magicus was there because King Alondo wanted her to succeed, so he commanded the Magicus to go as well. Sera wouldn't go back on the plan, though. Her vows meant something. Promises meant something. And King Alondo was offering the Cyroki help. It'd be foolish to turn him down, despite the risks of going to battle. Along with the Falcon Knights and the Redclaws, the king was dispatching half of his army to accompany them. If they could join the Camel Clans, they'd be unstoppable.

With the sun high, warming the fields, they left Andora amid cheers and well-wishes from the townsfolk. The king even saluted them from atop the repaired city wall.

They marched for several hours, heading into the jungle, following a wide dirt path. An hour into the jungle and one of her frontrunners pointed out fresh horse tracks—the Camel Clans. It seemed they were on the right path to encountering the clans. Sera felt both relief and apprehension. Relief, because she'd brought Villic the Imbuer along. Having somebody who could vouch for her, and the goals of those with her, would hopefully help in securing an alliance with them. Apprehension, because, if the Camel Clans weren't interested in an alliance, a battle could occur between the two armies—a battle Sera was sure they'd lose.

"Cyr Seradal," Renard said, running up the line to catch up to her. He'd been relaying her orders to the Bloody Duchess. He took a moment to suck in several gulps of air. "The Bloody Duchess agrees to settling down for the night."

"Wonderful, I'm glad we agree." She almost rolled her eyes. "Thank you for informing her. Take a moment to gather your breath, then go see if any of the scouts have any news to report."

"Yes, cyr."

She switched her attention to Villic, who, as usual, was beside her. "Cyr Villic."

He snapped to attention, eyes drifting away from hers to stare at a nearby tree. His camel, Dunecrest, following in his wake. Villic hadn't ridden the camel, nor would he allow anyone else to ride him. She didn't question it—she questioned nothing Villic did because the man was strange. There wasn't another word for it.

"Do the Camel Clans travel during the night?"

Villic shrugged. "Sometime."

"If you went ahead of us, do you think you'd be able to catch them?"

Villic nodded.

"Great. Catch up to them, see if they'll wait. I'd like to discuss our potential partnership."

Villic said nothing, just mounted Dunecrest and rode off. She hoped she'd made the right decision.

With summer only days away, Villic looked forward to the hotter weather. He also looked forward to being out from beneath the bush trees.

"They're just trees. Trees and bushes are different."

Speaker could claim to know about plants, but Villic had been living in this world long enough. He didn't need help. He gripped Dunecrest with his thighs, letting the animal guide itself down the trail. Villic wondered if he'd meet anyone he knew. Or if the Splintered Manes still existed.

He rode the camel until it got too dark, and dangerous, to continue. Then he let Dunecrest wander while he made a small fire, snacked on some dried bread, and went to sleep.

He woke early and, after cleaning up his camp and eating more of the bread, hopped back onto Dunecrest and continued.

What happened? What was that power? Villic thought back to the siege. When he'd summoned darkness, stabbed the man, and felt rejuvenated. He wasn't sure why he thought about it now, or why he hadn't thought about it much after. *I know you said calling darkness wasn't something you knew how to do, but what happened to me when I used it?*

"It felt like—this is speculation, mind you—the sword drained the life from the man you stabbed, and, somehow, that life entered you. Whether this has any long or-short-term effects on the body isn't something I know. I imagine it's a temporary effect that heals the user, and then dissipates. However, I'm unsure as to the validity of this information. Calling to darkness, though, doesn't sound like it'd be great for an individual's health. I would advise against doing it frequently."

Villic didn't understand several of the words Speaker used, but he understood the vibe. Don't call darkness unless it is necessary.

He spent another day and a half chasing the Camel Clans. And then, out of nowhere, he rounded a bend in the jungle's trail and entered a clearing where hundreds of men, women, and camels lounged about.

Upon seeing Villic, they sprang to their feet, drawing weapons. He saw Imbuers calling to unique elements, altering their weapons, forming a half-circle in front of him. When they recognized he was a clansman, they calmed themselves. A moment passed and the half-circle opened.

A dirty shaman with long braids appeared, and Villic swallowed. The crowd made him nervous, but now a shaman was going to speak to him.

"Don't lose focus, Villic."

The shaman chewed her fingernail for a moment, then spat. "What make you come here?"

Villic clenched his jaw, saw the sea of people staring at him, waiting for him to speak. "I—"

The dirty shaman stomped her foot, impatient. "Yes?"

Villic cleared his throat hoping to expel any frogs. He didn't want to croak. "I'm Villic the Imbuer," he said while the other clansmen gasped and applauded. Villic knew they didn't know who he was, more that they were impressed he'd made his way back to them.

"I'm Uva the Shaman," the dirty woman said. "What clan do you originate from?"

"The Splintered Manes."

Murmurs passed through the gathering.

The dirty shaman bit her fingernail and spat again. "It make me sad to say it, but that clan is gone."

Villic nodded, looking at the ground from atop Dunecrest. His heart lurched at the thought Jedkah was gone, and the other brothers and sisters he'd lived with, dead. He hadn't formed connections with them, even disliked talking to all of them, but he still felt bad they'd all died. Villic was alone, though he'd always felt alone. Now, though, nobody knew him.

"It took you a long time to find us," Uva the Shaman said.

"I was in the city." Everyone's eyes were still on him. Dunecrest snorted, stamped a foot. Villic felt just as uncomfortable. Sweat formed on his forehead and under his arms.

"Doing what? And don't touch Lurzal," she said.

Lurzal, god of deception, Villic recited to himself. He couldn't remember the gods without their title. "I won't go against the gods. Killiak, lord of lords, would slay me."

Uva the Shaman nodded, watching him with a strange expression.

"She wants you to keep speaking. Her expression is one of interest."

"They captured me. I work with them. We're friends. They're good people. Sir Seradal wants to talk to you. She sent me here."

Some clansmen shouted insults or laughed at him, while others whispered to one another. Uva the Shaman's face scrunched up.

"She's angry. Watch her."

I don't want to anger the godspeakers. I don't want to call down the wrath of the gods. Anaia, goddess of light, help me.

"You betray your kin. It make me angry!" Uva the Shaman raised a wooden staff into the air. "Killiak, lord of lords, demands you answer to him!"

Villic felt his skin go cold despite the profuse sweating.

"Answer for your betrayal, Villic the Imbuer," Uva the Shaman said. She shook her staff in the air. To Villic, it looked like she was about to call upon the power of the gods to strike him down.

"Wait!" Villic, panicked, slid off Dunecrest and held his hands up, collapsing to his knees. "I don't betray the clans. I come to help!" Tears rained from his eyes as though he was a storm, great cracks of thunder came from his throat.

Uva the Shaman paused. "Help?" she asked, quirking her head to one side. "Help how?"

"Camel Clans want to destroy Calrym. Sir Seradal wants to destroy Calrym."

"This make things interesting," Uva the Shaman said. "Bring him to me."

"Sir Seradal is like you," Villic said. "Sir Seradal is a woman."

Uva the Shaman smiled. "The gods bless us."

46

EDELBROCK BRENDIS

Lochwall, Calrym

Edelbrock and Seeker Korran stood at the head of a large group of former gladiators from the five Houses, all freed. Now they were discussing a plan: where to go, what to do. And somebody had mentioned something about blowing up Lochwall, though Edelbrock wasn't sure what they were talking about. A bloodied Magicus stumbled into the group. "Ced's not dead," he said, laughing and pointing at himself.

"Shame," Magicus D-Four said, sighing, though Edelbrock doubted anyone else noticed.

Magicus Demri shook his head. "B-Blessing in d-d-disguise." He lay in a cart, the former Velvet Mother—a man named Caius—next to him, nursing a wound.

"No matter. We need to get as far away from here as possible," Magicus D-Four said. She turned to the gladiators. "You'll come with us. It's not far to Hidehedge and you'll be fed well. I can't promise lodging, as there's a lot of you. I can promise freedom, though—as long as you offer your services to us. A war is on the horizon, and you're going to need to pick a side. Far as I see it, there are two. You can side with him and the other nobles, along with the Ashmount Magicai," she pointed at Scayde Haklon's manor, "or you can side with us, the Elkavich. A group of Magicai who have exposed Ashmount for its corruption, lies, and hypocrisy. Much like the nobility I'm sure you're all eager to slaughter."

Most of the gladiators nodded and shouted their agreements.

Edelbrock glanced at Seeker Korran, who seemed hesitant. Edelbrock shared his feelings. "I can't go," Edelbrock said. "But I'd like to thank you for freeing us. I have business in Lochwall." He wanted to sprint over to Scayde Haklon's manor, but he knew the man would be gone. Jaylena, too. *Cowards.*

"Lochwall's going to be gone after today," Magicus D-Four said. "Your best bet is to come with us. The city is about to go up in flames."

"I have people to kill." He thought of Scayde, Jaylena. The barrister, Chardaine. Killing Marshal Deywin wasn't enough. And he hadn't even killed the marshal. Not really. He'd caused the man to choke to death. There wasn't any satisfaction with the kill. He needed to *feel* like he'd gotten his revenge.

"Lochwall is still gone after today," she said.

"When?"

"At sundown."

"Thank you." Edelbrock, sore, tired, pained, and near broken, turned and walked away from his saviors.

Footsteps followed. Seeker Korran tapped him on the shoulder with the haft of one of his hatchets. "I'll tag along. Never liked big groups, anyhow."

"If you change your mind," Magicus D-Four called after them, "find a man named Tolsec Cabranth. He goes by C-One. He'll be masquerading as a jester in the city square."

delbrock and Seeker Korran entered Lochwall amid questionable looks from distracted gate guards. Dirty, wet, garbed in plain clothing, and marred with wounds and scars, the pair didn't look like the usual citizens. The guards, however, seemed more concerned with whatever they were whispering about than stopping and questioning them.

According to the Elkavich, Edelbrock had until sundown to complete his mission, which gave him several hours.

"Where are we headed?" Seeker Korran asked.

"A law office by the name of Roachford and Singleton's. There's a barrister I need to meet with."

Edelbrock led the way through sections of Lochwall. He passed through the residential area he used to live in—even noticing his old house. Somebody was living in it. He gritted his teeth and walked by. There wasn't time to worry about it, and anything left inside was surely gone by now. They walked through the city square where, just as Magicus D-Four said there would be, a jester laughed and danced for a group of spectators. Then they came to the largest section of businesses in Lochwall. Halfway down the street, the sign appeared for Roachford and Singleton's. Etched into the wooden block—carved in the shape of a sheet of parchment with a quill sticking out the side—a man sat behind a desk with his customer jumping for joy.

"What do you plan on doing to this barrister?"

"What he did to me," Edelbrock said. He walked through the door and was met by a dainty girl behind a counter.

She smiled at him. "Hello, welcome to Roachford and—"

"I'm here to see Chardaine."

"Do you have a scheduled appoint—"

"No. Which office is he in?" Edelbrock asked. Two hallways broke off from the entranceway, several doors in each hall with placards mounted on the wall next to them. "Never mind, they appear to be labeled."

"Sir, Barrister Hugomes is with a client. I must request that you schedule a *proper* meeting and return during the allotted time." The girl opened a ledger. "Your name?"

Edelbrock stared at her. "There won't be time to schedule anything because at sundown, Lochwall is going to be destroyed."

The girl giggled. Upon seeing Edelbrock's stern expression, she stopped. "What do you mean?"

"It's going to disappear."

Worry etched itself on the girl's face. "Like what happened with the University of Arcanical Arts? I thought that was just a rumor."

"Exactly like with the university. Get out of the city. *Now,*" Edelbrock said.

The girl blanched, realized Edelbrock was serious, and then ran out of the law office.

"Now the entire city will be in a panic," Seeker Korran said.

"Let's get this done." Edelbrock marched down the first hallway, reading the placards. Halfway down, he read the one he wanted: Barrister Chardaine Hugomes. Despite having hired the man, Edelbrock had never been inside his office. He'd met Chardaine out in the law office's entrance, when Chardaine was preparing to go home one night. Instead of returning to his room, Chardaine offered Edelbrock a meal where they could discuss business. Edelbrock obliged and thought he'd hired somebody who would aid him. Unfortunately, Chardaine was in the pockets of Scayde Haklon.

The door was unlocked, and Edelbrock opened it and strode inside.

Surprised, an elderly woman and a man who appeared to be her son turned and looked at the intruders. Behind the desk, Barrister Chardaine Hugomes had a glass of whiskey halfway to his mouth.

Chardaine didn't recognize Edelbrock. "Excuse me, I'm with clients. Make an appointment with the secretary up front." He shooed Edelbrock away.

"I recommend you vacate this office and come back later," Edelbrock said to the two strangers. He walked into the office, sword and shield in hand.

Taking his advice, they gathered their things and hurried out.

Chardaine stood and slammed his glass onto his desk, spilling whiskey on the half-filled out documents splayed across the surface. "Who in the—"

"This is Seeker Korran," Edelbrock said, waving his companion in. "And I'm Edelbrock Brendis."

"Oh no," Chardaine said, collapsing back into his chair.

"You screwed me."

Chardaine shook his head. "No, no, no. I *had* to Mr. Brendis. If I hadn't, Scayde—"

"Would have killed your son?" Edelbrock said, walking up to the desk. "Married your wife?" He pulled the desk away from Chardaine, sliding it against another wall. "Thrown you into a gladiator arena where he tried to have you killed countless times?" He leaned down, putting his face in Chardaine's. "Tortured you?" Edelbrock raised the sword, pressing the point into Chardaine's stomach. "Carve your body with his initials? Cut your ear off?" He poked the sword harder.

Chardaine gulped and cleared his throat. "Mr. Brendis," he held his hands up, nervous smile displaying clenched teeth.

"Barrister."

Edelbrock heard a thump behind him. A glance told him it was just Seeker Korran sitting in a chair, propping his feet up on Chardaine's desk.

"Don't kill me. I have kids."

"*I* had a kid!"

"I have four," Chardaine said, eyes flicking back and forth between Edelbrock and Seeker Korran. Searching for help.

"It'd give me great pleasure to force you to bring me to them," Edelbrock said, his forehead bumping against Chardaine's. "I'd make you watch as I cut each of them to pieces."

Chardaine winced, a tear rolling down his cheek. "No," he whispered.

"I'd laugh and have a drink, like you did."

"Please . . ."

"You took everything from me."

"You were breaking the law! You'd committed murder! Don't kill me. Don't be who you were, Mr. Brendis. Please."

The barrister was right. Edelbrock had killed a good man. "That doesn't justify what you did to me, Barrister Hugomes." He spat the name like it disgusted him. It did disgust him. If Chardaine's family were here, Edelbrock knew he'd follow through in murdering them, too. Just to make the barrister feel what Edelbrock had.

"No, it doesn't. And what I did doesn't justify this!"

Edelbrock sneered. "You don't even know what happened to me."

"I watched you fight in Buzzard's Bowl. You did great, truly, a spectacular performance. You made my family a lot of money, Mr. Brendis. I could give you some—a lot. I could make you rich. Just don't kill me."

"I don't want your money," Edelbrock said. He threw the sword on the ground.

Chardaine breathed a sigh of relief. "Then what is it you do want?"

"Vengeance." He slammed the shield into Chardaine's face, breaking the man's nose and shattering his front teeth.

Chardaine screamed, tipping over in the chair as he

attempted to push away from Edelbrock. His head cracked against the wall, and he screamed again.

Edelbrock stepped over the chair, leering at the whimpering barrister.

"Pleath," the barrister said. "Doan kill muh."

"I won't," Edelbrock said.

The barrister sighed in relief. "Thank—"

"Yet." Edelbrock brought the shield down with both hands. It ricocheted off Chardaine's ribs with a loud snap. Chardaine raised a hand to stop Edelbrock. He brought the shield down on his forearm next. The limb collapsed to the floor, limp.

Chardaine closed his eyes, sobbing. Tears streamed down his face, dripping onto the rug. "Pleath, pleath, I'm thowwy."

"Apologies don't bring back the dead. For the record, I'm sorry, too."

Chardaine screamed, eyes bulging in terror as Edelbrock brought the shield down as hard as he could on the barrister's neck. He choked, coughed, and spluttered. Edelbrock repeated the attack again and again. The third blow crushed the barrister's windpipe, and he gasped for air, moaning and weeping.

Edelbrock straightened, watching the barrister gargle for air. It was a long and painful death that took many minutes, and Edelbrock didn't hasten it.

<hr>

They left Roachford and Singleton's, and in the street, Edelbrock stopped.

"You good?" Seeker Korran asked. The man had both his hatchets in his hands. Edelbrock wondered if he was expecting trouble from Edelbrock or locals.

"I'm good." But he didn't feel good. He'd killed the barrister, but the barrister was nothing compared to Scayde and

Jaylena. Marshal Deywin didn't deliver the satisfaction of revenge, either. "I need to find Scayde."

"I doubt he's hanging around here after what happened at the Bowl."

"No, I'm sure he's gone." Edelbrock knew Scayde was a duke appointed by the king. He assumed the nobleman was fleeing to Anepolis to beg for assistance.

"Perhaps we should pay the jester a visit? Find the Elkavich?"

Edelbrock sighed but agreed with a nod. Hanging around Lochwall was a foolish endeavor and he didn't want to die before finding the last two people on his list. "Let's find Tolsec Cabranth."

They returned to the city square where the jester was dancing, throwing balls in the air.

Edelbrock and Seeker Korran approached the man, who smiled at them.

"Candy? Or are you here to offer a tip?" he asked with a wink.

"We're here for information. Tolsec Cabranth, right?"

Tolsec's expression turned serious. "How did you know that?"

"Magicus D-Four told us after she freed us from Buzzard's Bowl," Seeker Korran said.

"I see. Well, what do you want?"

"How can you be so cheerful?" Edelbrock asked. "You're pretending to laugh and dance and entertain, but you're going to die if you stay."

Tolsec smiled. "It's because of me the city will cease to exist. Well, myself and a few others. We believe in propelling Cedain into a new beginning."

"By killing everyone?" Edelbrock asked. It made little sense to him. Kill thousands to do what?

"It's not pretty, and yes, it's very radical, I admit," Tolsec glanced around, waiting for a happy couple to walk out of earshot. "To start anew, things need to be erased. The Elkavich have operated for hundreds of years, fighting oppression, lies, and deceit. Trying to expose hypocrisy, show the people they've been lied to for as long as Ashmount has existed. But it's never worked. Nobody ever believes. And we're sick of living in darkness."

"But you're going to die," Edelbrock said. "Living in darkness isn't as bad as death."

"It's a sacrifice, yes," Tolsec said. "But one I'm willing to make. One every member of the Elkavich is willing to make. If we don't reset the world, we'll always be hunted."

Edelbrock couldn't argue about that. People had always feared the Elkavich, always assumed if they were real, they were evil. Until they'd freed him and admitted they were the Elkavich, Edelbrock wouldn't have believed they even existed. He still wasn't sure they did. Perhaps a bunch of crazed Magicai got together and formed a neurotic, psychopathic group.

"Why are you here?" Tolsec asked.

"We need directions to Hidehedge. Magicus D-Four said you'd provide them."

"All right. You can have the directions, but you need to leave as soon as I give them to you. Plan is moving ahead of schedule," Tolsec said.

"Why? It wasn't supposed to happen until sundown," Seeker Korran said.

Tolsec shook his head. "The Elkavich are smart enough not to relay the true plans to anyone outside of the plan. Otherwise, corrupt members could expose it. Magicus D-Four, despite her being in charge of the plan, isn't aware of the exact time."

Seeker Korran laughed. "I'm noticing you have a lot of good luck, Edelbrock."

"It's well overdue," he said.

Tolsec gave them the directions and bid them farewell.

They left Lochwall and headed north, towards the town called Pinecrest, near the location of Hidehedge.

"Strange man, Tolsec Cabranth," Seeker Korran said.

"Indeed." Edelbrock didn't feel like talking, too preoccupied thinking about Chardaine, and what he was planning on doing to Scayde and Jaylena. Many people might feel bad fantasizing about torturing and murdering their ex-wife. Edelbrock, however, did not.

"I don't see how he could think killing himself would make the world a better place. I mean, yes, I can understand the logic from their perspective—the Elkavich get to live in peace. But he doesn't. He'll be dead. Why care?"

"Some people," Edelbrock said, thinking of his son, Gordane, "would die to help those they love."

"Yes, I suppose you're right. I'm not one of them, though."

Edelbrock didn't think he was, either. And then his son had been thrown off a balcony. They continued walking in silence when, about a mile up the road, they heard the first explosion in Lochwall.

"Rest in peace, Tolsec Cabranth," Seeker Korran said.

47

ASHEN HYREL

Calrym

Ashen still hadn't gotten used to Rooftop's height. The horse towered over everything. Falling would be a death sentence. She and Tallas had ridden for days towards Lochwall, the city where she planned to start a new life. Her home of Anepolis held too much sorrow and pain— the death of her parents, her life as an urchin, the betrayal of Jaspard, and ghosts of the dead. Memories of the slaughter brought on by Tallas Taybold's halberd haunted her.

"Gets easier, My Lady," He still seemed incapable of calling her "Ashen".

"Huh?"

"Dealing with the death. I've seen the distant look on your face countless times. It gets easier."

She looked at Rooftop's bobbing head, avoiding Tallas's gaze. Though only one-eyed, he had a stare fit for four.

"Don't worry, once we get to Lochwall, I'll set you up. Won't have to deal with me," he said.

Tallas had been saying that since they'd left Anepolis. It sounded like he meant well, like he thought she didn't want him around. But that wasn't true. For most of her life, Ashen had been alone. Once they reached Lochwall, she'd be alone again. The fresh start appealed to her, but not alone. She didn't want to like a child begging him to stay, though. That, she assumed, would only drive him further away, quicker.

"Look," he said. His one eye squinted forward. She followed his gaze out across the plains, beneath the orange glow of the setting sun. All she saw was orange tinted grass reflecting the sunlight. "A caravan."

She squinted, looking down the dirt road. Saw nothing but ruts and small stones. "Well, ain't you an eagle-eyed blind man?"

"Heh. When you're in constant danger, you develop a keen eye."

She frowned, wishing the mercenary understood her past. "I've been in danger."

Grinning, he looked over at her and nodded. "I wouldn't doubt that. But you grew up in a city. Never left, right?"

"Aye."

"Then you could never look further than the next building. And buildings aren't too far apart in most of Anepolis."

She thought about that for a moment. "No, I guess they're not. At least not compared to out here." Ashen glanced around at the fields stretching as far as the eye could see, fading into the horizon. At first, the view mesmerized her. Now, she just wanted to get to the end of the plains. They were, Ashen thought, aptly named—she called them "plain plains", something which had made Tallas chuckle.

"There's beauty in the open air," Tallas said, a faraway look on his face, grin plastered across his lips like he'd just eaten an entire custard.

Ashen wouldn't call it beauty, but it felt different from being inside a city full of buildings, noise, people, and odor.

When they got closer, Ashen saw the caravan was really

just two covered wagons, pulled by a pair of mules each, and a group of people walking alongside, some of them armed.

A rearguard stepped in front of Tallas's horse, hand reaching for his sword. "What's your business?"

"Just passing through. On our way to Lochwall," Tallas said.

"Coincidentally, so are we," the guard said, eying the halberd Tallas balanced on his legs. "Any good with that?"

Tallas shrugged.

"You seem the sort," the guard said. "If you're willing to ward off any hostiles, you can travel with us. Safety in numbers and all. I'm sure the caravan master would pay you an equal share of the goods, too. Once we sell them in Lochwall, that is."

"Safe passage would be welcome. Unless you're opposed, Ashen?" Tallas asked, glancing at her.

"Aye." Safety in numbers sounded good, though she doubted anyone here would help protect them against Anepolis guardsmen. She didn't raise the point to Tallas, then. Figured there were other potential threats on the road that it didn't matter.

"Good."

The guard nodded. "Just check in with the caravan master. He's riding in the first wagon."

Tallas and Ashen rode past the guard, and several others, then the first wagon. The second wagon, Ashen noticed, had a more extravagant covering. While the first wagon was fancy compared to most wagons, the second wagon had a solid exterior, complete with a wide door, steps, and windows. An armored man sat on a small platform attached to the rear of the wagon, sitting just to the side of the door. He watched them approach.

Rich men. Ashen remembered being a rich person for a while, herself. It was nice, she admitted, but being herself was nicer. The constant worrying about the king's perception of her was gone. As was the concern over the political battles always taking place between the dukes and duchesses.

The armored man didn't look like a normal caravan guard. His armor was shinier and fancier than everyone else's. He sported a well-groomed beard and a giant—and loaded—crossbow. Across his back, he carried a case of bolts and a long sword.

"Who might you be?" he asked, spitting something at the churned-up mud.

"Tallas Taybold. And this is Ashen. A rearguard claimed this caravan was heading to Lochwall, and if we wanted to tag along, we could." Tallas held his halberd up. "As long as we contributed, of course."

"Course," the man said. He reached into a pocket, retrieving some seeds and threw them into his mouth. "I'm expecting you want to talk to the bossman?"

"Well, ain't you a—"

"Ashen," Tallas said, cutting her off and giving her a stare.

She gave him her sweetest smile, though Ashen didn't know what that might look like. Judging by the faces of both Tallas and the guard, it wasn't pretty.

The man thumped on the door twice. A moment later, Ashen heard a bolt sliding open, and the door cracked open an inch.

"What is it? Don't tell me one of the idiot mules broke a leg already, ah-hah." Duke Velturo Ondakka opened the door wider, peering at first at the guard, then at Tallas and Ashen. A noticeable wet stain was spreading down his trousers, red in appearance. Ashen surmised he'd been drinking wine. Upon seeing Tallas, Velturo squeaked, screamed, and slammed the door. "They'll kill us all! Don't let them get to me, ah-hah." He grunted and groaned and after a few seconds more of audible struggling, Ashen heard the bolt slam shut.

She didn't know what to say. *How the fuck did he survive?*

Ashen wasn't angry about it, just surprised. She gathered herself back together. "We ain't here to hurt you."

"They tried to kill me, Captain! Don't let them in, ah-hah."

The guard captain spat some shells out of his mouth again, finger tapping on his crossbow. "Boss says you should leave."

"Not a problem," Tallas said, urging his mount forward.

Ashen steered Rooftop after Tallas and, when her head reached one of the open windows, she said in her noble voice, "Cithrial Hyrel offers her apologies and best wishes, Velturo." No response came.

When they passed Velturo's wagon and weaved through the people walking, Tallas brought himself alongside Ashen and Rooftop.

"Let's get some distance from them," he said. "I'd rather not remain close to those who think us enemies."

"Aye."

He urged his mare into a trot, and Rooftop kept pace.

They hadn't gone far enough, Ashen figured. She could see the glow of several fires behind them. Although she'd never liked Velturo, she couldn't help feeling guilty about what happened.

"We should go back," she said.

Tallas turned his good eye in her direction. "Why?"

"Because you almost killed him and I orchestrated it. We need to apologize."

"That'd be a first—apologize to somebody about not killing them properly." Tallas shook his head. "What do I always say? Honorable people—"

"Die young," Ashen finished for him. "I know."

"Rule breakers also tend to die young."

She didn't dispute that. Ashen had recited her Five Rules

of Survival before bed every night since her father had died when she'd been a little girl. If she hadn't stuck to them, Ashen wouldn't be alive now. She was certain of that. *But if I hadn't of broken them, I wouldn't have found Jaspard.* Though that fixed her homeless issue, it was now why she was in the company of a gruff mercenary, riding a horse in the middle of grasslands, contemplating whether she should return to a man she'd tried to have killed in order to say she was sorry —again.

"We can get to Lochwall faster without them," Tallas said.

"Aye."

"Good night, my lady."

"Good night, Tallas." She looked up, watching the smoke from their campfire swirling into the midnight blackness. Little dots of starlight spattered the sky as far as she could see in any direction. It was an unfamiliar sensation outside the city. Peaceful. Quiet. They were alone and Ashen didn't have to worry about other urchins chasing her down, trying to steal her food. Or her. Lochwall never slept. Out here, the only sound was the crackling fire, a bit of wind, and the eerie silence. *Yes, silence is a sound.* She'd determined it was loudest before falling asleep.

Ashen woke before Tallas. The fire had died down to embers, though the darkness of night hadn't yet abated. She'd had trouble sleeping; her mind kept returning to Velturo. Tallas breathed in and out, eliciting a slight snore with each breath. She wasn't getting back to sleep now, between the snores and her restless mind. She needed to talk to the duke.

She slipped out of her bedroll, pulled on her traveling cloak, double-checked to make sure her knife and two pouches of Black Dust were on her, then as quiet as she could, tiptoed out of their camp and away from Tallas.

She found Rooftop, guided her towards the road and, when she thought she was out of earshot from the camp, climbed atop the horse and headed towards Velturo's caravan.

There was enough moonlight to travel by and she let Rooftop take a gentle trot. Ashen wasn't in any hurry.

The fires of Velturo's camp were well lit, and as Ashen got closer, she could see the two wagons and plenty of lumps lying around the fires. She didn't see anyone awake. Realizing she didn't have a place to tether Rooftop, she slid off the horse and hoped Rooftop wouldn't stray.

Ashen crouched and, reminding herself of being an urchin, snuck towards Velturo's carriage, where she assumed the man would be sleeping. A warm breeze tousled her hair and caused the fires to sway sideways for a moment. She worried the blaze would catch a blanket on fire or singe somebody, waking the camp.

The door to Velturo faced the fires where everyone slept, the guard with the crossbow sleeping nearby. If she wanted to go through the door, she'd have to sneak through a bunch of people, and then get through the crossbowman, which seemed risky. Instead, Ashen circled the outskirts of their camp, searching for an open window. The wagon would be stifling without any.

Sure enough, Ashen spotted exactly that. She judged the distance between the window and the ground to be seven or eight feet. *This might be tricky.*

Ashen had climbed and navigated buildings in the city, and was adept with grappling, scaling, and jumping. The carriage was no different. She climbed a wheel, using its spokes for leverage. Atop the wheel, the window was too far away to reach out and grab. She'd have to jump and hope she could grab the frame without slamming into the side of the wagon and waking everyone.

Don't fuck up.

She jumped. Both her hands found their way into the wagon, but her midsection thumped off the wood, knocking the wind out of her. Gasping, she flailed her legs in the open air, trying to propel her way through the window. Ashen flopped inside, landing on something soft. The thing grunted and yelled out.

"Who's there, ah-hah?"

She'd fallen on Velturo. "It's me," she whispered. When she realized he wouldn't know who "me" was, she said, "Cithrial."

A chilled silence met her, followed by what sounded like a nervous gulp. She realized a moment later by the stench it wasn't an oral noise. "Did you just shit yourself, Velturo? Fuck."

Ashen leaped out of Velturo's bed and stood. If he'd shit himself, she didn't want to be anywhere near it. If he hadn't shit himself, she still wasn't keen on laying atop the Duke of Many Stains.

"No, ah-hah. Ah-hah." Clearing his throat, Velturo sat up in his bed, and a fresh wave of odor breached Ashen's nostrils.

She wrinkled her nose.

"Don't kill me, ah-hah."

"If I wanted to kill you, my knife would be in your gut by now. I wanted to talk."

This time, Velturo made a nervous gulping noise. "What do you want, Duchess Cithrial? And where's the murderer who killed . . . everyone? He'll kill me, ah-hah."

"Tallas? He ain't going to kill you. He was only following orders from . . ." she almost named herself. "Lord Couliac. Jaspard. You know who that is?"

"I know who he is . . . stole a ring from the king's lifeless body, ah-hah."

"Figure he's probably in charge now. Might fix everything to be king himself."

Velturo snorted. "The people would never have it. Alyst Garcovi is the closest living relation to the king. He would be the first choice, ah-hah."

"Speaks about the quality of the people, then, eh? Anyway, I wanted to apologize for what happened, Velturo." Ashen wasn't what she should say. The idea of sneaking into Velturo's wagon, waking him, apologizing for not murdering him—even though that was the obvious plan—and hope things would go well enough that she'd be able to walk out alive seemed increasingly foolish in that moment. "I'm sorry. For letting Jaspard manipulate me. I ain't a killer." That wasn't true. She'd killed once before she lived with Jaspard. Ashen assumed she'd kill again, too. "Jaspard betrayed us and put us in jail to await Alyst's arrival. I assume he meant us to hang. But then somebody freed us and handed over a note from Jaspard. I think he felt guilty. You know, if I wasn't so used to betrayal and shit people, I might've considered him a father figure. Huh. Well, ain't that a dawning realization correcting an unaware fool? Sometimes, even the clueless make discoveries." She didn't like calling herself clueless, but you also have to keep yourself honest.

"It's fine, ah-hah." However, Velturo sounded anything but fine. He sounded scared and also a little annoyed. She could tell he didn't believe her.

"I'm telling the truth, Velturo. I lived on the streets," she said. Ashen launched into her history before meeting Jaspard. She explained what a homeless life really was like. She told him of her Five Rules of Survival, how her parents died, and how she'd murdered to avenge her father's death by killing the urchin who'd taken his life. Ashen explained her chance meeting with Jaspard, how she'd returned to his house, and how he'd taken her in. And after all that, she recited how she became Cithrial Hyrel, how she'd trained to act noble, how the plan had always been to assassinate the nobility, and why she'd done it—she'd just needed a place to live. When she finished telling her history, she figured three-quarters of an hour had passed and the purple and pink hue of sunlight was appearing on the horizon.

Somebody knocked on the carriage door.

"Duke Velturo? That murderer came back, and he's not looking to talk. Should I shoot him?" The crossbowman's voice.

Velturo looked at Ashen, lost in thought.

"Duke Velturo?" the man asked again.

"Give me one good reason I don't have him killed, ah-hah."

"He can kill," Ashen said. When Velturo didn't look convinced, she continued. "For you. Let us journey to Lochwall together. You'll be safer. We'll be safer."

"Duke Velturo, are you all right?"

"Yes, I'm fine. Don't kill him, ah-hah."

Ashen breathed a sigh of relief.

Tallas Taybold stood in the center of Duke Velturo's guards, halberd at the ready. His stance and expression softened when Ashen and Velturo exited his carriage.

"It's okay," Ashen said. "I'm fine."

Tallas took a step forward and the guards tensed. The one with the giant crossbow took aim at Tallas.

"What are you doing here?" Tallas asked.

"I needed to explain myself."

"You could have waited for me, my lady."

"Lower your weapons, everyone. There will be no killing today, ah-hah."

The guards sheathed their swords and returned to their business, though Ashen noticed the one with the crossbow had lowered the weapon but was staring at Tallas.

"Come, murderer, let us talk, ah-hah." Velturo waved Tallas over, taking a seat by a campfire, and shooing away the pair of men it had belonged to.

Ashen shivered at the touch of a cool breeze and sat across from Velturo, warming her feet. With summer looming on the horizon, it seemed strange to feel so chilled, but Ashen had learned nights in the wilds can get colder than in the city—it was the wind.

Tallas found his way next to Ashen and for the next few moments, there was an awkward silence permeated by the occasional crackle of wood or the sound of a guard talking.

"I have no interest in killing you," Tallas said, breaking the quiet. "Jaspard paid me to do a job. I did the job. And apparently, I failed at it." He gave Velturo a pointed look. "But Jaspard sold us out."

"Then he freed us and told us we'd probably end up executed if we hung around," Ashen said. "But I told Velturo the story already. He knows it wasn't personal."

"Why did you flee the city?" Tallas asked Velturo. It was something Ashen had wondered as well, though she hadn't found an appropriate time to ask.

"The new king will be installed on the throne, ah-hah." Velturo's eyes shifted and his mouth contorted into a nervous smile. "Can you imagine if they realized there was only one survivor? They'd blame me for their deaths immediately! I knew I couldn't stay in Anepolis or I'd see the gallows, ah-hah."

"What about your wife and her brother?" Ashen asked. "Your kids?"

A dark looked seeped through Velturo's otherwise normally passive and childlike face. "They can all rot, ah-hah."

Ashen glanced at Tallas who was already looking at her. He raised his eyebrows, and she bit her lip. There wasn't much to say.

48

DEMRI SLARN

Demri and Caius limped their way into Hidehedge, stumbling up the stairs to collapse in their respective beds. The return journey had been tiresome. Aside from Demri's weak legs, the uncomfortable nature of the wagon bumping along the road, and sleepless nights due to celebrating gladiators, both Demri and Caius were miserable, exhausted, and ached beyond belief.

Demri fell asleep battling his mind—his brain kept slipping back to Doram Quandis and how, now that Demri had his powers returned, he should go kill the man, while Demri tried to keep forcing thoughts of Myri into his head, and how beautiful she remained, despite her aging appearance.

In the morning, Demri woke to Caius munching on a platter of food, still in bed. A similar platter rested on a small stand which must've been carried into their room.

"Mornin'," Caius said, chewing around a hunk of buttered bread.

"Ghosts d-d-deliver this? I d-didn't hear shit."

Caius grinned after swallowing his mouthful. "You were out like a bitch after having a litter of pups."

They ate in silence. No sooner than Demri had finished his fill and placed the platter back on the stand than there was a quick rap on their door, followed by a man entering the room.

"Are you finished, sirs?" he asked.

"Yes," they both answered.

"Very well, then," he said, bowing. The man didn't dress like a gladiator or Magicus, and Demri couldn't figure out what he was supposed to be. The Elkavich didn't allow servants or slaves or caretakers or anything of that sort in Hidehedge. He took their dishes and the stand, somehow bowed again, and then left without another word.

"Strange man," Caius said.

"Indeed." Demri shifted in his bed to better look at Caius. "We need to f-figure out our next m-move."

"We need to wait until we're able to make a next move, Demri. I took a hit in the gut. Gonna need some time."

"We'll wait until the f-f-first day of summer. Should be enough time t-to recover."

Caius nodded, then pulled out a knife and went to work on his fingers.

One late spring afternoon Demri and Caius sat outside Hidehedge and watched two men come stride down the road. One armed with a pair of hatchets, the other a sword and shield. As they came closer, Demri recognized them as the two gladiators who'd left the group at Buzzard's Bowl.

The gladiators approached Demri, who was sitting on the ground, back against a tree. It wasn't comfortable, but there was only one chair nearby, and Caius needed it more. For the first time since meeting Caius, Demri had to sacrifice comfort because his friend was worse off.

The scarred one gave each Demri and Caius a nod. Edelbrock, if Demri wasn't mistaken. "Pleasure meeting each of you again," he said.

"Did you complete your business?" Caius asked.

"I did."

"Did B-B-Buzzard's B-Bowl b-blow up?"

"I don't know. But part of Lochwall did," Edelbrock said. "If not, the entire city. Can't say we wanted to stick around."

The man with hatchets hanging from his belt said, "Is that the plan for the rest of the world?"

"Yes," Demri said.

"Seems extreme."

"I d-don't d-d-disagree. If you ever went to Ashmount, p-perhaps you'd understand, though. The M-Magicai have corrupted this world with false b-b-beliefs. And, no matter what anyone d-does, it seems everyone ignores the Elkavich. Been this way for hundreds of years."

"So, after Lochwall," Edelbrock said, "what's next?"

Demri felt stiff skin on the burned side of his face stretch as he frowned, having just learned the plan on the wagon ride back to Hidehedge from Myri. "B-Better sit d-d-down." No matter what they thought it was, Demri knew the shock of the truth would be worse.

The two men obliged, and Demri told them.

49

QOTHE

In Sultiva . . .

Groma woke. Groma cleaned Groma. Then Groma waited. It was the last day of spring—the day in question. Groma knew what needed doing. Groma strong.

"Mother Avani bless Groma," he said. Groma looked out the window of the second-floor room he was staying in. Groma watched the civilians going about their business. Going to work. Ignorant of what was about to transpire. If Groma had taken the time to meet them, Groma might've felt bad. He saw the limestone buildings of the city clustered together. It was a good thing Groma was young. Sultiva was the largest civilized place in Qothe. And, now that Ashmount was gone, the most powerful.

"Groma is sorry," he said to himself. But Groma wasn't. Not really. The importance of what they were doing, fixing Cedain, was something many wouldn't understand. The five Elkavich leaders had explained this, made Groma see reason. Made all the Elkavich see reason. Without the Ashmount-taught Magicai, without the propaganda and false knowledge everyone had, they could restart humanity. Groma wasn't smart enough to know how. It didn't matter. Groma wouldn't be around for it, anyway.

Groma's last meal was simple, because Groma liked simple things. Lukewarm water, dry bread, and a pear. He splurged and added a handful of dates to his plate. No point in letting them go uneaten.

Groma ate. Groma took a final piss. He walked outside, enjoyed the hot sun, though he didn't enjoy the way the air caught in his throat. When the sun reached its zenith, Groma knew it was time. Navigating through the few citizens milling about—at midday, most tried to be inside as much as possible in Sultiva—Groma found the building he was looking for. A half-built domed church dedicated to Mother Avani. A fitting end, truth be told.

Groma walked around the church, marveling at the architecture. Though he knew very little about architecture, the circular building mesmerized him. A ladder led to the second story, where Groma knew another ladder would lead to the third. He'd scouted it before. He started climbing.

The Church of Mother Avani had started construction after Ashmount's destruction. Sultivan citizens voted to tear down an abandoned brewery in order to build the church. Groma wished he'd seen it finished. But Groma had orders.

Groma was important, even though Groma was only fourteen years old. Groma had been on his own until the Elkavich had found him. He hadn't known he'd had any powers until they showed him. Groma had just wandered away from Pinecrest and gotten lost in the forest, and by sheer luck, he'd stumbled upon somebody. Groma knew it was at Mother Avani's hand, and since that moment, Groma had vowed to serve both the Elkavich and the Mother. It was his duty to perform whatever task he was called to.

He climbed the third ladder, dirt and sand dust raining down beneath him with every step.

"Hey, boy! Get down from there. It's not safe!"

Somebody had noticed Groma.

Groma waved to the man, smiling. Groma saw the vast city stretching out from him in all directions. If Groma had been older, he wouldn't have the powers to reach everything. But Groma was young, and the Elkavich trusted him. And Mother Avani had guided him here.

"Get down from there, son!"

Groma waved to the man, smiling. Then Groma consumed his Well. Groma became the sun, burning from the inside out. Groma screamed, battling against the agonizing pain. His flesh blackened and burned, and Groma glowed—his skin sizzling, then bubbling and popping, and then, melting. And at Groma's zenith, he evaporated Sultiva, its citizens, and himself.

In Argate . . .

Taressa brushed her long locks out of her face. The wind, she'd determined, wasn't favorable when wearing long hair. And the wind brought an aroma that made her sick: the stench of the sea. Taressa hated the ocean. She hated ships. But most of all, she hated the smell of salty water. It made her nauseated. In order to get to Qothe, she had to travel on a ship, through the ocean, smelling the vile vomit-inducing stink the entire time. And to make matters worse, the Elkavich had assigned Taressa to Argate. A fishing town located on the northern tip of Qothe. Sitting right next to the ocean.

"Pfftah." She spit, gagged, and wanted to die. Taressa laughed, realizing today was that day. She was supposed to wait for the sun to reach its peak, but Taressa wasn't patient. And who would it affect?

"Nobody!" Taressa ignited.

In Qelt . . .

Hargrim was old. Toothless, bald, hard of hearing, and unsure if he was up to the task. Perhaps his heart would give out, or he'd not have enough power—his actual concern. But Qelt was a village filled with more people than buildings, and Hargrim knew it wouldn't take much. The battle was living until today.

He walked through the wide-open town. Hargrim had been sleeping on the ground, under the stars. As a non-resident and visitor, he wasn't important enough to stay inside. Those were the rules, so he listened to him. His eyesight was diminishing, he realized. Everyone was blurrier than they were a few weeks ago. Say one thing about Hargrim though, and that was his back was still straight 'n strong. But not for much longer.

Today's the day I giveaway my vertebrae. Hargrim chuckled.

A pair of boys ran over to him. Triff and Gom were their nicknames, if Hargrim remembered right. The pair had a habit of bothering him when he went for his walks.

"Mr. Hardgrimes," Triff said. Or was it Gom? It irritated him they couldn't pronounce his name. The irony he couldn't remember theirs wasn't lost on him. "Wansta play?"

"Yeah, Mr. Hedgerhymes, play," Gom said. Or was it Triff? He held a ball made from the inflated bladder of some animal their parents had hunted.

Hargrim sighed. Every day he said no, but the boys were persistent.

"Please, Hardgrimes."

"Yeah, please, Hedgerhymes."

"Yes, let's play," he said.

The children cheered.

"But we're playing my game, with my rules."

"We wansta play balltop."

"Yeah, balltop."

Hargrim didn't know what "balltop" was and didn't care.

"Let me show you a magic trick instead," he said. Hargrim felt a little guilty, but the damned kids had plagued him for weeks.

"Magics?"

"Ma says only Mother Vonee can do that."

"Your mother's a fool," Hargrim said. "Now, watch closely."

Hargrim reached inside himself, grabbed hold of his powers, and unleashed them all. He turned yellow, then orange. The children began to scream and cry as he engulfed himself in flames. Then, while the children stood and started running away, Hargrim let everything go, blowing himself, the children, and Qelt apart. He smiled the entire time.

In Yordiv . . .

Dust and limestone, dirt and sand. Ursulas couldn't help thinking the same damn thing every time she stepped outside. A slight breeze wafted more of the dry earth through the streets, and Ursulas had to pull up her cowl. This was what she expected the deserts of Vessia to be like, not Qothe. She knew Qothe was a dry and warm place, but the dirt. *Why so much dirt?* According to locals, the dirt was blown from the mountains where Ashmount used to stand. Since the university had expired—by some of Ursulas's own closest friends— a hole in the mountain excreted large volumes of dirt, which landed outside Yordiv.

Ursulas had been waiting for the right time. She'd been living in Yordiv since before Ashmount had blown up. She wanted to join her friends, wanted to further the Elkavich cause. But she couldn't. Not until the right time—the last day of spring.

People walked, heads bowed, ignoring her. A once joyous place, Yordiv was now dismal, its people depressed and sullen. Without Ashmount, there was no reason for foreigners to arrive. Yordiv's economy, and that of Qothe in general, plummeted. Although Ursulas didn't understand, most of Qothe was already poor, so why should this change anything? It was the Magicai who profited. And yet, the people thought they'd lost more than just money. Their identities. Their sense of self-worth. Which, Ursulas figured, was humorous, because the Magicai didn't give a shit about these people. Never had, never would. She found it revolting how often the average person bowed and worshiped at the foot of an Ashmount trained Magicus.

Another gust of debris blew past her, and she choked on some flecks of dust. *Dust and limestone, dirt, and sand.* A vile place, Yordiv.

Ursulas found herself in Yordiv's center, a cross section of dirt paths which led to each corner of the city. She smiled, looking over at a small building a local Healer operated out of. He'd disappear, just like everyone else. She hated the Ashmount Magicai, loathed them. And now, it was time for vengeance for their lies, hypocrisy, and corruption. Every Magicus followed the rules, the laws, and the falsities of their teachings. They needed to be rooted out.

Ursulas stepped into the center of the cross section. She held her arms out, looked into the sky. A civilian bumped into her left arm.

"Excuse me," he said, continuing on his way.

She consumed her Soul Glyphs, one at a time, reveling in the slow, exhilarating intensity of her power building up to its ultimate crescendo.

People noticed.

"That lady's glowing!"

"What's she doing, Mother?"

And the voice of the Healer. "Everybody, run!"

Nobody listened, but it wouldn't have mattered if they did. Ursulas exploded.

In Warwin . . .

Hillion Stoole removed his apron, snapped it once to knock excess flour off of it, and hung it on the rack. It was time for lunch. He walked outside, meeting his apprentice, a boy—no man, now—his son had once been friends with, before his unfortunate death. With his wife dead, and now son, Hillion was alone. He'd mourned for two weeks before going back to work,. Hillion's first day returned to the bakery had felt liberating. Baking had become Hillion's passion.

"Come on, boy," he said to Graylan, who had grown his hair long. Hillion disliked long hair in the bakery, but Graylan would roll it up and pin it to his head like a woman when they worked, so Hillion didn't much care. "Time for lunch."

"Your house, or mine?" Graylan asked.

Often, the two would go back home, eat together, and reminisce about the old days. Today, Hillion wanted to do something different.

"Let's go to Helathi's," Hillion said, smiling. "I'll pay." Helathi was a kind old woman who survived by selling food cooked from her kitchen. She was the closest thing Warwin had to an official restaurant.

"You don't have to do that," Graylan said.

"But I want to, my boy. Come." Hillion led the way across town, towards Helathi's.

"We're going to have to be quick, or we'll be late," Graylan said.

Hillion laughed—he was always a stickler for time. But not today. "We have plenty of time. I've realized that I have been driving us too hard. We need a break." Graylan smiled.

Outside Helathi's a strange, robed man stood, eating a kabob. He inclined his head in Hillion's direction.

"Hillion Stoole, baker extraordinaire," the robed man said. Hillion recognized the voice as the new person in town. A man named Lynko.

"Lynko! What're you doing in them robes?"

Lynko took a moment to sink his teeth into the kabob, ripping a toasted bit of pepper off and chewing it. The smell created a rumble in Hillion's stomach.

"Go place an order—I'll have one kabob, you get whatever you want, Graylan."

"Thanks," Graylan said, leaving with the eager haste of youth. Hillion missed those days.

"Just remembering," Lynko said, having swallowed his mouthful. "Today's a good day for remembrance."

"Indeed," Hillion said, thinking of his son, Kelden.

Lynko ripped a piece of red meat off the kabob. Then, while chewing—which Hillion found to be incredibly rude—said, "It's time, I suppose. And I'm sorry."

"Sorry? For what?"

Lynko began glowing. "For killing you."

Hillion frowned. The world exploded.

50

SERADAL WINTLOCK

Remeria

Sera wakened by a nudge with a boot. She rolled over, saw Renard staring down at her. It was still dark. *Like a bird, we rise with dawn.*

"Cyr Seradal," he said. "A scout from the Camel Clans came and accepted your offer to parley."

"Parley? We're not here to fight them."

"Their words, cyr, not mine."

She grunted. If the Camel Clans already thought of her as their enemy, this could be a tough negotiation. "I'll meet with them at once."

"She's already gone, Cyr Seradal," Renard said, eyes shifting to his feet. "She came, delivered the message to a patrolman. Before I could alert you, she rode off. I'm told Villic wasn't present."

"They don't trust him to return. All right, rouse the men. Tell the Bloody Duchess and the Magicus about what's happening. And if you see Patrika, tell her I'd like to talk." Sera climbed from her bedroll and started packing her stuff.

She could have assigned this job to her page, of course, but Sera didn't need a slave.

"Yes, cyr," Renard said, saluting. He hurried off to carry out her orders.

She smiled, watching the boy. He performed his duties as well as one could ask, and she appreciated him for it. Renard's loyalty and devotion to her—in Sera's mind—was unwarranted. One day, she hoped she could make it up to him.

As Sera was finishing up clearing the campsite, Cyr Patrika Jorst arrived, looking disheveled and exhausted.

"Cyr Seradal," she saluted.

"Didn't sleep well?"

"Didn't sleep a wink, Cyr Seradal. Knowing the Camel Clans were near, I wanted to ensure our safety."

"That's why we have patrols, Cyr Patrika." Sera splashed some water on her face in order to flush the drowsiness she was still feeling away. "Can we keep things casual when we're alone, Patrika? Call me Sera."

Jorst blanched. "Cyr Seradal, you may call me whatever pleases you, but—"

"Call me 'Sera', Patrika. That's an order."

Visibly annoyed, Jorst nodded. "Yes, cyr."

"How about 'yes, Sera'?"

"Yes, Sera."

Sera gave a tired smile. "Good." Being in charge was becoming exhausting and mentally draining. "We're meeting with the Camel Clans today."

"I know. Renard informed me."

"Good. I would like you by my side, should things sour."

"Of course, cyr."

Sera gave her a pointed look.

"Of course, Sera."

The Falcon Knights and the Redclaws made it to a bend in the road, where two Camel Clansmen were waiting, both atop their mounts.

One of them had held up his hand and said, "Stop. Keep your army." Sera assumed he meant for the army to halt their progress, so she gave the order. The Camel Clansman seemed happy about this.

The Bloody Duchess and her poetic Captain Althier sauntered over to Sera, Patrika, and Renard. The Magicus was also not far away.

It took a moment for the Camel Clansman to work through the language, but he got the words out after a moment. "Only four with come."

"Renard, you stay here. Keep things in order," Sera said.

"No problem, cyr."

"Patrika, the Bloody Duchess, and the Magicus will attend with me."

The Bloody Duchess poked Captain Althier in the shoulder with her claw. "Ya best be makin' sure the Redclaws behave, aye?"

"At your beck, at your call, worry not 'bout the Redclaws at all."

"Prick," the Bloody Duchess muttered as Captain Althier marched off. "The poetry gets a bit annoyin' after a while, I say."

The silent Camel Clansmen let out a sharp whistle, then waved at the group to follow him. Around the bend they walked, and a big clearing opened up in the jungle.

Inside the clearing, the Camel Clans stood in a half-circle facing the road and Sera. A dirty woman wearing braids sat in the center of the clearing. A wooden staff lay in front of her crossed legs, and she was watching Sera and her party.

"Uva the Shaman," the talkative Camel Clansmen said, pointing at the sitting woman. "Leader of all Camel Clans."

"I'm Cyr Seradal Wintlock, leader of the Falcon Knights and Redclaws."

Sera heard the Bloody Duchess clear her throat. She ignored the woman.

"My companions are the Bloody Duchess, Cyr Patrika Jorst—my second-in-command, and this Magicus whose name I confess, I do not know."

The Magicus bowed to Uva the Shaman. "Call me the Last Magicus, Uva the Shaman. More a symbol than actual reality. I'm sure there are plenty of Magicai out there. However, I don't know if any are as dedicated to restoring the teachings of Ashmount, the university which—"

"Quiet! You make me ears bleed," the shaman said.

The Magicus bowed again.

"We're here to discuss—" Sera began, but Uva cut her off.

"I make you all quiet! Come," she said, waving to the crowded Camel Clansmen behind her. "Come!"

Villic appeared from the crowd, looking very nervous. He approached Uva the Shaman, standing beside her.

"Are these the people?" Uva asked Villic.

Villic stared, open-mouthed, at the grass beneath his feet. A moment later, he nodded.

Uva spat. "I make conversation. Villic back of line. Sad, sad, sad. Boy is too nervous for his own good. Something make his mind not work," she said, tapping her temple. "Gods, maybe? Maybe the Imbuer spirit? Maybe Villic always be that way, I not know. Not care."

"Villic the Imbuer told us about your desire to get revenge in Calrym," Sera said.

"Yes, yes, yes," Uva said, grasping the staff in front of her and shaking it in the general direction of Calrym. "They make Camel Clans suffer. Remeria bad, Calrym worse. Both need hurt, pain, revenge."

"Left Remeria sort o' early if ya thinkin' you've gotten revenge, no? What type o' revenge ya lookin' for?"

Sera winced at the Bloody Duchess's words.

"Ha!" Uva the Shaman leaped into a standing position, thrusting the staff over her head. "The Camel Clans make Remeria know we strong. Remeria no longer fight. We do same to Calrym. Calrym worse."

"Calrym destroyed my home," Sera said. "The Calrite army murdered our governess. They're the reason my mother and brother are dead. They killed thousands of innocent civilians. And after we left, who knows what other atrocities they committed? Their intention was to kill us." Then, whispering to herself, she said, "They probably succeeded."

"We stuck in desert our lives because of Calrym. We live in Vessia, hoping one day the gods deliver justice. Camel Clans wounded," Uva the Shaman said. "Camel Clans need friend if the clans are to live. Uva the Shaman vow to not attack. But you must vow to help kill Calrym."

"The Falcon Knights won't rest until Calrym's power is overthrown," Sera said. "Together, we will create a new power. One that doesn't bow to King Mikas."

Uva the Shaman nodded, smiling.

Next to Sera, Patrika said, "I hope this works, Cyr Seradal."

"The gods deliver. We make alliance!" The Camel Clansmen cheered. "We ride!"

51

VESSIA

In Argoa . . .

Dolphic's foot slid through the sand. His shoes, he realized, weren't conducive to sand. And sand was everywhere. The sand seemed to jump right into his shoes, and every half hour he had to empty them because of how full they'd become—even after walking around the meager town he found himself in. The sand rubbed against his feet, ripping the skin, and blistering his toes. Dolphic was, to say it plain, miserable.

Aside from the sand issues, the temperatures soared on the last day of the second spring cycle, and sweat made regular appearances across Dolphic's entire body, causing an awful stench, frequent itching, and stinging moist patches to spring up in many of his crevices.

But today was the day.

Dolphic had, along with four other Magicai, infiltrated Vessia. At least, Dolphic assumed the others had succeeded. The Camel Clans were a simple folk, and most of them weren't home. As far as he gathered, they'd gone off to war with Remeria. He admitted he could be wrong, though. He wasn't the most well-versed in their awful language.

In Argoa, he'd arrived, found a dozen invalids, a couple of women, and a few children. There wasn't a single solid building in the "town". Just tents. Why he was here was beyond him, but Erasure had been adamant. It was a named place on most maps; it needed removal. All major cities and towns in every country. The only way to bring about the changes the Elkavich desired.

Dolphic wondered how his comrades were doing. He knew them only by their code names, of course. Except for Vianna. Dolphic had always had a special connection with her, though. And now, during their last days, they found themselves separated. It was for the Elkavich cause, but it still hurt.

After stumbling through the awful sand, Dolphic reached his tent. Despite Argoa being near empty, Kaivana—the woman who was in charge—had refused him closer quarters, claiming they were reserved for clansmen. Clansmen they both knew weren't returning soon.

Anytime Dolphic needed something, he had to traipse across the rows and rows of endless and empty tents. But now was the last day of spring, and he couldn't be happier, aside from missing out on one last kiss with Vianna.

"Today, Vessia burns," Dolphic said, with spite and anger. "I suppose that makes it like any other day."

He'd returned to his tent because Dolphic hadn't the willpower to combust yet. He wanted to take a moment to himself, change into his preferred clothes—he'd selected the cloak which choked his neck and was a touch too tight around the waist, and he wanted to wait for the two elders who'd gone riding to return. It wasn't required by the Elkavich that he kill them all. Just eliminate the town's existence. But it angered Dolphic how he'd been treated.

After changing his clothes—and wrinkling his nose in

disgust at the stagnant odor emanating from his genitals —Dolphic exited his tent. By the time he hiked back to the main tents, he was sure the two clansmen would have returned. He left his tent, wondering if it was worth the trek just to feel more comfortable during the last few moments of his life.

The blistering sun bled its warmth on to Dolphic, causing irreparable damage to happiness. He thought of Vianna again. Wondered how she was faring in the capital of Vessia, Hathoran. Wished he could be with her. Feel her skin, taste her lips, see her walk. He'd loved her. Admitting this freed Dolphic. He'd never admitted it before. Hadn't realized it until that moment. He *loved* Vianna. He'd always thought it was more of a lust relationship, but he'd been fooling himself.

A brighter smile on his face, the sun no longer Dolphic's concern. He started whistling.

Sure enough, when he reached the center of Argoa, the two elders were back and grooming their camels.

It was bittersweet for Dolphic to reach his goal. He no longer had any reason to delay his end. He took a moment to breathe in a breath of dusty air, wishing he was back at Hidehedge. And then it was time.

Dolphic started consuming his Soul Glyphs, emptying his Well. He began glowing. The Elkavich shouted in panic. He laughed. They probably thought he was a god reincarnated or something just as foolish.

He released all his life force. Argoa disappeared. He thought of Vianna as his body fell apart.

In Hathoran . . .

Vianna rolled her sleeves back up to her elbows. No matter how many times she repeated the process, the ends loosened, and the too-big sleeves collapsed back, falling past her fingertips. She was an honored guest in Hathoran because she'd arrived under the pretense of being a diplomatic envoy from the Magicai in Ashmount—a ruse she'd concocted without the approval of the Elkavich. If she was going to suffer for several weeks, she was going to do it in style.

She wondered how B-Six in Valakur, C-Seven in Ilidros, or D-Fourteen in Kelm were doing. She assumed they were all miserable if they hadn't yet combusted. By the end of the day, they would have died. Then she thought of Dolphic in Argoa. If there was one good thing about journeying to Hathoran, it was to escape the creepy man who'd pursued her since they'd first met. At first, Vianna thought him nice and friendly. They'd even shared a few intimacies, and he did, at one point, moisten her lips—and not the ones she kissed with. She had almost complained about Dolphic when plans arose to send them to Vessia. To die. She couldn't have been happier.

The Elkavich wanted every major settlement in both Vessia and Qothe eradicated. The places that made it on maps. If they removed all significant civilization from Cedain, things could start over. Vianna couldn't agree with the methods necessarily, but the ends sometimes justified the means. In this case, the means were a little more evil than Vianna expected. But what did the world expect the Elkavich to do? What did the Magicai who knew about the Elkavich think was going to happen? They couldn't let the fake narrative spread by Ashmount continue. It was damaging, oppressive, and vile.

She rolled her sleeves up again—they'd collapsed—and glanced across the table at her host. The elder had a graying beard and scars depicting different symbols covered his face. According to the Camel Clans, these were tattoos carved into their skin and then ash would be rubbed into the wounds to make the markings permanent. To Vianna, she found them repulsive and unnecessary. She knew the Camel Clans thought them to be a mark of strength. She disagreed, though, finding them to be more of a mark of the foolish. Vianna would, of course, not say this.

Vianna took a sip of peshi—a drink made from fermented cacti juice—and resisted the urge to grimace. The bitter taste didn't resonate with her.

The old man across from her smiled as she sipped, thinking he'd done her a great honor in providing it. The pair of them had met every day since Vianna had first arrived and discussed possible peace treaties between the Camel Clans and Magicai in each meeting. Vianna would've felt bad about lying to somebody she wasn't about to blow up, but since that wasn't the case, she didn't. After the first couple of meetings, they grew tiresome. She had to keep inventing additional issues and problems for them to workshop, to avoid arousing his suspicion.

"Are there any other issues the Camel Clans need to be aware of, Mistress Vianna?" the old man asked, smiling. His usage of her language had been unexpected, but welcome when she'd first met him. Now it irritated her. And what irritated her further was his insistence on calling her "Mistress".

She smiled to match him. "I'm going to kill you," Vianna said.

The old man, still smiling, took a moment to process her statement. "Quick alliance," he said.

The threat didn't seem to bother him. Perhaps he was old enough he didn't care about death. Seemed like that happened often, especially with nomads. Maybe they grew tired of their harsh lifestyle.

"I'm going to kill you and everyone in this place."

"Hathoran?" the old man asked, chuckling. "Do it. Killiak would curse you, condemn you to Flaytz's realm. Flaytz is the god of death, you know."

"I'm sure," she said. Vianna knew who Flaytz was. She hadn't arrived in Vessia without the proper knowledge.

"Why tell me?" The old man took a deep drink of peshi.

He seemed calmer now than at any other moment she'd been around him.

"I thought it was the polite thing to do." And she meant it. Vianna didn't like surprises, and she didn't like surprising people.

The old man laughed. "You have some bravery, Mistress Vianna. Alhexa, goddess of truth, must inhabit your heart."

"Perhaps. Or maybe Lurzal." Lurzal was the god of lies, which is what she'd been doing the whole time she'd been in Hathoran.

"Yes, maybe," the old man said. "Lurzal prefers to not show himself so easily, though. Is there no way to prevent you from killing us all?"

"I'm sorry, no." Vianna stood. "Thanks for the drink," she said, drinking the dregs.

The old man remained sitting, smiling. "You're welcome, Mistress Vianna."

She pitied him. She pitied all the Camel Clans. Their foolish beliefs, their foolish pantheon of gods. Everyone knew Mother Avani was the one and only goddess. The Mother. That's how Vianna's parents raised her, anyway.

"Goodbye," he said. The old man leaned back in his chair, closing his eyes, and angling his head up at the sky.

"Goodbye," Vianna said. Her plan had been to curse the old man and come clean about her ruse, before blowing up. To gloat and display how brilliant everything had been. But he wouldn't have cared. And she didn't feel like it was right to do. He accepted his fate.

Now it was time to accept hers.

She ignited. Her last thought was of Dolphic and how glad she was to be free of him.

52

VILLIC THE TRIBELESS

Villic the Tribeless wondered who he belonged to now. Uva the Shaman had confirmed the fate of the Splintered Manes and now he belonged to no clan. He was an Imbuer, but he didn't belong to a group of Imbuers. The Falcon Knights accepted him, but he wasn't a Falcon Knight.

He didn't feel any different. Same Villic as all the others. Perhaps it was good he didn't belong to any group. Villic had always been alone, even when he had family. He had Dunecrest and Speaker. That was good enough.

Uva the Shaman had commanded Villic to ride with her. She didn't trust him and told him so. They'd ridden through Remeria, and tomorrow they'd be just outside Calrym's official borders on the first day of summer. The approaching summer made Villic smile. The hotter it became, the happier Villic felt. He missed the heat of the desert.

They'd exited a jungle, crossed the Elderspikes mountain

range, and had been riding across the plains that separated Calrym from Remeria. Some claimed the plains belonged to Remeria, while others claimed they belonged to Calrym. The Camel Clans knew they belonged to Vessia. At least that's what the shaman said. And Villic always listened to the shaman.

Late one evening, one of Uva the Shaman's scouts rode into camp. The look on his face was grim.

"Uva the Shaman," the scout said, leaping off his mount. "Half a day's ride, we come to a forest."

Uva the Shaman smiled, tossing her dirty braids over her shoulder. "Good, good. That make me happy. Means we're almost inside Calrym."

"Yes, but there's a problem," the scout said.

Villic wondered why the scout didn't just say what the problem was.

"He's nervous. Surely you can sympathize."

Oh, I didn't realize he was nervous like me.

"Not like you."

This confused Villic, but Speaker didn't speak anymore, which was odd. He refocused on the scout.

"We ventured into the woods to see if we could find a road," the scout said. "A quarter hour's ride into the forest and we heard noise, so we dismounted and, by the blessing of Zarn," *Zarn, god of shadows,* "we went unseen."

"What did you see? Don't make me wait!"

"We saw an army."

Uva the Shaman's face erupted into a wide smile and a hideous laughter came cackling out of her mouth. "Have all the other scouts return to us. We'll wait for them to emerge tomorrow. And then we'll kill them."

Villic's heart started racing. He was both nervous and excited about the battle ahead.

"Go tell your friends the news," Uva the Shaman said.

It took Villic a moment to realize she was talking to him. Nodding, he stood and exited the camp.

Villic hiked through the spread-out encampments of the Camel Clans and, by the light of the campfires, navigated his way into the Falcon Knight encampments. At first, he was stopped by a patrolling perimeter guard. It seemed the Falcon Knights didn't trust the Camel Clans. When they recognized Villic, they let him pass after he stammered through an explanation with Speaker's help.

He found Sir Seradal's campfire, where she was sitting with the Bloody Duchess. Her page, Renard, slept nearby in his bedroll. Sir Patrika must've been patrolling. Villic decided right then that he liked Sir Patrika and was sad she wasn't around. He wasn't sure why.

"Villic the Imbuer let out o' his cage, eh?" the Bloody Duchess asked as he approached. Speaker translated her words to him, as he always did. Her scarred hand pointed at him, and she angled her head so she could wink at him from beneath the strange hat with the wide brim she always wore.

"Please, sit, Sir Villic," Sir Seradal said. He followed her command. "What brings you here?" A moment passed and Sir Seradal then said, "Not that I dislike your presence."

"You need better control over your face. She thought you were upset by her question."

I was upset by her question.

"You misinterpreted it."

There are too many people and rules.

"And you're only just getting started."

Villic frowned at Speaker's words.

"Did I offend you?" Sir Seradal asked. "I apologize. I didn't mean to."

Villic shook his head. "No!" He swallowed, realizing he'd yelled. "Sorry," he muttered. "Uva the Shaman send me. Scouts find army. Fight army tomorrow." He still didn't have a good grasp on their language and wished they spoke the Vessian tongue.

"I suppose that's my cue to leave," the Bloody Duchess said. "I'll get the Redclaws in fightin' order, o' course."

"Thank you, Sir Villic," Sir Seradal said. "We'll be ready."

Villic nodded, smiled, stood, and returned to the Camel Clan encampments. Before he went to sleep, he made it a point to hug Dunecrest around the neck in case it was their last night together.

In the morning, Villic ate a light morning meal with the Camel Clans. When the sun rose high enough where they could ride the camels without fear of injuring them, they departed, the Falcon Knights just behind. The smell of last night's smoldering fires chased them in the breeze. As they rode, he noticed several streams of smoke. A few of the fires must've reignited.

They rode across the hilly grasslands, back the way they'd come from and, after a few hours of travel, crested a tall hill, entering a valley.

"They won't expect us here," Uva the Shaman said. She sent a pair of scouts to the top of the hill to wait and watch for the approaching army.

Midday passed, and Villic wondered if the army was coming after all. When the two scouts came running down the hill, he knew they'd arrived.

"Mount up!" Uva the Shaman said. The Camel Clans arranged their forces in front of the Falcon Knights, Imbuers in the frontline.

Villic sat atop Dunecrest, patting his friend's side.

They waited for what felt like an eternity. Then, he heard something. A horse neighing. The unmistakable sound of galloping.

The Calrite forces crested the hill, stopping at its peak. For a moment, the two sides stared at one another.

"Attack!" Uva the Shaman said.

The Camel Clans surged forward. The Falcon Knights followed. Villic, along with the other Imbuers, called to various powers.

It was then Villic decided he wasn't really tribeless. He was Villic the Imbuer and he belonged to multiple groups.

53

INTERLUDE
VELTURO ONDAKKA

Anepolis, Calrym

After Jaspard had left the Great Hall, leaving Velturo alive and quivering under the table among the bodies, Velturo waited. He knew he had to be careful about when he chose to leave. And leaving too early would likely end up with him in Jaspard's custody. Or killed. If he was in charge, he'd have lined the hallways with guards and prevented anyone from coming or going until he had control of the situation. If the wrong people found out at the wrong time, Jaspard would be next. Velturo knew he couldn't let anyone identify him. Nobody important, anyway.

His back had cramped from crouching under the table for who knew how many hours. Velturo's stomach rumbled, and he considered climbing out to eat from the remaining food on the table. He realized there would be blood and bodies contaminating it, though, which made him nauseous.

At one point, Velturo drifted off to sleep. When he awoke, he had shifted, and his face stuck to the floor. Peeling his cheek away, he felt sticky residue. A glance at the floor showed him he'd fallen asleep in a stream of blood flowing from Chancellor Bertrand's body. Velturo spit several times, just in case. His saliva was clear—something which he was grateful for.

The giant double doors to the Great Hall opened, and Velturo flattened himself to the floor. Peering through chair legs, he saw several young men enter the room—each pushing a wheelbarrow—groaning and moaning in disgust. He realized they were the cleanup crew he'd been waiting for. Behind them, the hallway was empty. No guards.

The men weren't like him, Velturo noticed. Though all were large, they were fit and strong, selected for the job because of their strength. They started throwing bodies into the wheelbarrows, bantering with each other as they did so.

"Look at the jewels on him."

"Don't even think about it. They'll hang you."

"I wouldn't! I was just saying."

"Ugh, Duke Hemmel. Pretty sure he fucked my cousin when he was ten."

"Pretty sure?"

"Well, my uncle found my cousin's body the day after. But I'm certain I saw him with Duke Hemmel the night before."

"You're full of shit."

Velturo believed Hemmel had done that. He decided he needed to make a move and started crawling out from under the table. "Hello, ah-hah," he said.

"Fuck!"

"Mother Avani save me!"

"He's alive!"

Velturo held his hands up, so they knew he meant no harm. "I need help, ah-hah."

"There wasn't supposed to be anyone alive!"

"No," Velturo said, "there wasn't. You," he said, pointing to the largest boy. "I need your clothes, ah-hah."

"What?"

"If anyone sees me, they'll turn me into that," he gestured

at the body of the king. "I'll pay you all well to get me out of here. I have a fortune. You know, I'm a duke, ah-hah."

"What's the deal?"

"We should go tell—"

"No, we can't tell anyone! He'll make us rich!"

"I will, ah-hah." It was the only way Velturo could escape. If he didn't make them rich, he'd be a dead man.

"You two stay here. I'll go get my father's cloak. It should fit you, My Lord. Erm, no offense."

"None taken, ah-hah." Velturo knew he was fat.

The young man left, leaving Velturo with the remaining two. They stood in awkward silence. After a few minutes, Velturo pulled a chair out from a drying pool of blood and sat. He glanced at his half-eaten lamb root pie, covered in blood and gore. And, despite that, he still wanted to eat. He didn't, though, because he wasn't foolish.

Velturo's stomach rumbled.

After a few awful attempts at initiating conversation, the boys went back to loading the wheelbarrows. *Incredible. They're about to become richer than almost every citizen in the entire city of Anepolis, and yet they're still loading bodies into wheelbarrows.* Perhaps it was because they didn't have the money in hand yet.

The third young man returned, carrying a bundled cloak with him, and winded from running. "Here," he said, huffing. "I brought you fresh clothes, too. They're inside the cloak."

Velturo could have kissed the man. He ripped his clothes off and put the new ones on. The scratchy yarn of a peasant's clothing immediately started itching and irritating his body, but Velturo was pleased. With the hood of the cloak up, he'd look the part of a nobody. "I'll reward you handsomely for this. Follow me to my manor, ah-hah."

"What about the bodies?"

"What about them? You're rich now, ah-hah."

The three men didn't argue. Velturo let them lead the way

out of the Great Hall, through the palace, and then through the city streets. They took a roundabout way to get to Velturo's, to avoid anybody he might know.

When they got to his home, Velturo said, "Stay here. I'll be awhile—need to gather my belongings. I'll bring you a sack of coin but you must be patient and you must remain here, ah-hah."

The three of them nodded.

Velturo had just left a massacre and was entering another.

<hr>

Velturo closed the door behind him and collapsed against it. He took a moment to breathe. For the moment, he was safe. He knew that was about to change, though. His wife and her brother were about to kill him.

He passed his children's room, saw both of his sons sleeping. Velturo considered waking the older one—Culbern—to say goodbye. He knew Benford, his younger, wouldn't understand. Whether it was an age thing or a stupid thing, Velturo wasn't sure. He let them sleep. They'd just create more noise and havoc.

He retrieved a large sack and collected some of his necessities. Then he swallowed, nervous, because he had to go into his bedroom. He thrust the door open. His wife, Glendys, and her brother, Ardus, were mid-fuck. Ardus's ass flailed up and down, his manhood penetrating Velturo's wife. The grunts and moans sickened Velturo and he cleared his throat. When they didn't hear him, he did it a second time, louder. His wife's moans drowned him out.

"I'm just going to gather some of my clothes, ah-hah!"

"Fuck!"

"What in the name of Mother Avani!"

They ducked beneath a blanket before Ardus noticed it was Velturo. "Damn it, Glendys, it's Velturo."

Glendys peeked her head out from under the blanket. "What are you doing in here? *GET OUT!*"

Velturo, since learning of his wife cheating on him with her own fucking brother, had remained complacent of their . . . vices. Mostly because of Ardus's threats to murder him. He didn't have time to worry about Ardus murdering him though, because if anyone discovered Velturo was still alive, they'd also murder him. So, he dropped the important information in as blunt and matter-of-factly as he could. "Somebody murdered King Mikas and all the dukes and duchesses, ah-hah." Perhaps if he hadn't of laughed, it might've sounded a bit more serious. It was, however, his fatal flaw.

Glendys looked at him like he was crazy, while Ardus's face turned a glowing red.

"I'm serious. I hid under a table, ah-hah." It occurred to Velturo if he explained everything, Glendys and Ardus might turn him in and allow him to die. "They suspect we are involved, ah-hah."

Implicating his wife and Ardus was the best way to invoke the panic he needed, for they both sprang their naked bodies from the bed. Velturo shielded his eyes from his wife's bobbing breasts and her brother's half-erect cock. It was an image he didn't need burned into his mind.

While they were dressing, Velturo gathered his favored garments and stuffed them in the sack.

"What's the plan, Velturo?" Glendys asked. He saw genuine fear in her eyes.

"I need to get my money together. There are men outside willing to help. You and Ardus need to get to the western gate. I'll meet you there with a wagon and we'll flee to Zemur —it's a small town by the sea, ah-hah."

"What of the kids?"

"Take them. Hurry, ah-hah!"

Glendys and Ardus sprinted from the bedroom, rousing

their children. Velturo went about the manor, collecting all his money from various caches. He separated the money into four bags—the first of which he threw into the already bulging sack. The other three he gathered in one arm, the other hauling his sack of possessions and he hurried through the manor, towards the door.

Passing Glendys, he said, "I need to pay some people. I'll get a carriage and meet you at the western gate. Don't forget—the western gate, ah-hah!"

"Yes, yes," she said. "Hurry up, Culbern! Benford!"

Ardus met Velturo at the door, a mean look in his eyes.

"You better not leave us," Ardus said. "If you do, I'll kill your children."

Velturo made a show of gulping. "I wouldn't dare, ah-hah." But he was daring. *Fuck Ardus and fuck Glendys.* She'd never let Ardus harm their children. He knew that.

Ardus nodded. "See you soon."

Outside, Velturo found the three young men. "Here, ah-hah," he said, dropping the three sacks of coin on the small patch of grass between the manor and street. He kept running.

"Hey, come back!" one of them said.

No pursuit occurred as whoops of joy and cries of, "we're rich, we're rich!" filled the air.

Now to get to the eastern gate. But before he got there, he'd need help.

<hr>

There was one noblewoman Velturo knew who needed to leave the city just as much as he did: Iadura Khyst, a noblewoman from Lochwall. She'd moved after getting married to a man who, Velturo heard, claimed he was related to King Mikas Garcovi. The king had dismissed the claim.

Now, with the king dead and Anepolis down a ruler, Velturo knew Iadura was in trouble.

Before he reached Iadura's house, Velturo stopped a horse-drawn carriage passing by. He paid the driver too much to go hire a wagon and have it stocked and outfitted by the eastern gate. And, just for insurance, he gave the driver the rest of his money for hiring a retinue of mercenaries and holding their—and the wagon driver's—services for several days, in case Velturo couldn't get to the eastern gate in time. He wasn't taking any chances. It was a gamble—the wagon driver might keep the money and ride off. Velturo took a moment to examine the man before letting him drive away. He felt good about the wagon driver.

He paused outside of Iadura's meager home—he expected something more extravagant—and thought about his approach before deciding honesty would be the best way to convince her of the danger she was in. He rapped his knuckles on the door, nervously bouncing in place. No answer came, so he gave the door a stronger few thuds.

A short young woman opened the door. "May I help you?" she asked.

"Yes, I'm looking for Lady Iadura Khyst. I have important information for her which could save her life, ah-hah."

The petulant girl laughed. "I'm sure she's fine."

Fuming, Velturo raised his hand and pointed his index finger at her, stabbing in her direction as he emphasized his words. "Now, listen, you little shit. She's in terrible danger and if you don't let me in to talk to her, the city might hang her tomorrow! King Mikas is dead. Now let me in, ah-hah!"

"Don't you dare speak to me like that!" the girl slapped Velturo, but her arm could only reach his neck.

Choking, Velturo stumbled back in stunned silence.

"Get inside," the girl said, stepping in the doorway and propping open the door. "Hurry!"

Velturo, still choking, rushed inside.

"What do you mean King Mikas is dead?" She shut the door behind him.

"He was murdered, ah-hah."

"That's not funny."

Velturo sighed. "It's not. I was in the room when he died. All the dukes and duchesses are dead, too. A madman came in and slaughtered them with a giant axe. I hid beneath a table! Duchess Cithrial was involved, ah-hah." He realized he hadn't explained himself. "I'm not laughing. Well, I am. It's a nervous thing, right? I always laugh when I stop talking. It's a habit, ah—" He cut himself off, swallowing his laughter.

"And why would *I* be in trouble?"

"You can't possibly be Iadura. You're much too young, ah-hah."

"I am Iadura Khyst. I'm almost fifteen years old, thank you very much." She harrumphed and snapped her head up into the air—almost a perfect imitation of the late Duchess Arena Hyrel. "I'm married to Baron Exildar Alcart."

Velturo blanched, unsure of how to rectify the situation. "My apologies for my ignorance and insulting behavior earlier, ah-hah."

"You've yet to explain why I might be in trouble, Lord . . .?"

"Velturo Ondakka. Until earlier today, I was one of the dukes on the King's Council. Now, I fear I'm a dead man, ah-hah."

Iadura led Velturo to a modest sitting room. Velturo sat in a stiff, barely cushioned chair and relayed what had happened in the Great Hall, how he'd escaped, and his plan to disappear. It seemed Iadura and Exildar might not be as well off as Velturo thought.

"I've heard your husband is distantly related to King Mikas, ah-hah."

"He is."

"Which means you're a contender for the throne. You need to flee, ah-hah."

"Exildar will never let me go."

"You must. You'll both hang. I've already hired a wagon and a mercenary contingent to bring me far away from here, ah-hah."

"Why not just leave without me?" A look of suspicion crossed Iadura's face.

"Because you're important enough to offer commands. Everyone will do as you say, while I can hide inside a wagon. I can't show my face. They're going to be searching for me. Alyst—the king's nephew—won't want any opposition to him taking over. Nobody is looking for you, ah-hah."

Iadura remained silent for quite some time. Velturo could see her mind racing. After agonizing minutes of waiting, she said, "All right. I'll go. But I want my own wagon."

"Done, ah-hah."

It took Velturo far longer to leave than he wanted. Iadura hid him in the basement of their house, having a servant deliver him food at odd hours. It seemed Iadura didn't have money, and Velturo had spent all his. The crew he'd hired was, like his money, gone. He had to rely on Iadura and, by extension, Exildar Alcart.

It was two weeks before Iadura convinced Exildar to give her enough money to pay for a pair of wagons and a decent mercenary crew led by a fearsome man with a large crossbow —one of her husband's men. Disguised, Velturo slipped out in the middle of the night and Iadura got them outside the city.

He'd lived.

1ST CYCLE OF SUMMER

232ND REIGN OF GARCOVI

54

INTERLUDE
JASPARD COULIAC

Anepolis, Calrym

It was as if Mother Avani herself decided the first day of summer should be scorching. Jaspard dabbed at his damp face with a damp kerchief. Despite the heat, discussions needed to be had.

Alyst sat in the king's chair. He'd returned the day before, delayed because one of his companions had fallen off a horse and broken an arm. Jaspard shifted to look at the haggard man. Blago Adavir's arm hung limp in a sling, half his face marred with scrapes and purple bruises. Why he was present escaped Jaspard—Adavir was hardly more than a violent vagabond.

The Golden Knight and the Watchtower of Calrym were also in attendance. Neither had left Alyst's side since he'd arrived in Anepolis, and Jaspard welcomed this decision. Alyst—the future king—needed protection. Though most of Anepolis's citizens had accepted Jaspard's word on what happened, there were few who protested. They wanted to see the culprit hung. But, because of an overwhelming sense of self-guilt, Jaspard had released them. He felt something for the girl. A kinship, if not love. *Certainly, not love.* She'd done as he'd asked, and he'd felt he owed her for that. So, Jaspard had let her free. And he'd freed Tallas to protect her. And if either of them showed their faces back in Anepolis again, he'd kill them himself. He'd have to. Jaspard wasn't concerned about them telling the truth. The citizens had heard the truth from him already—and if there was one thing he learned about the general populace, it was that they believed the first truth they heard. Counter information, even with valid proof, rarely overturned this. He was safe from them.

Jaspard had issued a public announcement assuring the few naysayers the criminals had died during a confrontation with Calrite soldiers. This waylaid most protestors, but there were still people—few though they were—spreading rumors Jaspard was vying for control over the city. With the arrival of Alyst, these rumors would soon be dispelled, though.

"With the dissolution of the King's Council—"

"Murder," Blago Adavir said, interrupting Alyst.

Through gritted teeth, Alyst turned to Adavir and said, "If you interrupt me again, your broken arm will be the least of your worries. Do I make myself clear?"

"Yes."

Alyst's faced morphed into an icy glare.

"Yes, sir."

"As I was saying," Alyst's face returned to the jovial expression he'd had since returning to Anepolis. "With the eradication of the King's Council, who's our current opposition? And I mean locally—opponents to my coronation, in particular."

Jaspard had spent the past years researching this in case his plan worked. "I think the immediate concern is Baron Exildar Alcart. He's a cousin of the king, I believe. Perhaps second cousin. Not as close in relation as you are, true. However, he could still throw his name into the ring. Another threat to your coronation—it seems the murderer didn't kill every member of the King's Council."

Jaspard cleared his throat, took a moment to retrieve a sugared honey chew—something to moisten his mouth. Something good to prepare him for the bad he was about to do. "Duke Velturo Ondakka is one. Perhaps he coordinated the attack. I can't imagine he's much of a warrior. Another missing body was that of Duchess Cithrial Hyrel—the newest member of the King's Council, and a child. I doubt she contributed. We subsequently arrested her and, shortly after her arrest, she, and her guardsman, escaped the prison. We have no indication as to how—there was no damage to the cells or the cell doors." Jaspard hoped Alyst would believe that last part.

"They must *all* be found and questioned," Alyst said.

"Baron Exildar Alcart is still in Anepolis," Jaspard said. He'd hoped it'd pull attention away from Ashen. Jaspard didn't want Ashen killed over his betrayal. He'd done enough to the poor child.

"The Watchtower and I will go at once, Your Highness," the Golden Knight said, shoving his chair back and rising.

"Zervan can handle this alone," Alyst said. "I don't want you leaving my side until I have this figured out."

The Golden Knight hesitated, then nodded and sat.

"Zervan, arrest the baron and bring him to me. We'll question him and see where his loyalties lie."

"At once, Your Highness," the Watchtower said. He bowed and left.

"Lord Garcovi," Jaspard said, hoping he wasn't about to offend the soon-to-be king. "It might be prudent to restrict language inferring you are already king. It might incense the people."

"Sound advice. Please don't call me that again. Thank you, Lord Couliac."

Jaspard dipped his head low, holding it for a moment longer than he had to.

"We'll search the city for Velturo and Cithrial and send riders out to see if they can locate them if they've attempted to flee. Any other local enemies?" Alyst asked.

"None of any immediate threat, Lord Garcovi," Jaspard said. "Though there is a preacher named Harkos who's been the loudest voice of dissention among the people. He's said nothing about you, Lord, but he has speculated *I'm* behind the uprising in a bid for power. I assure you, nothing could be further from the truth."

"I'm well aware of your loyalty, Lord Couliac, and I thank you for all you've done for me. When I'm king, you'll feel my favor."

"It won't be long, Lord Garcovi," Jaspard said.

Alyst turned to Adavir, who'd shrunken in his chair to avoid Alyst's ire. "You will find this preacher and bring him to me."

"Yes, sir."

It didn't take long to locate and arrest Baron Exildar Alcart and Preacher Harkos. When they were both in custody, Alyst called another meeting. This time, Alyst commanded Adavir to guard the entrance. Adavir sulked as Jaspard passed him by in the hallway, refusing to meet Jaspard's eyes. The Watchtower was also in the hall, the two prisoners in chains, sitting against the wall. Jaspard smiled at the preacher.

At the table, only Alyst and the Golden Knight were in attendance. The Golden Knight gestured Jaspard to sit at Alyst's immediate left. Jaspard was moving up the hierarchy.

"It's time to begin," Alyst said. "Bring them in!"

Nothing happened.

"Bring them in!"

Nothing.

"Damn it. Go find out what's happening," Alyst said to the Golden Knight.

Alyst's right hand walked over to the door, opened it, and said, "Zervan. Get in here. Yes, bring the prisoners." Then he returned to his seat.

The Watchtower, baron and preacher in tow, entered the Great Hall. "Sorry, Lord Garcovi. Never heard the call." He tapped his helmet.

"Adavir didn't hear me?"

The Watchtower shrugged.

"I hate that man. Bring forth the preacher," Alyst said.

The Watchtower unchained Preacher Harkos. The thin, almost emaciated man rushed over to Alyst's feet, and bowed until his forehead touched Alyst's boot. "Please, sir, have mercy!"

Alyst kicked the preacher. "Get your dirty face off my foot."

"My apologies, my apologies."

"You're charged with sedition and inciting violence against the state. What have you to say to my good friend, Lord Jaspard Couliac?"

Preacher Harkos glanced at Jaspard, face paling. "You can't be serious, Lord Garcovi. This man is a monster! He murdered your uncle. He ordered the deaths of every member of the King's Council. You *must* arrest him!"

Alyst rubbed his eyes with thumb and forefinger. "I'm already exhausted and I haven't been crowned yet."

"You're made for fighting," the Golden Knight said, a low chuckle echoing inside his helmet. Jaspard wondered what the man beneath the golden armor looked like. Would Jaspard know him?

"Yes, I am," Alyst said. "Preacher Harkos, you've just suggested I kill—arrest, but we'll be frank and just say kill here, because that's what would happen if your allegations held any merit—one of my closest advisers and, dare I say it, friends. How fucking dare you?"

Preacher Harkos dropped to his knees, whimpering and kissing Alyst's boots.

"Get. Off. Of. Me." Alyst lashed out with his other foot, kicking the preacher in the chest. He kicked a second time, connecting with the preacher's face. A spurt of blood spilled from his mouth, and he spit a tooth fragment out. "Jaspard, you'll be in charge of dealing with this wretched man. Carry out whatever sentence you wish."

"No," Preacher Harkos said. "No, please!"

"Zervan, chain this imbecile up and release Baron Exildar. And remove the preacher from this room. Lord Couliac can deal with him later," Alyst said.

"Yes, sir," the Watchtower said. After releasing Baron Exildar, the Watchtower had to chase the preacher to chain him back up. When he secured the fool, the Watchtower dragged him out into the hall.

"My apologies, Baron Exildar. Some men have very little civility," Alyst said.

Baron Exildar Alcart, though dirty from his cell and wearing a few more bruises, smiled and bowed. "Not at all, Lord Garcovi. Or is it Your Highness now? I confess the news has slowed to a trickle the last few days. I was rather . . . indisposed." He chuckled and everyone laughed.

The baron impressed Jaspard. He was charismatic and possessed good humor, despite the fact he was at death's door.

"Sit," Alyst said, pointing at a chair at the far end of the table. It was a great courtesy, but also demonstrated the baron wasn't a friend. The baron complied. "And it's just 'Lord Garcovi' for now, though I appreciate the respect."

"Absolutely," Baron Exildar said. "I suspect I'm here because of my relation to the late King Mikas. I want to make it absolutely clear I have no aspirations of kingship. At the moment, I only want to find and recover my missing wife, Iadura. I fully support your bid for the throne and would endorse you as King Mikas's successor, and the rightful heir to Calrym."

"What's happened to your wife?" the Golden Knight asked.

"She disappeared after requesting a significant sum of money. After asking around, I discovered she took off in a wagon, destination unknown. I found myself in a jail cell shortly after learning this, so I haven't been able to pursue it. Should you let me free, that would be my single goal."

"Did she leave with anyone else?" Alyst asked.

"I'm told she left with a contingent of mercenaries and a second wagon, though I do not know who rode within."

Silence swept through the Great Hall. Jaspard wondered if either Velturo or Ashen were on the wagon. He didn't care if Velturo was—the man wasn't a threat anymore, as long as he didn't return to Anepolis—but he would've been happier if Baron Exildar hadn't mentioned this information.

"Have Zervan find out where she was headed," Alyst said to the Golden Knight. "Then send out riders to bring Lady Alcart back to Anepolis. Before doing so, ensure she's questioned about the missing duke and duchess. She may have important information. I'll issue a full pardon to her for fleeing the city if she turns either of them in."

"Yes, sir," the Golden Knight said.

Baron Exildar stood and bowed to Alyst. "Thank you, Lord Garcovi. I will voice my favor for your immediate coronation, assuming you let me free."

"Objections?" Alyst asked.

Jaspard had none. Nobody spoke.

"You're free to go, Baron Exildar. Thank you for your loyalty."

After the meeting ended, Jaspard had Preacher Harkos

brought back to his manor. The Watchtower chained the preacher in Jaspard's den, and Jaspard turned his favorite sitting chair to face his prisoner. He got many days out of making the preacher suffer, and when Jaspard grew bored, he cut various appendages off the man, cooking them, and making the preacher consume them.

People would think twice before trying to kill Jaspard again.

55

THE INVASION OF CALRYM

For a moment, it seemed nobody heard him. Calrite soldiers lined behind Sergeant Wickam did nothing. Their enemy lined up in the valley below them, ready and waiting for the Calrite soldiers to crest the hill, had paralyzed them. *Calrym must be defended from invasion.* Then Sergeant Wickam saw past the Camel Clans, saw Remerian soldiers in the backline. *What? They can't have joined forces . . .*

"To arms!" Sergeant Wickam screamed, again, and more panicked, giving his horse a kick. The Calrite soldiers followed suit and they charged down toward their foe.

The thundering horde of camels was already storming up the hill as Wickam drew his sword. The ringing of steel being drawn pierced the deafening sounds of the Camel Clan war cries and their charging mounts. Behind the Camel Clans, Wickam spied a group of soldiers with various colored capes he recognized as Falcon Knights from his campaign in Cyrok. Adjacent to the Falcon Knights was another body of armed soldiers, though they appeared to be peasants.

"Tauven, bring around the rear! Trap them!"

Tauven turned his horse around and galloped back through the army to carry out his orders.

Wickam saw the enemy coming, swords aglow with power. He swallowed, wondering if they stood a chance with no Magicai.

Before Wickam could process another thought, the first wave of invading scum was upon him.

A woman rode past on his right, her flaming sword slashing his side. He jerked back, hacking her sword away from him. Flames spit into the air, singeing Wickam's fingers. Then the charging camel carried her past him, disappearing into the rows of Calrite soldiers.

Then more of the clansmen were upon him.

Villic urged Dunecrest faster. When he came within range, he threw his spear, impaling a soldier through the neck. Then he drew his sword. Calling to the power of water, his scimitar morphed into a blade which couldn't be blocked. Dunecrest smashed through the first line of Calrite soldiers. Villic's water blade passed through his foe's. He called to fire and both stabbed and incinerated the soldier. Melting and screaming, he fell off his horse, only to get trampled.

Villic glanced around, searching for Magicai. The glow of Imbuer weapons made it difficult to spot any Magicai powers.

Three Calrite soldiers rode towards him. Villic called to the power of lightning. The sword became a glow of crackling energy and when it passed through the first soldier's sword; the lightning traveled through the metal and into his arm. Slack-jawed, the soldier toppled onto the plains, fried like an egg.

The other pair of soldiers slowed their mounts, glancing at one another, hesitating.

Villic drove his feet into Dunecrest, urging the camel

forward. Surprised, the soldiers' reactions slowed, and Villic slayed both in quick succession.

A twanging Villic wasn't familiar with sounded, and Imbuers dropped. Villic saw projectiles sticking out of bodies lying on the ground, though they weren't arrows.

"Crossbows," Speaker explained.

Sera observed ranks of camels clash into horses. Several hundred feet away, the Bloody Duchess stood, staring in Sera's direction, waiting for her signal.

"Where's the magic?" Patrika asked.

"What?"

"The Magicai. There's no magic. Nothing happening. Not that I can see, anyway. I only see Imbuer weapons."

Patrika was right. Sera hadn't noticed before, but nothing was happening. No balls of fire, no pillars of earth, no sudden pits in the ground. Nothing.

"Maybe they don't have any," Sera said.

"Seems too lucky."

Sera didn't argue.

Braids whipping over her shoulder, Uva the Shaman followed the Imbuers to battle. *Today's the day Uva the Shaman leads the greatest battle in history. Today's the day we fight back against our oppressors and liberate Uva the Shaman's people. Today, Killiak, the Lord of Lords will deliver us better land, a place where we can live without desperation. We leave the desert, we enter paradise. Uva the Shaman has been blessed by the gods and will lead her people to victory.* She led the regular warriors of the Camel Clans, spears held up, ready to throw. When they closed the gap, Uva the Shaman launched her spear.

"For Killiak, lord of lords!" Her battle cry disappeared in the chaos of war and the sounds of animals stomping and people dying, weapons clashing and armor scraping, bellowing orders and screaming winds.

She watched her spear fall into the ranks of Calrite soldiers, couldn't tell if she even hit anyone.

"Push forward and kill the Calrites! It make the gods happy!"

The clansmen roared, or maybe she imagined it. She was too busy drawing her scimitar and finding her first victim to notice.

***

"To me, to me!" Corporal Tauven Shekt screamed. His low voice didn't have the volume necessary to garner anybody's attention, though. "*TO ME!*" Nobody heard him.

"To me, you bastards! To me!" He waved his arms over his head, and he attracted the attention of maybe five people.

"To me!" He remembered the small horn he carried. Pulling it out, he gave it two quick successive toots. "To me, you fucking idiots!" He blew the horn twice more. Finally, he got their attention, waved for them to follow him.

"To me!" Tauven led the cavalry away from the battle to circle the hill and ambush the Camel Clans from behind.

***

Wickam parried another blow, then another. The Imbuer didn't seem to change tact—keeping his sword a bloody icicle. Every time the sword connected with Wickam's, or his shield, ice chips sprayed the air.

The clansman's face contorted in fury, and a brutal couple of swings followed. Wickam struggled to keep his sword in hand. Blocking, blocking, blocking. His wrist already ached, and the battle had just begun. Wickam feinted, swinging to the clansman's right. At the last moment, Wickam shifted his momentum, driving the blade up and into the clansman's guard. Wickam's sword ripped through the clansman's throat, and a plume of scarlet poured forth.

A crossbow bolt thumped into the clansman's chest, throwing him off the camel.

The annoying soldier, Rickets, appeared on his horse, reloading.

"Looks like you got him, sir," Rickets said.

"Yes."

"Looks like there's more coming, sir."

"Yes."

"Best get to it, sir," Rickets said, pulling the crossbow up and pulling the trigger again. Another clansman fell from his horse.

"Yeah." If Wickam didn't need every soldier, he might've killed the idiot then and there.

Rickets knew Sergeant Wickam hated him. He didn't care, though. He liked the sergeant. Rickets bent, retrieved another bolt from one of the two cases he kept on either side of his mount's saddle. He placed it in the groove, cranked the pulley until he heard it click, then placed the stock against his shoulder and searched for his next target.

Rickets monitored Sergeant Wickam, who was fending off a regular warrior. He knew the sergeant could handle that and waited. A moment later, and a woman wielding a sword made of rock rushed towards Sergeant Wickam. Rickets lined the shot up, fired.

The bolt soared through the air, slamming into the woman's shoulder and throwing her off the camel. Grinning, Rickets reached for another bolt.

"Saved your life, sir!" Rickets said. Sergeant Wickam grunted, though whether that was in response to Rickets or because he was mid-fight, Rickets didn't know.

The Bloody Duchess waited, though waiting wasn't her favorite thing to do. She wanted to send the Redclaws in. But walking into a horse and camel fight seemed like a bad idea. None of the Redclaws had a mount. It was a damn shame. So here she was, cape billowing behind her shoulders, wide-brimmed hat tipped up so she could see, ruined hand resting on the pommel of her stiletto, making an impressive image, she figured.

She tipped her head, craning her neck, popping her ear. She swore she heard something—a crashing sound coming from elsewhere. "Somethin' ain't right," she said. "Ya hear that?"

Captain Althier shook his head. "The battle atop this good grassland hill has changed my attention to prevent my blood's spill."

"Well, focus on the here and now, ya great buffoon. Somethin's happenin'."

"I can't hear shit, and I'm sick o' it."

"There," the Bloody Duchess said. She pointed with her claw at the base of the hill where a cavalry unit raced in her direction. Drawing her stiletto with her good hand, she thrust her claw into the air. "Fuck Calrym!"

The Redclaws echoed her cry. Without giving Sir Seradal Wintlock a thought until it was too late, the Bloody Duchess was already running toward the approaching cavalry unit.

Sera's jaw dropped. "Wait!" she said, again. But the Redclaws weren't listening. "Shit," she said.

The Redclaws collided with the cavalry. Or the cavalry ran through the Redclaws, spilling blood and trampling bodies. They'd need help. But Sera's job was to reinforce the Camel Clans. *There won't be a line to reinforce if this cavalry gets past the Redclaws, though.*

"Stop them!" Sera said. "Attack!"

Patrika echoed Sera's command and the Falcon Knights swept across the plain to reach the base of the hill.

The Redclaws regrouped on the other side of the Calrite cavalry. The Falcon Knights moved to surround them.

Sera drew her sword; Patrika had hers out already. *Renard. Where's Renard?* Panicked, Sera swiveled her gaze, but didn't spot him. Then, the fight became too close, and she had to concentrate on surviving.

Renard tripped, face planting into ground churned up by horse hooves, camel feet, and soldier boots. Spitting a mixture of bitter grass and gritty dirt, Renard clambered back to his feet. "Cyr Seradal!" Horses whinnied, snorted, screamed. Swords clashed, rang, and scraped. Men killed. Men died. Blood ran.

Being a page, Renard didn't have any soldiering gear. He drew the large knife from his belt. "Cyr Seradal!" Falcon Knights in front of Renard engaged with the mounted Calrites. Renard took a step back, examining the battlefield.

Wonderful. I've lost my charge. My one responsibility is to remain at Cyr Seradal's side. And now . . . Now he was on the perimeter of a battle.

He searched for blue cloaks as Cyr Seradal was a Falcon. Problem was that a majority of their force were Falcons.

"Cyr Seradal!"

A Calrite soldier broke through the Falcon Knight line and galloped toward Renard. He ran, but not fast enough. The rider tried veering around Renard, but the horse either didn't listen or couldn't do it in time. The horse crashed into Renard, sending him sprawling, then thundered up the hill.

Renard bounced off the ground, his head ricocheting off an abandoned helmet. He came to a halt. Groaning, he tried to lift his head. His vision went black, and he lay back. Warm fluid dripped from his forehead. *I'll get up as soon as I catch my breath . . .* Renard lost consciousness.

***

The Last Magicus watched the Falcon Knights follow the Redclaws into battle. He didn't follow, at least not at their pace. He meandered in their direction, observing the deaths on both sides. The Last Magicus wasn't there to contribute to the battle unless necessary. King Alondo had given him specific instructions—observe, advise, and make sure the Falcon Knights or Camel Clans weren't intending to betray Remeria. To follow these commands, the Last Magicus couldn't kill himself by consuming his powers. He needed to wait for opportune times to use them if he decided to use them at all.

The Last Magicus crossed his arms and watched, waiting for the battle to end.

***

"Slow down. Check your injuries."

Speaker was right. Villic slowed Dunecrest, taking a moment to look over his body. Streaks of blood stained his clothing and sweat matted his hair. He saw a deep leaking gouge in his arm from the last soldier he'd fought. Painful, but his arm would recover. Otherwise, he was unhurt.

"It's a slaughter."

Villic looked around at the dead and dying. Many more Calrite soldiers had fallen than Camel Clansmen.

"Good."

"It's not over yet."

Villic glanced towards the Calrym army. They'd regrouped. The Imbuers were finishing off the stragglers.

"Over here!" Uva the Shaman said. "We must help our allies!"

Villic looked downhill, where Uva the Shaman was pointing with her staff. The Falcon Knights and Redclaws were fighting horsemen. Snarling, Villic redirected Dunecrest.

Uva the Shaman lowered her staff, turning her camel, Windglider, around. Abandoning the Calrym army, the Camel Clans, charged down the hill to help their Remerian allies.

Windglider swept through an opening in the Falcon Knights, crashing into the ranks of Calrite soldiers. Uva the Shaman bashed a man's face in with her stick, cackling to herself as she did. "To the realm of Flaytz, you go!"

She clubbed another soldier atop his helmet. Dazed, he dropped to his knees as another camel swooped in, trampling the man into grass. A collarbone had snapped, piercing the soldier's skin, and he sputtered, struggling to move. His leg jutted out at an odd angle, too.

"May pain and suffering make you atone for the sins of your forefathers!" Uva the Shaman grinned. "It make me happy to end your weak country." The soldier wasn't listening. His eyes drifted closed. He'd made it to Flaytz.

Uva the Shaman urged Windglider forward, further into the fight.

Captain Althier wiped blood from his eye. A cut on his forehead just above kept leaking into it, blurring his vision. He imagined the entire right side of his face was a mess of red, all from a single cut on his head. "The head bleeds more'n most folk figure; makes you woozier than drinkin' six quarts o' liquor. Not my finest rhyme, I must confess. Gotta press forward, nonetheless."

He waded through the dead, striving to return to the Bloody Duchess's side. A Calrite soldier noticed him and blocked his way.

"Get out o' the way," Captain Althier said.

Snorting, the soldier surged forward.

Not one to skip out on finishing a rhyme, Captain Althier muttered, "Okay." He noticed the soldier wore a fancy overcoat—something he'd want to pilfer should the fight go his way.

The soldier's blade crashed against Althier's shield. Grunting, Althier battered the soldier back, lashing out with his blade in return. The point snagged on the soldier's overcoat, tearing a hole through the sleeve. *So much for the coat.*

Fueled by battle lust or rage over the coat, the soldier bellowed and, dropping his shield, bludgeoned Althier with his sword, two-handed. The blade reverberated off Althier's shield once, twice. Althier waited for the third blow, and when it came, ducked beneath it, thrusting his sword into the battle-frenzied man, gutting him. With a shudder and groan, the soldier collapsed.

Althier took the man in a hug, whispering in his ear. "A spectacular, wonderful, and enchantin' fight. Please, my friend, be off to the light." He twisted his sword, then pushed the soldier off him. The dead man dropped to the mud and grass.

Captain Althier jogged towards where he thought he'd find the Bloody Duchess.

Shadows, messages, scouting, and horses were more Whisper's style. He'd lingered near the back of the fighting—at Sergeant Kolb Wickam's orders—and now was waiting for fresh orders. The Camel Clans had retreated down the hill to help the Remerians.

"We should help them, sir," a soldier said to Sergeant Wickam. Whisper believed the man's name was Rickets, the one who annoyed the sergeant.

Sergeant Wickam sighed, appearing both worried and weary.

Somebody else chimed in. A corporal. Jafe, Whisper thought. "We can't leave Tauven," he said in his squeaky, high-pitched voice. "They'll come for us next." Although the corporal was rather tall, Whisper couldn't help but see the man was terrified. It was clear he was putting on a brave face.

"You're right," Sergeant Wickam said. "Corporal Valendar, lead half of the men for the flank. I'll take the other half and help whoever needs it."

"Sir," Corporal Valendar squeaked, saluting. Though petrified, he rode off with his assignment, half of the remaining army following.

Whisper urged his mount closer to the sergeant. He needed to convince the man to let him go. "Sergeant Wickam," he said.

"Yes, Whisper?"

"I should get word back to the capital. They'll need to know an invasion has occurred." Whisper almost smiled. He knew the information was mandatory, and he was the person who could deliver it fastest. He'd live.

"I couldn't agree more, Whisper. I'll deliver the news myself. We'll leave at once. This fight is lost."

"What about the others, sir?" Rickets asked.

"What about them?" Sergeant Wickam asked in return.

Whisper didn't care how it was happening, he was just glad to be in the party leaving.

***

Duty and honor meant a lot to Sergeant Wickam, but living meant more—or, at the very least, having a worthy death, not a sacrificial one. Needlessly throwing away his life would aid nobody. Fleeing the battle would damage his reputation, but it would also allow him to deliver crucial information to King Alyst. They would need Magicai if King Alyst intended to win this war and push back the invasion. Wickam wasn't sure Whisper could convey that information well.

Also, he wanted to flee. *Mother Avani, forgive me.*

He waited until Corporal Valendar's cavalry disappeared before issuing the order to retreat.

"Good luck," Sergeant Wickam said. Although, if anyone survived, it'd make for an awkward reunion. It'd be preferable to having the Camel Clans running rampant in Calrym, though.

"We're going home, sir?" Rickets asked.

Sergeant Wickam ignored the annoying man and the question he'd already answered. If he'd been thinking, he would've sent Rickets to die with Corporal Valendar.

They rode back toward the forest they'd exited.

***

Corporal Jafe Valendar and his regiment collided with the Camel Clans. Sword met sword. Either the Imbuers were elsewhere or most were dead, because Jafe didn't see any transforming weaponry or flashing colors from the various powers he knew they possessed. Another possibility was they weren't using their powers, but that wouldn't make sense. Then again, the Camel Clans weren't the smartest people. Not in his opinion, anyway.

"Die!" He drove his sword into a passing warrior. Even among the shouting, crashing, thundering, banging, he heard the high-pitched squeak of his battle cry. He'd gotten used to the sound, but every once in a while he still felt shame.

Scanning the battlefield, Jafe searched for Tauven. He knew Tauven would need backup, and fast. "Further, push further!" Then he saw them, the Imbuers, with their colorful weapons. His soldiers hesitated. "We need to save our brothers!" His soldiers cheered along with him, and they pressed inward, towards the center of the colliding Camel Clans, Calrite soldiers, peasants, and Remerian forces.

J afe couldn't find his friend Tauven. He found himself unhorsed, weaponless, and aching. But alive. After charging into the battle, he'd slain several Camel Clan warriors, encountered an Imbuer, watched his mount lose its head, fallen to the ground and engaged in close combat, lost his weapon in the battle, ran, and now, he searched for a suitable weapon.

"Fuck," he said, in that irritating high-pitched voice.

Jafe turned at the sound of hooves. Dozens of Camel Clansmen were heading in his direction.

"Fuck!" he said. Jafe couldn't outrun them, so he grabbed the first weapon that caught his attention—a halberd. It wasn't his preferred choice, but it was better than a sword for fighting mounted warriors.

The battle-frenzied man leading the charge raised his

scimitar and Jafe swallowed, nervous. He lifted the halberd, ready to die. Then reality became even more horrifying. The Camel Clansmen's weapons all lit up different colors—they were Imbuers. Fire swords, rock spears, and ice-tipped arrows.

A Vessian battle cry rang out and the lead rider raised his flaming sword. Jafe couldn't fight an Imbuer one-on-one. He'd lose. With a shout of his own, Jafe lifted the polearm over his shoulders, then swinging it as hard as he could. The axe head bit into the camel, which issued a pained scream, and the rider flipped over the top of the camel, landing in the field.

Jafe didn't have time to relish his victory. Another rider's camel bumped into him, and he was thrown off his feet. More hooves ground him into the dirt, and he screamed. Bones snapped and skin bruised. His high-pitched scream, for once, was drowned out by other sounds. He screamed and screamed, and then a hoof landed on the back of his head.

More hooves pounded on and around Jafe Valendar, scattering his brainy, bloody pulp across the battlefield to mix with other concoctions of gore.

<hr>

Sera pried her sword from the dead Calrite with an awful squelch. *Point to me.* Blood, and battles, and fighting. She hoped leaving her homeland, Cyrok, would've ended much of this. With Cyrok under the control of Calrym, she assumed the fighting would be over for a while. She was mistaken.

"Cyr Seradal!" A Falcon Knight hurried to her. "A scout has reported that a significant portion of the Calrym army has retreated. We've won."

She looked around at the skirmishing. It didn't feel like a victory. At least, not yet. "We still have work to do."

"Yes, cyr," he said.

"Fall in with me," Sera said. She pointed at a group of outnumbered Redclaws with the tip of her sword. "Let's reinforce our comrades."

"Yes, cyr!" her soldiers replied.

As Patrika—nursing a bloody cut on the side of her head—regrouped at Sera's side, Sera wondered where Renard had gone and hoped he was all right.

***

The Bloody Duchess snarled as her stiletto scraped off a Calrite's shield. Her foe backed up, waving his sword in front of him as if that would do much other than confirm what she already suspected—he didn't know how to fight well. With this knowledge, she grew more confident. The soldier had already lost the battle.

She feinted, and the soldier threw his weight into another block. Off kilter, he wasn't able to recover fast enough before the Bloody Duchess jabbed the stiletto into his throat. Gargling, he dropped to the ground, revealing a pair of Redclaws making their way towards her. She recognized Captain Althier as one of them. They'd lost each other earlier.

"Captain Althier," she said, placing her right foot on the dead man's corpse and making a victorious pose. The wind whipped her red cape behind her back and she stuck the stiletto in the ground at her side. "How's the fightin' been for ya?" she asked.

"This battle's victory is about to be in the past. One thing's for sure, I fear it won't be our last."

"Thinkin' we've won?"

"No doubt about the win, Bloody Duchess. Only question remainin' is what's left of us?"

The Bloody Duchess looked around. Corpses, everywhere. "Aye. Lot o' dead folk. Let's go find Sir Seradal, eh?"

Villic followed Uva the Shaman downhill, bringing her warriors into battle. They outnumbered their enemy, and Villic knew they'd be dispatched before he reached them. He glanced around.

"Imbuers."

Speaker was correct. The Imbuers rode towards another group of Calrite soldiers. Villic urged Dunecrest forwards, merging with them and leading the way. Around him, weapons glowed with various powers. He whispered a quick prayer to Shymai, goddess of protection.

Give me fire.

Speaker honored the request, and Villic's blade roared to life.

A lone enemy soldier stood in Villic's way, hefting an axe so long it had a tail.

"A halberd."

Villic didn't care what it was called. He bared his teeth and urged Dunecrest faster, tightly gripping his flaming scimitar, wanting to get to the soldier.

The soldier lifted the axe. Dunecrest got closer.

The axe swung toward him. Villic misjudged. He would not be close enough to deflect the blow.

"Dunecrest!"

Villic tried to steer Dunecrest away from the soldier, but the camel didn't alter his direction.

The soldier swung the axe. Villic reached out with his scimitar, to block. But he couldn't reach. He watched as things slowed down. The blade got closer to Dunecrest, closer, closer. The camel, Villic's best friend, kept his pace up. But it wasn't fast enough.

A sickening crunch as the blade met camel flesh. An awful, gut-wrenching cry issued from Dunecrest. Villic felt the gods punching him in the stomach before he was thrown from his camel.

Villic changed his sword from fire to force, swinging it midair, slowing his fall. He landed on his back, bounced twice, and came to a stop. The Imbuers thundered past, the soldier with the axe gone to mush.

Another cry from the camel. *Dunecrest.* He had to get back to Dunecrest, mend his injury.

Villic ran, passing the trench on the ground his sword had made. He found Dunecrest lying on his side, blood gushing from a wound in his side.

"Dunecrest," Villic said, kneeling at his best friend's side. He pressed his hands against the bleeding wound. Then he noticed Dunecrest had a broken leg and a hole the size of a hundred birds in his chest from something else. Or Villic guessed it was a hundred birds. He didn't know measurements too well.

"Dunecrest," Villic said, again. His eyes watered.

"Bind his wound. Staunch the bleeding, Villic!"

In this, Villic knew more than Speaker. A broken leg was a death sentence.

"Dunecrest . . ." Villic pressed his head against Dunecrest's. He looked into Dunecrest's eye. Saw the pain his injuries were causing him. "I'm sorry." Tears dripped from his eyes, running down his cheeks as they looked at one another.

Dunecrest let out another whine, his own tears of pain rolling down his face.

"Villic, help the poor thing."

"I'm sorry, Dunecrest. I'm sorry." He drew his knife, placing the knife tip at the camel's neck. "I'm so sorry." His hand shook, the knife wobbling his in grip.

"Villic, stop. You can save the poor animal."

"No," Villic said. "I can't." He drove the knife into Dunecrest's neck, piercing the vein which held an animal's life.

Hot blood pumped out of Dunecrest's wound. The life slowly drained from his eyes and, after one last breath, he slipped into oblivion. Flaytz, god of death, had claimed another.

He looked up at the sky, up to where the Lord of Lords himself, Killiak, was likely watching him in his misery. Villic had no words for the god. Nothing other than rage and sadness. He screamed as loud as he could. His cries of despair wouldn't bring Dunecrest back. No, nothing would. He screamed, anyway. Everything he'd struggled with in his life came out. His social problems, his shyness, the way everyone in his clan made him feel, his frustrations with Speaker, but mostly, he screamed for Dunecrest. His best friend. All the other problems didn't seem so bad, when Dunecrest was around. And now . . . now Dunecrest wasn't around. And Villic had to face everything alone. He screamed, again, then pain gripped him and he collapsed back against Dunecrest.

Villic closed his eyes and hugged his best friend's lifeless body. He sobbed, closing his mind to Speaker. Life felt emptier already.

***

Corporal Tauven Shekt knelt in the grass, arms raised. *Sometimes, you need to admit you've been beaten.* Several soldiers, all restrained and kneeling alongside him, had found themselves captured by a much larger group of Falcon Knights. From what Tauven had gathered by keeping a sharp ear focused on the whisperings of the enemy, they were awaiting orders from "Sir Seradal".

Hours dragged on, and the Falcon Knights, Camel Clans, and peasant fighters—people called "Redclaws", apparently —continued depositing prisoners near Tauven. He noticed none of them were ever severely injured and assumed the people with injuries were being dispatched. It's what he would've done. Well, not really. When fighting in Cyrok, they didn't take prisoners. He would've followed his orders to kill them all.

Tauven guessed it was six hours after his capture when the army's leadership arrived. The knight, Sir Seradal, was female, much to his surprise. Sir Seradal was joined by another female Falcon Knight, a pair of peasants—one with a mangled hand—and a quiet, but crying, warrior of the Camel Clans.

"What are ya thinkin' o' doin' with the prisoners?" the peasant with the mangled hand asked Sir Seradal.

Sir Seradal appeared tired and wiped her dirty face with her hand. She swiped at the sweaty hair matted to her forehead, brushing it out of her eyes. "The same thing they did to us, I expect. Mercy is for the inexperienced."

The other peasant who stood aside the woman with the injured hand spoke next in a rhythmic voice. "The thing about war is that it's not pretty. There's blood, there's guts, there's gore, and it's gritty."

"Aye, that be the case," the clawed one said.

Sir Seradal nodded but turned to the other Falcon Knight. "Patrika? What do you think?"

The other Falcon Knight—Patrika—sighed. She seemed dazed and unable to focus. She closed her eyes, took a moment to breathe, then reopened them, and, to Tauven, seemed much more present. "Repay them for Cyrok."

"Cyr Villic?" Sir Seradal asked the sad man.

The man, teary-eyed, studied the prisoners. For a moment, Tauven swore Villic met his gaze. Villic swallowed, then whispered so low Tauven could barely hear him, "Kill them all."

"Today is a day of reckoning," Sir Seradal shouted so the prisoners could hear her, as well as her soldiers. "Today is the day we begin taking back that which was stolen from us. Our homes. Our lives. Today, we strike back at the people who destroyed Cyrok." She paused, looking over the prisoners. Noticing their fear. "Execute them all."

"Wait," Tauven said. "Wait!"

But it was too late. A blade pressed against his neck and cut deep. He choked, struggled to breathe, and his blood ran free.

After issuing more orders about where to set camp, taking reports from various officers, and determining how many wounded and dead there were, Sera grabbed a quick meal. Keeping her eye out for Renard, Sera's exhaustion had reached its limits and, reluctantly, she crawled into her bedroll under the stars.

It dawned on her, as she lay there, how many people she'd ordered dead. The old Sera, the one who'd grown up raising gyrfalcons, the one who still had a mother, and a brother, the one who'd still been innocent to the workings of the world, she'd have not done so. Old Sera would have felt terrible, worried about the affected families. Worried about how soldiers are innocent people, just carrying out the orders of their commanders. But she'd seen what soldiers had done of their own volition. Many of them enjoyed murder and rape and other sadistic pleasures. And, she was certain, all of them would've executed her, had she been their prisoner. She felt her heart icing, right then. Shifting into the cold brutality of a leader. Shifting into what she'd been fighting. Sera didn't like that. Didn't want it. But she had to look out for her people, nonetheless.

She went to sleep, dreaming of the soldiers she'd executed.

When she woke, dawn had just broken. Climbing out of her bedroll, Sera noticed Patrika sleeping nearby. She was sitting half-upright by the fire and it was clear she'd fallen asleep while trying to remain alert. Sera stepped around her, hoping not to stir her from her rest.

Sera smiled when she caught sight of an eagle flying overhead. It reminded her of before the fight, when the Old Vulture, Royal, and herself were discussing their plans. The yellow beak, bright white feathers, and crisp black ones made her appreciate the bird even more.

She made the rounds, checking in with officers and informing her subordinates they'd be marching in a few hours. She relayed this information to the Bloody Duchess and the Redclaws, relayed the information again to Uva the Shaman and the Camel Clans, and consoled a weeping Villic who appeared not to have slept at all. Then she checked in with the injured to see if she could find Renard, checked in with the deceased to see if she could find Renard, and, once the sun was in the sky returned to her bedroll to prepare to leave.

"Cyr Seradal."

She turned at the man's voice, heard Patrika stirring.

"I'm sorry," the Falcon Knight said. In his hands, a corpse. "Looks like he took a nasty hit to the head and drowned from the blood."

She took a step closer, saw it was a boy. "Renard?" The Falcon Knight laid the boy on the ground and his head turned in her direction. Renard. "Oh, no." *I never should have lost him.*

Renard, the page who'd been by her side since becoming a Falcon Knight. Renard, the boy who'd become family. And, once again, her family died. Because of war.

Sera closed the gap between herself and Renard and took the boy in her arms, holding his lifeless body against her. She cried. Not just for Renard's death. She was also saying goodbye to her mother and brother. Sera hadn't been able to. And now she could grasp something physical. Hold a body against her and sob.

A hand placed itself on her shoulder. "I'm sorry, cyr." Patrika said.

Sera tried to regain her composure, but she couldn't. The

sobs came and more tears ran down her cheeks, dripping on the poor, dead boy. This was just further affirmation she'd done the right thing to those prisoners. She'd think no more about them.

———

The Last Magicus had disappeared into the ranks of the common soldier. He observed their injuries, their losses. He listened for dissent—there was none. There wasn't any disloyalty, either. Not from what he could tell. He'd not had to use his powers, not had to intervene at all. They'd won the battle, and he'd done nothing. Victory. Now, though, they were about to press further into Calrym. The road would become more dangerous, for the chances of running into other Magicai would increase. And, if they made it to the capital, was certain. He didn't trust the Imbuers could deal with all of them. But they'd have to.

———

Two days later, the Calrite army had completed their retreat. No sign of pursuit. Sergeant Wickam had relaxed and allowed the soldiers a rest. Much to the dismay of his men and their horses, they had rested little during their flight. He had to get to Anepolis. He had to get to Anepolis fast. If all was going as it should be there, Alyst would be king. Alyst would listen to Wickam. He had to. If he didn't, all of Calrym was lost.

56

EDELBROCK BRENDIS

The battles, imprisonment, and torture disappeared with the end of spring. With the first summer cycle beginning, Edelbrock had a new lease on life, although scars from his past would remain forever etched on his body. It didn't feel like long ago that Edelbrock had been looking at a mirror, examining Trigg Gelbrandy, wishing to be away, a deed to Buzzard's Bowl firmly secured in his pocket. Now, as Edelbrock looked in the mirror, all he saw were an S and an H carved into his skin. Everywhere.

A few days into the new season, somebody cleared their throat in the doorway. Turning, Edelbrock saw a Magicus he didn't recognize. The man was tall, pale, and squinted eyes glanced over Edelbrock's scarred body.

"You're not as handsome as you once were," he said.

"No," Edelbrock agreed. Before Buzzard's Bowl, Edelbrock might've said something condescending in return, a slight for a slight. But now, it seemed pointless. Let the man get his barb in. There was a reason he was here, and Edelbrock's curiosity piqued.

"They call me E-Two. But," he said, stepping into the room and closing the door behind him, "I think it's fair to introduce myself properly if you're to undertake the task I'm going to request of you. May I?" he gestured at a chair in the corner.

"By all means." Edelbrock sat on the edge of the bed he'd been sleeping on, facing the chair.

"My name is Doram Quandis. I used to be a professor at Ashmount."

"Edelbrock Brendis. Former officer in Calrym's military. I achieved—"

"I apologize, Edelbrock, but I know your background already," Doram said. "I have already questioned the man you arrived here with. Seeker Korran. He filled me in."

Seeker Korran and Edelbrock had discussed each other's lives plenty since arriving at Hidehedge. There wasn't much else for them to do other than talk. "Not a problem," Edelbrock said. None of this information was sensitive to him. In fact, Edelbrock felt a sort of relief over not having to repeat much of it.

Seeker Korran hadn't mentioned meeting with this Magicus, though, which concerned him. Edelbrock wondered if Seeker Korran just didn't find it important, if he'd been sworn to secrecy, or if he didn't trust Edelbrock enough to tell him. Edelbrock wagered on the middle option. Something about how Doram carried himself, the way he spoke, made Edelbrock consider his every action. Betraying this man didn't sound like a smart plan. Additionally, Doram had introduced himself as E-Two, which was a very high-ranking position within the Elkavich.

"How much do you know about the Elkavich and their goals?"

"I have a vague understanding of both." Demri Slarn had filled him in on many of the Elkavich's goals and rules, but he wanted to hear more from this man's mouth.

Doram leaned forward in his chair, analyzing Edelbrock. "You seem unconcerned with the hard truths. Former military, then gladiator. Practicality works on you, I assume. Facts, not feelings."

"Sure," Edelbrock said. It wasn't completely wrong. However, if Edelbrock knew where Scayde Haklon or his former wife was, it wouldn't matter what he was doing, he'd abandon it. Anger, revenge, a lust for righting wrongs. He was driven by his emotion, though it only focused on the one specific goal.

"The Elkavich have exposed many lies taught and told by the Magicai educated by Ashmount's teachings."

"And so, you blow up the school?" Edelbrock asked. He didn't care about the school. The University of Arcanical Arts-taught Magicai guarded Buzzard's Bowl. They helped create the arenas he fought within. Edelbrock had little love for them and the riches they generated. Nor would he ever have the finances to hire one, and that made them inaccessible. And, if Edelbrock was honest with himself, that made him hate them even more.

"A plan has been in place for a long time, Edelbrock. To reset civilization. To scrub the lies from our histories and our texts. We want to relearn. To relaunch humanity. The only way to do this, the only way to ensure things are taken seriously, is to destroy the pillars that support Cedain. Erase the Magicai and their supporters. It may sound drastic, apocalyptic, even, but in order to fix society, to even out the playing field—this pertains to nobility and rich folk alike—is to remove any trace of them."

Doram paused. He leaned back in his chair and watching Edelbrock's response. Edelbrock maintained a neutral expression, considering the man's words. He'd heard most of this from Demri already. "It sounds extreme," Doram continued. "Most people won't understand it. I get that. It's why the Elkavich organization is, all things considered, relatively small. And, once our plans are enacted, it'll be smaller yet, as a good many of us will have blown up. All in the name of the greater good. But I digress—I have a request for you. Though, before we get to that, I should offer a chance for you to leave. Sometimes speaking about this directly upsets people. Others don't understand that, though our goals mean well, we're prepared to do unthinkable things to attain them. You won't be harmed if you wish to leave." Doram crossed his arms and continued watching Edelbrock, waiting.

Edelbrock considered what Doram had said. He had nothing to live for in this world. Edelbrock's life was missing anything . . . good. He had no family. No job, no home. No money. He had no aspirations, no desires, nothing. Other than a need, a craving, a responsibility to pay back those who'd ruined everything for him. Scayde Haklon. Jaylena. The nobility, the king. The Magicai. With the plan Doram was outlining, the people who'd been ignored, the peasants, the farmers, even minor nobility like Edelbrock would find power, maybe. A life. He never thought about starting or joining a rebellion. His plan had always been to join the elite, the powerful. Become one with money. But that landed him in Buzzard's Bowl, and if these people hadn't freed him, he'd still be there. Or dead.

"What's the plan?" Edelbrock asked. Bringing down the upper class was always going to be one of his goals. This might afford him the opportunity to do just that.

Doram smiled.

<hr>

A day later and Edelbrock, along with Seeker Korran, was on the road. Their destination was Anepolis, the capital of Calrym. Their goal was to establish themselves in the city, get close to powerful figures, if they could. And, when the time came, assist the Elkavich Magicus, or

Magicai, who would arrive in the future to, Edelbrock assumed, blow up the city. Edelbrock had an alternative goal for accepting this mission, however. If he was going to select a place a bunch of noblemen would flee after their home blew up, it'd be Anepolis. He hoped to find Scayde Haklon.

Half a day into their travels, they merged onto a road where hundreds of people lay about resting, their belongings scattered. Dirty, ragged, poor. They had a downtrodden look to them, as if they'd suffered defeat after defeat. And, after scanning faces for a moment, he realized he recognized some of them. Lochwall's blacksmith, a bouncer for a local tavern, and a drunk everyone called Nonsense, because he said nothing of substance and he'd told nobody his name. Nonsense sat alone, propped up by a small sack of belongings under his back. He wasn't drunk now.

"Nonsense, good to see you."

Seeker Korran gave Edelbrock a confused look.

Nonsense stared at the road.

"What are you doing here?" Edelbrock asked.

Nonsense continued staring, his fingers tapping against one another.

Edelbrock moved on. He found somebody else he recognized who wasn't preoccupied. Another minor nobleman, C.K. Todlin, a former neighbor of Edelbrock's. The man always used his initials and Edelbrock, despite knowing the man for many years, never learned what they stood for.

"C.K., what's going on?"

C.K. turned towards Edelbrock, and when he did, both Seeker Korran and Edelbrock gasped. The usually immaculate C.K. Todlin looked a disheveled mess. A large bloody wound stretched down the man's face, and half his nose was missing, along with the corner of his upper lip. His pristine, bushy white mustache was now coated in soot and a snarled mess. When he opened his mouth to speak, Edelbrock noticed three of his incisors were missing. His voice made a slight whistling noise as it passed through the gap.

"Brocky Brendis, is that you?" he asked. Aside from the whistling, C.K.'s voice had the same stiff, regal, forced sound he always had.

Edelbrock held back a retort. The Todlins had always called Edelbrock "Brocky" for some reason Edelbrock still didn't know.

"You look like shit," C.K. said.

"So do you."

"Lochwall exploded. Almost everyone died, Brocky. The survivors," and C.K. splayed his hands out, gesturing at the surrounding people, "are here. They're all that's left."

"And you're staying . . . here?"

"Lochwall is gone. Any surviving nobility fled with Duke Scayde to Anepolis. They didn't invite us. They didn't invite *me*." C.K.'s mustache twitched in anger, scrunching up his face. It reminded Edelbrock of how he used to feel as a forgotten nobleman. Disrespected, ignored, dismissed. "Bastards," C.K. said, face scrunching up again. This time the act caused the wound on his face to crack, and he winced, blood snaking down his cheek.

"I know of a safe place," Seeker Korran said. He gave C.K. directions to Hidehedge. "Bring everyone. They have more than enough room."

"Thank you," C.K. said. "Thank you, sir."

"You're welcome. We must go, though." Seeker Korran turned, and Edelbrock followed him after shaking the hand C.K. Todlin proffered.

Once they'd put some distance between themselves and the Lochwall refugees, Edelbrock confronted Seeker Korran. "Any reason you're giving them the location of their secret hideout? They'll kill us if they learn it was us who gave it away."

Seeker Korran shrugged. "How? We're going to be in

Anepolis, learning about the city, setting up a place for them to stay. They couldn't do anything to us even if they wanted to. Besides, it's their fault those people are refugees. If they want to start over, now's the time. They can't kill *everyone.*"

"Fair enough," Edelbrock said. He wasn't sure he agreed, but he didn't oppose it, either. It'd be a problem for the Elkavich. His thoughts drifted to the knowledge C.K. Todlin had offered. Scayde Haklon would be in Anepolis. Jaylena, too, Edelbrock assumed. He pictured them, bound and gagged, as he carved into their skin with a knife, etching E.B. into their skin.

57

ASHEN HYREL

Ashen didn't notice the seasons change. It's not like she had any experience in the wild to notice the signs. Inside Anepolis, she never cared about the seasons until she started living with Jaspard. Before Jaspard, she cared about few things other than safety, food, and shelter. Velturo, being the rich and lazy man he was, cared little about making any actual progress and preferred to rest more than they traveled. Tallas, too, had started relaxing.

During their travels, neither Velturo nor the guards outside the second carriage would answer questions about what, or who, was within. Ashen had been suspecting another person, had considered sneaking up to the window and peering in late one night, but ever since breaking into Velturo's carriage, the guards had redoubled their efforts to remaining vigilant at night.

Instead of sneaking around, Ashen recited her Five Rules of Survival every night before closing her eyes.

Never forgo food because it appears dissatisfying. Starving to death isn't worth it. *Yes, I've done this.*

Never accept a helping hand. You never know who you'll owe, and you have nothing to leverage. *Except we're accepting a helping hand with Velturo right now. Safety in numbers. Or, perhaps, we're helping him more than he's helping us. I don't know.* She'd have to think about that some more.

Never display your belongings, however meager they may seem. Somebody always has less than you. *I have very little, and what I have is hidden.*

Never assume you're returning to the last place you felt safe. Unforeseen circumstances could mean you won't be able to. *Glad I listened to that one.* They weren't even in the same city anymore. Now she was on the road, unsafe, in the open. And yet, with Tallas and the other guardsmen around, she'd never felt safer. Ashen felt like she belonged.

Never trust anyone, even those you trust. In matters of life and death, your life is meaningless even from your friend's point of view. *And even though I feel safe, anything can happen. Even when I felt safe, Jaspard threw me in prison and planned to execute me.* It was only by the grace of Mother Avani he'd discovered a slight bit of guilt and had them freed. But the words of Jaspard's letter rang true in her mind, *"If you come to my home or inquire about anything that has transpired—if I'm to encounter you at all, that is—I will be forced to have you arrested and returned to the jail to await the justice of the future king."* If Jaspard would do that to her, what might anyone else be willing to do? What would Velturo do? Tallas?

Never let them know you're a girl, even after dark. Girls find themselves at the violent hands of angry men, and never leave them unscathed. *An outdated rule.* Yet one she couldn't quite let go of. She hadn't hidden her identity since moving into Jaspard's home. Ashen was more capable now.

When the young girl exited the second carriage, Ashen felt a pang of surprise. Another girl. Another person who appeared to be around the same age as Ashen. The girl, upon meeting Ashen's eyes, brightened, skipping to Ashen's location.

A guardsman said, not too quietly, "A bit improper, don't you think, my lady?"

"Well, hello there," she said, ignoring the guard.

Ashen noted the girl's short height and snarky stance. It was like she was trying to imitate Duchess Arena Hyrel. The thought of the duchess made Ashen feel guilty, so she pushed the thought from her mind. "Hello," she said, unsure of how to address the stranger.

"How old are you and what's your name, commoner?" the girl asked, crossing her arms and staring at Ashen in a most rude way.

"I'm fourteen, and until recently, I was Duchess Cithrial Hyrel." She put on her proper accent, assuming it would be needed with this girl.

The girl blanched. "I apologize for the insults, my lady."

"Nonsense. I've been demoted," Ashen said, offering a polite giggle. As part of her training with Jaspard and Alora Couliac, Ashen knew giggling with ladies often endeared oneself to them.

The girl giggled too and Ashen smiled. She was making headway.

"Well, Lady Hyrel, my name is Iadura Khyst, um, I mean Alcart. *I'm* married to Baron Exildar Alcart," she said, clearly impressed with herself.

"My real name is Ashen. Call me that, please, Lady Alcart."

"It's a pleasure, Ashen. Call me Iadura. We're all friends here. And too young to play at politeness for too long!" Iadura giggled and Ashen giggled, too. "I'm fifteen, so we're not too far apart."

Ashen's eyes widened. She would've guessed Iadura was younger than her, merely due to her size. Iadura made up for it in attitude, though, for she was already standing with a frown and hands on her hips, neck craned like a genuine lady.

"Shall we retire to my carriage, Ashen?" Iadura asked.

Ashen wasn't sure why Iadura would want to return to the carriage. She'd just left it for the first time in days. But Ashen was also smart enough to know this was an invitation to socialize and "socializing with anyone that has a title in front of their name can never hurt" Jaspard once told her.

Together, the pair retreated into the carriage and spent the afternoon gossiping about the guards, the politics of Anepolis, Velturo and the other dukes and duchesses, and debating whether the guard with the large crossbow or Tallas Taybold was the most capable fighter in the camp. Once the gossip ended, Iadura explained how she'd come into fleeing Anepolis with Velturo. And Ashen ended up dropping her proper ways because it felt natural, even if Iadura remained just as proper as Duchess Arena Hyrel had.

Having somebody to connect with might've made it the single greatest in Ashen's life since her mother's death.

***

When night approached, Ashen and Iadura left the carriage and gathered around a fire with Velturo, Tallas, and some guardsmen. As Ashen took a seat on the warm grass, she noticed Velturo and Tallas were in the middle of a discussion regarding the invasion of Cyrok.

"The king attacked Cyrok because they sold gyrfalcons?" Tallas asked, sounding absolutely perplexed.

"No, Tallas, you've misunderstood me, ah-hah." Velturo took a bite from the leg of a roasted chicken, fat and gristle dropping from his mouth and drooling down his chin. He wiped it with the back of his hand before speaking again. "It was a strategic advantage. The birds were just an excuse for Remeria, should there be spies or questions. As soon as we launched the ships, we knew they'd be suspicious. The actual goal was to conquer Remeria, ah-hah."

"Everyone knows that," Iadura said. "My husband, Exildar, told me so."

"Your husband has loose lips, ah-hah."

Iadura shot Velturo a glare, complete with pursed lips. "I won't tolerate negativity directed my husband's way."

"You're not inside the capital anymore, Iadura," Velturo said, dabbing at more chicken grease on his face. "You don't have to be afraid of what anybody might say. We're on the same side, ah-hah."

Iadura bit her lip but stayed her voice. Ashen got the impression the girl wasn't sure how to answer—either in favor of her husband, or, perhaps, the way she truly felt.

"What's the plan, then, eh?" Ashen asked. They'd been traveling two or three hours per day and "resting" the rest of the day and night. She didn't mind the slow pace—it was nice to be in a community of people who didn't ignore her, didn't find her annoying, and she wasn't lying to.

"We go to Lochwall to hide. I know a noble there; he runs the gladiator arena. Scayde Haklon was just promoted to duke recently by . . . everyone who's dead, ah-hah." Velturo glanced at Tallas. "I'm sure he'll aid us, ah-hah."

Tallas looked unconvinced. "Let's hope he's not better friends with the people we left behind."

Although they'd planned, Velturo still restricted traveling to five hours per day. The pace was slow, methodical, and if Ashen had anywhere to be, she might've lamented this. She had nobody outside of Tallas and Iadura, though. Velturo and the guardsmen, but her relationships with them were cordial acquaintanceship, nothing more.

She spent her days learning more about the political

schemes of King Mikas and the dukes and duchesses of Remeria. Any guilt she'd felt about participating in their deaths quickly erased itself. Velturo confirmed they'd committed many more atrocities than Ashen had learned about in her short tenure as Duchess Cithrial. Everything they did was to enrich their families, and that was all. Ashen knew this already, but to hear it from Velturo's mouth was enlightening. Ashen socialized with Iadura daily, and it wasn't long before she was living in the carriage with the young lady instead of outside with Tallas. Tallas, for his part, remained quiet, protective, and watchful. She realized he wasn't pleased with her reallocation, but he didn't argue about it. He did, Ashen noticed, relocate where he slept from the perimeter of the group, to just outside Iadura's carriage. This warmed her heart more than she cared to admit.

A journey that should've taken less than a week took many weeks because of Velturo's leisurely directions. They'd never make it to Lochwall, however.

58

DEMRI SLARN

Hidehedge, Calrym

With the dawn of the first cycle of summer, Caius's injuries were still too painful for him to do much. And Demri, with being his own injuries, didn't wish to stray too far from Caius. They lounged and talked, Caius whittled at his fingers while Demri read various books and tomes stocked in Hidehedge, and the first few days of summer included several visitors—all of whom Demri wished hadn't.

Although they spent a lot of time together, Demri also found himself separated from Caius. Caius slept far more than Demri did—a part of his recovering—and Demri took these opportunities to either study something which fascinated him or limp outside and get some fresh air.

A humid forest wasn't the best place for fresh air, but inside the Hidehedge building, Demri often felt even more stifled. Despite the number of people staying in Hidehedge, there wasn't any outdoor furniture. Part of this was to protect their secrecy—though at this point, Demri didn't think there was much they could hide. Far too much traffic had made it obvious there were plenty of people here. Dozens of horses and a few carts littered the area. He'd had enough of trying to lean up against tree trunks and avoiding sitting on gnarled roots. Bugs and grasses tickled his body and he could never get comfortable.

Demri consumed some power and ripped a pair of stumps from the ground. He moved them, then did the same with a log, propping it across the stumps. Then he constructed a back and armrests with smaller fallen trees and logs. To get the construction to stay together, he created mud by ripping dirt from the ground and conjuring water—a waste of his power with so much rain in the forest, to be sure, but when Demri made his bench, it wasn't raining. And he wanted his bench now. The mud he packed into the cracks, cementing the logs together, then he used a small flame to dry everything out. It wasn't hard work, nor did it take a ton of power, so it didn't age or tire him.

When Demri completed his bench, he watched and listened to the multitude of birds and squirrels. Loud, squirrels were with their chittering. But he didn't mind. He could both think and be alone. He was sitting on the bench for approximately a minute of time when she arrived.

"C-C-Couldn't have shown up a few minutes ago and helped?"

"No," Myri said, turning to face Demri. "I'm far too old for that now." She grinned, newly wrinkled lines forming at the corners of her smile—he noticed the crow's feet at her eyes had gotten larger, too. Demri felt a familiar pang of longing and desire in his chest. He pushed it aside.

"Young enough," Demri said. "There's still p-plenty you c-c-could do. Your m-mind is younger than your b-b-body. Young enough to have a happy life, young enough to b-b-be just like the foolish children running around, p-pretending at marriage."

She took a moment to look at him before answering. He wondered what she was thinking, and if she caught the implication. "Young people do foolish things, Demri. And not just children."

"We seem to f-find ourselves sitting next to one another often. Always p-playing with our words, always t-t-toeing the line. Always wondering if the other one will break."

Myri turned away. They sat in silence for several minutes. Then, she said, "It seems so. And yet, you're brave enough to call it out. Why now?"

"Why are you here?"

"You're right, Demri—I shouldn't be here. I have things that require my attention." She stood and walked off.

Demri wouldn't call after her. He wanted to, but he wasn't begging. He wasn't pleading. Demri had done enough of that.

The next visitor was even more unpleasant. Another day, another evening spent sitting on his crafted bench, thinking about the ancient magics Demri had read about —Veckheimism, the extinct blood magic cult being the one which fascinated him most. Then another figure sat on the bench, disturbing Demri from his thoughts: Doram.

"Demri, Demri, Demri. I heard your powers returned. I don't believe I have the words to express my disappointment. However, D-Four's report was positive. You exceeded expectations." Doram closed his eyes a moment, putting his head in his hand, as if considering something. To Demri, it seemed a false show. "I suppose I'll allow you to keep your powers, as long as you remain . . . controllable. Is that understood?"

Demri glared at Doram. He strained against his will, which was driving him to obliterate the man, but in doing so, Myri would die. And Demri wouldn't risk that.

Doram noticed the restraint and laughed. "Ah, Demri,

never change." He patted Demri's shoulder and leaned back on the bench. *My bench.*

"Do you ever take a moment to sit here and relax? So much"—Doram waved his hand at the forest all around them—"nature. The animals, the vegetation." He slapped his arm. "The bugs you wish would stop pestering you." In Demri's peripheral vision, he saw Doram glance at him. "Sometimes it behooves a man to sit back and relax—especially the wounded and broken. Let nature happen. The strong will breed and thrive. Survival is for the strong. That's how nature intended it."

Demri said nothing. He wouldn't humor the idiot. They sat, wordless, for a quarter of an hour.

Doram rose from the bench. "I have a private dinner with Myri. Do you want me to let her know you're thinking of her?"

Demri's jaw trembled as he clenched it, teeth clicking as they reverberated against one another. His fingers wrapped around the edge of the bench seat, fingernails clawing at the bark.

"I'll tell her you're doing well," he said.

An hour later, Demri found he was still clenching both his teeth and the bench.

———

Three days into the first summer cycle, a hoard of ragged refugees. Clothing in tatters and covered in dirt and blood, the people stumbled towards Demri with renewed vigor.

"Help us!" one of them said.

Demri stood, unsure what to do. *Should I kill them?* He didn't even know who *they* were. He placed his pair of Examiner spectacles on scanning the crowd of people, searching for any Magicai. There were none.

"B-B-Back!" he said.

"Help us!" the stranger said again. Others picked up the cry. "Help us! Help us!"

Demri stepped back, searching for help. He didn't know who they were or what they wanted. Nobody came to rescue him. "Remain where you are."

"Help us! Help us!" they chanted together.

"Who are you?" Demri asked.

A man with a battered face stepped forward. Part of his nose and lip were missing. "We come from Lochwall," he said. "It's gone. We were given instructions to come here. Said you could help. Brocky Brendis and a friend of his pointed us here. Help, sir. We need help. We're hungry and thirsty, we're exhausted, we have wounds."

"I'm sorry."

"There are *children* here!" The man raised his voice, but the conviction wasn't in his eyes. Demri guessed he was more concerned about himself than the children. The man sighed, then closed the gap between them. In a low whisper, he said, "I'm important. I can offer you money. My name is C.K. Todlin, of the Todlin noble family. I have connections. I don't care about these people. If there's a way I can—"

Demri raised his hand, pressing it against the man's chest. "I understand," he said. Then he consumed some of his Well, drawing from a Soul Glyph, emitting energy from his palm.

C.K. Todlin's chest burst, blowing blood, bone, and gore out of his backside. A stunned look graced the nobleman's face before he toppled over. Bits of Todlin sprayed Demri's face, and a sizeable chunk stuck to his hand. He wiped it off on his cloak, then faced the shocked crowd of refugees.

"Go away," Demri said. "There is nothing f-f-for you here." Feeling comfortable there were no Magicai in the crowd, he removed his spectacles, placing them back in the pouch on his belt.

A disheveled figure emerged from the crowd. Somebody, Demri thought he recognized.

"You'd confine me to death again, Demri?" the man said. His voice shook, and his slim figure trembled. Nevertheless, the man made a show of putting on a brave face. "You owe me," he said, taking another step forward. "You owe me, Demri. Both you and the *Velvet Mother*," he said, sneering. "I gave everything for that family. Everything. I would have sold my home and given the Velvet Mother every coin. And you"—he raised his hand, pointing at Demri—"you handed me over to *him.*"

Demri realized then who it was. His jaw dropped and his eyes widened. Somebody Demri had condemned to death. Stanton Brick, the man who'd helped Caius run the organization for the small time they'd been in charge. "I thought you were d-d-dead," Demri said. When he and Caius had left Scayde Haklon, he remembered a distinct sound. The sound of a dying man's shrieks.

"No," Stanton said. "Just hurt." He stepped closer and Demri saw the evidence of Scayde Haklon's torture. An S and H were carved into the man's face, cuts and bruises hid under dried blood, and he squinted through a swollen eye. The way he walked spoke of many other aches and pains, too. Demri could sympathize. "Let us live. You owe me that much."

"It's not my choice," Demri said.

"Welcome to Hidehedge," a jovial Doram Quandis shouted. "We'll take care of everyone's needs."

Demri turned, saw both Doram and Myri approaching. Doram's arm was around Myri's waist. *Bastard.* Demri ground his teeth against one another, resisting the urge to access his Well and incinerate his adversary. *Why is she letting him touch her like that? He doesn't deserve her. She doesn't deserve that slimeball touching her.* A brief wave of nausea floated around his stomach and throat, he swallowed some saliva, pushing it away and shifted his focus to what Doram was now doing.

Doram's boot connected with C.K. Todlin's arm and, looking down, he made a disgusted face and kicked the arm out of his way. "That won't happen to anyone else," he said, addressing the crowd. "Everyone, come with me. We have much to talk about!" Doram caught Demri's gaze and grinned, giving Myri a slight slap on the ass as he guided her back to Hidehedge with the refugees in tow. She made no sounds of resistance, no indicator she disapproved.

Left alone, Demri returned to his bench, sickened, and feeling betrayed.

The smell of C.K. Todlin's corpse got worse as the afternoon dragged on. Demri ignored it.

The sun had drifted below the tree line when Demri had another visitor.

Stanton Brick lowered himself onto the bench, visibly wincing in pain as he did.

"I know how that f-f-feels."

"I remember watching you," Stanton said.

"What d-do you want?"

"An apology, for one."

"I'm sorry," Demri said. "I was just looking out f-for myself and C-C-Caius."

Stanton nodded. It must've caused him pain because he grimaced and stopped mid-nod. "I understand. There was a time I would've done anything for the Velvet Mother or any member of the Corbéo family. I somewhat regret my feelings now, as both a Velvet Mother and Corbéo family member betrayed me."

"He's here. C-C-Caius is here."

Stanton sighed. "I figured that would be the case."

"We c-could use your help."

He snorted, shaking his head. "I'm no fool, Demri Slarn. The moment it suits you, you'll leave me to die. Again."

"He almost d-died. Took a crossbow b-b-bolt to the stomach."

"If he died, Khlaux Corbéo would be the sole remaining member of the family. And I don't even know if he's alive. I'm glad Caius is alive, for the sake of the family, at least."

Once again, Demri sat with somebody he didn't like, in silence, waiting for the conversation to progress.

"I'm not sure what to do, Demri. These people, the Elkavich—a group of people I thought didn't exist—seem strange. And yet, I have nowhere else to go."

"They'll make room for you. Everyone has a use to them. B-B-But, you c-could help C-C-Caius and me again."

"Demri, please," Stanton said, itching at a red mark on his neck—another injury. "I could never trust you again."

Demri didn't like Stanton Brick, but the man had a lot of information. He figured Caius would like Stanton around, too. *Perhaps he could still be useful to us.* If Demri wanted Stanton Brick on his side, he'd have to convince him. The only way Demri thought he could convince the man was with a lot of spilled secrets. And Demri had them to spill. The world was ending and nobody was going to give a damn about them, anyway. "We wanted to return and claim the organization for ourselves. B-B-But when we returned, it blew up."

"That doesn't matter to me."

"C-C-Caius never wanted to rid himself of the Velvet Mother. We wanted t-to takeover B-Buzzard's Bowl and k-k-kill Scayde Haklon. We never got the chance."

"I don't care what your plans were, Demri." Stanton rose from the bench. "I hope you have a wonderful night."

"Wait," Demri said, gesturing for Stanton to return to the bench. "I have so much more to t-t-tell you."

"I said—"

"D-Doram Quandis sold Healers into slavery. He contributed to the Blind Sisters." Demri had to drop a significant secret to keep Stanton's attention. He wasn't sure if it would be the right secret, wasn't even sure why he dropped that particular secret. It's just what came out. But it worked.

Stanton Brick plopped back on the bench, looking intrigued.

"I have a lot more to t-t-tell. About whatever you want. Ask, and I will explain. Anything."

Demri and Stanton talked for hours. It was dark when they retired that night, Demri feeling good about not having to relinquish the more sensitive information he had, while Stanton seemed to feel reassured.

The next day Stanton asked the hard questions.

59

SERADAL WINTLOCK & VILLIC THE IMBUER

Calrym

Her heart ached. People Sera loved and cared about continued dying. Her mother and brother, Governess Stasia Falconel, The Old Vulture, Renard. She wondered if her father had died, too. And regretted parting ways with him but was also glad they'd done so—if he was here, she'd have nothing but fear and worry over his wellbeing.

The air in the plains smelled of blood and flowers. The stench of sweaty soldiers mixed with the fresh breeze of grasses and hays of the fields they'd marched through.

The wounded needed some time to heal, some time to figure out who would die and who'd be able to continue into Calrym. Sera had called for a week of rest. And so, she, along with the other able-bodied survivors, dragged hundreds of corpses—men, women, horses, and camels—into large piles and burned them far from their encampment, to prevent disease. She and her soldiers worked themselves to limits Sera didn't think any of them had before felt.

Patrika became a lifesaver, taking over command when Sera was too tired, or sad and depressed to do so. Despite Sera's feelings of inadequacy, soldiers offered constant reassurance, complimenting her on the way she handled herself.

The Camel Clans, under the leadership of Uva the Shaman, took on the duty of providing food for the army. They left on regular hunting missions and supplemented the camp with much needed fresh meat and foraged vegetation.

The Redclaws assisted Sera. The Bloody Duchess even hinted that they were making fine Falcon Knights themselves.

And Villic. Villic didn't hunt with the Camel Clans. He remained near Sera, helping move bodies. He refused to allow anyone to move Dunecrest's body and took time to dig a grave. Villic spoke no words to anyone. He remained silent, withdrawn. She wanted to help him but knew what he was feeling—for she felt the same loss. She let him mourn and mourned herself. But the difference was people continued to approach her, asking her questions, requesting orders, and praising her work. Sera had to interact.

On the afternoon of their fifth day at rest, Sera had just returned from working in the fields when she found herself surrounded by Patrika and several officers.

"Cyr Seradal," Patrika said. "We were victorious. Now that we're inside Calrym, we plan on continuing, yes? To the capital?"

"We must put the king on a spit and see him roast!" an officer said.

Another one chimed in. "Annihilation. We must do what has been done, or at least attempted—some of us still live. It is only fair."

"Yes," Sera said. "We ride to the capital and demand answers. We ride to deliver retribution."

Nods and cries of "yes" echoed around the perimeter of people surrounding her.

"Can I please retire now? I am exhausted," Sera said.

"Not quite," Patrika said. She turned to the oldest officer, a Grouse in the standard yellow cloak.

"Cyr Seradal, you have impressed everyone," he said, nodding in deference to her. "We are awed and inspired. You were thrust into this leadership role and have exceeded expectations. The rest of the officers and I have elected you as a potential candidate for the next governess of Cyrok."

Sera laughed. "You can't be serious."

"You have everyone's respect, cyr," Patrika said, "and more importantly, the respect of every group—the Redclaws, the Camel Clans, the Remerians, and the Falcon Knights. You unite the forces. King Alondo endorsed you. The Old Vulture endorsed you."

"The Old Vulture did not—"

Patrika interrupted Sera. "He did. Not to you, but to us. He mentioned he favored you when we arrived in Remeria. We've all watched for enough time to have decided."

"The Cyroki need somebody to rally behind," the Grouse said. "You are that person."

The other officers agreed. She was to become the next governess.

———

Villic tuned Speaker out. He ignored everyone. If Sera talked to him, he half-listened and did what she requested. He didn't listen to Uva the Shaman. His thoughts were on Dunecrest. Always. Since Villic had been a young boy, he'd grown up with him. Rode him, befriended him. His best friend was gone and Villic was the only one who cared. To everyone else, Dunecrest was another camel. Another casualty of war. To Villic, Dunecrest was his entire heart, his reason for living. Now what?

Sometimes he'd catch himself staring at the bush trees. Occasionally, he'd watch somebody care for their camel or horse and the pain of losing Dunecrest would rip a fresh wound in his fragile heart. Uva the Shaman had offered him a replacement camel, but he denied it. Villic would walk with the other foot soldiers, for he couldn't think of trying to bond with another creature.

Speaker became an echo he ignored. Villic tuned him out just as he'd tuned everyone aside from Sera out—and her only out of necessity. He wanted to fulfill his promises to her. And she was in mourning, just as he was. He felt bad for her, felt bad for anyone who'd lost somebody close to them. Felt bad for the people he killed and the people who had fled the battle. And he felt bad for Dunecrest. A loyal camel and friend that didn't deserve to die like that.

Villic's days drifted by in a haze of monotony and sadness.

"Villic, answer me."

Sometimes he heard Speaker but pretended not to.

———

"You have to decide what bird will represent you, what color, and select a new last name," Patrika said, for the third time that day.

"I know," Sera said. "But it's too fast."

"It'll rejuvenate the soldiers. Give them motivation. It'll make us feel like the Cyroki still live." Patrika paused but appeared eager to say something more.

"Yes?"

"It's just . . . it'll feel like we're home. I know we won't be, but it'll give us a sense that we are. It'll feel like when Governess Stasia Falconel was still alive."

Sera grimaced. "Hardly. Now *she* was a leader."

"An admirable woman, yes," Patrika said. "But you make a fine one yourself."

"With your help, that is."

"Yes," Patrika said, grinning. "With my help, cyr."

Sera considered her options. The albatross was a coastal predator she'd always admired. Thinking of birds reminded her of the eagles she'd seen and how beautiful she thought they were. *The Eagle Knights. Cyr Seradal Eagle. Eaglest? Eaglen? Eagleton. Cyr Seradal Eagleton.* She liked that but wasn't sure what others would think.

"Patrika," she said. "What about Seradal Eagleton?"

"The Eagle Knights?" Patrika's face lit up. "They're gorgeous, smart, and true hunters. Perfect. But what color cloak?"

Sera considered that. The Falcons wore blue, Hawks green, Grouse yellow, and the Vultures, when there had been any still alive, had worn gray—meaning she could select gray if she wanted to, but wanted something fresh. Something vibrant. Something accurate to their times.

"Red," she said, not happy about it because of its relation to the Redclaws but with all the deaths, the killing, the wars, and their current purpose, it couldn't be any other color. It had to be red.

"Red," Patrika said. "It's a bold color, bright. And I understand the significance. Fitting, sad, but honest. Red. The Eagle Knights. I'll spread the word, cyr."

"Thank you, Patrika."

Villic stood with everyone else, watching Sera, Patrika, and the other important Falcon Knights. They were speaking and talking, and the crowd was cheering and smiling. Villic stood, numb. *Dunecrest, I miss you.*

"I miss you, Villic."

He ignored Speaker, closed his eyes, focused on Dunecrest. But all he could see was the dying camel's eyes fading, the bloodied knife he'd used to put his friend down, easing his suffering. *Take care of Dunecrest, Flaytz, god of death. Please.*

Villic stood, watching, but not taking part. His focus was elsewhere. He'd become a loose grain of sand, blown by the wind wherever Hytrok, god of storms, willed him to go.

The army regrouped and entered the large, forested area in Calrym. Trekking through here took time, as everyone had to condense themselves into columns of no more than two or three bodies. In the narrower parts of the forest, they sometimes had to go single file.

At least it's not the jungles in Remeria. There were still bugs, and it was still hot, but it wasn't as bad on either front.

They passed several deserted small villages, and hamlets in forest clearings on their way to Anepolis. Each one they looted what they could, any forgotten food or water, clothes, and other supplies. The Bloody Duchess even found several dyes, and along with Patrika, fashioned a makeshift red cloak for Sera. Now she wouldn't stop making jokes about how Sera was a true Redclaw. She wasn't fond of the fact they shared the same color now, but she liked the color and it fit their cause, so that was that.

They pressed on, marching. Anepolis was their goal. And all along, Sera couldn't shake reminders of Cyrok from her mind. Images of the abandoned villages combined with memories of Cyrok's citizens fleeing Gyrloft. Countless innocents slaughtered. Panic, fear, death. She didn't want to bring the same level of decimation to the citizens of Calrym. She wanted justice for her country and her people. And for her family. Her mother, Yudri; her brother, Fezzel; the page, Renard; the former Falcon Knight leader, Governess Stasia Falconel; and her mentors, the Old Vulture and Ilic Strickland, came to mind.

She would find vengeance for all of them.

Everything passed in a blur. When they finally emerged out the western side of the forest, it took several more hours of marching before Villic even realized it. Back onto plains. *It feels like Zarn, god of shadows, has possessed me. I am silent. Not seen.*

"Welcome back!"

Villic heard Speaker and focused elsewhere. In an effort to ignore him, Villic thought of other things. Dunecrest popped back into his head and he remembered all the good times he'd had with his loyal friend. He remembered how they'd bonded when they were both young, grew up together. Until Flaytz, god of death, took him. Teeth grinding against one another, Villic suppressed his rage and sadness, and marched on.

Shouting is what shook Villic from his . . . Otherness.

People pointed, some shaking their heads in surprise. He looked and saw nothing. After listening, he realized why. There was supposed to be something there.

An entire city was gone. Lochwall had been eradicated.

He didn't know anybody in Lochwall and had never seen the city. Didn't care. Villic returned to Otherness.

60

DEMRI SLARN

Caius was feeling better, so both Demri and Caius sat on the bench Demri created, enjoying each other's company and being outside. When Stanton Brick showed up, Caius tensed—though he couldn't have been surprised, Demri had warned him of this inevitable moment—and Demri sighed. The last thing he wanted to bother him was Stanton Brick. Or Doram. Or Myri. Really, he didn't want to deal with anyone.

Caius apologized, Stanton accepted it. An hour went by while they fixed their issues. Once they'd settled their differences, Stanton focused on Demri.

"You said you'd answer questions I had," he said.

"Yes."

"I have more."

Demri sighed. "Let's hear them."

"I heard you and the Elkavich don't get along. Why?"

"Because Demri's too much of an ass to be silent and take orders," Caius said.

Demri glared at Caius. "No. You know that's not why. It's . . ."

"It's what?" Caius asked. "It's because you want to kill that fucker in there"—he jabbed his finger over his shoulder at Hidehedge—"but they won't let you. Which makes you hate both him more, and the leadership. Erasure, Catastrophe, all of them."

"You know—"

"Yes, Demri. I know. We've been at this for a long time. I'm not saying you're wrong—I'm still here, aren't I?" Caius paused. He took out his knife and started picking at his fingernails. "You could be a little more tactful."

"The Elkavich and I d-d-don't get a long because they work with a b-bastard," Demri said, turning to Stanton. Caius issued a grunt at being ignored, but Demri ignored that, too.

"But that's one person."

"I know that, Stanton. I'm not a f-f-fucking idiot." But he felt like one. At first, he'd been careful around the Elkavich because he hadn't known them and the organization was shrouded in mystery. Then Doram Quandis showed up and he found out Doram was a high-ranking and respected member of the group. Since then, Demri had been too busy trying to kill him than trying to work with the Elkavich. He wouldn't stop trying to kill Doram, but he needed to be more careful, more covert. He couldn't upset the Elkavich more. Demri didn't think he'd have Myri to fall back on if something happened. She seemed to be cozying up with Doram, returning to her old ways. Demri replayed his time at Ashmount, remembering her and Doram, happy together and tormenting him.

"Demri?" Caius asked.

"I'm fine," he said. Both Caius and Stanton were looking at him, expecting an answer to something. "What d-did you say?"

Stanton glanced at Caius, unsure, before answering. "I

heard the Elkavich can access multiple classifications of powers taught at the University of Arcanical Arts." Demri winced at the name non-Magicai referred to Ashmount as, considered offensive to anybody who'd attended. Ashmount wasn't a university, a school—not like other learning, anyway. "One could be an Enforcer and a Healer. Or, I guess, all five. Is this true?"

Demri nodded. "Yes. I am b-both an Enforcer and Examiner." He retrieved the pair of spectacles he carried upon him. "See?"

"But how?"

"I d-don't know that I c-c-could explain it. I researched, and through self-examination, I isolated various . . . threads within me. This allowed me to t-t-tap into a p-part of the Trace I've never had access to. One day I had Enforcer p-powers, the next, I had Examiner. I've yet to replicate this, b-but the Elkavich are, with training, able to d-do it to anyone."

"Why doesn't everyone have access to all five powers, then?" Stanton asked.

Caius snorted. "Trust. Even organizations like this, those that preach new beginnings and want to bring down evil hier-archies—the Magicai, the nobility—have their own hierar-chies. It's hypocritical."

"I would agree," an unfamiliar voice said behind Demri.

Startled, Demri turned and saw a masked man standing there.

"Don't worry, I'm not angry," the man said. A letter B was stitched onto his cloak. *Bloodbath.* A leader of the Elkavich had just overheard them. Demri had talked to the leaders, or heard them talk, several times in Hidehedge, but he'd never noticed how old Bloodbath was. The man, somewhat hunched Demri noticed, ambled around the bench, and patted Caius's shoulder. "You wouldn't mind, would you?"

Caius slipped out of his spot and Bloodbath sat, sighing with relief. "Getting too old for this," he said. "And boy, it's warm out here." Without a care in the world, Bloodbath reached up and pried his mask off, setting it in his lap.

Caius caught Demri's eyes, and Demri knew he was ready to act if need be.

"Oh relax," the old man said. He lowered his hood, exposing a nearly bald pate. Liver spots dotted his blotchy skin. "What you've said isn't untrue. It's something we've always been aware of, but it was necessary to contain our secrecy. There's no need, now. Qothe, Cyrok, and Vessia are all neutralized—we didn't even have to involve ourselves with Cyrok."

"What d-do you mean by 'neutralized'?"

"At this point, every major city or town is . . . gone. Outside of Calrym, anyway. We're still working on that," Bloodbath said. "Look at that," he chuckled, looking at the forest. "Nature is beautiful."

Demri followed his gaze, saw a pair of bright blue butter-flies. "B-Butterflies?"

"Yes, butterflies. Gorgeous creatures, aren't they?"

"Going to blow them up, too?" Caius asked.

"Maybe," the old man said, nodding. Serious and sad, he looked away from the creatures. "Unfortunately, the side effects of what we do are very real." He itched the top of his head, flaking dry skin everywhere. "We're considering opening all branches of power to all Elkavich members. Even the less . . . trustworthy ones. In the days that follow, we're going to need all hands. Magic is going to be consumed at a rapid rate. People will die. But tomorrow, perhaps, people can live in peace. And our descendants can know a happiness we have yet to experience—acceptance. Understanding."

They remained silent until Bloodbath stood, nodded at each of them, and, putting his mask back on, slowly returned to Hidehedge. Stanton took Bloodbath's spot and they sat in silence.

61

EDELBROCK BRENDIS

Calrym

They made good time. Buzzard's Bowl had hardened their bodies, given them the stamina and muscle they needed to travel far and fast, without concern for resting. They carried light rations and foraged and hunted —they'd taken a pair of bows with arrows for their journey. The days they didn't find food weren't awful. They'd experienced true starvation before and were able to go hungry without being too uncomfortable. Anything they ate, they ate in appreciation and savored.

Edelbrock found he had more in common with Seeker Korran than he'd guessed. Seeker Korran, who preferred to go by his gladiator name and wouldn't offer his birth name, had also ruined a relationship by cheating. He'd been about to propose to the woman of his dreams but he hadn't realized how perfect she'd been. One night, drunk and horny, he lost himself to the whims of a street whore. When his beloved found out, she left him for a potato merchant and spent the next five years in turmoil before dying of heartache.

The roads were busier than they normally would be. Most

people preferred not to engage in conversation with Edelbrock or Seeker Korran, and a few had warned them that if "they came closer, they'd be riddled with arrows". At one point, a family of four passed Edelbrock and Seeker Korran, armed with bows, and weren't shy about notching them. Edelbrock let them pass—for they were in a wagon pulled by a set of mules—and continued on the road following them.

The few snippets of conversation they had with travelers willing to speak to them, or overheard others saying, was that the lands weren't safe anymore. It sounded like many of the travelers were also on their way to Anepolis. Many of the travelers were from the unnamed, small hamlets close to Lochwall. Some said they were from Pinecrest. Edelbrock was certain he recognized a family by appearance from Lochwall, but they refused to talk to him. Everyone's sense of danger and self-preservation had heightened.

Edelbrock couldn't blame the people he encountered. Both Seeker Korran and he had one outfit of clothing they both traveled and slept in. After only a day of travel, they'd gotten dirty. After a few days, they looked like armed vagabonds.

Once they'd gone through the Valkrynd Mountains pass, travelers spread further across the plains, keeping safe distances from one another. Edelbrock could count at least nine different fires their first night on the plains. The second day on the plains, they met a strange group of people fleeing Anepolis, traveling in the direction Edelbrock and the rest of the travelers, had fled from.

62

ASHEN HYREL

Calrym

The plains in Calrym were endless. It didn't help that they were traveling an hour or two per day before Velturo tired of the bumps and ruts, because he refused to walk.

Ashen spent her time divided. In the mornings, she was usually with Tallas listening to him complain about their pace, Velturo, and the hired guards. In the afternoons, she joined Iadura, where they discussed the other men journeying with them, politics, Anepolis, Iadura's husband, and Lochwall, along with what they planned on doing.

Iadura wanted to get word to her husband about what had happened. Ashen had warned her to send a discreet message if she had to send one at all, and Iadura promised to let Ashen read it prior to sending, which allayed Ashen's fears about being discovered. She doubted anyone would intercept delivered messages in Anepolis—there were far too many more important things for Alyst and the city to focus on.

Ashen wasn't sure what she wanted to do upon reaching

Lochwall. She didn't know anyone. She wondered if Tallas would leave her somewhere to fend for herself, though that didn't seem like something he'd do.

The slow pace normally would've been concerning. Lack of food, water, and other supplies on an open road, in a group this large, could've been a death sentence. However, Velturo had—*of course*, Ashen thought—been overindulgent in the amount of supplies he'd purchased and stocked. They weren't close to running out.

They'd been stopped for several hours when Ashen noticed increased traffic on the road. More travelers than normal passed them by.

Tallas approached her and Iadura, issuing a warning to them. "It might be safest for both of you to retreat into the carriage," he said.

"Why?" Iadura asked.

"I don't know what's going on, but this looks bad. Something has happened. Everyone is on edge. You'll be safer in there."

"I don't want to hide," Ashen said.

Tallas swiveled his one eye in her direction. "'Honorable people die young.' Remember?"

She grumbled her assent and followed Iadura back to the carriage. If she were honest with herself, she didn't mind hiding away. After watching the massacre that occurred in the Great Hall by Tallas's hand, and having a part in it herself, she wouldn't mind avoiding violence or confrontation for a while.

Inside the carriage, Iadura and Ashen peered out the windows, watching various groups of disheveled travelers pass by. They wore dirty and bloody clothing, several nursed injuries, and had very few possessions. One pair of travelers passed close to the carriage, and she caught a fraction of their conversation.

"Don't know what we're going to do now," a man said to the woman he marched along.

"Me either. Anepolis is our only hope."

"King Mikas will help, I'm sure of it," the man said.

"Nobody knows that the king is dead yet," Iadura said.

"Well, ain't that gonna be a rude awakening on the wrong side of the bed?"

"What?"

"Never mind," Ashen said, forgetting who she was talking to. Iadura was a nice, proper lady. She didn't understand the simple folk. Even so, Ashen found her to be good company.

"Why is everyone staying so far apart from one another?" Iadura asked. She leaned against the window and looked at the various groups of travelers.

Ashen hadn't considered that and noticed she could see four different groups. All remained a respectful distance from each other, though the pair who'd passed by Ashen's carriage seemed to care less about maintaining any distances from the others.

Each day they traveled, the passersby became more frequent, more ragged, more distraught. Ashen started preferring her time hidden in the carriage with Iadura more, because there were so many grim travelers.

<hr>

The mood in the traveling party soured. Everyone adopted the dour attitude the other travelers carried with them. Two days after first encountering them, Ashen noticed discussion becoming less frequent. Everyone was retreating into themselves, something Tallas noticed and grumbled about with fervor. Although, Ashen noticed Tallas becoming crankier each day, so even he was affected by the change.

"We should travel more, not less," he'd said to her when

Velturo called for a halt a mere hour into traveling. "And look at everyone," he said, nodding his head towards the grumpy guards. "Everyone's miserable. We don't know why we're miserable, but we're all going to brood. It's unprofessional."

Ashen stared at him.

"How're things with Iadura?" he asked.

"She's fine. Doesn't seem too affected by the mood."

"Well, that makes one of us." He snorted and shook his head.

After that, Ashen dismissed herself and remained with Iadura, secluded inside the unmoving carriage. Even Iadura seemed distant, claiming fatigue, and they talked little, which made Ashen feel like a liar to Tallas. Eventually, Iadura decided to nap, leaving Ashen to sit alone.

Later that day, an alarmed shout from a guard outside the carriage woke Ashen from a doze. She glanced at Iadura who offered her a nervous smile of reassurance.

Ashen drew her knife and a pouch of the Black Dust she carried and snuck to the door of the carriage. She heard a guard shouting at someone to turn away.

She opened the door and slipped out.

"Don't leave me!" Iadura's voice called.

Ashen ignored her. If there was something to worry about, she'd return and protect Iadura.

The guards had formed a perimeter, protecting the carriages. Velturo posed, half in the carriage and half out, as if he'd started fleeing to safety and then curiosity got the better of him. He watched what was happening before him with wide eyes, likely deciding whether to hide.

She focused on Velturo's guard—the one with the heavy crossbow—who was talking to a pair of men. One had his hands resting on a pair of axes on his belt. The other one had scars riddling his face and arms and a sword hung at his side, though his hands were nowhere near it. Ashen also noticed Tallas lurking nearby, halberd readied.

"We're just trying to pass through," the one with the sword said.

Velturo's guard pointed with his crossbow. "Plenty of room that way," he swiveled the crossbow in the opposite direction, "or that way."

"Your carriage is heading in the direction we just came from. I strongly suggest you turn around."

"If you don't leave, I'll put a bolt through your eye."

The traveler with the sword looked at his companion and shrugged. An icy chill went down Ashen's spine. Something was off.

"Wait," she said. Nobody heard. "Wait!"

All eyes turned to her. "Let's at least hear them out." Nobody said anything. "Ain't gonna hurt us."

The traveler with the sword glanced at the crossbow guard, who was looking at Velturo, waiting for approval.

Velturo shrugged. "Let them in. But kill them if they do anything suspicious, ah-hah."

The two men, under the watch of several guards—and Tallas—entered the camp, approaching a fire set in-between the two carriages. Velturo remained in his doorway but Ashen followed, meeting the travelers at the fire. On the way, she loosened the ties around the pouch of Black Dust. Just in case.

"Where are you from, ah-hah?"

"Lochwall," the one with the axes said.

"Our destination," Ashen said.

The travelers gave each other a grim look.

"You can't," the one with the sword said. "It's gone. Destroyed. We just came from there."

"How could a city be destroyed?" a guard asked.

The sword traveler nodded. "Magicai blew it up. Survivors are heading to Anepolis, hoping the king will save them. Others dispersed to other locations near Lochwall, but I don't believe they're safe."

"Anepolis isn't safe, either," Ashen said. Tallas shook his head "no" at her, but she decided she didn't care. "Ain't no king to speak of."

"What?"

"The king was murdered," she said.

The strangers glanced at each other again. Perhaps she'd given away too much information, but she wanted more. The best way to gain was by offering.

"Have you seen a nobleman pass by? Scayde Haklon?" the sword traveler asked. "He probably had other noblemen with him."

"I wouldn't know. Everyone's keeping to themselves," Ashen said. "How do you know Lochwall is gone?"

"I watched it explode," he said. Then, after a moment, he held his hand out to her. "My name is Edelbrock Brendis."

"Ashen Hyrel," she said, shaking his hand. His grip was firm, but she could tell he was being gentle for her sake. Like she was a fragile girl. *I am a fragile girl.*

"Seeker Korran," the man with the axes said. He nodded to her. She nodded.

"Got any food? We're hungry. And we'll answer all your questions," Edelbrock said.

"Well, ain't that a deal fit for a cheap bastard?" she said, grinning.

63

INTERLUDE
VITHOR BANE

Anepolis, Calrym

He was under no illusions that people found him revolting. Rotund, blunt, and, by all accounts, rife with disgusting habits, he'd made a name for himself. In Cyrok, anyway. In Calrym, Vithor Bane was unknown. The fact he stood here was a testament of his social prowess. Or, perhaps, the weight of coin in a sack.

He shifted his weight from one hip to the other, leaning against the wall for support. He wasn't a man who enjoyed standing for long, nor was he one to disgrace himself by sitting where peasants walked.

In Cyrok, he'd had to disappear. So he'd adopted a new persona: Vithor Bane, that of a cartwright. He'd become a disgusting man who used his trousers as a kerchief. But after fleeing Cyrok and escaping the grasp of the Falcon Knights, it was time to reform his identity.

The Falcon Knights, and by extension Vithor Bane, docked at Maceport. He immediately chartered another ship to whisk him and a few loyal men to Bryn, a port city in Calrym. He worked a while, buying new clothes and forming himself into a proper man. A man of means and nobility. He trashed his old disgusting clothes, stopped picking his nose, and eating with his fingers, and didn't commit any crimes—all things he did in Cyrok.

Vithor Bane was a name in the past. In Cyrok, he chided people who only used his first name, saying, "Mum gave me two names. I like to hear 'em both. Otherwise, you're wasting one of them." He enjoyed that saying, felt it gave him power over other people. He'd need to come up with something different. Something both respectable and powerful.

He'd created a new name, letting Vithor Bane die like the name before that, and the one before that. His new name, Lord Dellevue Vaston, had a more regal feeling. A respectable nobleman who'd fled Cyrok during the war. He thought there was a decent chance they'd murder him as soon as he told them he was Cyroki. He hoped not. Lord Dellevue Vaston didn't want to die. *Ah, maybe that's my new line. 'A dead Dellevue is an avoidable dilemma, I hope,'* he'd thought. Now, standing outside the Great Hall, waiting for his chance to meet with King Alyst, he wondered if he should've thought of a better one. *No time to reform yourself. You know who you are now. Stick with it. Sell it.*

It took many days for Dellevue to become comfortable in his new identity, and that was before he'd ever stepped outside the room he rented. It took several more weeks of interacting with other people before he felt truly comfortable. Now, he was answering to "Lord Vaston" as if he'd always been this identity.

"Lord Vaston," a guard said from the doorway of the Great Hall. "King Alyst is ready."

He cleared his mind, nodded to the guard, and strode forth.

The guards held the door open to which he gave them each a nod—Lord Vaston wasn't impolite—and entered the Great Hall. Magnificent as it was, his eyes didn't wander. He didn't care about the spread of luxurious foods, or the new marble table and extravagant chairs with their fancy carvings. Lord Vaston had eyes for one person: the man at the table's head.

"Your Highness," he said, offering a graceful bow. He made a show of letting his left arm flair enough to demonstrate he wasn't accustomed to Calrym's requirements. Though, of course, long ago he'd studied every country's mannerisms.

"Sit," the king said, gesturing to a chair. Lord Vaston noticed the king's crown rested crooked on his head—slightly too large—meaning he'd not yet had one forged. A fresh king, looking for respect and validation of power. He'd have to navigate this with care and caution. Lord Vaston had discovered the last king and most of his advisers had all been murdered.

Lord Vaston sat, noticing the other faces in the room. He'd done proper investigations before requesting a meeting and knew who the identities of the other people sitting at the table.

At the king's right-hand side was a nobleman named Jaspard Couliac. From what he'd learned about Jaspard, the man had somehow risen from minor nobleman to important king adviser. Even more rumors suggested Jaspard had somehow been behind the former king's murder. Lord Vaston noticed him sucking on something—a sugared honey chew if his information was reliable.

Next to Jaspard was an armored giant of a man. Zervan, The Watchtower of Calrym. People said there'd been no one taller, nor would there be. Across from the Watchtower was the Golden Knight. Both the Watchtower and the Golden Knight were Calrym legends. He wondered if he should've come dressed in the Falcon Knight armor he'd received as payment to smuggle people out of Cyrok to impress the king. Then he considered Alyst would see him as an enemy before he uttered a single word. Best not to cause any offense.

Sitting to the Golden Knight's right was "Captain" Blago Adavir, the former brigand who'd caused plenty of trouble in Cyrok. He hadn't needed to research that man. Why he was sitting so close to the king was a puzzling matter Lord Vaston hadn't yet cracked. Adavir's tongue darted across his mustache—a habit Lord Vaston expected to see.

His gaze flickered beneath the table and he swore he saw a thin streak of dried blood. This unnerved him more than any of the living people in the Great Hall. A reminder of the past, a warning of his current situation, a promise of the future. Lord Vaston swallowed his fear and adopted a confident and knowing face of arrogance—a typical noble know-it-all.

"Lord Dellevue Vaston, is that correct?" Jaspard asked, his words slightly slurred by the extra saliva the sugared honey chew was creating.

Lord Vaston nodded his assent. Before the meeting he'd decided he'd only speak when necessary, to appear more powerful and knowledgeable than he was. He assumed King Alyst would respect him more.

"From Cyrok?" Jaspard asked, eyebrows raising, as if waiting for an answer.

Lord Vaston nodded once again, setting his mouth into a stern smile. Let Jaspard think him irritated. Perhaps this would encourage them to skip questions they already knew and offer pleasantries they didn't mean.

"Let's get to the point," King Alyst said.

If Lord Vaston felt it safe to smile, he would've. Instead, he nodded to the king. Always nodding. Let them believe him an agreeable man.

"You insult our king by not offering words," Adavir said.

Lord Vaston stifled many things—a laugh, a scoff, a snort,

a grimace—and nodded once again. "I did not wish to offend His Grace."

"Let's dispense with this . . . nonsense," King Alyst said, waving a hand to stifle Adavir's protests. "Nothing has ever been accomplished by formalities. The truest alliances, the truest information, the truest friendships have all been less about respect and more about comfortability. Call me Alyst."

He knew the king lied. Alyst Garcovi was a man who demanded respect, demanded worship from his followers. But he'd play the game. "Call me Dellevue," Lord Vaston said. "And I wholeheartedly agree," he said, nodding. He noticed the king's head nodding slightly in return. *Finally, we're getting somewhere.*

"I'm Jaspard, that's Blago," Jaspard said, then glanced at the two guardsmen. "They're . . . irrelevant."

Alyst glared at Jaspard. "They're important," he said, gesturing to the Watchtower. "This is Zervan, the Watchtower of Calrym." He shifted his finger to the Golden Knight. "He's the Golden Knight. No name. No identity. But he's a damn good fighter."

Throughout the introductions, Lord Vaston nodded to each man.

"Now, why are you here?" Alyst asked. Lord Vaston detected a hint of impatience. *Best get to the point.*

"After the unfortunate but necessary," Lord Vaston paused, emphasizing the last word, "loss of my home, I fled with the remaining Falcon Knights." At this, several in attendance grumbled in disgust. In the silence, Jaspard made a sucking noise. He couldn't determine if this was in reaction to his words or if the man was enjoying his candy a bit too much. "It's of no matter. I have my money and the men that matter to me." A sigh of relief passed through the room. As if they were all expecting Lord Vaston to accuse them of something egregious and demand reparations. As if they'd pay them. "I think we can all agree that's all that truly matters," he said, nodding.

Everyone in the room nodded back, a few chuckled.

Lord Vaston continued, "We've all heard the rumors, out there," he said, tipping his head towards the door leading outside the Great Hall. "We know the Falcon Knights are coming. They're coming here. I'm also well aware that you, Sir Alyst, personally led the attack—and what an effective one it was, might I add—on Cyrok. I came to offer my any advice and knowledge on the Cyroki military you may be interested in."

"We know enough about the Falcon Knights," Alyst said.

Adavir jerked in his chair, giving Lord Vaston an icy glare. "He already has somebody who knows about the Falcon Knights," he said. "I am also from Cyrok, but I am trusted. You're a nobleman with no Cyroki military experience. Your knowledge is useless." He leaned back in his chair, a self-satisfied smile worming its way across his ugly face.

Everyone watched Lord Vaston, waiting for a response. The silence deafened the room, and Lord Vaston glanced around the room, observing each member at the table —Adavir smirked, as if he'd won a battle, while Alyst's eyebrows had arched up, and he appeared to be waiting for Lord Vaston to lunge across the table. Everyone else sat still. A hand clenched, a throat cleared, but everyone waited for him to make a move. After a moment, he did what he always did and nodded. Disappointed looks graced the faces of those he could see—the Watchtower and the Golden Knight had helmets on and were remaining silent aside from the creaks of metal as they shifted their bodies to watch whichever person was speaking next. They had expected Lord Vaston to anger, but he would not anger at such a pathetic attempt to discredit him.

"Your Grace," Lord Vaston said, "with respect," he glanced back at Adavir, wanting to watch the man's reaction as he dropped his information, "I would not place my trust in a leader of bandits. A man who couldn't sack a small village correctly."

Adavir's face morphed from smug smile to fiery red and puffing cheeks. "You dare . . ." he started, trailing off in stunned anger. He glared at Dellevue then almost made a comical expression as he licked his mustache while trying to appear furious and intimidating.

"Clarify," was all Alyst said.

"Was it not the *captain's*," he let that word out like a slur, as everyone in the room knew that Blago Adavir was no officer, never had been, "orders to dispatch Gyrloft? Was he not supposed to capture the gyrfalcon business? What happened to that? He botched any attempt at salvaging that business, and, bafflingly enough, somehow didn't kill every citizen he'd had *bound and captured*. How would one trust anything this man says if he can't figure out how to kill someone who's tied up?"

Adavir threw his chair back and lunged to his feet, fists slamming on the table. A half-full cup of wine spilled. "How dare you!" His tongue flickered out, licking his mustache, and he glared at each of his comrades before turning back to Lord Vaston. "How dare you!" he said again.

"Stay yourself, Adavir," Alyst said. "Dellevue speaks the truth."

Adavir, shaking, sank back into his chair, eyes glued to his feet, tongue darting across his mustache several times. It appeared he was too angry to be civil but not foolish enough to stay silent.

"What would you require, Dellevue?" Alyst asked.

"For?"

"To join me as an adviser. We need all the help we can get," Alyst said.

"Why," Lord Vaston said with a smile and a nod, "the

same thing any man of note wants. Money, manpower, and a fine bit of prestige."

Alyst returned the nod with vigor. "I know exactly what you mean."

Lord Vaston knew he did. That's why he always did his research.

64

SERADAL EAGLETON & VILLIC OF OTHERNESS

Lochwall, Calrym

With Lochwall obliterated, they spent a day rummaging through the remaining rubble. By the day's end, it was clear others had already done this. The Falcon—*no Eagle*—Knights set up a camp of soldiers with the Redclaws integrating themselves. The Camel Clans, weary of the destroyed city, traveled a couple of hours west to camp in the open plains. Villic remained near Sera, but he only spoke when necessary and otherwise seemed more withdrawn than normal.

When the sun set, Sera collapsed near the fire Patrika had started. Patrika knelt by a copper kettle, stirring a bubbling stew of some sort.

"Hungry, Governess?" Patrika asked.

Sighing, Sera shifted in her bedroll to glance at Patrika. "We're alone. No formalities—it's tiresome enough dealing with everyone else's respect."

"Very well, cyr," Patrika said, grinning.

Sera groaned and flopped over, putting her backside towards Patrika.

A moment later, Patrika was kneeling in front of Sera, holding out a bowl of stew. "Here, eat."

She took the bowl, spooning a mouthful of the brown slop into her mouth. It was better than it looked. "What is this?" she asked, steam billowing from her mouth.

"You'd be happier not knowing," Patrika said, dishing herself some.

The tender meat tumbled from Sera's mouth back into the stew with a *plop!* "What is it?" Flashbacks of the last time she didn't know what she was eating entered her mind. Her stomach turned, and she vomited.

"Are you okay?"

Sera took a swig of water from her canteen, swished her mouth, and spat, relieving herself of the burning, acidic leftovers.

"It's horse meat," Patrika said. "We harvested what we could."

Though gross, it wasn't what Sera had been fearing. "Horse is fine," she said. Though the fact she was eating a horse killed in battle also turned her stomach, she was hungry and needed something hearty. She spooned another mouthful, chewing quickly and swallowing. She repeated the process, not focusing on the taste or her memories, and stared into the fire, watching the wood crackle and snap. When she finished her stew, she set the bowl aside. "Thank you, Patrika. I need some rest."

"Cyr," Patrika said. "I'll be here if you need me."

Relieved to know she could still count on Patrika, Sera closed her eyes and slept. She dreamed of the cold, bandits, her murdered family, and Captain Blago Adavir. In the middle of the night, her eyes opened and she stared into the fire again, thinking through the best ways to enact her revenge on the traitorous asshole. *Don't swear, Sera,* she chided herself, before drifting back into her dreams.

Villic of Otherness closed his eyes at night but didn't sleep. He dragged his feet instead of walking like a proper warrior should. He ate enough to live, but not enough to give his body proper fuel. Villic of Otherness was empty. He trailed behind Sera and her group when on the move. At night, he'd find a quiet spot and sleep alone. When they met with the Camel Clans, he ignored Uva the Shaman. It might've been an invitation or request for him to rejoin her. He only caught a small bit of the conversation, and between his nervousness at talking with anyone at all and his grief, he caught little.

Sometimes Villic the Imbuer would return for a moment, interrupting the muttering of Villic of Otherness. Villic of Otherness mostly whispered prayers to the gods, or sometimes curses. Villic the Imbuer drowned in misery and mourning and actively worked to return to Villic of Otherness. The quiet, dark emptiness was what he needed now. He wasn't sure he'd ever want to leave the darkness.

"Don't think like that, Villic."

Villic the Imbuer ignored Speaker, despite the pleading tone of thought. He returned to Villic of Otherness.

Sir Seradal, though now it was Eagleton, and Sir Patrika walked in front of him, issuing orders. He noticed they were talking to him less every day. Or he wasn't noticing their words.

The plains rolled by and days blurred together. He thought of Dunecrest's cheerful face, chewing on grass, giving Villic his "leave me alone" stare. He remembered hugging the camel and growing up together, isolating themselves from other people.

One foot in front of the other. A mouthful of water from his canteen. A spoonful of the bland porridge he made at night. It all blended together. Soon, Villic the Imbuer stopped returning. All feelings ceased. Villic of Otherness became a true minion of Flaytz, god of death.

65

DEMRI SLARN

Hidehedge, Calrym

It wasn't long before the Elkavich's supplies waned. The expansive group of Lochwall refugees and the freed gladiators of Buzzard's Bowl had claimed all the spare clothing, filled every room in Hidehedge, cleared out a significant portion of the surrounding forest to create better living spaces outside, eaten and drank most of the food and wine stores, and consumed all the stockpiles of raw materials. Stanton Brick had been absent since their discussion because his questions had been answered or he'd been busy, or maybe he'd had no interest in associating with Demri and Caius again. Demri hoped he would remain absent.

Demri and Caius spent their time speculating on what would happen, sitting on the bench, watching people carve more of the trees away, constructing small huts and other buildings. With Lochwall's destruction, the Elkavich weren't as concerned about being discovered. Pinecrest, the closest significant human settlement, was too small a town to offer any threat.

"Things are going to happen soon," Caius said. "I've overheard a few people whispering about having their powers unlocked."

"They're going t-t-to find a lot more resistance in C-C-Calrym and Remeria than they did elsewhere. There are t-too many M-Magicai loyal to Ashmount's teachings who still live. And they didn't work in Cyrok or Vessia."

"It's not looking like Cedain is going to come through this without a few bruises," Caius said, looking at a pair of men chopping down a tree.

Demri appreciated the allegory the two men made. "The world has already b-b-been bruised b-by us. Cedain will b-be lucky to come through without several broken b-bones. If not more."

"Say goodbye to the world as we know it," Caius said.

The tree fell, crashing through the limbs of its neighbors and smashing into the ground.

***

Two days later, Demri lay awake in his bed while Caius snored. Some Elkavich members were less reluctant about sharing that they had fresh access to new powers, because of jealousy it had caused between those who'd been lucky enough to receive them and those who hadn't. Demri wondered if he'd have his own unlocked. He considered how useful it would be to heal oneself, or to replenish his Soul Glyphs. If he had the abilities of a Collector, it was possible he'd never have to spend his life again, which led him to wonder why the Elkavich kept using their powers instead of vials. Perhaps they were also hoarding them, like Ashmount had.

Thinking back to when he'd unlocked his Examiner abilities, Demri closed his eyes and searched within himself. He'd attempted this countless times in the past and knew he wouldn't figure it out now, but he tried anyway. Accessing his power was like consciously thinking—he just needed minimal effort. Each Soul Glyph attached itself to his life, and each one felt like a separate tendril, an additional tendon of the body. When he'd unlocked the Examiner thread, he somehow *saw* or *felt* a foreign . . . thing. Like an extra limb. Somehow, he reached out and grabbed it. The entire process had never made sense to him. After securing the link, he had a new feeling—almost like having a too-long fingernail. He knew he'd opened up another power. Since then, however, he'd not been able to replicate the process, which was too bad—Examiners were the least useful to Demri.

He reached, he prodded, he thought. Demri couldn't find anything foreign, anything unusual. It was just like the other hundreds of times he'd attempted this.

The door to their room opened and Demri opened his eyes as Myri entered.

"Were you sleeping? Everything okay?" she asked.

Demri raised a brow, confused.

"I knocked several times, but nobody answered," she said.

"I was—"

"It doesn't matter," she said. "Can we go for a walk? We have things to discuss."

He stared at her a moment, wondering if he should bother now that she was close with Doram again—it could be a trap, or other bad news. He decided to at least see what she wanted. Demri climbed out of the bed and hobbled after her. *Damn these legs. Damn Doram. Damn all the awful shit that keeps happening to me.*

He gave a last look at Caius. The man's mouth hung open, and he was in the dead of sleep. Then Demri closed the door behind him and Myri brought them to her room.

"Erasure has given me permission to unlock your full potential, Demri," she said.

Demri, for once, stuttered because he was taken aback,

and not because of his impediment. "T-T-Today? Wha—Why?"

"Everyone needs to prepare themselves. The Magicai will not sit back and watch us blow everything up." She sighed, collapsing on her unmade bed. "We've lost contact with many of the Calrym and Remerian Elkavich who've infiltrated the major cities in the countries. We assume they've lost sight of their goal. That the vast amount of citizens caused them to abandon the goal. Or they found other, well-paying, people of power to renew their loyalty to. Either way, we're looking at starting the infiltration in many of these cities over again or launching an open attack."

"And with the Falcon Knights attacking C-C-Calrym, there's already going to b-b-be p-plenty of mistrust and chaos as it is. Might as well join the attack."

"Right," she said. "But it's not just about destroying major settlements. It's about eradicating the Magicai teachings of Ashmount. Even if our agents were still within the cities, we'd want to ensure we killed as many of them as possible."

Demri agreed with that. Regardless of the Elkavich plans, every Ashmount-taught Magicus Demri considered an enemy. All had taken part in hunting him down. None had stepped up to assist him. They were all complicit in the lies, even when information exposed those lies. They disgusted him.

His thoughts switched to the potential power he was about to have. The potential to heal his own wounds and refuel his own Well through either Soul Glyphs or Collector vials.

"Give me the p-power."

She narrowed her eyes. "Not until we go over a few things."

"Like your rejuvenated friendship with D-D-Doram?"

"Excuse me?" Myri asked. She sat up in bed and looked as if she were about to stand and slap him.

"It seemed as if you were b-b-becoming friendly again."

Her eyes narrowed even further and her lips pursed, then her arms crossed each other. *Well, fuck.*

"How dare you," she started, then suddenly she was standing. "How dare *you*?"

"How d-dare me?" Demri asked. "Are you not forgetting what you and he b-b-both p-put me through? I'm a fugitive *b-b-because* of that man and you d-didn't give a fuck!"

"I've done more for you than you could possibly imagine," she said, glaring at him. Her cheeks reddened and her eyes moistened. "I saved your life, Demri. You don't have a clue what I've risked." Myri's hands danced around her body in sharp, exaggerated motions as her voice pitched higher and higher until the real cutting words flowed from her mouth. "Everything we pretended, everything we did so others wouldn't suspect you. The fake relationship? I . . . *I* kissed you!" He saw the disgust wash over her face and, for a brief moment, found himself transported to his past.

"I hadn't realized it was so d-d-difficult for you," Demri said.

"Not difficult, Demri! Dangerous. Foolish. We could've both been killed!"

"Killed?" Demri laughed. When tears flowed from Myri's eyes, he laughed harder. "We c-c-could've been k-killed? That's b-been my entire life since fleeing Ashmount, you selfish b-bitch. I've b-been injured, living on the run with C-C-Caius and C-Caius alone. Limited supplies, limited p-power. You have no clue what I've had to d-d-do."

"You've had to murder innocent people, Demri? Is that it?" Her finger jabbed him in the shoulder, over and over, accentuating each of her points, every sentence. "Was that so hard for you? Because nobody has seen a lick of remorse from you. Not once, you twisted, sad man." Her pokes became harder, more hurtful. "All you care about is your power and your revenge. I'll give you your power—you can have that.

But don't you come to me for anything else. Don't stay here. Don't even think about hurting Doram."

His teeth clamped together, and he looked at the floorboards, avoiding her face. His heart throbbed in his chest with both anger and heartbreak.

"Here," she said in a much softer tone. She grasped his hand, closed her eyes, and a moment later, an explosion began inside Demri's body. He knew she'd unlocked all the schools of power for him. "I need to go," she said, and her tone turned into a much more cutting one again. "Doram needs me." And she pushed past him, exiting her room.

The door slammed shut behind her and Demri felt as if his chest were bursting, but he wasn't sure if that was because of the newfound power or the absolute devastation she'd caused.

66

ASHEN HYREL & EDELBROCK
BRENDIS

Calrym

They'd traded information. Edelbrock Brendis and Seeker Korran had told their story. They were, to Ashen's best guess, truthful with everything they said. And, because Ashen trusted them, despite Velturo's and Tallas's and Iadura's protestations, Ashen told them everything in return. She included everything she knew about Velturo, Iadura, and Iadura's husband, Baron Exildar Alcart. She was, just as they'd been, completely honest.

By the time they'd finished relaying their histories to one another, day had faded into night, and everyone went to sleep; though Ashen noticed the guards were on alert. Despite Ashen trusting Edelbrock and Seeker Korran, it seemed nobody else did. She noticed Tallas was relaxed around them and reassured her.

Ashen slept inside Iadura's carriage once again. Ashen noticed the girl had become quieter since Edelbrock's arrival. She hoped she'd done nothing wrong.

"Iadura?" she asked, while spreading her bedroll on the carriage floor. It was much too warm to sleep bundled up in but would make for decent padding between her back and the floorboards.

"Ashen?"

"You're quiet."

Iadura slipped into her bed. "I'm mulling over some things. There was a lot of information passed about today." She paused, then said, "Not all of it willingly so."

"I'm sorry, I—"

"It's of no consequence, Ashen. I assumed we could speak to each other with a certain amount of discretion and confidence in one another's ability to keep sensitive information to ourselves. Instead, we're apparently allowed to blather it off to any muddied traveler with an interesting tidbit of their own information. Sleep well." Iadura flopped over, turning her body away from Ashen.

"I'm sorry," Ashen said. Iadura didn't respond. *Well, aren't I the unwanted dog to somebody looking for a cat?*

Ashen felt frustration, for although she'd used Iadura's information, she knew they'd received a lot and felt she owed it to Edelbrock and Seeker Korran to return quality intelligence. Despite her irritation for betraying Iadura's trust, it didn't take long for Ashen to drift into deep dreams.

The man called Tallas Taybold led Edelbrock and Seeker Korran to a fireplace on the outskirts of the camp. Tallas, Edelbrock noticed, had a grizzled appearance. A scar crossed the top of his head, another crossed his chin and through his lips. Mottled pink skin surrounded the man's blind eye. He looked like someone who belonged in Buzzard's Bowl, though Edelbrock would've feared to face him. Tallas didn't release the halberd he lugged around with him everywhere.

"You may stay here with me," Tallas said. He kicked the

coals of the fire with a boot, and an orange glow appeared for a moment. Kneeling next to the coals, Tallas started the fire back up and hung a kettle over it. "I have enough food to make a pot of soup for everyone. Vegetable soup, but it's something. I also have some smoked ham to go along with it. Will that be satisfactory?"

"That'd be wonderful," Edelbrock said, and he meant it. They hadn't been eating the best food on their journey from Hidehedge, foraging and hunting for what they could along the way. Edelbrock and Seeker Korran had agreed it wasn't worth taking too much food from Hidehedge since the gladiators from Buzzard's Bowl added extra mouths to feed at the Elkavich hideout. Upon meeting the Lochwall refugees, this reaffirmed their decision, so they subsisted on whatever they found. The last few days hadn't been very lucrative.

Tallas threw a variety of vegetables and herbs into the pot of water, then left it to cook. While waiting, they sat in silence. Multiple patrols of guards passed by, keeping a watchful eye on both Edelbrock and Seeker Korran. Edelbrock nodded to each, but never received the same courtesy.

Once the soup was simmering, Tallas put three slabs of ham on a rock by the fire and browned the meat up. When it was ready, he dished three equal portions of soup and ham both, and they ate in silence. Edelbrock didn't mind. He'd had plenty of silence during his time in Buzzard's Bowl. He knew Seeker Korran didn't mind it, either. And Tallas, if Edelbrock were to guess, also didn't mind it. Then again, anyone with a face like Tallas's must've gone through some shit.

The ham, cooked to perfection, fell apart in Edelbrock's mouth. The soup, a flavorful pot of leeks, onions, carrots, and beets wasn't half bad, either.

"Seeker Korran tires of silence."

Confused, Edelbrock turned to his companion.

Tallas sighed. "There's always one." He shifted his body to face Seeker Korran. "Well, let's hear it."

"You bring us to the outskirts of the camp. Why? It would be safer if we were in the center, surrounded by armed men," Seeker Korran said.

"There are only two people who should concern you in this camp," Tallas said, nodding towards Velturo's carriage. "The man with the huge crossbow and me. This is my spot. I like the perimeter. I don't have to rely on incompetence, like some people," he said, nodding towards Velturo's carriage again. "If that's your reason for interrupting the peace of this night, I beg you not to do so again."

"No, that's not why. I wanted to know what you plan."

"With what?" Tallas asked, sounding perplexed.

"If you can't go to Lochwall and you can't go to Anepolis, what then?" Seeker Korran held out his hands, as if waiting for answers to be placed in his palms.

"I don't have the answers you're looking for. I tag along and fight when needed. Talk to the fat one if you want some answers." Tallas relocated to the other side of the fire and lay down. "And don't make too much noise," he said.

Edelbrock and Seeker Korran sat in silence for another few minutes until they decided they'd join Tallas and talk to Velturo the following day.

As Edelbrock settled down, he considered his goal: infiltrating Anepolis. But with the king and all the dukes and duchesses either dead or deposed, did he *need* to help the Elkavich? From what Ashen had told them, and what he already knew of Calrite politics, Alyst Garcovi, Jaspard Couliac, and the others who'd claimed power weren't better than the former king. Things could, and Edelbrock believed they would, become much worse.

Tomorrow, I'll convince them to return to Anepolis.

It turned out they wouldn't need much convincing.

"What do you mean?" the guard with the crossbow said. Shouted was a more appropriate word, since Ashen heard him across the camp.

They hadn't started that morning's travel because Edelbrock and Seeker Korran were meeting Velturo—a futile attempt to turn the caravan around. Ashen had left them to it. She'd eaten—according to Iadura—an unimpressive meal of stale bread, a pungent cheese, and a kind of smoked meat. Somebody claimed it was lamb. To Ashen, who'd grown up on the streets of Anepolis, it was both filling and delicious. After finishing her meal, she'd gone behind Iadura's carriage and took a piss with what little privacy could be had on the plain.

Upon reentering the camp, she saw several strangers being waylaid by the guardsmen. One, she noticed, had his arms chained behind his back, loose brown robes concealing what appeared to be a very frail man. A snobby-looking, middle-aged woman leered at Velturo's guards, while a plump man held his prisoner's chains in one hand, a drawn sword in the other. The woman must've been noble. The way she carried herself and her general demeanor, combined with her rich clothing—a silk tunic stretched across her thin frame, and despite the warmth, she wore a thick sheepskin cloak—persuaded Ashen. Her companion, the plump man, wore a regular guardsman's outfit made of leather, though it wasn't fitted to his size; his stomach pressed against his tunic, while his trousers clung to his legs.

"I demand you step aside," the woman said, pressing her hand against a second of Velturo's guards and pushing him. The man gave a slight wobble but didn't move otherwise. "I am Lady Umara Missleton and if you *don't* step aside"—she glared over the guard's shoulder, looking at the encampment, eyes passing across Ashen as she approached

—"you will find yourselves without the favor of King Mikas!" Lady Missleton shoved her finger into the air, punctuating her point, and a delightful and victorious smile crossed her face. "Now, move," she said, shoving the guard once again.

The guard, unmoving and unwavering against the threats of Lady Missleton, held up his hand to stop her from progressing through their camp. "Lady, who is your prisoner?"

"None of your concern. My property, my concern." Angry, she turned around. "Do something, Packard. Do something right now!"

"Lady Missleton," Packard said, a low, monotonous voice filled with calmness and, to Ashen's ears, years of strained patience, "let's circle around them. Or answer their questions and perhaps they'll share a meal with us."

Ashen stepped beside the guardsman Lady Missleton was shoving. She felt the sun beating on her, and though it felt nice, it was almost too warm.

"How dare you question me, Packard?" Lady Missleton's cheeks flushed, and she stamped her foot. As Ashen observed her, she realized Lady Missleton was much older than middle-aged, though she was, clearly, prone to tantrums. "I will not suffer such disrespect!"

"We need to go," Packard said. "Arguing with commoners isn't helping." He lowered his voice, and whispered not too quietly, "They're coming." Ashen noticed now that Packard wasn't calm—he was very much the opposite. Sweat had formed on his forehead and a finger kept tapping on the chains he held.

The guard Ashen stood next to pointed at the prisoner. "Lady, who is that?" he asked a second time.

She heard the guard with the crossbow sigh, and out of the corner of her eye, saw him hefting the weapon up, taking aim with it. "Answer," he said.

"How dare you aim that at us?" Lady Missleton said. "I am a *lady* and you dare—"

A thump quieted her words, and she stared in shocked silence. Her guardsman, Packard, lay gurgling on the grass, the bolt protruding from his sternum.

"I'll ask you again," the crossbow guard said, reloading his crossbow. "Who is the prisoner?"

"This isn't right," Ashen said. "You can't kill people over nothing."

"Let me do my job," he said, cranking the winch. "And have some faith. I know what I'm doing."

"Aye," she said, unwilling to argue with the man, but Ashen didn't think so. Packard's body stilled and Lady Missleton let out an uncouth wailing sound.

"One more chance," the crossbow guardsman said.

"I will have you hung, you psychopathic, murdering scum!" Lady Missleton drew a small hunting knife from her belt, raising it above her head. "I will see you—"

Another thump. Lady Missleton's body collapsed, the crossbow bolt in her head.

Ashen's jaw dropped. "What the . . . what . . . fuck." She'd seen plenty of people murdered cold before, and that was before her mission in the King's Council. But this was a level of cold killing she didn't understand. Urchins would kill one another over some food. A guard would kill an urchin for stealing or committing a serious crime. Criminals would murder each other over the competition. There was always a reason, a purpose, for the murder. This, though . . . Ashen saw nothing to gain.

"Trust me," the crossbowman said. "They were not good people."

The second guard was already rifling through their possessions. He produced a key and held it up. "I think I found the chain's key."

The crossbowman nodded. "Give it to her. She'll learn the good deed which was performed today."

He delivered the key to Ashen, who took it, still bewildered by what just happened.

"Free the man and ask who he is. Ask what they made him do," the crossbowman said. "We'll be over there if you need us," he said, gesturing to Velturo's carriage.

Key in hand, Ashen approached the prisoner. He reeked of urine and unwashed filth. She was right—he was a wilted frame of a man, body wasting away. He stood silent, hands chained behind him. Removing his hood, she saw he was both blindfolded and gagged. Disgusted, she tore off the blindfold, revealing a pair of sunken, amber eyes, surrounded by spider webbing wrinkles. He blinked at the sunlight and as his eyes adjusted, Ashen untied the gag. The man breathed deeply, inhaling the fresh air. His teeth were golden yellow, dotted with black rot. He exhaled and Ashen choked on stagnant breath. He tried speaking, but only a raspy noise exited his throat.

Ashen took the key to his backside, slotting it into the keyhole, and turned. The lock clicked, and she removed the manacles from his thin wrists.

The man rubbed at the few wisps of hair on his empty head, and he grinned. She noticed he was missing a tooth. Looking around, the man caught sight of his dead captors. With a sound somewhere between a strangled gurgle and a muffled yell, he was atop Lady Missleton, slamming his fists into her.

"She's already dead."

The man didn't seem to care, bashing her face into the ground repeatedly until it came up a bloody pulp. He wiped his gore-coated hands off on Lady Missleton's silk tunic before returning to his feet. He opened his mouth, tried to say something, choked, and pointed at his throat. "Wa . . . ter . . ." he said.

Ashen handed over her waterskin and the man guzzled it, spilling half on the ground in his eagerness.

"Thank you." He took another deep breath, sighing. "Thank you," he said, again. "I thought I'd live the rest of my days in chains and slavery."

"Slavery?" Ashen asked. Slavery wasn't something she thought occurred anywhere in Cedain. Nobody talked about it, anyway. She heard of the gladiators of Buzzard's Bowl before Edelbrock had arrived, of course, but they were people being punished for crimes—mostly. Edelbrock's information suggested Scayde Haklon used it as a place to dispose of his enemies, too. But regular slavery? There weren't slaves.

The man nodded, despite what Ashen had learned while growing up. "I'm a Magicus from Ashmount. A place, I've heard, that no longer exists." He glanced at his feet, depressed and downtrodden. Or maybe he was used to not looking people in the face. Ashen didn't know how slavery might change somebody.

"Ashen Hyrel."

"Chance de Gault," he said, trying to smile, but it seemed he found the action hard to complete. "The Lady Missleton always said, 'For a name of luck, you could certainly use a spot of it'. It seems I finally have."

"You'll have to thank him," Ashen said, pointing out the crossbowman guard.

"I shall do that."

"How does a Magicus become a prisoner?" she asked. Ashen knew the Magicai were powerful. More powerful than anyone else in Cedain.

"I'm a Healer," de Gault said. "We're only able to help people, not hurt them. Ashmount, for a long time, has run a secret slave trade. They sold us to the rich, who would keep us locked up and force us to heal whomever they chose. They called us the Blind Sisters. If I didn't comply, they tortured me. Fortunately, I only needed to heal twice while in captivity. I think they did more damage to my body with the imprisonment than the aging caused by healing another." He glanced at Lady Missleton's body and spat. "She deserved worse."

"I'm sorry."

"Well, I'm free now. And for that, I thank you. Please, I must express my gratitude to the man who killed my captors. And also, I confess, I must offer a dire warning."

"Of course," she said, leading him to the pair of guards, both confused and worried.

After de Gault had thanked the crossbowman, he launched into a worried ramble referring to Remerians and Camel Clans. She caught something of war and invasion, and like the other guardsmen, didn't pick up on much. De Gault began anew, slowing his explanation, and once he'd formed comprehensive sentences, Ashen abandoned the discussion and sprinted for Velturo's carriage.

V elturo's carriage was, in Edelbrock's estimation, twice as hot as the weather outside. Why the man insisted on conducting his business inside was beyond Edelbrock's understanding. What little air could be felt outside never made it inside the carriage, despite there being windows.

Duke Velturo and Tallas Taybold sat in too-small wooden chairs across an even smaller foldup wooden table, which struggled to contain the four glasses of wine. Edelbrock, sitting in his own too small and too stiff wooden chair, wondered how wooden his body would feel upon rising. The fat and lazy Velturo, somehow, didn't seem bothered by the uncomfortable furniture.

The glass chinked against Tallas's as Edelbrock picked it up to sip from. Setting it back on the small table, he knocked

Seeker Korran's glass this time. The table was simply too small.

He sniffed, catching a whiff of stale men, stale wine, and stale air.

Seeker Korran had his forehead in his hand. "Lochwall is destroyed," he said, clearly frustrated. "We told you yesterday."

"It matters not," Velturo said. "We'll just pass through and proceed to another location. Pinecrest, perhaps. I hear that's a nice, small town, ah-hah."

"The Elkavich blew up Lochwall," Edelbrock said. "They plan on doing the same to other cities and towns. Pinecrest isn't safe."

"Nonsense," Velturo said. "Why would anyone destroy Pinecrest? Furthermore, what could the Elkavich have against the *entire* country? It makes no sense, ah-hah."

"They want to destroy *everything*," Edelbrock said. "Calrym, Remeria. All of Cedain. They want to start everything over again."

"You've said that, ah-hah."

Tallas remained silent, listening to the conversation, but every time Edelbrock glanced at the man, his face became more and more stern. He, at least, seemed to believe them.

"Then why don't you believe us?" Seeker Korran asked. They'd explained the plans of the Elkavich twice over. Velturo wasn't getting it. Or just didn't believe it. Or, maybe, he was delusional enough to think Calrym had proper security.

"It makes no sense, ah-hah," Velturo said, sipping some wine. A dribble of red trailed down his chin, and he dabbed at it with the cuff of his sleeve, staining it. "If you kill everyone, you won't have anyone to repopulate with. They have to keep some people alive. Perhaps we should go to the Elkavich, ah-hah."

No. I need to get to Anepolis. I need to find Scayde and Jaylena. They both need to die. Edelbrock could've taken Seeker Korran and left by themselves, but traveling in a larger group would be safer and more pleasurable. If he couldn't convince them, Edelbrock would go on by himself, but he wanted to try.

"If we return to the Elkavich—" Edelbrock started, but the door to Velturo's carriage opened and somebody thumped in.

A moment later, Ashen Hyrel appeared, out of breath and looking anxious. The girl impressed Edelbrock. For someone so young, he couldn't believe her story that she'd served as a duchess for the king—but he knew it was true. Everyone had confirmed as much.

She said two words. "They're coming."

"Who, ah-hah?"

Ashen's words flowed fast and concise but panicked. "The Remerians have invaded. They're almost here. The Imbuers are with them. We need to return to the capital and round up the Magicai. We need to leave. Now." After she speaking, the panic seemed to transfer from her to the four sitting men.

"We can't go back to Anepolis," Tallas said.

Calmly, she stood straighter and said, "There isn't anywhere safe now. Pack your things. It's time we apologize to Alyst and tell him what we know. And hope he doesn't kill us."

Eager to leave, Velturo announced they'd not be following his rigid travel restrictions any longer. Instead, they'd travel double-time and hope to beat the invaders. They left an hour later.

67

INTERLUDE
SCAYDE HAKLON

Anepolis, Calrym

Capes were annoying, but they were also a sign of nobility. They struck a powerful figure. One couldn't miss a swish of a brightly colored piece of clothing. And nothing had more flair that a dramatic sweep of the cape. Travel had damaged the cape with several holes and dirt stains, but he'd not had time to replace it. His black boots —once shined, but now covered in muck—clicked on the Great Hall's floor as he entered the chamber, stroking his mustache, which, he admitted, had also become unruly during his journey to Anepolis.

Scayde took his seat, flinging his arms out to ensure the cape draped itself over both sides of the chair. The last time he'd met with the king, it was a different person. And this time he was the only duke in attendance—a first. *A frightening time of incompetence and insecurity when an entire leadership is upended by an urchin and a mercenary.* He'd heard what had happened. It made him sick. He'd even had the chance to interview one of the investigating soldiers who'd viewed the carnage himself. Blamed it on Black Dust, a tool of street thugs. *Street thugs.* He almost scoffed at the idea, even now, days after learning about it.

King Alyst Garcovi appeared unhappy, angry, and impatient. His fingers rapped on the table, his face contorted in a permanent snarl, and the noise from his elevated breathing seemed to have silenced everyone else.

"Your city is gone," the king said. "Destroyed, I hear."

"Yes." It wasn't a question, but Scayde wouldn't be frightened to silence.

"The Elkavich?"

"Yes," Scayde answered the king. He'd reported what happened in Lochwall to both the Golden Knight and the Watchtower of Calrym two days previous.

"We need to prepare the city's defenses if the Elkavich are blowing cities up and the Remerians are invading," somebody said.

"I know, Wickam, I know."

"Your Highness, with respect," Wickam said, "I fought them. They *will* destroy us."

"You've told me," the king said, sighing. "Please introduce yourselves to Duke Scayde. I want everyone familiar with each other so the coming days are more . . . manageable."

A man sitting on the king's right spoke first. "Duke Jaspard Couliac," he said, correcting Scayde's earlier assumption.

"Captain Blago Adavir."

"You aren't a captain," Wickam said.

"Fine," the man grumbled, "Blago Adavir, Cyroki mercenary." Adavir explained how he'd helped Calrym initiate the war in Cyrok as a ruse to reposition their military in order to attack Remeria and how he was a great friend of the king's—something the other men at the table rolled their eyes at.

"Sergeant Kolb Wickam," Wickam said, then launched into an explanation of the battle he'd fled, the Invasion of Calrym, and what happened. Followed by a lengthy analysis of the Remerian soldiers, including the Falcon Knights, the Camel Clans, and the Redclaws.

"Dellevue Vaston," the next man said. He explained his experiences in Cyrok, his expertise in Cyroki culture and understanding the Falcon Knights and detailed how he fled the war.

"I'm Baron Exildar Alcart," the last man sitting at the table said. "You've heard of the massacre that took place in this very Great Hall?" The baron didn't wait for Scayde's answer. "We've been investigating what occurred. Unfortunately, my wife aided in the escape of Duke Velturo Ondakka, for reasons that aren't clear. Assuming my wife would flee to Bryn or Zemur, we concentrated our search in that direction. It seems Velturo convinced her to go southeast. However, with the continuous string of bad news, I have elected to remain in Anepolis. Both for my safety and for the good of the king. I'm of far more help to him here than off yonder, searching for a wife who wishes to rid herself of me."

Coward just doesn't want to be out in the open with the invasion happening. Though neither did he. However, he was no coward. Was he? *No,* he decided. *Definitely not.*

"I am Duke Scayde Haklon," he said. And then he launched into a retelling of what he'd already explained to the Golden Knight and the Watchtower of Calrym about the destruction of Buzzard's Bowl and Lochwall.

"So," King Alyst said. "It is clear to all of us. In order to survive, we must lockdown the city. Nobody in. Nobody out. We *must* require all Magicai in Anepolis to report to me, no matter who they serve. We must prepare ourselves for a siege."

"Thank you, my King, for allowing me to seek refuge here," Scayde said. "I'll pledge my loyalty and that of my men. A few Magicai accompanied me here."

"You are welcomed, you and the forces you've brought,"

the king said. "But I feel it may not be enough. There is too much chaos out there."

Scayde's skin crawled with that icy declaration. Alyst Garcovi was a renowned military leader. If he was this pessimistic, Scayde's hope ceased to exist. "I will do my best to help," he said, without hesitation. For if they failed, they would all die.

68

SERADAL EAGLETON & VILLIC OF OTHERNESS

Calrym

Governess Seradal Eagleton woke refreshed and ready to perform her duties as a leader of the Eagle Knights. *The leader,* she corrected herself. Rising from her bedroll, Sera, though rejuvenated herself, saw the soldiers looking weary. Sluggish and grouchy looks met her as she walked through the camp, searching for Patrika. She found Patrika in the Redclaws encampment, talking to the Bloody Duchess and Captain Althier. Sera also noticed the Last Magicus among them—somebody she hadn't concerned herself with since they'd departed Remeria.

"Gov'ness Eagleton," the Bloody Duchess said, tipping her hat.

"A leader bequeathed herself upon thee, a pretty one, no doubt, with a fine sword arm, army soldiers, and plenty of clout," Captain Althier said, bowing to her. "Your Excellence," he said. "Perhaps too much reverence." He winked.

"Governess," Patrika said. "I was preparing everyone for the march."

Sera shook her head. "Redact those orders, Patrika. I think everyone has earned a reprieve. We'll resume tomorrow."

"We should continue to make haste. The longer we wait, the more organized Calrym will become," the Last Magicus said. "It's important we reach Anepolis. Otherwise, the king could pull in militias from surrounding towns, bolstering their defenses."

"If we strain ourselves, we'll be too weary to fight," Sera said.

The Last Magicus frowned but nodded his assent.

The Bloody Duchess pointed her claw at the Last Magicus. "Fuckin' strategists always overthinkin'. Have some care, aye? Some o' us have weak limbs." She shook her arm in the air. "See?"

"Once we get to Anepolis, what's your plan?" Patrika asked.

"Same thing that happened in Remeria. Surround the capital, have the Imbuers break through the walls, and enter," Sera said. "This time, though, we'll need to take control. Perhaps we won't have to kill everyone. Just the people who deserve it."

Everyone agreed.

"Good, Patrika, please bring the news to Uva the Shaman. I want her to know we're taking the day off before they pack everything up."

"Yes, cyr," Patrika said.

The remaining afternoon was quiet and restful.

***

Zarn, god of shadows, was who Villic of Otherness thought of. Like Zarn, Villic retreated into darkness, but not the darkness seen in shadows. The darkness in his mind. With the outside world ignored, Speaker ignored, and now the Killiak, lord of lords, and the other gods ignored, Villic had found his place.

With the army halted for the day, Villic didn't have to do anything. No marching, no talking, nothing. He sat on the grass and disappeared into his thoughts.

After the first half of morning passed, a Remerian soldier approached Villic. He said something Villic didn't hear, then dropped something at Villic's feet. When Villic looked, he saw a bottle of brown liquid. Alcohol, he knew, from his days in Andora, where Royal was always drunk.

Villic popped the top off the bottle. He sniffed, winced, pulling his nose back. It smelled worse than a sick camel shit. *Dunecrest was sick once.* Images of his friend flashed through his mind again. He pushed them away, retreating into the shadows in his mind again. Dunecrest followed.

He tipped the bottle, sticking his tongue into the liquid to taste it. A burning sensation spread through his mouth and he rammed the squishy brown piece back into the bottle.

"A cork," Speaker said. *"It's used to stopper—"*

Villic stopped listening. He wanted to forget it all. Wanted to stay in the shadows. Dunecrest's face followed him. He retreated further. Dunecrest was still there, watching him with his beady eyes.

He remembered Royal once mentioning alcohol and how it could erase terrible memories, at least for a time. He reopened the bottle, sniffed, winced, took another small taste. The burning was bad, but not as bad as the first time. He'd been expecting it. Villic took a sip. It burned like Tabashi, god of fire, was sliding down his throat. Villic's eyes watered. He almost spit the liquid out.

Villic took another drink. Then another. And another. Half the bottle was gone several minutes later and darkness returned. He slept without Dunecrest appearing in his dreams.

69

DEMRI SLARN

Hidehedge, Calrym

Demri spent his first day with newfound powers as a Glyphist, drawing tattoos all across his body which enabled access to all of his Enforcer power. He remained in his room, in bed, across from a resting Caius. He had no wish to venture outside and risk encountering Myri.

It was the second day when he realized he could speed Caius's healing. He was now a Healer; he could help whomever he wished. Even himself. He approached Caius, reaching the beside, and then Caius's eyes opened.

"Something wrong?"

"Going t-to speed this along," Demri said, reaching out and grasping Caius's arm.

"I'll be fine. Fix yourself."

"No," Demri said. "This is a much easier fix. Repairing c-crippled limbs c-c-costs t-too much. You're almost recovered, anyway."

"So, let's wait it out. I can do almost everything I could before. No heavy lifting, traveling, or fighting."

"Right. We have t-to go. You need to b-be able t-t-to t-travel."

"Go?" Caius asked.

Demri ignored the question, focusing on what needed to be done. He closed his eyes, searching the various strands of power he could sense within his body. The all-too-familiar Enforcer and Examiner ones. Then there were strange connections. The ones enabling him to heal, to collect vials of power from dead Magicai, and to draw his power out with tattoos. He grasped the healing connection, feeling a strange sensation, like he'd grown an extra appendage overnight, then felt the tug at his life force, almost like whenever he consumed a Soul Glyph, but this felt different. It lacked the constant feeling of power he had with the Enforcer strand. There was no power here, just life ready to transfer. He consumed.

Caius gasped. His internal wounds closed up, and Demri let go of his arm. Demri felt weak for a moment, his eyes blurred. He closed his eyes and his vision cleared. The weakness faded. He knew he'd aged. "B-Better?"

"All good," Caius said. "Thank you, Demri. Why do you want to leave?"

"How old d-d-do I look?"

"You haven't changed. Maybe a new wrinkle on the bridge of your nose. Otherwise, nothing."

Demri nodded, wondering how it'd feel to bring somebody back from death and age in actual decades. The life transfer from healing felt much different than consuming from his Well.

"Why do you want to leave, Demri?" Caius asked, pulling out the knife and filing away at his finger. "Huh. Look," he flashed his fingertips at Demri. The cuts and scabs and rough skin that'd built up because of all the nicks Caius gave himself had disappeared. Demri had healed those, too.

"We need to stop these p-p-people."

"From?"

"Destroying the world."

"I don't think we can, Demri. There's a lot of them. And they're all Magicai. And look at what they've already accomplished."

"We've always b-been outnumbered."

Caius shrugged. "Yes."

"We're still alive."

"Yes," he said again. "Let's not test that. We've got a good thing going."

"D-Do you like the p-people here? Honestly, C-C-Caius? Ced? Does anyone like Ced? Erasure?"

"Myri?" he said, eyebrow arched.

Demri looked away, teeth grinding against one another.

"Another falling out. You need to stay away from her. She's terrible for your health."

"I know that!" Demri said, slamming his fist against the wall. His knuckles rapped on the wood, scraping the skin off the top and he felt bruises forming. A dot of blood slipped from the scrape. "F-Fuck!"

"Demri."

Demri closed his eyes, reached out for the healing strand, tapped into it for a moment, and focused on healing his throbbing hand. The skin closed and his pain ceased.

"Demri, you can't spend your life like that. You're going to age yourself too quickly."

Demri didn't care.

"We're leaving, C-Caius. P-Pack your things."

"Of course," he said.

In silence, they gathered their few belongings together.

70

ASHEN HYREL & EDELBROCK BRENDIS

Calrym

The caravan had turned itself around and they traveled as much as they could. A few hours in the morning to break camp, eat, and pack, and an hour of daylight in the evening was what they were allotted. They slept through the night, woke weary and sluggish, and repeated the forced march.

On one of their days of travel, which blended together, she found herself walking alongside the escaped gladiator, Edelbrock. He launched into a detailed description of Scayde Haklon, asking if she'd encountered him on their travels—to which she said no. They trudged along behind Velturo's carriage for a few minutes before he opened his mouth again.

"Are you sure he didn't pass you?" Edelbrock asked her.

"No," Ashen said, sighing. She'd tire of him quickly if the questions continued in this repetitious fashion. "I wouldn't have a clue. We saw so many people and the plain is big."

"He's an arrogant man. He would've let you know if he was nearby, I'm sure."

"Then no, we didn't see Scayde Haklon," she said. "No

yellow capes, no over-the-top speeches. Just people trying to survive. If I had seen him, you'd be the first to know. Don't question my memory again." She realized she was speaking like her alter ego, Duchess Cithrial Hyrel. Snooty, in command, and, if she admitted it to herself, over-the-top. "Apologies," she said. "Ain't sure who I should be nowadays. Lost between my old self and whatever I became."

"I know what you mean," Edelbrock said, but he wouldn't elaborate on the matter and she didn't press him. Something to do with being an imprisoned gladiator, she was sure. After her limited experienced being imprisoned herself, she couldn't imagine what cycles of the experience would do to her.

Ashen wished she could ride inside the carriage, but too much extra weight would tax the animals. *Though, considering Velturo's size . . .* she restrained a laugh. Both Velturo and Iadura rode inside every day while the rest of them ended up walking. The first few days were the hardest. Ashen's calves burned, her thighs ached, and by the end of the day, she slept sounder than any baby.

She found herself enjoying Edelbrock's company, spending a few hours walking at his side every day. Tallas remained observant, more focused on watching their rear than having any conversations. "Conversations can drown out even the sound of an army," he'd said, so she left him alone while traveling.

She hadn't kept track of time after leaving Anepolis, but with the pace they set, they returned to the city in mere days compared to the weeks it'd taken them to travel the same distance.

T he city of Anepolis was a place Edelbrock always aspired to live in. To be so near the king, the other important nobility, and the center of a booming economy, was his dream. Riches, power, beautiful women. It all spoke to him. The gates, though, had been barred shut. A line of guardsmen stood in a row above the gate, peering down at them. Several, Edelbrock noticed, had loaded crossbows resting on the wall, angled down at them. Below the gate archway, a cobblestone street they'd been following for several miles led into the city.

"Anepolis is closed!" a guardsman said.

"Ain't accepting refugees?" Ashen asked.

"No. Nobody comes in," the guard said. "We've locked the city to prepare for a siege."

"You should let us in," Velturo's crossbowman said. "We can aid in the city's defense, in defense of the country. Remeria has many allies."

"We're not to let anyone in, specifically *because* of that," the guard said. "Now clear out or die."

"If you kill us, our bodies will rot out here," Ashen said. "Rot brings disease. You'd have to open the gates, anyway."

"We'll find somebody to do it. Whoever leaves the city won't be allowed to return," he said. "And if they choose not to move the bodies, we'll kill them and start over. My apologies, but my orders are very specific. We are not to allow anyone inside."

Edelbrock needed to get inside Anepolis. Scayde and Jaylena were in there. The Remerians were invading with the help of Cyrok and Vessia and being caught outside would be a disaster. He needed safety and he'd pledged his loyalty to the Elkavich. Would he? He didn't know. But he needed to find Scayde and Jaylena. Needed to feel a knife between their ribs as they squirmed and begged for their lives. And so, with a heavy heart, he sighed, knowing how to get inside the city and wishing there was another way. *Sometimes, I'm a bastard of a fellow.*

"Get!" the guard said, raising his crossbow. "I won't warn you again." He sniffled, as if he had allergies.

Before Edelbrock could speak, Velturo showed himself. "Open the doors, Mikaeus. Let me in, ah-hah."

"Velturo?" Mikaeus asked, clearly surprised.

"Yes. I escaped uninjured, though with a bruised ego perhaps, ah-hah."

"We can't let you in."

"I am a duke, ah-hah!"

"Not anymore," Mikaeus said, sniffing again. Edelbrock thought he saw the man shrug. "King Alyst has started a new panel. Made it clear anybody with a former title has had it expunged. You're a citizen now, Velturo."

Edelbrock closed his eyes, took a breath, and stepped forward. "Mikaeus? My name is Edelbrock Brendis, and I require somebody above your station. I have information they'll want—no, need—to hear. From soldier to soldier, I can't stress how important a matter of state this is."

"Very well," Mikaeus said. "It better be worth it or I'll have you killed."

Mikaeus disappeared, but not before hawking some phlegm and spitting it over the side of the wall, followed by another sniffle. Edelbrock heard the wet splat on the cobblestone street.

"What are you doing, ah-hah?"

"Edelbrock?" Ashen asked.

He glanced at them. "Trust me. I used to be a noble." He returned his gaze to the wall, feeling even worse.

A few minutes later, and Mikaeus returned. With him stood an unfamiliar figure towering over the other guards.

"This is the Watchtower of Calrym," Mikaeus said. "He will judge your information." He sniffed again, and Edelbrock saw him wiping his nose with a kerchief.

"You can call me 'Zervan' if it pleases you," the Watchtower said.

"Zervan," Edelbrock said. "I've traveled long and far. I've seen the destruction of Lochwall, I've heard of the Remerian invasion, and I've learned of a king's assassination. There's a wealth of information I could deliver from what I've seen and heard, but I think there is one thing you might be most interested in. I have delivered the king's assassins to you."

"Traitor," Tallas's voice hissed behind him.

Edelbrock turned to face Tallas. "I'm no traitor," he said. "I'm getting inside that city."

"At what cost?" Ashen said.

Edelbrock looked into her eyes and felt a pang of remorse. Their time together had been nice. He'd enjoyed the company of people who weren't trying to kill him. But he'd carried one lesson from Buzzard's Bowl and Lochwall: look out for yourself and nobody else. Scayde Haklon had taken everything he'd cared for. Now, he had to use similar tactics to get the revenge he wanted.

"I'm sorry," Edelbrock said.

"Kill him!" Velturo's crossbowman shouted, raising his huge crossbow. Half a dozen crossbow bolts slammed into the man and he screamed, falling to the ground.

"Run, Ashen!" Tallas said, and he and Ashen raced to their horses.

The city gates opened and a swarm of guards exited the city.

"Arrest them!" Mikaeus said.

Edelbrock looked back at the people he'd traveled with, feeling his heart lurch. As they were subdued, he wondered if any of them would survive past tomorrow.

The looks he found stared at him with hatred. They stared at him like he stared at Scayde Haklon. He had become that which he hated: a monster.

71

SERADAL EAGLETON & VILLIC OF OTHERNESS

Calrym

The Remerian army marched. The Camel Clans took the lead and flanks, the Eagle Knights and the Redclaws formed the main body of the army, and the Remerian soldiers took the rear.

Patrika arrived with a report from a Camel Clan scout—they were nearing Anepolis and would arrive within a day if they kept pace. Sera didn't want to arrive late in the day, with little light, and near a city packed with hostile people. They'd end their march several hours away from Anepolis and resume in the morning. That would give them plenty of light to negotiate with the city, and also to set up encampments.

She searched for Villic the Imbuer but couldn't find him. He'd become more absent as the journey progressed and she worried about him. The death of his camel had ruined him. This surprised her. Coming from a nomadic warrior, she assumed they would all be used to seeing their mounts perish in battle, or from the excruciating heat.

She dealt with various reports and questions throughout

the day—a duty she'd dealt with since finding herself in command—but seeming to double since becoming the governess. An official role came with official responsibilities, she supposed.

Once she'd finished with them, another person approached. The Last Magicus.

"Governess," he said with a somewhat mocking smile—though she could tell it was in jest and not rude.

"The Last Magicus."

"We've almost arrived," he said. "I accompanied you at the request of King Alondo."

"I know."

"To make sure you'd follow through with your promises."

"I have," she said, annoyed. It irked her the king hadn't trusted her. The Calrites had obliterated her homeland. Of course, she wanted them dead.

"You've done an admirable job. However, I wonder if you'll be able to stomach what comes next."

"Taking over Anepolis? I can handle that," she said.

"Killing those who'd resist," he said, grimacing. "Ruling can be a particularly brutal occupation. And if you invade the capital city where the country's most loyal citizens live? You may have to murder not just soldiers, but common folk who feel the need to rebel from their shacks and sheds. People, I might add, who did not contribute to the destruction of Cyrok, but are still enormous threats." He cleared his throat, averting her gaze. "People," he said, in more of a whisper, "who need to die for you to succeed."

"I know what's at stake," she said.

"Very good, cyr." And the Last Magicus bowed his head to her, then turned away, and disappeared into the throng of the soldiers.

She wondered if she could do it. If she could strike down a child who was thwarting her and her people. In the end, she decided, yes, she could. Too many innocent Cyroki citizens died in the invasion. If she had to murder a few herself, it'd be just. Painful, but just.

D runk, he stumbled past Cyr Patrika. A few steps on, and he'd passed Cyr Seradal.

"Eagleton, Villic. Cyr Seradal Eagleton. She's a gover —"

Villic of Otherness shut Speaker out. Took another swig of whatever was in his bottle. He'd stolen it from a soldier. Ran out of the first one and craved more. If he got drunk enough, he remembered nothing. He couldn't hear Speaker, or anyone around him. Sometimes, he slept. The gods took care of him when he slept.

He enjoyed his new form. No care about how people looked at him. He didn't worry about talking to anyone because he wasn't listening to them.

"Villic," somebody said.

He heard them. At least, he thought he did. He looked around, saw nobody speaking to him. *Perhaps a god . . .* later he realized there were hours of distance between when somebody had spoken to him, and when he searched for them. Villic of Otherness wasn't paying attention to what happened. There was no need. No reason.

He blinked and day became night. His head hurt. Villic of Otherness felt clarity returning. He reached for the bottle of alcohol and downed the second half. Drunkenness returned, and comforted by this, Villic of Otherness slept.

The following day, Villic of Otherness couldn't find any alcohol. Nobody had any, or if they did, nobody was displaying it.

His mind was clearing up, and he felt pain and devastation again. Dunecrest's saddened face, those glistening black orbs glaring accusations at Villic, returned. Tears welled up in Villic's eyes and streamed down his face.

One foot in front of the other, he followed the marching army.

"Villic," Speaker said.

Villic tuned him out and cried.

72

INTERLUDE
FAITH ENNINGS

Anepolis, Calrym

"Have faith," people would tell her. She always scoffed and answered with, "Faith is what you make of it, and unfortunately, my parents made a person. I choose to make nothing with faith." Faith Ennings was an atheist, which had greatly upset her parents. "Mother Avani loves you, even so," they'd said each time she informed them she didn't believe in the goddess.

Faith had left her parents in Lochwall. Now, she believed them dead. It was both a time of mourning and a time of relief. During her entire life, her parents had hounded her about her religious beliefs. They'd pressed her to marry a man of faith, a man named Adelbroad who she also assumed died in the destruction of Lochwall. Another relief.

"Faith," a Magicus said, nodding to her and sitting in the chair at her booth.

She was one of several Glyphists drafted in the employ of the king. "Anepolis has a need," the king had said. "*You* are that need." And so, here she was, using her Soulpen to give Enforcers the ability to draw upon their powers.

Faith had been a Glyphist-for-hire for fifteen years now. She didn't even think about her job anymore. So she thought of other things: her parents, her lack of faith, her future. She wondered sometimes if she'd ever find a husband who didn't make her sick. Somebody she actually enjoyed being near. A rarity today, it seemed. Her parents had explained their lives growing up and Faith wondered if she was an old soul born too late. It sounded majestic. People cared about one another more in the past, she thought. Or maybe she just was around the wrong people. Had society changed? Maybe her parents had just grown up lucky and the world—as well as its people—had always been shit.

"Left arm first?" she asked the Enforcer sitting across from her.

"Makes no difference to me," he said, stretching his arm out.

She went to work. Faith had made a name for herself. Though Glyphists were talented at drawing intricate and pleasing-to-look-at images, Faith had exceptional style and skill when compared to other Glyphists. She had a natural talent; it seemed. And thus, people lined up for her, waiting extra just to have her do their Soul Glyphs.

Most people requested nothing specific. They just sat and watched as Faith let her imagination do its work. And everyone left pleased. This business was how she was getting away with what she was now doing. The art distracted people too much to notice anything amiss.

She started with a mouse in mid-jump. She even added crumbs of bread she imagined the mouse nibbled on. Then she followed that with a snake lunging towards the mouse. The snake trailed down and around the man's arm, its tongue weaving around the Magicus's elbow, its tail ending halfway down his thumb.

"You do fantastic work," the man said.

"Thank you, Junipo," she said, recalling the man's name. Faith thought little of most of the Magicai she serviced, but she knew their names. Needed to if she was to get away with what she wanted to. "Other arm," she said, and Junipo stretched it across the table.

When Faith had graduated from Ashmount, she'd believed in the Magicai's teachings. She'd gone to work, fulfilling the duty of a Glyphist. As the years dwindled away, and she learned more of the Calrym leadership and politics, she felt worse and worse. She, Faith Ennings, had directly affected the invasion of Cyrok. She, Faith Ennings, had supplied many of the Magicai who'd gone over there with their powers. And Cyrok never stood a chance—they didn't have many, if any, Enforcers or Collectors to defend themselves. Guilt had permeated her mind due to that. And now they were here. The Cyroki who escaped had joined forces with the Remerians—another country they oppressed—with yet other people they'd oppressed more so, the Camel Clans from Vessia.

So Faith drew intricate designs on skin. She made them look pretty. She smiled, she talked, Faith showed everyone she was in their corner, on their side. But she never completed her tattoos. This was something they didn't teach a Glyphist at Ashmount—for why would any Magicus want to train a Glyphist they could screw over an Enforcer? That would lose incalculable amounts of money—and a gigantic loss in reputation. And now, with Ashmount gone, the world was shaping itself in new ways, and Faith was trying to right a few wrongs.

Instead of connecting the strands of power to the Soul Glyphs, Faith had learned how to create the feeling they were by latching the connections to nerves near the Soul Glyphs, but not the Soul Glyphs themselves. If an Enforcer tried to draw upon their power, they'd find themselves tapped out at the last second. It'd be like turning on a faucet which had run water before but was now dry. A spittle of magic, maybe. But not enough to do anything.

"All set," she said to Junipo. He stood, admiring the design on his right arm—the outline of a castle under siege by several soldiers.

"Beautiful," he said, marveling at his arm and walking away from her table. He passed a Magicus coming in to replace him at the table and waved his arms up to show his new designs.

"She does amazing work," the next Magicus said. Mallix, she was pretty sure, was his name.

Mallix sat at her table, but his arms were covered in Soul Glyphs already. "Can we do it on my back?"

"Of course," Faith said, smiling. "We can do it wherever you want."

Faith continued her work. She hoped Calrym wouldn't slaughter the invading army. She didn't want to die, but she couldn't bear to watch entire groups of people killed over nothing. Midway through working on Mallix, ringing alarm bells echoed throughout Anepolis. The enemy was there.

"Hurry," Mallix said, "I'll need access to it all."

She bit her lip and went back to work.

73

DEMRI SLARN

He wanted to heal his legs, but knew it'd cost him far too much life. And one thing Demri wasn't short on was things to do in his remaining years.

"So we're leaving," Caius said.

"Yes. Fuck these p-people." He'd been lured into another corrupt group of Magicai. First Ashmount, now the Elkavich. They were all the same. It was always about power. Ashmount wanted to control the world and its people. The Elkavich wanted to stop this and control the world and its people once they killed the ones Ashmount had control over. They were starting a new cycle of the same things all over again.

He'd said as much to Caius, who agreed. But Caius didn't care. The man followed Demri wherever Demri went. *Except when he became the Velvet Mother*, Demri reminded himself. But that was a family matter, and, as Demri had heard from far too many people, family is everything. Too bad he'd never had a family he liked. Or did he? *Caius is family.* Aside from Caius, there wasn't anyone he cared about anymore.

Myri. He wouldn't see her again. He was leaving without saying goodbye, but after their last meeting, he didn't think it mattered. Demri focused on the task at hand. He'd asked Ced to come to their room. Ced would deliver them a few supplies Demri had discreetly requested. Though Ced wasn't a discreet individual, Demri had told Ced it was for an Elkavich-assigned mission. That shut him up.

A gentle knock followed by, "Sirs? It's me. Yer friend Ced."

"Come in," Caius said.

Ced entered, carrying a bag on each shoulder. He hefted them over to Demri's bed, dropping both. "Bunch of food, a kettle, bedrolls, and those glass bottles you requested, along with some other helpful traveling knickknacks." The high-pitched voiced grated on Demri's ears, which made the next part of his plan easier.

"Wonderful," Demri said, limping to the door and closing it. "Wonderful. We have to go soon, b-b-but I want to thank you for your aide. The Elkavich w-w-wanted me t-t-to t-t-t-t—damn it—navigate in the direction of Remeria." A round-about way of saying "travel," but for some reason Demri's stutter was worse than usual.

"What's yer quest?" Ced said.

"It involves the glass b-bottles. Where are they?"

Ced turned to the bag, slipping in hand inside and feeling around. A moment later, he pulled one out. "Here it is," he set it next to the bag. "There are several more in there. Six total, I think. What's yer plan with them?"

"I'll show you," Demri said. He hobbled to Ced. "Stand still." He tripped, placing his hand on Ced's shoulder to stabilize himself.

"Whoa, careful there!" Ced said, grabbing Demri with both hands—occupying both hands. He'd fallen for the ruse.

Demri's second hand reached out, pressing itself against Ced's chest.

"Demri? What are—"

Demri consumed a Soul Glyph, pulling a force of energy against Ced's back. The energy tore through Ced's skin in a desperate attempt to reach Demri's hand—he'd done this before at a tavern where he'd killed many people. His ribs snapped and his chest erupted, creating a wide chasm in his body. Ced's eyes widened, then closed, and he fell, lifeless, smoke trailing from the hole.

Demri turned, grabbed a vial, and knelt beside Ced's smoking carcass. He'd never collected the essence before, but it was almost habitual. He *saw* tendrils of a Magicai's power trailing from his body. Using the glass bottle, Demri held it in the path of the leaking power and filled the bottle with a clear liquid.

"Housekeeping won't be impressed with the mess," Caius said.

Demri glared at him. Caius tossed a coin onto Demri's pillow. "Hope that covers it," he said.

"Sometimes I c-c-can't d-deal with you."

Caius shrugged. "Same."

"You c-can't d-deal with yourself?"

"I can't deal with you," he said, glancing at Ced's dead body. "Now the Elkavich are going to be pursuing us. And we haven't even left their headquarters."

"We'll have a head start," Demri said. "P-Push the bed over his b-body."

"Like that'll stop the smell," he said, but he followed Demri's command, and shoved Demri's bed over Ced.

"Now we have a vial, C-Caius."

"And we're wanted criminals. Again." He sighed, hoisting their traveling gear over his shoulders. "Well, we best get leaving."

Demri nodded. Together, they left the room. Demri caught

a glance of Doram Quandis walking arm-in-arm with Myri on their way out of Hidehedge. A flare of anger rose and he quickened his pace. When they reached the outdoors, they almost knocked over Bloodbath.

"Ah," the old man said behind his mask, "leaving?" and gesturing at the bags Caius carried.

"I c-can't remain here."

"Because of the girl? We all have our roles to play," Bloodbath said. "Perhaps some aren't as willing as they might appear."

"Right," Demri said. "Goodbye, old man."

"Goodbye, Demri. Goodbye, Caius. I hope they don't kill her for this infraction, but you are free to go."

For a moment, Demri paused. Then he remembered her cutting words. "I d-don't care if they d-do." He pushed past Bloodbath, making his way to the stable.

It occurred to Demri that they didn't actually own any horses.

The same thought must've occurred to Caius because he asked, "Are we stealing their horses, too?"

Demri gritted his teeth. He should've planned better. But life as a fugitive was lived in the moment, with very little planning. Reactionary, rather than plotted.

"We'll take two horses and leave them more c-c-coin."

"They're going to come after us once they discover Ced's body."

"Quiet, f-f-fool!"

Caius quieted, but Demri realized nobody could've heard them. Between the breeze, the forest wildlife—birds chittering and peeping, woodpeckers pecking, and squirrels chattering —they were safe.

When they made it to the stable, they loaded their belongings onto a pair of horses. Caius helped Demri mount his horse, then leaped astride his own. He tossed their pouch of money on the ground. "Just in case they don't mind losing Ced," Caius said, grinning.

Where they were going, they wouldn't need money, anyway. They had all the currency in the world: information.

A shadow flickered across the sunlight illuminating the stable. Demri, turning, saw Stanton Brick standing in the entrance. *Wonderful.*

"You're not leaving me here," he said.

"Grab a horse then, Stanton," Caius said. "We best be leaving quick."

Stanton shrugged. "Nobody'll care where we're going until we've been gone a while."

Demri didn't mention Ced's body. He also didn't want to deal with Stanton at all. However, Stanton Brick cared more about the Corbéo family than Caius did, so Demri trusted him. He just didn't want to deal with him.

And with that, the trio steered their horses onto the road, galloping away from Hidehedge toward Andora, Remeria. Their new plan was to meet with King Alondo Sedoa and warn him of the Elkavich.

74

ASHEN HYREL

Anepolis, Calrym

They weren't gentle when they caught her. She was thrown to the ground, face in the dirt, and several knees kept her planted there. Somebody's hands searched her body, groping her private parts, and the rest of her body.

"Knife," the groper said, tossing her knife into the grass. "And some Black Dust," he said, tossing the pair of small sacks containing the dust next to her knife. "Otherwise, she's harmless."

The knees remained on her back, and she coughed, trying to inhale. She felt cold metal on her wrists and then they lifted her to her feet. Somewhat unnecessarily, they attached her ankle to a ball and chain. As if she had any hope of escaping without it.

They were rougher with Tallas and gentle with Velturo and Iadura. The rest of the caravan's guardsmen, to Ashen's horror, were executed. The guard captain, Mikaeus, had arrested Edelbrock, but he just wore a loose pair of manacles and wasn't being manhandled. Seeker Korran stood nearby, also in manacles. Also without being harassed.

She, Tallas, Velturo, and Iadura were led past Edelbrock and Mikaeus—who had his arm over Edelbrock's shoulder and was whispering to him. Ashen glared at him, wanted to say something insulting, bit back her insult and held her tongue. Edelbrock wasn't looking in her direction, anyway.

The guards, led by the Watchtower of Calrym, split them into two pairs. They led Velturo and Iadura one way while the Watchtower brought Ashen and Tallas back into the jail they'd once been in. He freed them from their chains and placed them in a cell together. Then, before he left, he said, "Your execution will be tomorrow." After pausing to close and lock the door, he looked at them one last time. "I'm sorry," he said, without a trace of remorse. Then he turned on his heel and left.

"I should have done better," Tallas said. He was sitting in a corner of the cell, legs splayed out in front of him. "I could have protected us. We never should have returned here."

"We never should have trusted that prick, Edelbrock."

"Throughout life we'll encounter many regrets, but it's not about wishing how we could've altered them, it's about coping with the results we've created for ourselves," Tallas said.

Ashen sighed, sitting across from Tallas. "Well, ain't that a bunch of poetic shit fit for a delusional mind?"

Tallas shrugged. "Perhaps. I suppose we won't know. Tomorrow we'll both be dead."

"Aye. You're a comforting man."

"And you're a comforting woman."

"I ain't a woman."

"You've been through enough. I can't exactly call you a girl."

She nodded. "Fair enough."

They slept. In the morning, they ate the provided meal.

No visitors arrived. They passed time by talking about nothing important.

Marching boot steps heralded their executioners.

A knot formed in Ashen's stomach and she felt an overwhelming urge to cry. Instead, she lunged toward Tallas and wrapped her arms around his waist.

"I don't want to die," she said. She thought of the fate that had befallen her parents—dead at such a young age. And now, here she was, about to die at a young age as well. She hoped they'd be proud of her.

Tallas's hand patted her back. "I'm sorry," was all he said.

She pulled away from him when she heard the key unlocking their cell door, wiping wetness from her cheeks.

"It's time," a guard said.

The Watchtower had returned, ready with the manacles. They were chained and led from the jail.

The guards marched them to a set of gallows. A small crowd had gathered, murmuring and gawking at them. When Ashen was young, she'd once watched an execution take place here. Somebody had gotten caught plunging a knife into a woman's neck after raping her. Ashen had known the young man responsible—a man she'd spent plenty of time avoiding. To watch him die was a blessing.

"Fuck," Ashen said. "You don't have to do this." Appealing to the Watchtower felt foolish. "Anepolis is about to be under siege. Why kill us?"

"I do what I'm ordered. I serve only Calrym and its people," the Watchtower of Calrym said, leading them into another group of guards. The executioner stood atop the gallows platform, next to the levers that sent so many people to their deaths.

And then she saw him.

Jaspard Couliac, hunched and sharing a joke with King Mikas's nephew, Alyst Garcovi, the new king of Calrym. A chill ran down her spine. *The king?* The king only ever showed up for extraordinary executions. High-profile deaths. Seeing the carefree way Jaspard interacted with the king angered her, and she clenched her fists. It also stirred up a healthy level of fear and sweat formed on her palms and under her arms. Ashen began to tremble as the guards hauled her closer to the platform. She noticed both Velturo and Iadura. Velturo looked worried, but not too worried to stop shoving pastries into his mouth. Iadura was smiling, talking to a man Ashen assumed to be her husband, Baron Exildar Alcart. *How can they be so calm?* But she knew how. When she'd been a duchess she'd seen what nobility did to one another. She'd participated. Her heart plummeted into her stomach. No matter what happened, she knew she couldn't count on any of them.

When they reached the staircase to the gallows, she struggled to lift her foot high enough to ascend, she was shaking so much. The guards tossed her limp body onto the platform, and a second pair of guards stood her up. Tallas walked up the stairs, obviously not as stunned into as she was.

"People of Anepolis," a man shouted. The crowd quieted. "I give you, the King of Calrym, Alyst Garcovi."

The crowd applauded, and the king rose to address them.

"I have only been your liege for a brief time," he began. The crowd cheered. Somebody whistled. Ashen felt like she was going to hurl all over her feet. Reality was setting in. She was about to hang. "Everyone knows that I've worked hard, and long, to be a fair ruler. Before we get to our event"—he waved at the gallows—"I'd like to take a moment to sing the praises of a few men who've served me, as well as all of you."

The king paced around the gallows platform, looking at various people, and if Ashen was in the crowd, she'd know it'd feel as if the king were talking to her directly.

"First," the king continued, "the Captain of the Guard in Anepolis, Mikaeus, who captured these villains!"

The crowd roared their approval.

The king nodded. "Yes, quite right. There are other soldiers who've helped protect you. I'd like to offer praise of both the Golden Knight and the Watchtower of Calrym. For though they served the previous king well, they have proven to be invaluable to both me and this city."

The crowd continued their cheering and clapping. A few whistles, too.

"A few other people I've been working with come to mind, and I hope you're as accepting of them as I have become. They will serve this city in the trying months to come. Sergeant Kolb Wickam fought with me in Cyrok. And, speaking of Cyrok, Lord Dellevue Vaston and Blago Adavir have defected to us and offered plenty of insight into the enemy."

More cheering. More clapping. Ashen wasn't sure why she was paying attention to the speech. She didn't want her last moments to be spent thinking about a king's words. She needed to free herself, but she couldn't and nobody was coming to her aid. She stole a glance at Tallas. He stood, head bowed. Defeated. She knew he'd want to die a warrior's death. That wouldn't be the case here.

"Coming here from the destroyed city of Lochwall, and joining me as one of my newest advisers, Duke Scayde Haklon—a man of many resources and of much knowledge. The city of Anepolis will only benefit from his relocation."

The king had made a full circuit of the gallows. He now ascended the stairs. *Closer to my death.*

"I'd also like to shed some light on a few locals who've done more than they could possibly imagine," the king said. "First, to Baron Exildar Alcart, a man who helped unravel an awful scheme."

The crowd cheered their loudest cheer yet.

The king held his hand up for quiet. "But wait, there's another. Duke Jaspard Couliac, a man without whom I would not be where I am today. Jaspard, will you join me for a moment?"

Jaspard followed in the king's steps, ascending the staircase. He beamed, waving to the crowd and avoiding her gaze. Ashen was sure she saw a sugared honey chew in his mouth.

"Without Jaspard, I would not be crowned," the king said. "Without Jaspard, the former king would still be alive."

The crowd went quiet. Ashen wanted to clean her ears out. She wasn't sure she'd heard that correctly. Citizens glanced at each other, horrified expressions of both anger and betrayal written on their stupefied faces. Ashen heard a few of them whisper condemnations against Jaspard, others praising the previous king's life. "Your Highness?" Jaspard asked, a hint of caution in his voice.

"Jaspard Couliac," the king said, ignoring Jaspard, and addressing the crowd, "has lied to me. He and he alone is responsible for the murder of the former king. And I have a witness to prove it."

"My King, no!" Jaspard said.

"Arrest this man," King Alyst said to the guardsmen.

Jaspard had no way to protect himself. He was quickly subdued, manacled, and pushed to his knees.

"I helped you!"

"Lies!" King Alyst said, slapping Jaspard across the face with his backhand. "Silence!" The king turned to where Ashen had seen Velturo, Iadura, and Baron Exildar. "Come up here, Velturo."

Velturo, wiping powder-dusted fingers off on his pants, rose and obeyed the king.

"This is Duke Velturo Ondakka. Most of you should recognize him. He's one of the few survivors of the Great Hall massacre that took place during the king's murder."

Velturo nodded.

"Velturo, tell them what you told me."

"Your Highness," he said, bowing. "Good people of Anepolis, ah-hah," he said, and bowed to them. Velturo turned, glancing at Ashen and Tallas, nodding to the crowd behind him. Ashen noticed his face was still powder-streaked. "I was there," he said in a whisper. She noticed he didn't laugh. "A man entered the Great Hall and slaughtered everyone before my eyes. I hid under the table, pretending I was dead. When it was finished, Jaspard Couliac showed up. He stole a ring from the king's hand. He set everything in motion. The guards—"

"That's enough," the king said. "The guards were following the orders of the man in charge and won't see any repercussions." Ashen wondered if that was because they didn't know who the guards that had taken part were. "Regardless, Duke Jaspard Couliac is charged with treason, murder, and conspiracy." He reached into a pocket and retrieved a ring. Holding it up for the crowd to see, he said, "We found this stashed in Jaspard's home. It was, I can confirm, one of the king's rings." He slipped it on his finger. "Evidence of guilt, no doubt. The punishment for these charges . . ." he looked out at the citizens.

"Hanging!" they shouted. Ashen could almost hear the seething hatred and anger they held for Jaspard.

"Correct," the king said, flicking his hand to the guards who'd restrained Jaspard. They dragged him over to the first noose, stood him on the raised dais, and slipped the noose over his head.

"Please, King Alyst. I've done nothing but aid you," Jaspard said.

"I've heard enough of his begging," the king said. He nodded at the executioner.

The executioner walked over to the lever adjacent the platform Jaspard stood upon. "Last words?" he said to Jaspard.

"I didn't do this! I have always been a man of the people, I swear it." Jaspard swallowed. Ashen wondered if he was swallowing the candy. Hope filled her. She figured there was now a chance that, since they'd uncovered Jaspard was behind the plot to kill the king, both her and Tallas had a chance of lesser punishment.

The crowd booed.

"I swear, I only meant to help you. And our spectacular king," he said, nodding to King Alyst.

"Enough," the king said. "Do it."

Ashen caught Jaspard's eye. "Well, ain't you about to drop faster'n a turd?"

Jaspard opened his mouth to respond, but the platform opened. His body dropped, the rope went taut. He jerked but his neck didn't break. The sugared honey chew flew out of his mouth during one of his gasps for air, dispelling Ashen's earlier assumption. Jaspard's death went on far too long. He struggled and gasped . She even thought he tried to say something at one point. His face went red, then maroon, then purple. Then, his body gave one last jerk, his boot kicked out, and his face went blue. He went still.

The king clapped his hands. "We are not done."

Ashen's heart jerked. She hoped for good news.

"As Duke Velturo kindly informed us, there was a butcher in the Great Hall. The Butcher of Anepolis—Tallas Taybold." The king swiveled to look at Tallas. "This man is a former king's guard, a trusted man who resurfaced to commit a revolting act. His punishment . . ." and Ashen's heart lurched. " . . .will be death. Have you anything to say?" She gasped as the faint remnant of hope she'd clung to was hopelessly swept away.

Tallas, head bowed, said nothing.

"Have you anything to say?" the king asked again, louder.

The crowd remained quiet, listening for Tallas to speak.

Tallas looked at the king. "Are you aware, Your Highness, that I was the original Golden Knight? That the current Golden Knight is an imposter who stole my armor after ambushing me? We were once good friends. In a fair fight, I would win."

The king laughed. "You expect me to believe you could best the Golden Knight?"

The crowd laughed with him.

"No, no, no," King Alyst said. "You won't have that opportunity. But, on behalf of the former king, I will pull the lever myself," he said, relieving the executioner from his position.

The guards dragged Tallas to another noose, standing him on the platform, and looping the noose around his neck.

Tallas looked at the crowd, addressing them. "When it comes to politics and power, underestimate no one. Especially those of us with the smallest stake in the game and the largest portion to gain. Find your voice, and people like the king won't have any power over you. It's time for you to stand up."

Tears welled in Ashen's eyes. Tallas, a man of few words, but often insightful ones. A man who'd been more a father figure to her than anyone else.

"Goodbye, traitor," the king said.

"Honorable people die young," Ashen whispered.

Somehow, Tallas heard her. He gave her a slight nod and a grim smile. The lever pulled. He fell without a sound, until the rope cracked, and his neck snapped. No struggling from Tallas. He died instantly.

More tears fell from Ashen's eyes, and the crowd cheered again.

Fucking Edelbrock.

And then she saw the man. Edelbrock Brendis in the middle of the crowd of citizens, staring at her. He wasn't joining the crowd's cheering. He looked morose, eyes not meeting hers, and he kept shaking his head slightly, back and forth, back and forth. She thought she spied tears running down his cheeks, but then her vision became blocked.

Two rough hands clasped her arms, dragging her to her doom. They stood her on the platform, looped the scratchy, uncomfortable rope around her neck. When it tightened, she nearly choked. She knew much worse was about to occur. She glanced down, saw her feet trembling, saw the cracks in the door that would drop open. Ashen wondered how long it'd take to die, dangling there. Her bowels let loose and warm urine trickled down her legs. More tears blurred her vision, streaming down her cheeks.

"This girl," the king said, standing near Ashen and interrupting her thoughts, "was in the Great Hall that day. Some of you might recognize her. Though she goes by Ashen, for a while, she went by the name Duchess Cithrial Hyrel. She served in the Great Hall, but lived with that traitor," he said, pointing at the swinging body of Jaspard. "Do we, as a society, believe in killing children?" the king asked. He walked to the third lever.

Ashen's nose ran and bubbles of snot formed from her nostrils, hanging in front of her in strings catching the sunlight, while more tears flooded her eyes. Humiliation. With her arms bound behind her, she couldn't wipe away the snot that had blown itself across her face. Jaspard and Tallas were dead. What was she to do? She had nothing. Nobody alive cared about her. Edelbrock had the shame to look at his feet. She wanted to scream his name, curse him, swear at him. But in the end, it wouldn't change anything.

"Do we, as a society, want to punish all murderers? Do we want to see this girl hanged?"

The crowd cheered again. "Yes," they chanted, over and over.

The king turned to look at Ashen. "And what says the girl?"

There was nothing to say. "Well, ain't this an unfortunate ending for one so sweet?"

The king and the crowd both laughed.

"She didn't actually kill anyone, ah-hah." Velturo said.

"But she was aware of the plan and plotted in everyone's demise," the king said, countering Velturo's point.

Velturo met Ashen's face. "Yes, though I'm not sure there was much she could've done about it, ah-hah."

"Me either," the king said. He pulled the lever anyway.

Ashen dropped. She jolted as the rope tightened and strained to hold her weight . Her throat closed, and she kicked, trying to propel herself up to get another breath.

She couldn't hear the roar of the crowd. Couldn't hear anything. The rope dug into her skin, choking her. Her eyes went black. She dangled. Her mind drifted back to when she was a child, when her mother and father still lived and how happy she'd been to have a family.

Struggling with a renewed burst of energy, she thrust her head forward, taking in a small breath of air. It didn't help. Ashen gurgled, gasped, and choked. She couldn't focus, couldn't think. Her vision went black, then her thoughts ceased. Then she was gone.

It took Ashen fourteen minutes—her years lived—to die. After her last shudder, the crowd once again cheered.

75

EDELBROCK BRENDIS

Anepolis, Calrym

Edelbrock had told Captain Mikaeus everything. The information was then relayed to his superior, which made its way up the chain, and then Edelbrock met with the king himself. The king interrogated him, asked Edelbrock what he wanted in return, and refused. He would not give up Scayde Haklon. The king was willing to give up Scayde's wife's location, though. She was hidden and the king knew where. Edelbrock settled with that.

He, along with Seeker Korran, were free to go. The king claimed they'd be watched, and under explicit command not to hurt Scayde Haklon. They could roam the city freely, but they would aid in its defenses.

They spent the night in a local tavern. Edelbrock struggled to sleep. Guilt riddled him with his decision to betray Ashen and Tallas. He was disgusted with himself. While he ate nice food and slept in a comfortable bed, they lay in a dungeon.

He attended that execution. Edelbrock didn't want to be seen by the king, or any of his advisers. But he felt he should watch the people he'd condemned to die. It was the right thing to do. When the moment came, his heart broke. He'd had hope when Velturo stood on the gallows platform that something would change. This just killed another person. When Tallas's neck broke, Edelbrock couldn't hold back his tears. When they killed the child, his soul shattered. Now he knew he was no worse than Scayde Haklon. When Ashen looked at him, he'd had to look away. Guilt and shame.

It dawned on him that being in Anepolis felt like being in Buzzard's Bowl. He was a warrior forced to do things he didn't want to do. Except he had the choice not to do those things. In order to live, in order to secure vengeance, he'd sacrificed people he'd known for a few days. He'd become a monster. And monsters should be put down. Problem with hunting monsters is they never cooperate, and they often fight back.

———

E delbrock and Seeker Korran were staying at the Dripping Bucket, a shady inn where the whiskey was cheap and the mugs weren't clean, but it cost little and was hidden in an alleyway far from anyone important. Neither Edelbrock nor Seeker Korran thought they were safe from the king. Confirming that Scayde Haklon was in Anepolis made it even less safe. Knowing King Alyst and Scayde were working together made everything much more dangerous.

They sat in a corner of the Dripping Bucket, drinking. Seeker Korran complained of a dark smudge halfway down the inside of his mug, while Edelbrock noticed a mark from a prior customer's lips on the rim of his. They drank the whiskey anyway.

From the patrons to the barkeep to the entertainment, the place was shoddy and unimpressive. The patrons, a gaggle of dirty-trodden, filth-encrusted, smelly-infested vermin, milled about together like a horde of rats, eagerly scooping up whatever they found and putting it into their mouths—whether it was food, drink, or the obviously diseased-riddled women stalking the bar. The barkeep, whose hands hadn't been washed in at least a week, kept sticking a white-stained-brown rag deep into the mugs, swishing the dirt around. The entertainment consistent of two dancing women—scantily clad but boasting nothing of interest, unless one enjoyed the many bruises and cuts on display, and reeked of syphilis—while the musician, a bard with barely a whisper of a mustache, sang offkey and played from a lute with half the necessary strings.

"You want to go do the deed today?" Seeker Korran asked. He meant to find the house Jaylena was staying in.

Edelbrock nodded. They finished their drinks and left the inn. Jaylena's house was on the opposite end of the city and it took time to navigate the streets, checking with passersby or vendors for directions whenever they lost themselves.

When the sun reached its zenith, they found it: a quaint, blue house tucked between two larger ones. Outside, a single guard. According to the king, the guard would admit them without hassle. Edelbrock didn't trust kings, nobles, or anyone in elevated positions of power, though. Too many had fucked him over. Instead of rushing inside, he and Seeker Korran spent several hours surveying the house.

They stayed hidden and watched, saw nothing of concern.

"Wait here," Edelbrock said to Seeker Korran. "If I'm not back soon or the guard follows me inside . . . well, you'll have to decide what to do. Either run into the house or run away."

"Seeker Korran would not abandon you, friend." He clapped Edelbrock on the shoulder. "Luck be with you."

Edelbrock, unsure if this was going to backfire, strode over to the house guard.

The man nodded, hand on sword hilt. "Something I can do for you?" he asked.

"I'm Edelbrock Brendis."

"Oh," the man said, frowning. "Oh! Right. Yes. Enter the house. I'll make sure nobody flees out the front door if you catch my meaning." The guard winked at Edelbrock.

"Thank you," Edelbrock said. He walked past the guardsman and entered the building.

The comely home had few possessions. A wooden chair with a suede cushion sat behind an oak desk. A staircase to Edelbrock's left led to the second floor. To his right, an empty kitchen, a layer of dust coated the floor—nobody had been in there for quite some time. A chill ran up Edelbrock's spine. Something wasn't right.

He glanced back at the chair and desk, looked at the floor. It was clean. He noticed that aside from a piece of parchment and a small, dust-coated mirror, the desk was empty.

Edelbrock walked over, eyeing the parchment. It was written in Jaylena's hand. He groaned. *Once again, they fucked me.*

His eyes scanned the letter and as he read, his rage ascended into betrayal. Of course the king hadn't kept his word. Nobility rarely helped one another, let alone somebody of *his* stature. The betrayal melted away, turning into heartbreak. Edelbrock had betrayed his traveling companions for a chance at revenge. And now Ashen was dead. A child had died because of him. He grimaced, thinking of Gordy. Edelbrock had taken a child's life, to pursue his personal interests. *I'm a terrible fucking person.* He'd done exactly what Scayde and Jaylena had done to him. *I may be a terrible fucking person, but I'm a terrible fucking person who's not going to stop being a terrible fucking person until I kill the other terrible fucking people.* He swallowed away his rage, the feeling of betrayal, and the heartbreak. Then he read the letter.

My Dearest Edelbrock,

I remember days past when you and I would curl against one another in our bed. Once, many moons ago, I loved you. What a mistake I'd made. It wasn't long after our marriage when you began disgusting me. I felt revulsion every moment we touched. And then, you cheated on me. WITH A MAN. If you weren't into women, why wed one? Why have a child with one? When I found out what you were doing, I went to Scayde Haklon. He freed me from you. Freed me from the obligation of taking care of the child which would have been a constant reminder of you and your betrayal. I am glad I don't have to deal with a little suckling Edelbrock at my breast.

The humor in all of this is that you felt betraying your traveling companions would gain access to me. Oh, yes, they told me all about it. You gave them all the information they wanted to, and for what? The chance to kill me? I'm more protected than you could possibly imagine, boy. Yes, boy. For that is what you are, Edelbrock. A petulant, emotional boy. And I'm glad I don't have to see you again. I'm glad you're pathetic enough to turn on people who care about you. It suited my husband well, and it wasn't me you were betraying. Perhaps you'll learn that betraying those you allegedly care about doesn't help you, but gravely hurts. Do you remember Buzzard's Bowl, Ed? It doesn't seem like those scars really sank in. Perhaps I'll have Scayde pay you a visit sometime to renew that pain. You surely could use it.

You do not get to murder me in cold blood, Ed. Forget about me,
Jaylena Haklon

Edelbrock crumpled the letter and flung it across the room.

"Fuck you," he said through gritted teeth.

He turned and caught the mirror just right. Edelbrock saw a stranger staring back at himself. A brutal, deadly killer, who would right the wrongs committed in the world—likely by committing more wrongs. *The ends justify the means.* He slammed the mirror on the desk, shattering it, then stormed back outside the house. The guardsman was gone. Seeker Korran was, too.

Ringing bells pierced the quiet afternoon, but not for the Church of Mother Avani, not to signify the closing of the gates. Something important was happening. He ran down the street, searching for Seeker Korran, or the guardsman. Finding neither, he watched a swell of armed soldiers sprint for the wall. Edelbrock followed them.

When he arrived, he wasn't allowed to ascend. He could, however, hear soldiers yelling.

"The Remerians are here! The Remerians are here!"

76

VILLIC OF OTHERNESS

Villic of Otherness lost himself to time. He didn't have more alcohol to drown his thoughts. Instead, he focused on the color black. He concentrated on thinking of nothing. And sometimes, it worked.

"Villic, are you okay?" somebody asked him.

He looked up, realized he'd heard her speak. He felt his face redden, and he looked away.

"Cyr Villic?" Sir Seradal asked.

"Don't call me 'cyr'," Villic said. Then, "I'm fine."

"Praise Mother Avani, you answered me."

"Villic, why haven't you been answering anyone?"

Dunecrest entered his mind. Villic closed his eyes and shook his head. "No, no, no," he said. "Make it stop." Dunecrest's eyes welled with tears. The camel was in pain.

"Villic, stop this!"

But he couldn't. His best friend, dead because of something he'd done. And now, there was nothing Villic could do to fix it. Tears flowed from the camel's eyes, and then the camel died. When Villic opened his eyes, he also cried.

Pushing past Sir Seradal, Villic kept marching. He ignored everyone.

"Villic, you can't hide from everyone forever."

Villic's mind remained foggy. He did things in a daze. If he had been traveling with the Camel Clans, he was certain they'd assume Lurzal, god of deception, touched him.

He didn't notice the distance traveled. Villic put one foot in front of the other. And then the air changed again. Like emerging from the desert into the jungle, or the jungle into the plains. The change brought him back to the present.

He saw a massive city, much larger than Andora in Remeria. Anepolis, the capital of Calrym, standing tall in front of him. He wondered if it was blocking the wind he'd been feeling. It was easily the size of twenty buffalo, maybe more. Villic wasn't good at distances or measurements.

A stone road he hadn't noticed he'd been walking on winded its way through the plains and through the city's gate. Bells sounded, soldiers shouted. He saw the tops of the walls filling with soldiers. Anger flowed through him. These were the people who'd killed Dunecrest.

"Villic, you're back."

Quiet, Speaker.

Sir Seradal approached the city. Villic hurried to catch up with her. The Last Magicus followed, though, like Villic, was uninvited. Villic caught Sir Seradal's gaze as she looked back, and she nodded. He returned the nod. In one hand, he gripped his spear. He drew his scimitar with the other.

A man with a hat of colorful stones leaned over the wall and shouted down at them. Somebody whispered he was a king. Villic had seen a king before, King Alondo Sedoa of

Remeria, but he never saw him wearing a hat with colorful stones.

"You won't break through Anepolis's walls," the king said. "I advise you to leave! We have many Magicai waiting for your approach. Return to Remeria and there won't be any retribution taken."

Sir Seradal laughed loud. "Your soldiers destroyed my home and murdered my family, and you want me to turn around? I think not."

The king glanced at the others standing next to Sir Seradal. "Who's in charge of the Remerians?"

"I am," Sir Seradal said.

The king shouted louder. "To all the Remerian soldiers—we have no quarrel with you. Return to your homes in peace. There is no reason for you to be here. Let us fight the Cyroki. It won't affect you. To the Camel Clans, stand down! I'm sure we can work something out. You want land, yes? We can offer you a significant portion of southern Calrym—just stand down! There's no need for any of this battle."

"There wasn't any need for you to invade my home, either," Sir Seradal said.

The Camel Clans don't flee from battle. And these people need to pay for what they did to Dunecrest.

Villic gripped his weapons tighter. He took a step toward the city.

"If you get any closer, they'll kill you."

I know what I'm doing, Speaker.

"Sorry, My King, but I'm no stranger to the lies o' a liege. The Redclaws know ya ain't honorable, and we're ready for a fightin'," the Bloody Duchess said.

Her captain nodded. "You can sit up there on your tall wall, but we'll be the ones laughin' when we see your ass fall."

Some cheers from the soldiers followed Captain Althier's words.

"You can try," the king said, "but we have the numbers. And the Magicai. Go home."

Villic snorted. The Calrites didn't care about all the damage they'd already inflicted. Not just on Dunecrest, but on all the other clansmen they'd murdered. They'd kept the Camel Clans pinned in the desert for centuries. Now it was time to take things back.

Villic walked towards the city.

"Halt!" the king said.

Give me the power of a sandstorm.

He raised his weapons over his head and waved them back and forth while closing the distance to the city.

Loosed arrows and crossbow bolts rained down upon him. The storm shifted their journey, and all were thrown aside.

"Villic, what are you doing?"

Ruining their lives as they have ruined mine. Give me the power to cut through stone.

"Villic—"

SPEAKER!

Villic's spear remained a storm, and he used it to ward off the flurry of arrows and bolts. His sword morphed into liquid fire.

"Lava."

The sword sheared through the rock, melting it. He tore the sword out, did it again, and again, and again. Cracks formed, stone rumbled, people screamed.

Villic cut stone. He lashed out with all his fury, Dunecrest at the center of his mind. Revenge filled his heart and his head.

The collapse happened mere moments after he began. A vast hole cratered the wall of Anepolis. Dozens of dying and wounded soldiers now lay at Villic's feet.

"I return you to Flaytz, god of death," Villic said, ending their lives.

77

SERADAL EAGLETON

Anepolis, Calrym

The gate and the surrounding walls crashed to the ground. Sera's jaw dropped. Nobody expected Villic to just walk in and open the city up. Negotiations, though poorly started, hadn't even finished. For a moment, everyone looked around one another in a state of stunned silence.

Sera drew her sword, and going with the flow, pointed it at Anepolis. "For Cyrok!"

"In honor of the oppressed, we'll be the best!" Captain Althier said, drawing his sword.

"Redclaws, follow me. We ain't lettin' the soldierin' type claim all the glory," the Bloody Duchess said. "We're just as capable, and more'n fierce enough to stand our ground." The Redclaws let out a battle cry and rushed toward the city.

The Camel Clans, mounted on their camels, surged forward with nothing other than a nod from Uva the Shaman, riding through the hole and into Anepolis.

"Attack!" Sera said. The Remerian soldiers and the Eagle Knights both followed her command.

Chaos blossomed, and Sera became lost in the throng of charging soldiers. After the initial confusion, she regained her senses and ran with the rest of them. The breach in the wall Villic had made was large enough for four or five people to walk through at once. The Calrite resistance was thin—most soldiers were still descending the walls.

The bottleneck at the wall slowed her progress for a few moments. Then she was climbing over rubble, forcing her way over dead bodies and through dust clouds. She emerged inside the city, coughing. Already she saw a house on fire, wounded soldiers screaming. Clashing swords, officers shouting commands, and the elemental destruction wrought by the Imbuers greeted her vision.

"Where to, cyr?" Patrika asked her. Sera hadn't even realized Patrika had remained at her side.

"We need to gain control of the city with as few casualties as possible. If we can secure the wall"—she nodded towards stairs where Calrite soldiers were descending—"we may have a chance. The king was up there. They'll surrender if we can find him."

"On it," Patrika said, raising a horn to her lips and blowing. The Eagle Knights and Remerian soldiers cascaded around Sera and Patrika. "Take the stairs," Patrika ordered. "Capture their king!"

Soldiers swarmed the bottom of the stairs, fighting the Calrite soldiers. Sera glanced up at the ramparts, searching for the king. She started where the breach began, tracing the wall back to the stairs. She couldn't see him. Sera returned her gaze to the breach and followed the other side of the wall. *There.* King Alyst was huddled against the wall, surrounded by robed men and women. *Magicai.* She noticed they weren't doing much. Occasionally one of them would step forward and direct his power, but many examined their bodies in what she could only surmise was confusion.

"Patrika!" Sera nudged her officer, pointing at the king. "We're at the wrong staircase."

Patrika blew the horn a second time. "Regroup, regroup! Other wall! The king is on the other side!"

Cries of "protect the king!" and "no quarter given!" came from the Calrite soldiers already engaged with her soldiers.

"Patrika, protect our flank. Keep them occupied!" Sera said, taking a majority of their soldiers and heading to secure the king.

"Yes, cyr!" Patrika turned, joining the soldiers already engaged with the Calrym army.

Sera and her soldiers headed to the other staircase. They had to cross three streets, navigate past two battles, and wind their way through a narrow alleyway shortcut to reach the other set of stairs. Like before, a flow of Calrite soldiers stampeded down from the wall.

"Yield!" Sera said. They didn't. Her soldiers threw themselves into battle.

A glow of orange in Sera's peripheral vision caught her attention. She turned, saw Imbuers with swords lit aflame, approaching. No Magicai interference occurred.

The Calrite soldiers saw the Imbuers and started screaming. Many tossed their weapons on the ground and kneeled in surrender.

"Come down," Sera said. "Leave your weapons behind. We won't harm you. We're not here for you."

Most of the Calrite soldiers mumbled to one another. Then, slowly, they funneled down the stairs. When the path to the wall opened up, she gathered some Eagle Knights and ascended, sword in hand. A few loyal Calrite soldiers remained to protect their king, but she and the Eagle Knights felled them without an issue.

At the top of the staircase, a small resistance had formed, but they, too, were quickly slain. Behind them, the king, armed with a sword and guarded by several soldiers, sneered. A second group of Magicai hid behind the king, huddled against one another.

"Betrayal," the king said to her. "That's how you're here."

"I'm sorry?"

The king glanced at the huddling group of Magicai. "Most of them don't have their powers and the ones that do are too afraid to fight." He waved at her army. From the wall, the army looked much larger than she'd thought. Bolstered by the Camel Clans, the Redclaws, and the Remerian soldiers, the smaller group of Eagle Knights seemed tiny in comparison.

"What now?" the king asked.

"You destroyed my home. My family has been destroyed because of you."

The king nodded. "I had a significant role in that. My name is Alyst Garcovi. King Mikas's nephew. I led the eastern forces."

"You killed Governess Stasia Falconel. And Cyr Ilic Strictland." Her hand clenched the sword hilt.

King Alyst nodded. "I did what was commanded. And I enjoyed it. Much like you're enjoying your role now, I'm sure."

She shook her head. "I do not enjoy murdering people who don't deserve to die."

"Well," the king said, "I don't know what to tell you. War is war. And if you're not strong enough to do what's necessary, you will falter. Are you strong enough to do what's necessary?"

Sera relaxed her grip on her sword. She knew what needed to be done. Without aid, the city of Anepolis wouldn't suffer an occupation. "Yes," she said.

"Good. Then you're aware that despite your desire, you cannot kill me. You need me."

"I know," Sera said. "Yield the city to me and you may live."

"But what becomes of me after?"

"We'll figure it out."

The king snorted. "I don't want to rot in a jail cell over the next decade. Either kill me here or allow me to remain in power. At your behest, of course. A new council has already been formed in the city. Let us continue to govern—with additions from you and your soldiers, obviously—and the city will accede to your demands. Nobody else needs to die without just cause."

She remembered the words of the Last Magicus. People would need to die for her to succeed. She wondered if that was now. Sera closed her eyes, picturing her mother and brother. She thought of Cyrok. All the innocent men and women and children, murdered. In no small part because of this man. Keeping him alive would certainly allow her to ease into control of Anepolis. But life wasn't easy. Calrym had seen to that, for the Cyroki, at least. She was here to mete out justice. And so, she would. No, she would not fall into King Alyst's ploy. The second she agreed to his demands, he'd be plotting to overthrow her and kill her allies. She knew this. Everyone would do the same in his position.

Sera switched her sword to her left hand. She held her right hand out to the king. "I'm Governess Seradal Eagleton, formerly Seradal Wintlock of Gyrloft, a lovely town that was razed by banditry under your employ."

The king offered a sad—and fake—smile, switching grips on his sword as well. "I apologize for the actions of my uncle," he said, stepping forward to grip her hand in his. "I only hope—"

She drove her sword into King Alyst's stomach. He lurched backwards and the guards surrounding him readied themselves.

"Don't," she said to them. "It's over." They looked at one another, unsure.

The king gasped, his hand dropping from hers. "You traitorous . . . whore."

"You murdering asshole," she said. She wrenched the blade from his innards. He groaned and fell to the floor in a growing pool of crimson blood. The crown he wore slipped from his head with a bang, rolling a few feet, and stopped before a Calrite soldier's foot.

"I . . ." the king said, then his eyes rolled up in his head and he stilled.

"Anepolis is mine," Sera said. She glared at the enemy soldiers, but none raised a fist to oppose her.

Anepolis had fallen.

2ND CYCLE OF SUMMER

1ST REIGN OF EAGLETON

EPILOGUE
ROYAL

Andora, Remeria

The people tending to Royal's broken leg claimed he'd taken exceptionally long to heal. "You've spent far too long lying in bed, drinking booze," one of them said.

Perhaps he had. But alcohol was a sweet nectar he just couldn't be rid of. Speaking of which . . .

Royal slipped his hand into the pocket of his officer's jacket and retrieved his flask. He unscrewed the top, tipped it to his mouth, and poured down a swallow of whiskey. Straight down the gullet. The back of his throat burned. Warmth descended through his body. He smacked his lips and licked his whiskers. No sense wasting any of it. Wiped his mouth with the sleeve of his jacket.

He stood on the ramparts of Andora's repaired wall, gazing in the direction of the ocean. He couldn't see it, but he imagined it. Missed it, even. In Cyrok, it'd been colder than a king's heart. But, despite that, Royal enjoyed it. He'd had a routine. Now, everything was fucked up. He wasn't even where he was supposed to be. Everyone he knew was off in Calrym, likely dying.

Royal tipped back more alcohol. The continuous wiping of alcohol-stained lips and hair had bleached the color out of his jacket. He'd need to have a new one commissioned. He wondered if King Alondo could help him. They'd become good enough friends, though Royal was sure the king had grown impatient with him. "You drink far too much, Royal. You're a royal alcoholic," he'd said the other day.

And now the king was busy meeting with a stuttering Magicus and his loyal knife dog. Royal had decided to stay out of the way. Some people had a look to them, and the knifeman had one. *So did the Magicus.* He went back and forth on which one was more dangerous.

Royal took a deep breath of fresh air. It wasn't sea air, but it was good enough. His tongue explored the hole in his mouth where rot had taken a tooth. "Huh," he said, enjoying the view. "Life could be worse."

He took another swig of alcohol. Straight down the gullet. The back of his throat burned. Warmth descended through his body again. He smacked his lips and licked his whiskers. No sense wasting any of it. Wiped his mouth with the sleeve of his jacket.

It wasn't so bad here. A few moments later and Royal drank himself to sleep, collapsing in a corner of the ramparts. Patrolling soldiers kicked him, but he was too unconscious to notice, or care.

He dreamed of conquering Calrym and ruling with an iron fist. Little did he know, it was already happening.

Acknowledgments

Anybody who has read this book has gotten past the first, and for that, you are fantastic people. I thank you all, and if you're reading this, perhaps consider dropping a rating or review on Amazon and/or Goodreads. It helps authors a ton. I appreciate all your support.

Thank you to my editor, Sarah Chorn. It's been a huge blessing working with you and I'm so glad. Sarah is a spectacular human and one of the nicest people I've encountered in this business. I am very grateful and hope to work on many more books together.

Thank you to my formatter, Amber Helt, and my cover artist, Dusan Markovic. Both of you do wonderful work and I greatly appreciate both of you.

I would also like to thank everyone who has read and reviewed the book, whether it be on YouTube, Amazon, Goodreads, or their blogs/website. All of it helps spread the word, and I can't thank you all enough. Special thanks go to Luke, John, and Sean, for your awesome reviews on Before We Go Blog, Grimdark Magazine, and FanFiAddict, respectively.

And now work continues on with the third novel in the Tragedy of Cedain series . . .

ABOUT THE AUTHOR

You've stumbled upon somebody who takes nothing seriously, not even author bios. It'd be a good guess to say John Palladino was born in 1988, lives in Avoca, New York, has a bachelor's degree in business management, and enjoys hibernating at home while writing. He might also lie and say he enjoys pets, long walks on the beach, and his hobbies include happiness and scuba diving. You'd see right through those lies, however, and notice he prefers the simpler things in life—reading, video games, and making ill-timed jokes. John also dislikes taking care of anything that excretes substances.